# SHERLOCK HOLMES: A YORKSHIREMAN IN BAKER STREET

## Robert V. Stapleton

### Edited by David Marcum

Paperback ISBN 978-1-78705-802-6
ePub ISBN 978-1-78705-803-3
PDF ISBN 978-1-78705-804-0

Published in the UK by MX Publishing
335 Princess Park Manor, Royal Drive, London, N11 3GX
www.mxpublishing.com

Cover design by Brian Belanger

Contents

The Penny Murders 5
From - **The Early Adventures of Sherlock Holmes Vol. II** (Belanger Books)

And From
**The MX Book of New Sherlock Holmes Stories**

Larceny in the Sky with Diamonds – Vol. II 39
The Pharaoh's Curse – Vol. VII 65
The Missing Empress – Vol. IX 94
Dr Agar and the Dinosaur – Vol. XII 120
The Mystery of the Green Room – Vol. XIII 145
The Turk's Head – Vol. XV 178
You Only Live Thrice – Vol. XVIII 213
The Whitehaven Ransom – Vol. XIX 249
Wolf Island – Vol. XXII 285
The Black Hole of Berlin – Vol. XXV 321

To Rosemary, my loving wife for nearly 50 years

## The Penny Murders
by Robert V. Stapleton

"I see you have discovered something of interest in the morning newspaper, Watson," said Sherlock Holmes as he surveyed me through the smoke of his early morning pipe.

I looked up from scrutinizing the pages of *The Times*. "How can you tell?"

"Simplicity itself, my dear fellow," came his rejoinder. "Whenever you come across an article worthy of note, you invariably shift in your seat and furrow your brow. Your entire expression grows decidedly studious."

I raised my eyebrows in surprise.

"What is it this time? Another bizarre death, like the one reported two days ago? A pig farmer in the Fens, I seem to remember, who was trampled to death by his own herd."

"Your memory serves you well."

He laughed.

"But you are quite right," I told him. "Today's article tells of a man, in rural Leicestershire, who has been killed and partially eaten by a Bengal tiger."

"In Leicestershire? Now that is indeed remarkable."

"It seems he was employed as a groundsman at the country house of a prominent peer of the realm. The article explains that his Lordship maintains a small menagerie in the grounds, and that this man somehow fell victim to the animal when nobody else was around. A singular coincidence, do you not think?"

"Two incidents too similar to dismiss as coincidence. I sense something darker in this matter."

It was a fine late spring morning in 1882, but I could already sense the shades of human tragedy invading the day. "Your imagination is proving as agile as your memory today,

Holmes," said I. "But what possible connection could there be between these two events?"

"It is too early to tell, but if there is one, then we shall undoubtedly hear from Scotland Yard when they finally admit themselves at a loss. Then we shall see."

A sparkle in my friend's eye displayed an appetite for action. I too can read expressions.

Holmes stood up abruptly and glanced toward the window. "Look sharp there, Watson. We have a visitor."

I put down my newspaper and turned my attention to events unfolding downstairs. I heard the doorbell ring, and then two female voices, one of which I instantly recognized as our landlady, Mrs. Hudson, but the other, sounding urgent and pressing, was unknown to me.

By the time the knock came upon our sitting room door, Holmes had changed out of his dressing gown and was standing before the unlit fireplace, dressed and ready to receive our visitor.

The door opened, and Mrs. Hudson announced, "Mrs. Elsie Horchester to see you, Mr. Holmes."

A woman in her mid-thirties hurried in. She stood approximately five-feet three-inches in height, wore a dark blue bonnet pulled down over graying-brown hair, and gazed at the world from brown eyes animated with urgency. Without a word of explanation, Mrs. Horchester hurried across the room to the window, from which position she looked down onto the busy thoroughfare of Baker Street.

Whilst I watched on in alarm at such an abrupt entrance, Holmes surveyed the woman with serene and dispassionate curiosity.

"They're still out there," exclaimed Mrs. Horchester.

"Who are still out there?" demanded Holmes.

"Why, those three men, of course. Can't you see them?"

We both joined her at the window, standing back slightly in order to make our surveillance of the street less obvious from below. On the opposite side of the road stood three men. They appeared bulky and robust, dressed in dark clothing, and all were watching our window with singular attention.

"A man of the sea, together with two London thugs," observed Holmes calmly.

Our visitor turned from the window. "How can you tell?"

"In the one case, mere observation, my dear lady," replied my friend. "He stands as though swaying with the rolling of the waves, whilst the others I recognize from previous encounters with London's criminal underclass. Those two ruffians go by the names of Withyburn and Smith."

"They sound like a firm of solicitors," I commented.

"Quite the opposite, I can assure you," replied Holmes dryly.

"I have no knowledge of their names," said Elsie Horchester, "but I think you must be close to the truth, Mr. Holmes. You *are* Mr. Sherlock Holmes, I assume."

Holmes laughed. "Kindly take a seat, Mrs. Horchester, and tell us the nature of the predicament that has brought you here on behalf of your husband."

The woman sat down, and looked up at him in amazement. "You know about my husband?"

Holmes took the chair facing her. "No, but the ring on your hand proclaims that you are married," observed Holmes, "and the urgency of your visit is only such as a troubled wife might make concerning her spouse."

Clasping her hands together, as though in urgent supplication, she began. "As you already know, my name is Elsie Horchester. And you are right, Mr. Holmes. My husband, George, does appear to be in some kind of trouble."

"And what does this misfortune have to do with those men out there?'

"My husband believes they are intent on killing him."

"For what reason?"

Elsie Horchester shook her head doubtfully and let out a deep sigh. "The full nature of that predicament has not yet been made clear to me, Mr. Holmes, but it has to do with the tragedy of the *Henrietta Baldersby*."

"A ship?"

"A fishing boat. Her home port was a famous fishing town on the east coast of England. The incident took place ten years ago, and was reported in all the newspapers at the time."

Holmes stood up and searched through his extensive and mysterious filing system. After several minutes, he returned, holding up a dog-eared and badly foxed newspaper cutting. "Here we have the contemporary report from *The Times*," he declared. "It tells of a certain fishing vessel breaking up in heavy weather and stranding the crew on an island in the North Atlantic."

"That is quite right, Mr. Holmes," said Mrs. Horchester.

"And you think this present business has something to do with that tragic incident?"

"It was certainly the reason why my husband came to London, but that was before we met and were married, so I am ignorant of the details."

Holmes steepled his fingers thoughtfully. "Am I to understand that your husband has sent you here to request me to visit him?"

Mrs. Horchester's look of embarrassment was as good as a nod. "But what about those men? They followed me all yesterday, though I managed to lose them in the end. They followed me again this morning, and they are out there now. I believe they are intent on following me home, in order to discover the whereabouts of my husband. And George is fearful for his life."

"Then we must evade them once again." Holmes slapped his knees decisively, and stood up. "I am intrigued by this story. Come, we must leave at once."

Immediately we were outside in the street, Holmes flagged down a cab, and we all climbed aboard, with Mrs. Horchester between us, concealed beneath the folds of her coat. But our subterfuge failed to outsmart the watchers, for as soon as we were rattling toward the far end of Baker Street, they bundled into their own vehicle, and were soon in hot pursuit.

Animated by the chase, Holmes called to the cabbie, "Lose them, and I'll give you another sovereign."

We all held on as best we could, as our cab rolled from one side to the other along the busy streets of central London. By the time we reached the street-end closest to our destination, the other vehicle was nowhere to be seen.

Holmes paid the cabbie and, staying alert to any sign of our pursuers, we followed Mrs. Horchester down the narrow alleyway adjacent to where we had alighted.

She stopped at a darkly-stained door, pushed it open, and led the way inside, slamming it firmly shut against the world.

The gloomy building held the smell of mildew and decay, and a thin ray of daylight, filtered in through an upstairs window, lit up motes of dust floating in the chill atmosphere of the hallway.

We followed Elsie Horchester into the parlour, where we discovered a man of approximately forty years of age, lounging in a badly upholstered armchair at the far end of the room. He looked up as we entered, an expression of suspicion showing in his dark eyes.

Holmes removed his hat but retained his coat. "Good morning, Mr. Horchester," said he, addressing the seated figure. "We have come at your wife's invitation. And at your own behest, I believe."

The seated man leaned forward in his chair. "Ah, yes. You must be Mr. Sherlock Holmes. People tell me you are a man who can be trusted."

"Trusted to uncover the truth, Mr. Horchester," he replied.

Then, as Horchester turned his gaze upon myself, Holmes added, "And this is my colleague, Dr. John Watson. He has my full confidence, and you can rely upon his absolute discretion."

"Very well, Mr. Holmes. Kindly take a seat." George Horchester pointed to two upright chairs standing in the middle of the room.

"Mr. Horchester," said Holmes, "your wife has told us a little of your present situation, and we have come here post-haste. I would be obliged, therefore, if you would please now come to the exact purpose of this meeting."

George Horchester sat back in his seat. "Then allow me to unfold to you my tale, Mr. Holmes – a story which takes us back ten years."

"You and your crew were castaways on an uninhabited island, I believe," said Holmes.

"Indeed. The place was known to the Viking seafarers as Dragon Island. Or so our Icelandic rescuers later informed us."

"Very interesting. Pray continue. Watson, take notes."

"I was skipper of the sailing trawler, *Henrietta Baldersby*, one of a fleet owned by our father, but managed and partly manned by myself and one of my two brothers, William. At this particular time, we were fishing in Icelandic waters. The weather was bitterly cold, and the North Atlantic was proving a particularly hazardous environment that season. Other boats had been lost, and our vessel suffered badly from the mounting waves, losing rigging and spars. Then, through the gloom, between the menacing sky and the mountainous sea, we saw a dark shape emerge. An island. A black rock, rising from the ocean waves, akin to a whale emerging from the depths. Massive in height, and rugged in appearance, with waves breaking white over sharp rocks where the island met the ocean. We fought with the helm, but the rudder was too ineffectual against the power of the water to direct us away from that approaching menace."

George Horchester looked around at us with wild eyes. "Mr. Holmes, we struck those rocks with such force that we were all cast overboard into the boiling ocean. The last I saw of my vessel, she was being smashed to kindling by rock and waves. We all gave ourselves up for dead."

"But you managed to reach the island."

"And a most accursed place it turned out to be, Mr. Holmes. At first, I was glad to discover gravel beneath my body, and to touch the security of solid land. But every stitch of clothing was soaking wet, and the cold Atlantic wind was set to chill each of us to the bone, and leach both heat and life from our miserable bodies. The high cliffs and jagged rocks kept us restricted to one small section of the island. From the gravel beach, we climbed to a ledge some five feet above, and there we discovered the entrance to a cave. It wasn't much, but at least it provided us with shelter, and a chance to take stock of our unenviable situation. We discovered that we had next to nothing in the way of resources. I had, however, managed to rescue the ship's papers, together with useful items including a clasp knife and a box of matches."

Horchester paused, staring fixedly into space, as though, for a moment, he had returned to that island.

"Pray continue," Holmes encouraged him. "How many of you had managed to reach shore?"

The man who had been unfolding this tale looked at us with haunted eyes. "We had lost two in the sinking, never to be seen again, and we remained a crew of four. Harry Winter, Jack Shelton, my brother Bill, and myself. As skipper, I was the one in charge, and it was my responsibility to do whatever had to be done in order to save the rest of my crew. We needed to light a fire, so I set the others to gathering together as much driftwood as they could find. The majority of it was wet, and we had to allow it to dry. So the wood came with us into the cave, as we sought what little shelter it might provide."

"You were fortunate to find such shelter," I told him.

"Indeed, Dr. Watson, we were extremely lucky. As I told you, it was an island known to the Viking seafarers a thousand years before we landed there."

"Dragon Island," recalled Holmes, with a knowing nod.

"And well named," said George Horchester. "The interior of the cave was dark, but when some of the wood had dried, I lit a brushwood torch and discovered that somebody had indeed been there before us. Along the wall, incised deeply into the rock, we found the depiction of a dragon. Its mouth began as wide as the entrance, and the carving ended with the tail at the far end of the cave, as though deliberately indicating where a small spring of fresh water trickled from the rock. We had water, we had shelter, we had the beginnings of a fire, but we needed nourishment. We were fishermen by trade, but we had neither nets nor line with which to feed ourselves. It was outside the breeding season for seabirds, so we took what little we could access, together with limpets we wrenched from the rocks, and concocted a few meagre meals."

Holmes nodded slowly. "Did you find any further signs of human habitation?"

"Indeed we did. Toward the far end of the cave, we discovered, huddled together in the darkness, the skeletons of three people. There was no way of telling how long they had been there, or by their shreds of clothing whether they were men or women, but they must have been there for some considerable time. The discovery came as a profound shock to us all, as it suggested that we might never be rescued from that ill-fated island."

"Loss of hope can have a terrible effect upon people," observed Holmes.

"That is the only explanation for what occurred next."

"Pray continue."

George Horchester's face turned a deathly pale. "We were dying, gentlemen. And even though we managed to light a fire, its heat brought us little in the way of comfort. For several days, we sat and merely existed. We very soon became nothing more than skeletons, every bit as pathetic as those we had discovered inside the cave. We now considered ourselves unlucky to have survived. The other three men looked to me for leadership, and for some way of escaping or even surviving this unenviable predicament."

Our story-teller stood up, turned to face the corner of the room, and continued his tale. "I put into words the thought that had been haunting each one of us. We would need to kill and eat one of our number. Perhaps more than one. Until a single man remained, to die there alone. None of us wished to be that final survivor. But neither did anyone want to take the lives of his companions."

"Great Heavens!" I exclaimed. "Whatever did you do?"

He turned, glared down at us, and shouted, "I was the skipper! I was the one to do the filthy deed. My responsibility. My job. My burden to carry for the rest of my days."

Hardly knowing what words to use, I asked, "How did you decide which one of the crew should be the first victim?"

George Horchester sat down heavily, and once again looked blankly into space. "We tossed a coin," he told us in a small voice.

"A coin!" I exclaimed. "That sounds damnably cold and heartless."

He glared defiantly at me. "How else should we have done it?" he demanded. "Drawing lots? That too is a horrible way for a man to learn his fate. No, I had to be seen to be scrupulously fair, otherwise they would never have accepted the outcome. There was no choice. It had to be done that way."

"Quite," said Holmes, leaning forward in his seat. "Then, pray tell us exactly what occurred."

"I had a penny. It was enough. The fact that it carried a picture of the Queen perhaps gave it added legitimacy at that moment. I don't know. But they agreed that I, as captain, should conduct the selection process." The man sitting in front of us looked around, as though requesting our acquiescence in what was to follow. In this he failed. "I decided that I would toss the same coin in the same manner for each man in turn. It seemed the fairest method. Each time the coin fell 'heads' upwards, the man would be saved. But the very first time the coin fell 'tails' upwards, that man would be our victim."

"Not a pleasant situation," muttered Sherlock Holmes.

"Not for any of us, Mr. Holmes," replied Horchester. "Despite our personal differences, I decided to give my brother the best chance of all of us to survive, so I commenced with Harry Winter, a particularly valuable member of our crew. His eyes held a deep fear as he watched me. I tossed the penny into the air, and we all watched it fall to the ground. The image of Queen Victoria saved Harry, at least on that occasion. He was a lucky man. Jack Shelton was the next to face the ordeal. I tossed the coin, and saw it fall to the ground. Once again, 'heads' showed. Then I tossed for myself. Again, the coin fell so that I was spared."

"That was unusual," I commented. "Three out of three tosses falling the same way."

"Not necessarily, Watson," said Holmes. "If all other things are equal, then each toss has an identical chance of landing either way up." Holmes gave Horchester a questioning look.

"I had done my very best to spare my brother, Bill," said Horchester, "but it was now his turn to face the toss of the coin. And it fell showing 'tails'. Chance had selected my brother to die, so that the rest of us might live. I would willingly have been the one, but fortune had dictated otherwise."

"Horrible!" I exclaimed.

"Indeed," added Holmes. "Pray continue."

George Horchester sat back, and looked around. "There is little more to tell, Mr. Holmes. As skipper, it was my job to kill him, so that we could all eat and live. I do not wish to relive the details of that dreadful day, save to say that I killed my own brother. When we had eaten enough to make us all sick, we buried his remains on the beach below the cave. Several days later, as we were beginning to consider who might be the next to die, an Icelandic fishing boat saw our fire and came to our rescue."

"It must have been awkward when you returned home."

"Indeed, it was, Mr. Holmes. I stood trial for murder, and was initially sentenced to death. But the power of the Press was on my side. Through the strength of public opinion, I was fortunate to serve only three years in prison, before being quietly released. My family, on the other hand, were less forgiving. The news of what had happened to my brother went down badly with them, and undoubtedly contributed to the death of my mother only a few months after my return. My other brother, my sister, and my father all blamed me for her death – perhaps with some justification. They ostracized me and, when I left prison, I was forced to leave home and build a new life in London."

"And what happened to the other members of the crew?"

"They were both forced to leave home as well. One found employment at a country house in the Midlands. The other went to work on a farm, feeding pigs – just like the Prodigal Son. I found work in London, as a jobbing longshoreman, picking up whatever work I could find along the river. I became like Cain: Cast out from home, with a mark upon my character, doomed to wander the earth as a man who had killed and eaten his own brother. Then I met Elsie, who agreed, in spite of knowing something of my past, to become my wife."

"How long ago was that?" asked Holmes.

"We have been together for five years. I imagined that, by now, the horrors of those days might have blown over, and that the painful memory of my sins might have diminished with time. Instead, it seems they are now catching up with me. They have already caught up with the other two."

"Those two recent deaths reported in the newspapers were your other men, were they not?" said Holmes.

"Indeed, they were. Even though it seems they both met with accidents, I am certain that they were both murdered. And that I shall be the next to die. You must help me, Mr. Holmes."

On our return to 221b Baker Street, Holmes and I discovered that we had another visitor. The moment we walked through our sitting room door, we were greeted by the sight of Inspector Lestrade, standing before the hearth, fingering his hat in an agitated manner.

"Ah, Mr. Holmes," he exclaimed. "I am very glad to see you."

"Why, Lestrade," replied Holmes genially. "To what do we owe the pleasure of this visit?"

We all sat down, with Holmes leaning back in his chair, and the inspector inclining forward, with an earnest expression upon his face. "Mr. Holmes, we need your assistance."

"Those two unusual deaths reported in the newspapers, I have no doubt," replied Holmes. "Jack Shelton, eaten by his pigs, and Harry Winter, eaten by a Bengal tiger."

"Indeed. Both extremely nasty. Both men were crushed and disfigured by the animals that attacked them."

"A coincidence?"

"I think it must be more than that, Mr. Holmes."

Holmes nodded. "Then there has to be something you are not telling me, Lestrade."

"You are quite right, Mr. Holmes. One detail which seems to clinch the matter, and which has not yet been released to the Press, is that each corpse was discovered with a coin pushed into its mouth."

"A coin?"

"A penny."

"So, two deaths, which might otherwise have been dismissed as unrelated accidents, are deliberately manipulated to raise the suspicion of the police," mused Holmes. "And to be publicized as such by the presence of those coins. And you naturally suspect murder."

"The evidence points that way. We need your assistance to help us sort out what is going on here. Are we definitely dealing with murder? And if so, what is the meaning of the coins? Are we dealing with a killer who wants to be caught? Or somebody with a decidedly perverted sense of humor?"

"And your next step, Lestrade?"

"I should like you to come with me to examine the bodies, Mr. Holmes, and see what you can make of the matter."

"Then we need to begin by visiting the scene of each of these tragedies."

"I have already arranged for the sites to be secured, but it might be more convenient to visit the estate first. The site of the latest death."

Holmes turned to me. "Come, Watson. Pack yourself an overnight bag, and we shall be off."

A train journey, followed by an uncomfortable five-mile jog in a rickety four-wheeler, brought us to the Leicestershire country house mentioned in the newspaper report.

The estate manager, dressed in tweeds and carrying a shotgun, greeted us at the main entrance to the grounds.

"This is indeed a distressing incident, gentlemen," said the manager. "I hope we can have this matter dealt with as quickly as possible. His Lordship is extremely upset at having the police swarming across his land, and asks that we should have the matter sorted out before his guests descend upon the place for a banquet this Saturday night."

"In that case," said Holmes coldly, "kindly escort us to the site of the death, and explain to us exactly what occurred there."

The manager showed us the place where the body had been discovered. A fence of iron bars bounded an area of grass, with a tiger glaring out through the bars of a brick-built animal house. The smell took me back to my days in India.

"The matter is simply told," said the manager. "Somehow, Harry Winter gained unauthorized access to the tiger pen. The animal attacked him, mauled him, and partially consumed his flesh."

"Has the site of the attack been left as it was?"

"No. The police surgeon who certified the death at first said it was nothing more than a tragic accident."

"What made him change his mind?"

"The discovery of the coin concealed in the man's mouth."

Whilst the manager kept his eye on the tiger, and his shotgun at the ready, Holmes stepped into the enclosure, and examined the area carefully. All the while, he was grumbling that the tiger had trampled the scene as clear of useful evidence as any number of policemen.

He finally joined us outside and shook his head. "I have seen all I wish to see here," he declared. "Now I should like to examine the body."

The corpse had been removed to the local police station, and the police surgeon was already waiting in a back room for us to arrive.

"We are being pressed to release him for burial," said the surgeon, as he pulled back the sheet to reveal the body. "But this has now become a coroner's matter."

"What exactly killed him?" asked Holmes.

The surgeon stared at Holmes with incredulity. "Man, can you not see? It's obvious to even a blind man what killed him. His flesh has been torn and partly eaten, and many of his bones have been broken. His life has been literally crushed from his body."

"And a coin was found in his mouth."

"True. But that was not what killed him."

Holmes looked to me, and I stepped closer in order to make my own examination of the corpse. "He is badly bruised, and a number of the bones have been broken," I reported. "The animal's claws and teeth have caused extensive injuries, but strangely with little consequent loss of blood. Mr. Winter's body is in a poor way, Holmes. He could never have survived such a mauling."

Holmes looked from me to the surgeon. "Gentlemen, I would be obliged if you would now kindly turn him over."

The surgeon looked to me. I shrugged, and together we turned the dead man's body onto its front.

"I fail to see anything new," I announced. "Apart from the dislocation of the fourth and fifth cervical vertebrae."

Holmes leaned closer, and lifted the hair at the nape of the man's neck. "Now, do you see it?"

"Ah, yes. A fragment of metal embedded in the base of the skull."

The surgeon leaned closer. "Good gracious! I completely missed that." He collected a pair of surgical forceps from the instruments on the side-table and, with some difficulty, grasped hold of the protruding metal. As he pulled, we saw a length of steel slowly emerge from the base of the man's skull.

"What is it, Holmes?" I cried. "It reminds me of a carpenter's nail, but it measures no less than ten inches in length."

"A nail of that length is not unknown among shipbuilders," said Holmes. "But I suspect this is not one of those."

"And what on earth is it doing inside this man's skull?"

"This object is undoubtedly the cause of his death," declared Holmes. "Thrust up into the brain from the base of the skull. But before I pass further judgement, I shall need to consult someone with expert knowledge of maritime matters."

"If this is what caused his death," I added, "then we must conclude that he was killed before the tiger launched its attack upon him. But why?"

Lestrade broke into the conversation. "In order to cover up the crime, of course, Dr. Watson. Somebody wanted us to believe that the tiger was the cause of his death."

"In that case," interposed Holmes, "why was the killing publicized by the coin inserted into the man's mouth? No, gentlemen, this was a carefully staged murder. And the man who committed it is telling us something."

"Granted, Mr. Holmes," said Lestrade. "But what exactly is his message?"

"That is what I intend to discover," concluded Holmes. He turned toward the surgeon. "Thank you for your cooperation in this matter, Doctor." Then, stepping toward the door, he added, "And now we must continue to the site of the second death."

On the map, the pig farm was not far away, but the journey led us along rough and unkempt country lanes and took a further couple of hours. All the way, Holmes sat with his hands resting on the head of his cane, and his thoughts lost in a world that I could hardly imagine.

The pig farm, where the body of Jack Shelton had been discovered, lay at the end of a long and rough farm trackway. The sound of unusual squeals and grunts, coming from somewhere beyond the farm-yard, greeted us as we reached the buildings.

After stepping down from the carriage, I followed Holmes and Lestrade toward the farmhouse. There we were greeted by a woman who appeared to be deeply distraught – and naturally enough, I thought.

"Good afternoon, Mrs. Shelton," said Lestrade, with genuine sympathy in his voice. "I have brought a couple of gentlemen with me this time, to examine the scene of this most tragic incident."

Mr. Shelton's widow nodded and then led us across the farmyard and between the farm buildings to a paddock of churned-up mud. This was obviously the site of the tragedy, and was identified as such by the presence of a uniformed police constable standing guard at the gate. But the paddock itself was empty.

"We had the animals moved," explained Lestrade, "in order to allow us to retrieve the body. The pigs are now in an enclosure on the other side of the barn."

The constable stepped aside, allowing us to enter the area. The lingering smell of the pigs might have proved too much for some people, but I was determined not to appear weak. Mrs. Shelton seemed not to notice. Only Lestrade's face turned a shade lighter in color.

"Please explain what happened," said Holmes.

"Late yesterday evening," said the widow, "I heard a terrific commotion coming from this paddock. With my husband out here, I assumed it was feeding time, and thought nothing of it. But after it had lasted for some time, I came outside to investigate. At first, I could see nothing untoward. Then I saw the figure of my husband, lying in the middle of the paddock. The animals must have trampled him to death. They had even started eating him." The poor woman shivered at the thought.

"The situation is clearly very different now," said Holmes.

"We could hardly leave the animals in there," said the constable, defensively.

"Quite." Holmes examined the paddock, and then the area around the outside. "Too much has been disturbed here to allow me to make out much of value." He turned to

Lestrade. "Except that one set of footprints appears to have been made by a man wearing sea boots."

"Sea boots?"

We all looked toward Mrs. Shelton for elucidation, but she shook her head.

"Interesting," said Holmes, without explaining the significance of the boots to the inspector. "We must now examine the body."

The mortuary at the police station proved to be little different from the one we had visited earlier in the day – a bare room with tiled walls and floor. The police surgeon had already laid the body out in advance of our arrival. On a side-table, close at hand, lay the surgical apparatus that had been used to carry out the *post mortem* examination. Alongside those, in a white enamel bowl, lay two distinctive objects. One was a penny. The other, a nail-like object, the twin of the one I had seen removed from the head of Harry Winter.

The surgeon, Dr. Blackstone, gave us his opinion. "Gentlemen, as you can see, the deceased suffered extensive physical injuries, which are consistent with his being trampled to death by a herd of swine. Their hoof marks are clearly visible on the skin. In addition, the animals had begun to eat away at the flesh, particularly at the extremities: The fingers, the nose, and the ears."

"Ghastly," I exclaimed.

Dr. Blackstone nodded, and pointed to the penny. "The corpse had this coin pressed into its mouth, almost certainly placed there *post mortem*. However, death was caused not by the animals, but by the insertion of that long object. I found it pushed up through the base of the skull, severing the spinal cord, and penetrating the brain to a depth of some ten inches. Although people have occasionally survived similar head injuries in the past, with the spine being severed, death in this case must have been almost instantaneous."

"Thank you, Doctor," said Lestrade.

"Indeed, a thorough and professional examination," added Holmes. He turned to Lestrade. "Now you have evidence of your connection, Lestrade. Both men were killed before their bodies were crushed. Each man was killed by having one of these nail-like objects driven deep into his brain. Both had their spinal cords severed. Each man had a coin of the realm pressed into his mouth. And it seems nobody saw anything, or can give a description of the murderer."

"That is indeed how it appears, Mr. Holmes," said Lestrade. "But where can we proceed from here? How can we find out who killed those men? And why?"

"The fact that both men were partly eaten by the animals that attacked them is suggestive. But I think the real breakthrough in this case will come when we identify the origin and true purpose of those nail-like objects that were used to commit the murders. Allow me to keep one of those instruments, Inspector, and I shall make every effort to answer your question."

"Very well, Mr. Holmes." said Lestrade. "The hour is late, and I have to contact the coroner before returning to London. Is there anything else that you need?"

"Only the name of a local inn, located close to a telegraph office," said Holmes. "We shall need an early start in the morning."

After smoking pensively late into the night, Sherlock Holmes was up with the sun, and roused me from sleep with news that he had received an answer to his telegram of the previous evening.

"The police have furnished me with a description of the third Horchester brother – the one called Albert. It confirms the identity of the third man we saw outside our window in Baker Street."

"How does that help us?"

"With his identity certain, everything now comes together."

"Well, I cannot can see it."

"Get dressed and find us a Bradshaw. The game is afoot, Watson, and time is extremely short."

We took the train and reached the hometown of the Horchester family by early afternoon. I stepped down from the railway carriage onto the main platform and accompanied Holmes out into the town. We found the place bustling. Fishing boats were coming and going from the harbor, and the smell of fish pervaded the air.

Holmes stopped a man in the street and asked if he had heard of Mr. Horchester.

"Heard of him? Of course I've heard of him," the man replied. "Everyone in the town knows the Horchester family. They own a large number of the fishing vessels that sail from this port. I reckon half the town depends on that family for their livelihoods. Jimmy's getting on a bit nowadays and, with the boys all out of town, people are wondering about the future of the firm and the security of their jobs."

"Then you will be able to direct me to where I can find Mr. Horchester senior."

Only a few minutes later, we were standing before a splendid front door, in a street of high-class residences. Holmes rapped the large brass knocker which adorned the middle of the door.

Presently, it opened to reveal a housemaid standing on the threshold.

"Good afternoon," said Holmes, handing over his visiting card. "I am here to speak to Mr. Horchester."

"You mean Miss Horchester."

"Perhaps I do," said Holmes. "Is she home?"

The maid invited us inside, and asked us to wait in the front reception room. A moment later, a woman in her middle years came in. She stood prim, and held her head with an assertion of pride.

Holmes removed his hat. "Miss Horchester, I presume."

The woman merely nodded.

"Good afternoon. My name is Sherlock Holmes, and this is my friend and associate, Dr. John Watson."

"And how may I help you, Mr. Sherlock Holmes?"

"We are currently assisting Scotland Yard with their investigation into a couple of recent deaths, and I was hoping Mr. Horchester senior might be able to help us with our inquiries."

The lady looked doubtful.

"He does live here, does he not?" asked Holmes.

"Indeed, he does."

"Then, may we please speak with him?"

"I don't see how you expect him to help you, Mr. Holmes. He is elderly and very frail."

"Even so. This is a matter of the greatest urgency."

The woman paused, as though deep in thought. Then she nodded slowly. "Very well, but we need to talk before you meet my father."

"So, you are the sister of George Horchester?" asked Holmes.

"Oh, you've been talking to George, have you?" she asked with a sneer in her voice.

"We fear that his life might be in danger."

"Huh! I'd be surprised if it wasn't. Did he tell you what happened all those years ago? Did he tell you what he did? He killed and ate my brother."

"But that was many years ago now."

"Not so many that I'm likely to forget. Please sit down, gentlemen."

We sat down, and Miss Horchester continued. "Mr. Holmes, you need to understand one or two things which have not yet been made clear to you. My name is Elizabeth Horchester. Since the day that our mother died, struck down by the news of her son's murder on that dreadful island, I have been holding together what remains of our family. My parents had one daughter and three sons: Myself, George, William, and Albert. Being the eldest of the four children, and with none of us having married, I was the only woman left in the family, so it was up to me to take control of the situation as best I could."

"I have heard of George and William," said Holmes, "but please tell me about Albert."

"Albert is the youngest. He took over all the hard work when we lost William, and after George was sent to prison. For many years now, Albert has shown himself to be the most valuable and reliable member of the family. Until recently."

"What happened to change him?"

"Albert took it into his head to visit Dragon Island, the place where our brother was killed. He didn't tell me what he found there, but whatever it was, it turned him into an angry and resentful man. He focused his bitterness onto those who had survived that ordeal all those years ago – the men who had killed and consumed our brother."

"Might he perhaps have discovered William's body?"

"I think he must have done, Mr. Holmes. There can be no other explanation for his change in personality."

"I have gained the impression," said Holmes, "that there had been some tension between the two older boys, George and William."

"Tension?" Elizabeth Horchester paused, as though choosing the right words to use. "Yes, you are right, Mr. Holmes. You see, they were both in love with the same girl. Evie Carstone, as she was in those days. But George and William were both wild for her. It caused bad feeling. Rivalry. Bitterness."

"Bad enough to kill?"

"You mean, on the island?"

"As one example."

"No, Mr. Holmes. Whatever happened there, it was the toss of a coin that took one of my brothers, and alienated the other from his family."

"And what became of this Evie Carstone?"

"When news of the events on that island were made public, she left town. The last I heard, she was happily married to a shopkeeper in Birmingham."

"Is there anything else you can tell me about your brother George?"

"George possessed a great many talents, Mr. Holmes. He was an illusionist, and was in great demand to entertain the children. He could tell stories, perform conjuring tricks, and loved to make the children laugh. He has been greatly missed, at least by them."

"Thank you, Miss Horchester," said Holmes. "That was most helpful. Now I need to meet your father."

"As you wish, Mr. Holmes," replied Elizabeth. "But try not to upset him too much."

We found Mr. James Horchester sitting in a wing-backed chair, gazing out of a bay window toward the harbor. He turned to face us when he heard us enter. He was thin and wiry, with a mop of white hair above a face alive with character.

"Father," said Elizabeth Horchester, "you have two visitors who would like to ask you a few questions."

"And about time too," grouched the elderly man. "Come along in, gentlemen. I don't like people hovering in the doorway. Find a seat, and tell me the nature of your business with me today. As if I cannot make an educated guess."

After Miss Horchester left us, my companion began. "My name is Sherlock Holmes, and this is Dr. John Watson. We are helping Scotland Yard in their investigations into a couple of recent deaths."

"And you thought these new deaths might be connected with that incident many years ago, the one that took away one of my sons, and ruined the lives of the rest of us."

"That is what we are investigating, Mr. Horchester."

"Then perhaps you are on the right track, Mr. Holmes. At the time of the tragedy, my other son, Albert, took the matter extremely badly. As did we all. Which is why George wisely decided not to return to his family home and business. Albert took on more and more responsibility for running the fishing fleet, and helped manage the company that I own. Then, recently, matters came to a head once more."

"What was the cause of that?"

"I decided to alter my will." The old man glared out from his piercing gray eyes, as he looked around the room. "I am growing old, Mr. Holmes, and I must make provision for the future. I decided to bring George back into the family firm, so I made legal provision in my will for the fishing business to be shared equally between my three surviving children – my two sons, and my daughter. Well, I have to tell you, Mr. Holmes, Albert took the news extremely badly. The bitterness he had bottled up inside him all spilled out. He told me he had recently discovered something significant about the death of William, and he said he was going to take revenge on each one of the survivors. Every one of those men who had killed and consumed his brother. I am horribly afraid, Mr. Holmes, that somehow those two recent deaths that I read about in the newspapers were the work of my boy, now in the grip of some insane spirit of revenge."

Holmes reached into his coat and drew out the steel object that had been used to kill one of the victims. He handed it to the old man. "Mr. Horchester," he said gravely. "Can you please identify this object for me?"

Mr. Horchester took the proffered nail-like object, and nodded. "It's a type of marlin spike, Mr. Holmes. It's commonly used by sailors, for a variety of purposes. To open knots, separate fibres, and repair rigging."

"So I thought. That confirms my suspicion."

"Wherever did you find it?"

"It came from the dead body of the man who had been trampled by his pigs. This is the object that killed him."

"And the man eaten by the tiger?"

"Killed in a similar manner."

The old man sighed. "That settles the matter. This is undoubtedly the work of my son. All three of my boys knew how to use these things. They were all marlin spike seamen."

Holmes retrieved the spike and stood up once more. "Thank you, Mr. Horchester," he said, decisively. "I shall leave you in peace now."

The old man hadn't yet finished. "Mr. Holmes, I have lost one son to the sea, and another will undoubtedly meet the hangman's noose. You must prevent any harm from coming to my other son, George. He may have done a horrible thing in the past, but a reasonable man can hardly refuse him forgiveness. And he is my son. Promise me that you will bring him safely back to me."

"I promise that I shall do everything in my power, Mr. Horchester," said Holmes, "but I fear that time is short, and we must leave immediately if there is to be any chance of rescuing your son."

Before we left the fishing port, Holmes sent a telegram to Lestrade, requesting that he find and hold the two men, Withyburn and Smith, who, with Albert Horcester, had initially followed Mrs. Horchester to Baker Street, suggesting he might discover them in the vicinity of George Horchester's residence.

On arriving in London, we drove directly to Scotland Yard, where Lestrade greeted us on our arrival.

"We have those two men, Mr. Holmes. Withyburn and Smith. Two of the most notorious thugs in London."

"Have they told you anything to help with the current murder inquiry?"

"Nothing at all, Mr. Holmes. I was hoping you might assist us with the interrogation."

"Very well. Lead the way."

We found the two thugs slouching in an interview room, with faces of stone turned defiantly upon the world. As we entered, I saw their eyes immediately show that they recognized Holmes. They had encountered him before.

"Now, gentlemen," Holmes began, as he sat down facing them across a table. "The police are investigating two murders. And they suspect you two of being involved."

Withyburn glared back at him. "We didn't kill nobody, Mr. Holmes. And that's a fact."

"And we've got nothing to say," added Smith.

"Then allow me to tell you want happened," said Holmes, sitting back in the chair. "A certain fisherman called Albert Horchester hired you to help him commit three murders."

"He might have done," growled Smith, "but we're admitting to nothing."

Lestrade leaned forward, and laid a drawing on the table before the two men – an artist's depiction of Albert Horchester. "Is this the man who hired you?"

Withyburn clearly recognized the man and seemed to realize that he was caught. "That's the cove. He told us what to do, and we did it for him. He promised us each a hundred quid when all three men were dead."

"But we didn't kill them," added Smith.

"Maybe not," said Holmes, "but you physically held down the farmer, Jack Shelton, whilst Horchester thrust a spike up into the back of his head. I have seen the bruises on his arms. Then you threw his body into the paddock, to be consumed by the pigs. You did a similar thing with the groundsman, Harry Winter. Again, I have seen his bruises. However, things failed to go so smoothly on that occasion. Winter failed to die as easily as you imagined, so you broke his neck before feeding him to the tiger."

"That was Horchester," said Withyburn.

"But you two did all the preparation, so that makes you guilty of assisting with those murders."

The two men glowered back at Holmes.

"Now we come to the third man," said Holmes. "Horchester's brother, George."

The two men looked back at him. One shrugged. The other nodded.

"Where is this third killing to take place?"

"Go down by the docks," said Smith, "and you'll find a warehouse owned by an old man called Schultz."

Lestrade rubbed his chin. "I've heard of it."

"But did you know that the place conceals a rat-baiting pit?"

"If it's hidden, how do we find the pit?"

"Go through to the back, pull up a trapdoor, and you'll find a flight of steps leading down. That's where you'll find them two brothers. And one of them's due to end up dead. Eaten."

"How do you know?"

"Because, Inspector Lestrade, we supplied the rats. Thirty or forty of the filthy vermin."

"When is this to take place?" demanded Holmes.

"Any moment now."

Leaving the two thugs in custody, Holmes and I, together with Lestrade and a couple of constables, took carriage toward the docks. The men had been right about the warehouse, and soon we were climbing down into a void beneath the building. There we were met by the lingering smell of dogs and stale human sweat, together with the enduring stench of rats. We found ourselves in a room with gas-lamps illuminating a rectangular pit almost twelve feet across. An unearthly squealing arose from the pit, and the squirming multitude of rodents it contained – the rat-pit. Here was the site of a cruel but popular blood-sport, which pitted dogs against rats, with bets placed on how many each could kill within a given time period.

A figure stepped into the light – the man we had seen in Baker Street with Withyburn and Smith, holding in one hand a marlin spike glinting in the gaslight, and in the other the woebegone figure of George Horchester, his hands tied behind his back.

"You must be Albert Horchester," observed Holmes.

"Quite right, Mr. Holmes. But you're too early for the main event of the evening, so we must make do instead with the death of just one rat." He gave his brother a violent shake.

"I think not!" shouted Lestrade, indicating his two constables. "Albert Horchester, drop that spike, and accept the fact that you are now under arrest for murder."

Instead, Albert pushed his knee into his brother's back, and thrust him over the edge of the rat-pit. With a shriek, George tumbled face-downward among the rats.

Whilst the constables took Albert in hand, I grasped hold of my Malacca and jumped down into the pit, where I pulled George to his feet, and beat off the rats which had already sunk their teeth into his flesh.

"Watson!" I looked up to see Holmes's hand outstretched toward me. A moment later, I had joined him on the rim of the pit, where Lestrade had also lifted George to safety.

Only now did we have a chance to inspect our murder suspect. It was evident that Albert and George Horchester were indeed brothers. There could be no doubt about their relationship – except that Albert's face was distorted by bitterness. He sneered at Holmes. "You have been very clever, Mr. Holmes," he said. "I would happily have swung for my brother, as well as for those other two. But somehow I was afraid that you would come along at the very last moment and rescue him."

Albert Horchester was hanged for the murders of Harry Winter and Jack Shelton, and for the attempted murder of his brother, George. The matter was widely reported in the press, and Inspector Lestrade basked in the fame of having solved the crimes so rapidly. The incident initially passed without comment from Sherlock Holmes.

A few days later, Holmes invited me to join him on a visit to the abode of the Horchester family, to which George had removed with his wife and household.

George welcomed us enthusiastically and invited us to sit down in his newly decorated parlour. "I must thank you, Mr. Holmes, for saving my life, and for bringing justice to my family."

"Justice?" demanded Holmes, with a sour note. "Is that what you think I have brought?"

"Why, certainly."

Holmes sat back, and fixed his gaze upon the newly-reinstated fisherman. "Indulge me for a moment, Mr. Horchester, by listening whilst I tell you a story. There once was a fishing boat which struck a rock and sank. Four members of the crew survived and managed to reach an island. As time passed, the crew began to starve. Eventually, it was decided that one of the men should die, in order to provide nourishment, and indeed life itself for the other three."

George Horchester's gaze remained riveted upon Holmes.

"The skipper took it upon himself to decide which one of the men should die," continued Holmes. "He decided to appear openly fair to all of the crew, and to leave the decision to the toss of a coin. The first to flip 'tails' would die. The skipper tossed the coin for the first man. It came down 'Heads', as indeed it did for the next man, and for the skipper himself. This was hardly surprising, since the skipper was using a two-headed coin."

Beads of sweat appeared on the face of George Horchester.

"When it came to the fourth man," continued Holmes, "the coin came down 'Tails'. Which is again hardly surprising, since the skipper, who was known for being adept at sleight of hand and illusionary tricks, had switched the two-headed penny for a coin with two 'Tails'."

"Of course," I gasped as the truth hit me.

"This is all pure speculation," growled George Horchester.

"Indeed it is," replied Holmes. "I told you, this is merely a story, and I have no way of proving that this is what really happened. But, allow me to continue. The man chosen to die was the skipper's own brother, and he wanted to be as merciful as possible in taking the young man's life. Consequently, instead of using his blunted knife, the skipper used a method which he considered more humane: A marlin spike. This he drove deep into the back of his brother's skull, bringing about what he hoped would be instant and painless death."

"Which we hope it was," said I.

I could see pain now haunting George Horchester's eyes. "This is all very interesting, Mr. Holmes," he said. "But you almost make it sound like murder. If so, then what possible motive might there have been for anybody committing such a terrible crime?"

"Jealousy," said Holmes. "The skipper in the story knew that one man on that island had to die, and who better than his rival in love, even if it was his own brother?"

George Horchester sat grim faced and silent.

"If I am correct in my interpretation of the facts," continued Holmes, "then the skipper was indeed guilty of the deliberate, premeditated murder of his brother. Years later, when the dead man's other brother discovered the body, and saw the cause of his brother's death, he flew into a vengeful rage. This was made all the more bitter when he discovered that the man responsible for the other brother's death would inherit an equal share of the family business and fortune on their father's death. Now, to pile one crime on top of another, when this younger brother confessed to a charge of murder, rather than admitting to what he had done, and providing mitigating circumstances which might have saved the man from execution, our fisherman remained silent. Now, to my mind, that is as good as murder."

"You have no evidence to identify this hypothetical cold-hearted villain with myself, do you, Mr. Holmes?"

"None at all," replied my companion. "It is all circumstantial. And as your brother has already pleaded guilty to the charge of murder, we shall never know what a trial judge might have made of my little story."

"Don't forget, Mr. Holmes, I have already been tried for the murder of William, and have served my sentence. If you could prove any of this new theory of yours to be true, and if you could convince the police of its importance, then you still could never have me tried for the same crime a second time. That would place me in double-jeopardy, and would be in violation of an Englishman's rights under Magna Carta."

"You seem to know your rights, Mr. Horchester."

"Ten years ago, I discovered that a man accused of murder had to be certain of where he stands in law, Mr. Holmes."

"Quite so. And that is the point of my tale. You could have saved Albert. But since he had discovered your secret, he had to die. Now, if the police were to hear of my story, and were to search the house of the man in question, they might come across those two incriminating coins. That would transform my tale from a hypothetical theory into an accusation with just ground for investigation. You may not be tried for the same crime twice, but if my suspicions were made public, then I can promise you, Mr. Horchester, that your life would quickly be ruined for a second time, but with no hope of ever returning to civil society. However, I promised your father that I would do my best to bring you home alive. That I have done, even if I find your actions on Dragon Island and since to be repulsive and uncivilized in the extreme. But be assured, one day the facts will be made public. One day, the story will be told."

It was on the day following this encounter with George Horchester that Holmes received a parcel. It was small but carefully wrapped. On opening it, he paused, and allowed an expression of satisfaction to cross his face.

"Well now, Watson. What make you of this?" He passed me two coins, which I examined with care. Both were copper coins of the realm. Pennies. Each measured one-and-a-quarter inches in diameter, but neither was like any that I had ever encountered before. One carried the design of the Queen's head on both sides. It was evident that two coins had been filed down flat, and sealed together by the application of intense heat. The second coin was different, in that it carried the figure of Britannia on both sides. The one had two "Heads", whilst the other carried two "Tails", just as Holmes had suggested.

I expressed my amazement, and passed the coins back to Holmes.

"I am assembling my own Black Museum, Watson," he told me. "And I shall add to it these two coins – the instruments of a man's deliberate killing of his brother."

"Whilst I gather together my notes."

"Have a care," cautioned my companion. "In view of the hurt it might cause, it might be wise to delay publication. As I suggested to George Horchester, the time for such revelations has not yet come."

"Very well. I have a box where it can be stored for the time being."

Holmes sat back, smoking his pipe. "The title is of course entirely up to yourself, Watson, but I might suggest, 'The Penny Murders'."

I mulled over my friend's wise and considered suggestion, nodded, and bent to amend my notes.

# Larceny in the Sky with Diamonds

by Robert V. Stapleton

I collected a glass of champagne from the waiter's tray, and looked around the room. A string-quartet was playing, elegant young couples were dancing, and I was in search of a victim.

It was the early spring of 1891, and I'd been invited to this society gathering a few miles outside London. For some reason, the hostess regarded me as a philanthropist, and I didn't like to disillusion her on that matter. Organised crime was flourishing, and my greatest adversary was on the run, but I was bored. I needed something to lift the gloom. Sherlock Holmes might resort to cocaine, but I needed a fresh hands-on criminal project to engage my attention. I knew the sort of person I was looking for. He or she would be alone, vulnerable, and brooding. I've discovered that there's always at least one such person to be found at every social event.

I spotted her at the far side of the room. The young woman was standing on her own, not touching her drink, and with her eyes fixed on the unfocused distance. Her mind was clearly on matters far away from this place.

"Her name is Lady Jacinta Pulmorton," the waiter told me. He was one of our men, and he'd noticed my interest in the woman.

"Of Oakenby Hall?"

"The same."

We retreated to an alcove where we could talk freely without being overheard.

"Ah, yes," I told him. "I remember we blackmailed her last year over some personal matter."

"We had some letters she wanted kept hidden from her husband."

"Indeed, a most unfortunate business, but we gave most of those letters back to her in the end."

"That's how I remember it, Professor."

"And my name never came into the affair."

"I believe not."

"Good. That's just as it should be. So, out of a sense of guilt, this lady will now be even more devoted to her husband than ever before. She can't still be worried about those letters. I wonder what's troubling her now."

Through the crowd of guests, I noticed Grimdale's mop of chestnut hair. He was lurking quietly beside the fireplace. He's a good man to have around: a first-rate dodger. He had also seen the young woman, and was watching her like a predacious cat eyeing a doomed mouse. Grimdale turned his hooded eyes towards me. I nodded, and we converged on her from our different directions.

"Good evening," I began. "It's Lady Pulmorton, isn't it?"

She looked up, startled by my interruption to her thoughts. "That's right." Her periwinkle blue eyes were enchanting, but they were clouded by sadness.

"We haven't been introduced," I told her, "but my name is Moriarty. Most people just know me as The Professor."

"Good evening, Professor," she replied. She'd obviously never heard of me before.

"And this is my colleague, Harold Grimdale," I said, indicating my companion.

She gave us each a melancholy smile.

"The evening's going well," I said, trying to break the ice with small-talk.

"Is it?" she said, looking down at her still-full glass of wine. "I hadn't noticed."

I decided to jump straight in. "Forgive me for approaching you like this, Your Ladyship," I said, "but I was concerned. You appear to be rather unhappy."

She looked up at me. "Is it that obvious?"

"I'm afraid so." I gave her a smile that I hoped would convey deep sympathy. It didn't matter if it was sincere or not, just so long as she thought it was. There was a mystery here that needed to be investigated.

Lady Pulmorton looked as if she was holding back from saying something important. I needed to gain her confidence.

"I can assure you, Your Ladyship," I told her, "we are both completely trustworthy." I can lie most convincingly when I want to. I gave her another warm smile.

She began to thaw. "It's about my husband," she began.

Grimdale and I exchanged glances. The signs of a profit here were already looking good.

"Is he making you unhappy?"

"Oh, we've had our ups and downs," she admitted, "but we have been extremely happy together. Until recently."

"Recently?"

"You see, Professor, over the last three years, my husband has developed an absurd interest in flying."

"Indeed? Flying?"

"It's become an obsession. He began by building a glider, and then testing it himself."

"That sounds a dangerous pastime."

"So it turned out. He crashed the thing on its very first flight. He was lucky to escape with nothing worse than a broken leg and a dislocated shoulder."

"All part and parcel of the adventure, I believe."

"Then he became obsessed with building a powered flying machine."

"People all over the world are experimenting with powered flight," I told her. "But to build a machine capable of taking a man into the air and then keeping him aloft, now that really is the aeronautical Holy Grail."

"Well, my husband has done just that," she said. There was a hint of pride in her voice. "He's built one."

"Really? You mean to say he's actually got the thing to fly?" I began to imagine the enormous income we might gain from this business.

"Oh, yes. It took off all right. Then it crashed, just like last time. He's been injured yet again."

"I'm sorry to hear that."

"That was nearly two months ago now."

"And has it put your husband off flying?"

"Not a bit of it. He can't wait to have another go."

"And how's his recovery going?"

"He's up and about again, but he still walks with a limp."

Tears welled up in Lady Pulmorton's eyes that would have melted any other man's heart. Pah! I almost felt sorry for the woman.

"I can see how that would upset you," I told her.

"That's not the only problem, Professor," she continued.

Out of the corner of my eye, I noticed our hostess bearing down on us. I was afraid she might make Lady Pulmorton clam up altogether. I needed to hear what more she had to tell me, so I sent Grimdale to occupy our hostess in some engrossing conversation. As a cockney born and bred, that's where his real talents lie.

Meanwhile, I put down my glass and took Lady Pulmorton out onto the terrace. We stood together, looking out over the greening fields of the Thames valley. The cool air was still, loaded with the sweet aroma of new life and fresh growth. The evening was delightful: if you like that sort of thing.

"You see, Professor," she continued, "the engineer who was working with my husband has gone missing. What's even worse is that he seems to have taken my husband's design blueprints with him."

I hesitated for a moment. Then I asked, "Have you informed the police?"

"No. My husband believes it's much more serious than that. He thinks the man might try to sell those papers to some foreign power, possibly to be used against this country. He is extremely upset."

"Naturally. So, it's becoming a matter of national security?"

She nodded. "With my husband confined to the house and grounds, I decided to consult Mr. Sherlock Holmes myself. But they tell me he's away from London at the moment."

"Yes, I believe he's somewhere on the Continent." I tried to keep the bitterness I felt for the man out of my voice. Holmes had been making life very difficult for me recently, and I was glad he was making himself scarce.

"I don't know who else to turn to." Her face clouded over again.

"As it happens," I told her, "I, too, am interested in crime and the criminal classes. Perhaps I could find this scoundrel for you." A criminal operating outside my sphere of influence was a personal matter for me. The man had to be dealt with.

A look of hope filled her ladyship's charming eyes. "That would be wonderful," she said. "Thank you, Professor."

"As time is clearly of the essence," I told her, "we'll come down to Oakenby Hall by the first train tomorrow."

"Moriarty?" said Sir Henry Pulmorton when we arrived at Oakenby Hall on the following morning. "I don't think I know the name."

"I am well known for my academic and charitable work," I told him. Well, at least that was half true.

"In that case, welcome to my home, Professor."

Sir Henry was in the Morning Room, sitting beside a window that looked out over the parkland in front of the house. He was a man of medium height, with dark hair, a pointed nose, and piercing brown eyes.

"Your wife has told me something of your problem," I began. "You think your engineer might have stolen the blueprints to your flying machine."

"Oh, there's no doubt about it," he replied. "I discovered yesterday morning that my safe had been opened and that those papers were missing. He's the only person with anything to gain from taking them. Now the rascal himself has disappeared."

An enterprising fellow, I thought to myself. "What's the man's name?"

"Jeremiah Silt," he replied, in a tone that implied utter contempt.

"Physical description?"

"He's a short, mousy sort of fellow, with grey hair framing a balding head. His most distinctive feature has to be his long sideburns."

"Your wife thinks he might try to sell those plans to some foreign power."

"That is highly likely," said Pulmorton. "He often talked about how useful flying machines might be in times of war. If he can steal from me, then he might well be capable of betraying his country."

"Will you allow us to investigate the matter for you, Sir Henry?" I asked.

"I can't do it myself," he replied, pointing to his ash walking stick, "So yes, please do whatever you can,

Professor. Get those documents back for me, and I'll pay you well for your time and effort."

I bowed graciously. I'd willingly have done the job for nothing.

"But first," I told him, "I'd like to see your machine."

"Certainly. Come with me."

Obviously still in considerable pain, Sir Henry picked up his stick, hobbled out through the front door and led us round to the far side of the house. There we approached a vast wooden tithe-barn. From the front of this building, a pathway of hard-packed earth led off across the garden.

When I stepped inside the barn, I was utterly amazed. The flying machine almost filled the place. It was a monoplane, shaped like some gigantic bat, with a wingspan of over forty feet. The bone-like structure of the wings was covered with a black silk-like fabric. The fuselage consisted of an open carriage on wheels, with a wooden seat at the back.

"The carriage would normally be enclosed," Sir Henry explained, "but we've been concentrating on repairing the wing mechanisms first."

"Even so," I told him, "it's a magnificent machine."

"It's based on a French design."

"By Clément Ader?"

"You've heard of him, Professor?"

"Indeed."

"Silt got the plans for me. The machinery is complicated and expensive to make, so I was glad of his engineering skills and know-how. He even made a few improvements of his own. Flight is controlled by adjusting the wings. You can alter the flow of air over the front edge of the wings, change their total area, or flex the end-sections."

"And the engine?"

"We're using a steam-powered engine," said Sir Henry. "It's situated just in front of the aviator, and powers a single propeller at the front. The engine is cooled by a radiator directly above. It's a light-weight apparatus, fuelled by alcohol-spirits. We store the alcohol in barrels at the back of the barn."

"Amazing!"

"Again, it's based on Ader's own revolutionary design."

"Did Silt get that for you as well?"

"Yes, but he refused to tell me how."

"In test-flights last year, Ader's machine proved to be underpowered."

"Perhaps, but this one isn't."

"You mean to say it really flies?"

"Oh, yes. It crashes spectacularly as well. While I've been recovering from my injuries, I've been busy putting the machine back together again. As I said, the damage was mostly to the wings. That's now been fixed, so I'm hoping to fly it again very soon."

"Tell me, Sir Henry," I said, "how do you operate the engine?"

"Put simply, you open the tap on the fuel-reservoir, light the boiler jets and wait for the water to boil. Then you allow high-pressure steam into the engine. This drives the cylinders, which turn the propeller."

"Just like boiling a kettle."

"Pretty much. Then hang on for the ride of your life."

Before Grimdale and I left for London, Lady Pulmorton stopped us. "We have yet another problem, Professor."

"Can I help?"

She looked flustered. "In two days' time, an important visitor will be coming to stay with us. A lady from Russia. The Countess of Felixburg."

My eyes lit up. "Isn't she one of the richest women in Europe?"

"I believe she is," said Lady Pulmorton. "It means that we're going to need some extra security here." She turned her heart-melting eyes onto me. "Could I possibly impose on you to take this extra duty on for us, Professor?"

I felt like an alcoholic who's just been asked to take charge of a brewery. "I would be delighted," I told her. "I have some business to attend to first, but I shall return the day after tomorrow."

In the train back to Waterloo, I sat alone with Grimdale in a First Class compartment. We had bribed the guard, locked the door, and drawn down the blinds, so there was little danger of anyone interrupting us.

"Are you really going to help this man?" Grimdale asked me.

"I don't see why not," I told him. "Especially now that the Countess is coming to stay at Oakenby Hall."

"As you say, she is reputed to be extremely rich."

"Indeed, but I'm going to need more details," I told him. "Contact our colleagues in the European criminal underworld and ask them for a description of her jewellery. Somebody will know."

"I'll get onto it the moment we reach the Smoke," said Grimdale.

I tore a sheet of paper from my pocket notebook, wrote a few brief words on it and handed it to my companion. "But first, I want you to deliver this message."

His eyes opened wide when he saw the address. "Are you sure, Professor?"

"Completely."

The message was simple: "Meet me in the Calcutta Room of the Century Hotel, Mayfair, at seven tonight. Come alone. Moriarty."

Sherlock Holmes and I have much in common. We are both chameleons: cold and calculating, whilst at the same time being masters of deception and disguise. He is a worthy but deadly opponent. But it was not Sherlock I'd asked to meet me that evening, it was his brother, Mycroft.

For this meeting, I adopted my persona as a cold fish. I stood at the far end of the room, placed my gloves and top-hat on the table beside me, and leaned on my silver-topped cane.

When he arrived, Mycroft remained near the door. It amused me to think that he didn't want to come any closer.

"I take great exception to being summoned like this," he told me.

"Regrettable, but necessary," I replied.

"I have important state business to attend to."

"No doubt, but I need to consult you on a matter of national security."

Mycroft raised one eyebrow in surprise. He can sometimes appear as unemotional as his brother.

"You may have heard about Sir Henry Pulmorton's obsession with flying-machines."

"He has made no secret of it."

"But what you might not know is that he has now succeeded in building one."

"Have you seen it?"

"Indeed."

"Have you seen it fly?"

"Not yet."

"Then it's a purely academic matter."

"But his assistant believes it can fly. So much so that he has stolen the blueprints. He may try to sell those documents to some foreign power."

In the fading light, I saw Mycroft's eyes sparkle. Now he was interested.

"The man's name is Jeremiah Silt," I told him.

"Someone of that name did make an initial approach to our government," Mycroft admitted, "but we didn't think it was a matter worth pursuing."

"So he may wish to try his luck elsewhere."

"He might."

"You know the diplomatic scene better than anyone," I continued. "Who is there in London who might be willing to pay good money for those papers?"

"What's your interest in this?"

"You may be under the impression that I have criminal tendencies, Mr. Holmes," I told him. "The truth is that I am an intensely patriotic man. I wish, as much as any other true-blooded Englishman, to see to all enemies of our Queen and country vanquished." I was putting on a very convincing show. I could easily persuade myself that all this claptrap really was true.

Mycroft looked pensively out of the window at the darkening sky. "The German Ambassador is expecting a visitor from Berlin," he said. "A man with direct access to the Kaiser himself. I believe he has a particular interest in flying machines."

"That has to be more than a coincidence."

"But whether the Kaiser is also interested is another matter entirely. However, if this fellow Silt is hoping to sell those plans to some foreign power, he might begin by taking them to the German Embassy."

"When?"

"Their visitor arrives tomorrow morning."

"Another foreign visitor!" I exclaimed. "It must be a sign of spring. But the cuckoos are a little early this year. In that case, I shall have my men keep a constant watch on the place until our man shows up."

"He might not."

"But there's a good chance that he will."

From first light, my men kept a discreet vigil outside the Embassy of the Imperial German Government. I'm pretty sure that Mycroft had his own people watching the street as well. I'd have been disappointed if he hadn't.

Later that morning, a young lad, who works for us as a runner, reported to me that the German official had now arrived.

"A posh toff, with a beard as long as Methuselah's," he said. "Came from the station in a carriage as if 'e was the King of Prussia 'isself."

I took a hansom to Belgravia and stopped across the road from the Embassy. Grimdale gave me his succinct report. "He's definitely in there, Professor."

"Then all we have to do is wait for Silt to arrive," I told him. "Are your men in position?"

"We've got a newspaper-seller, a road sweeper and some men pretending to work on repairing the road," he replied.

"He mustn't be allowed to reach the front door."

"Don't worry, Professor. The moment Silt turns up, we'll have him."

"Very well," I told him. "I'll wait here."

I made no secret of the fact that I was watching the place. Leaning on my swordstick cane, I stood with my eyes fixed on the front door of the Embassy. All afternoon, diplomats came and went, but I never for one moment took my eyes off that door.

The lamplighter was already doing his rounds by the time Silt arrived. The engineer's sideburns were almost undetectable in the fading light, but I can recognise a guilty man when I see one. There was no mistaking the furtive way he shuffled along the street towards the Embassy building.

The front door of the Embassy opened, and a tall man with an impressive white beard stood in the entrance. But it was too late. Before he could come within twenty feet of the place, my men took Silt in hand.

I crossed the road towards him. "Jeremiah Silt, I believe."

"How dare you treat me like this!" he snapped.

"Because I know all about you."

A look of concern crossed his face. "What do you mean?"

"We both know that you stole those blueprints to Sir Henry Pulmorton's flying machine."

"Stole? I was the one who got them for him in the first place," said Silt. "If I stole anything from anyone, then it was from the Frenchman. I adapted his designs. I added more power to the engine. I was the one who made the thing fly. I am a genius!"

"No doubt," I replied coldly, "but we also know that you came here hoping to sell those blueprints to the German government. You're a traitor to your country, Silt."

"I tried to interest our government in my machine," Silt sneered, "but they didn't want to know. I wanted to develop the design further, but for that I needed money, more than Sir Henry could give me. This country ought to celebrate me as a hero, not condemn me as a traitor."

"Sir Henry wants his documents back," I told him. "Hand them over to me immediately."

He thrust his hand beneath his coat, drew out a bundle of papers and handed them to me, muttering darkly to himself.

Mycroft Holmes now arrived in his own cab. He was looking very pleased with himself.

"At least now those plans won't be used against this country," he said.

"You regard the Germans as potential enemies?" I asked him.

"They are a growing threat in Europe," he replied. "One day, Professor, they will become a direct threat to us."

That was very interesting.

"Give me those plans," said Mycroft. "I'll make sure they get safely back to Sir Henry Pulmorton."

"Do you still not trust me?" I asked, trying to sound offended.

"Not in the slightest," he replied.

I handed over the plans.

"I'll keep Silt," I told him.

"This isn't a police matter," Mycroft told me, "so I'm sure I can safely leave him in your hands."

Oakenby Hall was in turmoil when we arrived there on the following afternoon.

"The Countess has arrived from Russia," said the butler. He sounded exasperated. "Together with her entire household."

"I was hoping to speak with Sir Henry," I told him.

"He's extremely busy, sir," the butler replied. "But he is expecting you. He hopes you will both join him at dinner this evening."

"As members of the security staff," I replied, "we shall certainly both be there."

"There are two bedrooms prepared for you and your companion in the south wing of the house," the butler added. "I hope you will find the arrangements to your satisfaction."

"I'm sure we will," I replied. "But where will the countess be staying?"

"In the Blue Room, sir. On the first floor at the front of the house."

After we'd settled into our rooms, Grimdale joined me to discuss our next step.

"What have you learned about the Countess?" I asked him.

"Following the death of her husband last year, she now owns a great deal of land in her native country," said Grimdale. "Her income is more than enough to keep herself and her entire household very comfortable indeed."

"And her jewellery?"

"She never goes anywhere without it."

"That's what I like to hear," I replied. "It gives us a realistic chance of taking it from her. Do you have any details?"

"There are several pieces large enough to attract attention if sold on the open market."

"Then we must concentrate on the smaller ones."

Grimdale laid the complete list of jewellery on the table in front of me. "There's one piece that looks particularly interesting," he told me. "It's described as a necklace made up of three strands of diamonds."

"I have no doubt she'll be wearing it tonight," I said. "So we must find out what happens to it after the meal."

"Sir Henry might lock it away in his safe."

"Perhaps."

Our luggage was light, suitable only for a flying visit, but we both managed to turn up to dinner that evening looking suitably turned out.

"Ah, Professor," said Sir Henry, when we met just before the meal, "it's good to see you again."

"And you, Sir Henry," I replied. "I trust you received your papers."

"Indeed. They came by special delivery from Whitehall this morning."

"That's just as it should be," I told him. I added modestly, "I have my contacts there."

Grimdale raised an eyebrow in surprise at such a pretentious statement.

I ignored him.

"I hope those blueprints are back where they belong."

"They are now once again locked away in the safe in my study."

"That's good to hear." It was indeed very good to hear. If some grubby little engineer could open that safe, then a criminal mastermind like myself should have no difficulty with it.

At dinner, I was seated opposite the Guest of Honour, the Countess herself. At first, we talked of unimportant things, but my attention was fastened on her necklace. It was just as my informants had described it. There were three strands of diamonds, no single stone remarkable on its own, but together undoubtedly worth a fortune.

"That's a magnificent necklace, madam," I told her.

"My late husband gave it to me," she explained. "The stones came from the private treasury of the Tsar himself."

"Indeed? They must be worth a great deal."

"Several millions of roubles, I believe."

"Then, as the man in charge of security here, I must caution you to be on your guard, Countess." I shook my head sadly. "There are thieves active in this country. Are you sure the necklace will be safe during your stay here?"

"I am quite sure it will be," she replied.

"Of course," I continued. "Sir Henry has a heavy-duty safe in his study."

She laughed, then fixed me with her steel-grey eyes. "It will not be in his safe, Professor," she said. "I insist on keeping this particular necklace close to me at all times."

"That is a very wise decision, madam," I assured her, "very wise indeed."

I had to get my hands on those jewels. But how? As I watched the wine waiter serving out the hock, the germ of a plan began to form in my mind.

I noticed that the lower button on the man's jacket was hanging loose. As he leaned over me, with the bottle in his hand, I grasped hold of the button and gave it a sharp jerk. It came away so easily that the man failed to notice that anything was wrong.

By the time the meal was over, my plan was complete in every detail. The below-stairs staff would be key to its success.

When nobody was watching, I left the dining room and descended to the servants' hall. There my eyes fell on a charming young chamber maid.

"Excuse me, my dear," I began.

"Yes, sir?"

"Would you like to earn a sovereign?"

She gave me a suspicious look. "What do I have to do?"

"Oh, nothing much." I took out a glass vial and held it in front of her. It's amazing the things a master criminal keeps concealed in his pockets. "All you have to do is to pour the contents of this vial into the Countess's last drink of the day."

"But why?"

"The Countess has had a long journey," I explained. "She needs a good night's sleep."

"Don't we all?"

"You must also make sure that her bedroom door is left unlocked tonight."

"It's the job of her lady's maid to secure the door."

"But not this time," I told the girl. "Tonight, her maid will have her mind on other things."

"What if someone sees me? Are you sure I won't get into trouble over this?"

"Quite sure," I replied. "If anyone does question you, just tell them that you saw the wine waiter loitering in the corridor outside her room. That should leave you completely in the clear."

I gave Grimdale the job of keeping the Countess's lady's maid occupied that night. He seemed pleased with the assignment.

"But first," I told him, "I want you to have a word with our coachman."

"Are we leaving tomorrow?"

"Most certainly. At first light."

"What do you want him to do, Professor?"

"Just make sure that our bags are on the brougham and that he's waiting for us at first light down by the old packhorse bridge."

"The stone bridge across the river?"

"That's the one. Then I want you to go to the barn and make sure the flying machine is fuelled-up and ready to go."

"Are we going to fly out?"

"If necessary. As you know, every good burglar prepares an alternative way of escape."

Grimdale nodded.

"Then, first thing in the morning, go back to the barn and light the boiler. Until then, the night and the girl are yours."

Shortly after midnight, I tried the door of the Countess's bedroom. The handle turned easily and without a sound. Inside, the air was infused with the smell of expensive cologne. The Countess was alone, lying on her back; a well-upholstered woman in a well-upholstered bed. She was snoring like a pig. The sleeping potion had obviously worked. It ought to have done. There was enough in that vial to put an elephant out for the count.

Now I had to find the necklace. But where would she have put it? The Countess had boasted about keeping it close to herself at all times. The idea of searching her person didn't appeal to me in the slightest, so I began with the bedside cabinet. I had a lantern with hinged shutters on all four sides. This was the only light I had to work with. In addition, I would have to rely on the well-honed sensitivity of my fingertips.

The top drawer contained only personal documents. I slipped these into my coat pocket. Then I tried the middle drawer. Nothing. Then a stroke of luck. I found the jewels in the bottom drawer. They were in an ordinary jewellery-case, hidden beneath a large fur hat. I took the jewels, returned the case and closed the drawer.

On my way out, I dropped the wine waiter's button onto the floor beside the bed. That would see his goose nicely cooked.

It was still dark when I reached Sir Henry's study early the next morning. The safe stood in its usual place, against the wall directly opposite the door. I lit my lantern and knelt down to examine the lock. It was a simple combination affair. I tried the number we'd extracted from Jeremiah Silt just before he died. It was no use. Pulmorton had obviously changed the combination number. I'd certainly have done the same in his shoes.

It didn't really matter. I had it open within five minutes anyway.

I was now glad that I was wearing my voluminous coat with the cavernous pockets. It might look an ungainly garment, but it is extremely practical for a burglar. Faced with a pile of jewellery-cases, and with no time to examine their contents, I transferred them all to the pockets of my coat.

At the back of the safe, I found what I was looking for. The bundle of papers we'd taken from Silt outside the German Embassy. I took them out of the safe and locked it again. Then I stood up and turned towards the study door.

There, in the gloom, I saw Sir Henry Pulmorton. He was standing in the doorway, holding a double-barrelled shotgun, and pointing it directly at me.

"Moriarty!" he exclaimed. "I've had a message from Whitehall warning me not to trust you. Now I see the truth of it. I've sent a telegram to Scotland Yard, asking what they know about you. I expect a reply imminently."

I'd anticipated something like this. That's the trouble with honest people; you just can't trust them. But it was too late now to protest my innocence.

"Damn you, Mycroft!" I hissed. "And damn you too, Pulmorton!"

"No, you're the one who'll be damned, Moriarty," he growled. "Put those things back in my safe, or I'll shoot you as an intruder."

Was he bluffing? Did he have the nerve to pull the trigger? In this world, I consider myself the measure of all things. If the hereafter brings judgement, then I shall have to face it in due time. But I had no wish to be sent to my doom by Sir Henry Pulmorton. Nor, on the other hand, did I wish to return my ill-gotten gains to his safe. The result was a tense stand-off.

It was now that Grimdale appeared. And just in time, as well. He opened the front door and called out, "Everything's ready, Professor."

Instinctively, Sir Henry turned his attention away from me and looked out into the entrance hall.

I am no gymnast, but today I had to act quickly. In the blink of an eyelid, I kicked out at the shotgun in Sir Henry's hands.

The gun went off, peppering the ceiling above us with the contents of both barrels, and bringing down a shower of plaster. The noise was loud enough to waken the dead. The fact that it would rouse the rest of the household was bad enough. Time was now extremely short.

When Sir Henry turned to face me again, I pressed the point of my swordstick blade tightly against his throat.

"Drop the gun, Sir Henry," I told him.

He dropped it onto the floor beside him.

"Now step away from it."

He shuffled to one side.

Without repeating Sir Henry's mistake of taking my eyes off my opponent, I spoke to Grimdale. "We have to get away from here quickly," I told him. "Go back to the barn and open the doors."

When my companion had left, Sir Henry turned his blazing eyes fully onto me. "You'll never be able to fly that machine, Moriarty," he growled. "It took me twelve months to learn, and then I crashed the thing."

"I'm a fast learner," I replied.

"Very well. Take the thing, and break your neck."

I could hear footsteps hurrying along the corridor. It was time to leave. I sheathed the blade, picked up the shotgun and rushed outside. There I dropped the weapon into the herbaceous border. I hoped that might give me enough time to get clear of the grounds.

When I reached the barn, I found that Grimdale had the flying machine ready for me. It was an impressive sight. The boiler was bubbling nicely, steam was bursting out through gaps in the machine's boiler-jacket, and the sweet smell of industrial alcohol was hanging in the morning air.

I climbed onto the seat and jammed the blueprints safely behind a couple of struts. Then I pushed my cane into a space beside the seat and pulled my hat firmly down on my head.

Pulmorton had been right about the controls. They were fiendishly complicated. I was now faced with a confusing array of valves, cranks, dials and foot-pedals.

I tried to remember what Sir Henry had told me on my previous visit. I cautiously opened a valve. High-pressure steam hissed into the engine cylinders. One of the dials indicated an increase in steam-pressure. The four-bladed propeller started to turn. The flying machine emerged under its own power and began to move slowly along the pathway. The wheels rattled noisily on the hard-packed earth.

Then I heard angry shouts coming from somewhere nearby. I needed to make a quick exit. I opened the steam valve still further. The pressure in the engine now increased rapidly, the propeller began to turn more quickly, and the machine shot forward, giving me a violent kick in the rear.

A gunshot rang out. Trust Sir Henry to have another twelve-bore. I was spared a direct hit as shotgun pellets peppered the structures around me. One of them hit the fuel cylinder, and alcohol-spirits began to spray out through the hole. I was lucky the entire thing hadn't exploded there and then.

As the flying machine picked up speed, a gust of wind caught the wings and made it swerve off the pathway. Fortunately, the wheelbase was wide enough to keep it upright when it landed on the lawn. On the other hand, it was now out of control, and careered across the front lawn like a demented chicken. Its wheels gouged unsightly ruts in the carefully manicured turf. I didn't know how to control the thing, let alone how to make it take off. All I could do was to hang on tightly.

The machine soon reached the end of the lawn, where it bounced against the raised edge of the gravel footpath and hopped across the ha-ha. No longer having any solid ground beneath it, the machine began to fall. Desperate to avoid a crash, I opened the steam-valve as far as it would go. The contraption immediately picked up speed, and just about managed to keep clear of the ground. I was flying!

I had no idea how to control the direction of travel. I was having to learn the basics of flying as I went along. At the same time, my mathematical brain was devising possible improvements to the design.

Using a mixture of cold logic and blind panic, I fiddled with the controls until the wings opened to their fullest extent. Then I managed to alter the camber of the leading edge of the wings. These, together with the early morning breeze and increased airspeed, made the flying machine slowly gain height.

But something was wrong. I sensed that the machine was overbalanced at the front. I looked down and saw Grimdale hanging onto the wheel struts for dear life.

"What are you doing there?" I shouted.

"I wasn't going to stay and have that maniac shoot at me," he hollered back.

At that moment, the morning sun rose from behind a nearby hill and bathed the countryside in its bright warming glow.

In its light, the harsh shadow of the bat-shaped flying machine swept rapidly and menacingly across the landscape beneath us. Seen from below, the spectacle must have been utterly bizarre. Black against the clear blue sky, a tall man in a top-hat and flapping coat-tails was riding a gigantic bat, whilst another man was desperately clinging on underneath.

The effect it had on the estate workers, who were coming out to begin their daily work in the fields, was startling. When they saw us coming, many of them ran away screaming. Others simply stood still, gazing into the sky, with eyes and mouths wide open in terror.

Superstitious minds might have thought that we were a vampire fleeing the light of the new day, and coming to suck their blood. Scaring people witless always gives me a great thrill.

The land was now sloping downhill. As I'd intended, we were flying towards the river in the bottom of the valley. More alarmingly, we were heading directly towards a line of trees on the far bank of the river. With the additional weight on board, we were flying so low that we risked going straight into them.

I knew I had to jettison something. I now had a choice. Either I choose to throw away the boxes in my pockets, together with the treasures they undoubtedly contained, or else I elect to drop Grimdale off as soon as possible.

It was no contest.

I noticed a willow tree on the nearside bank of the river and decided to direct the machine towards it. I flexed the ends of the wings and leaned over to my left. The machine began to turn. My colleague's extra weight helped, and we were soon making our way directly towards the willow. We flew so close to the treetop that Grimdale became entangled in the upper branches. He released his grip on the undercarriage and fell ten feet into the water below.

Now free from its destabilising load, the machine quickly gained height. Indeed, it rose so steeply that it rapidly lost airspeed. With the fuel also running low, the propeller lost power, and the flying machine plummeted towards the ground.

I struggled frantically with the wings, trying to direct the falling machine towards the far bank of the river. I had no intention of getting wet like Grimdale, but I didn't want to kill myself either, so I looked desperately for somewhere soft to land.

Then I spotted it. Along one edge of the riverside meadow, just in front of the trees, stood a large haystack. My only hope now was to I reach this without hitting the trees. I flexed the wings, held tightly onto my hat, and prepared to hit the ground.

The flying machine landed in the haystack with a tremendous crash. It immediately broke up. The impact threw me out of my seat and into a pile of soft grass. Some might think I didn't deserve such an easy landing, but they can keep their opinions to themselves. I admit I was shaken, but I was also relieved that I was able to walk away from the wreckage.

Which was just as well. A few seconds later, the remains of the flying machine burst into flames. The pall of black smoke drifted across the fields, turning the sweet morning air acrid with the smell of burning hay and scorched textile fabric. The heat was so intense that it forced me to back away. At least I still had my hat and cane with me.

The estate workers, having overcome their initial shock, now came running. They used anything they could lay their hands on to try to beat out the flames and save what was left of the haystack.

As arranged beforehand, our carriage was standing beside the old stone bridge. The coachman now opened the door and helped me climb aboard. Once inside, I sat down and heaved a sigh of relief.

A moment later, Grimdale joined me there. He was soaked to the skin. I had no time for sympathy; my mind was already on other things.

"To the German Embassy," I announced. "Let's hope their government official still wants to buy the plans to Sir Henry's flying machine."

It was only as I looked around for the blueprints that I realised where they were. For safety, I'd pushed them behind some struts on the machine. They were still there, already burnt to ashes.

I roundly cursed my bad luck.

"All that work for nothing," said Grimdale.

I felt like throwing the man back into the river.

"Drive on," I told the coachman.

As we rumbled out of the estate, I took off my hat and pulled something out from beneath the lining. It was the diamond necklace belonging to the Countess.

The sight of the jewels cheered us both up as nothing else could have done at that moment.

Grimdale gave a low whistle. "It must be worth a king's ransom," he gasped.

Then I took out the jewellery boxes I'd removed from Sir Henry's safe. We opened them one by one and took out their contents.

"You must have got every piece of jewellery the Countess owns," said Grimdale.

"She is indeed a very rich lady," I replied.

"Or at least, she used to be," added my companion.

"Scotland Yard are already making plans to arrest me," I said. "This is going to stir them up like a nest of hornets."

"They'll scour the entire country looking for us," Grimdale told me.

"In that case," I replied, "we're going to need a vacation. Somewhere abroad, I think. Possibly Switzerland."

# The Pharaoh's Curse
by Robert V. Stapleton

I had never before seen the eyes of my friend Sherlock Holmes sparkle with such rage. He was sitting beside the empty fireplace, staring directly into the face of a young woman in the chair opposite him. The moment I walked in through the door of his rooms in Baker Street, I was in no doubt about the depth of his feelings.

"Are you telling me, Miss Venton," said Holmes, "that you want me to help you find a bag of old bones?"

Her bright blue eyes stared back at him, inflexible and unrepentant. "Hardly any old bones, Mr. Holmes. It's more a matter of finding the mortal remains of a First Dynasty Egyptian king. Pharaoh Amkotep, no less."

"It is as I said. A bag of old bones. I'm sorry, but I can do nothing to help you."

I stepped forward, to try to bring peace between them. "Now, Holmes," I said, "you can hardly turn the young woman away so abruptly when she's come to seek your professional help."

Without looking up at me, he waved vaguely in my direction. "This is my colleague, Dr. Watson. He wanders in here from time to time."

She acknowledged my presence with a slight tilt of the head.

I smiled in return.

Holmes now turned his gaze fully on to me. "You deal with it, then, Watson. You know my methods. Although I hardly think you'll need them in this case. Without having any other facts to go on, I should say the matter is perfectly straightforward."

He turned away, picked up his violin, and began to pluck a tune, pizzicato, on the strings.

I dropped my evening paper onto the table, pulled up a straight-backed chair, and sat down facing the young lady. "I'm sorry for my friend's rudeness," I said. "Am I to understand that your name is Venton?"

"That's right. Beatrice Venton."

"Then, Miss Venton, perhaps you'd like to tell me your story."

She gave Holmes one more poisonous look, and turned to face me. "Very well, Dr. Watson. But I don't think anyone can help me now. Mr. Holmes was my very last hope."

"Sometimes it can help simply to share a problem with somebody else."

She looked down at her hands, folded in her lap. "Very well." She took a deep breath. "You might have heard of Dr. Seymour Venton."

"The famous Egyptologist? Of course."

She looked up at me. "He's my father. He has spent much of the last fifteen years searching for, and unearthing, the relics of people who lived in Ancient Egypt. Especially their mummified remains."

"That's very interesting."

"For the last five years, I have been my father's constant companion and co-worker in Egypt."

Without interrupting his tune, Holmes said, "Hence your tanned skin, caused by constant exposure to the sun. And the scarab beetle ornament on a chain around your neck."

"The scarab?" I hadn't noticed that.

She gave a self-conscious smile, and held the necklace out so that I could see the fine workmanship of the scarab. "From the tomb of Pharaoh Ramses."

I nodded. "Please continue, Miss Venton."

She gazed into the unfocused distance. "For a long time, we had been searching specifically for the remains of

Pharaoh Amkotep. Trying to fill in the blank pages of the mysterious period of history covering his brief reign."

"With no success?"

"Oh, we did indeed have success. Initially, at any rate. We worked hard to find the burial place. We scoured the archives, researched the history of ancient rulers, and dug in numerous locations. Then, we found him. Still in his sarcophagus, in a stone-lined tomb in the desert of the Upper Nile valley. But no sooner had we uncovered the remains than a band of grave-robbers came along one night and removed the mummified remains of our pharaoh. One of our Egyptian workers had betrayed us. We thought we would never see his remains again."

"But?"

She abruptly turned her gaze onto me once more. "Dr. Watson, there is just a chance that the pharaoh has been brought to this country. For what reason, I have no idea."

"Why do you say that?"

She became agitated. Then she stood up, stepped over to the window and looked outside. Not seeing the daily activities of Baker Street, but some horrible scene painted by her own imagination.

"We had a stroke of luck. We knew a man who worked at the docks in Alexandria. He told us of a cartel that specialised in exporting mummified remains. To places all over the world. It's nothing new. There are reports of mummies being sent to the United States, to be used for a whole list of frivolous purposes. Some have even been fed into the paper mills. Can you believe it?"

"And I suppose it's all quite legal."

"Legal, yes. But morally reprehensible. As far as I'm concerned, anyway. Well, our friend told us that some of the mummies were being exported to England. So we turned our search back to London, on the off chance, but the trail went cold. Now, all we have to go on is a name. Dackford."

Holmes interrupted his playing. And looked up at her. "Dackford? Mr. Cornelius Dackford?"

"Have you heard of him, Mr. Holmes?"

"It's a name whispered in hushed tones among the lower classes of society." He stood up. A light had now entered his eyes. The light of a chase. "But I don't know where he resides at the moment. Perhaps this is a case for the Baker Street Irregulars."

Within ten minutes, the leader of the band of street urchins was standing in front of us. "What can we do for you, Mr. Holmes?"

"I want you to find somebody for me, Wiggins."

"We're good at that kind of thing, Mr. Holmes."

"I know you are. So you should have no difficulty finding this individual." He looked to Miss Venton. There was now a fragment of hope in her eyes as well. "I want to know the whereabouts of a man called Dackford. Cornelius Dackford. It seems he trades in exotic goods."

"Usual rates, Mr. Holmes?"

"Usual rates. And double if you manage it by breakfast tomorrow morning."

The following morning, we called on Mr. Dackford. He owned a warehouse down by the docks. It was a disreputable place, with water dripping from a broken pipe in one corner of the building, and rats scuttling around in dark holes and murky shadows. Not a suitable resting place for a ruler of ancient Egypt.

A man answered our knock. He was thin, balding, and had skin as yellow as parchment.

"Mr. Dackford?"

The man glared at us through narrowed eyes, and blew a cloud of tobacco smoke into our faces.

"Hmm," mused Holmes. "I see you smoke a German brand of tobacco, Mr. Dackford."

"Here. Who are you?"

"This is Mr. Sherlock Holmes," I replied, "and I am Dr. John Watson."

"And the young lady?"

"Miss Beatrice Venton. The daughter of an eminent Egyptologist."

Dackford cast his dark eyes suspiciously up and down the back lane.

"And what do you want with me?"

"We're looking for the mummified remains of a pharaoh," said Holmes. "Amkotep."

"Doesn't mean anything to me," said Dackford, giving an exaggerated shrug. "Can't tell one of them blighters from another. What does it matter, anyway? They're all dead and gone."

"It might matter if you were working for a gang of smugglers."

Dackford looked offended. "Now listen, Mr. Holmes. Everything I do here is quite legal, whatever else you might think of it."

"I'm glad to hear it. But the police might still be interested in some of your other activities. At the very least, they might want to search your premises here."

"You can't frighten me."

"Then perhaps you can help us in our search."

Dackford gave a non-committal sniff, and pointed to a wooden chest in the far corner of the room. "Have a look through that lot. They're a load of charms and bracelets we've taken from some of them mummies. Nothing of much value. If you're lucky, you might just find something to keep you happy."

Whilst Holmes wandered around the storage area, his eyes scanning every inch of the place, I stood beside Miss Venton as she searched through the collection of trinkets.

Most of it was rubbish, but after several minutes she stood up again, holding a delicate fragment of cloth in her hands. "Look. This piece of fabric. There's an ancient cartouche still visible on it." She looked at me. "The name of Pharaoh Amkotep."

I looked down at the material in her hands. "Are you sure?"

"Of course I'm sure, Dr. Watson. I've spent years looking for these hieroglyphs. They're branded into my memory."

Holmes turned towards Dackford. "So, even if it isn't here now, that mummy certainly has been here in the recent past."

The man gave a sour look.

"To whom did you supply that mummy?"

"I don't remember. And anyway, I often send them to auction. Sell them anonymous, like."

"I only need a name."

Dackford turned nasty. "Well that's all you're getting out of me."

Holmes sniffed the air. "Tell me, Mr. Dackford," he said. "Those German cigarettes. Did one of your clients supply them to you?"

Dackford's eyes bulged in anger as he wrestled to control his temper.

"But there's something more on this cloth," said Miss Venton. "Along with the cartouche, there are other hieroglyphs." She looked up at us with concern. "It's not unknown to find them in such tombs, but it tells of a curse on anyone who disturbs his bones."

Holmes shook his head. "A curse only has power over you if you believe that it has."

But Dackford was interested now. "A curse, you say? I'll be able to charge at least twice the going rate for something like that. Now, clear off, all of you. I've got work to do."

As we left the warehouse, Miss Venton looked deflated.

"Cheer up," I said. "At least we know that your lost pharaoh passed this way."

"Yes," she said, "but we've no idea where the trail leads from here."

"Perhaps not," said Holmes. "But the initial indications are suggestive."

After we had escorted Miss Venton to her lodgings, Holmes and I took a cab to Oxford Street, and decided to walk the rest of the way. During those next few minutes, Holmes stopped at every newsstand and kiosk within sight, and collected a copy of every different newspaper edition he could find.

The moment we stepped through the door of his rooms in Baker Street, Holmes tossed the newspapers onto the carpet in front of the fireplace, cast aside his hat, coat, and cane, and knelt down amongst this array of newsprint. He divided them between us, and we began to search through them.

"What exactly are we looking for, Holmes," I asked him.

He looked up at me as if I were stupid. "You know what unscrupulous people do with mummified remains, don't you, Watson?"

I gave him a bland stare.

"You'll be aware of an interest among the general public in viewing grotesque exhibits. The fairgrounds and amusements parks are full of them. Charlatans and tricksters make a great deal of money from catering to the morbid curiosity of the general public."

"Of course. And the unwrapping of mummified remains has recently become one such ghoulish entertainment. Yes, I've heard of them, but I've never been to such an event."

"Then perhaps you need to broaden your horizons," said Holmes. "We're looking for any report of an unwrapping occasion. It will probably appear as an advertisement, inviting those with a macabre taste to attend a scientific event, or some such poppy-cock."

We searched.

Holmes was the one who found it. An invitation for members of the public to gather for an unrolling event. In was to take place in a basement room attached to a teaching hospital on the south bank of the Thames. Tickets to be purchased in advance from a certain Professor Tobias Powell. No address was given.

Holmes tossed the newspapers to one side, and began to search through his own collection of cuttings and documents. The storage system rapidly descended into chaos. Mrs. Hudson would once more be kept busy re-establishing order there.

"Here he is," said Holmes. "Professor Tobias Powell. An entrepreneur who describes himself as a scientist, a dealer in the extraordinary, and a collector of the exotic."

"Perhaps we should have a word with this Professor Powell."

"Well, you'll certainly have to do that if you want to buy a ticket for that unrolling event. Fortunately, we now have an address."

"I am indeed honoured to meet you, Mr. Holmes," said Tobias Powell, as he ushered the three of us in to the study of his modest town-house.

I looked around the room. A vase of flowers stood on a side-table. It held a single red rose, a single white carnation, and several green leaves of lily of the valley. The sweet smell filled the room, and helped to cover the smell of tobacco-smoke that lingered in the air.

Powell turned to face us. "Won't you please sit down, gentlemen and lady?"

We did so.

"Now, why would a great detective like you, Mr. Holmes, be interested in my humble affairs?"

"Merely helping out our client," said Holmes. "Miss Venton here is trying to discover what happened to the mummified remains of a certain Egyptian pharaoh."

"I'm not sure I can help."

"But I understand," said Holmes, 'that you organise events at which mummified remains are unwrapped."

"I have indeed organised such occasions in the past. And I make no secret of the fact. But we are very particular about whom we allow to such evenings. We advertise widely, but we select with extreme care."

"Very wise," said Holmes. "But we are looking for one particular mummy. The Pharaoh Amkotep."

"I'm not an Egyptologist, Mr. Holmes. So I really cannot help you. But, if you would like to attend one of our sessions, then I'd be very pleased to add your name to our list. Perhaps you might like to attend the event we are holding on Thursday of this week."

"That is very kind of you," said Holmes. "But I shall be busy with other matters on that particular day. However, I think my friend, Dr. Watson, and my client, Miss Venton, would be happy to attend."

"There is just one problem," I told them. "I happen to be a married man. I can hardly escort Miss Venton there on my own. It just wouldn't be right."

"Then I have perfect the solution," said Powell. "Lord Elstack will be joining us that evening. Perhaps you could come along with him."

Miss Venton looked at me, and smiled. "It sounds like the ideal solution."

"Then that's settled," said Powell. "Seven o'clock at the hospital entrance. Oh, and refreshments will be provided afterwards."

As we were leaving, Holmes turned to face Powell. "Would you mind my asking one particularly pertinent question, Professor?"

"Of course not."

"Of what are you a professor?"

"Modern and Ancient Sciences."

"Of course. Thank you, Professor." Holmes turned away. "It is just as I thought."

On the evening for the unrolling of the mummy, a black brougham pulled up directly outside 221b Baker Street. A man stepped down – rotund, ruddy of complexion, and with a winning smile. He wore a top-hat and a frock-coat. Here was Lord Elstack, an important member of Lord Salisbury's Conservative government.

"Good evening, my Lord," I greeted him.

"Ah, good evening, Dr. Watson. Mycroft Holmes asked if I wouldn't mind calling to collect you this evening. I don't normally act as a taxicab service, but, to tell you the truth, I'd be glad of some company this evening. And some female company at the same time." He smiled at Miss Venton.

"That's very good of you, my Lord. Sherlock Holmes has gone off on business of his own. Again."

The brougham drew up outside the teaching hospital. We climbed down and joined a small group of people already assembled there.

We now numbered eight in total. Four were unknown to me, two ladies and two gentlemen. Then there were the three of us, and the man we had come to know as Professor Tobias Powell.

"Good evening, my Lord, ladies, and gentlemen," he said. "It seems that we are now all present and correct. I would therefore like to invite you to follow me."

He led the way in through the main hospital entrance, and then down into the basement area of the building. At the bottom of a flight of stone steps, he pushed open another door, and welcomed us all into a small underground room. The walls were whitewashed, the floor was covered in green ceramic tiles, and a gas-light hissing above a small stone mantelpiece. A second door, on the far side of the room, was shut. A cupboard stood in one corner, and a large table took pride of place in the middle of the room. On this table lay a figure, wrapped in a white sheet. It had the outline shape of a human body.

We gathered around the table.

The door opened again, and an elderly man, bent with the deformity of age, shuffled into the room. He was wearing the overalls of a hospital porter. The man coughed loudly, and introduced himself. "My name's Jenkins. I work for the hospital. They've asked me to come and represent them this evening."

Powell wasn't pleased to see the old man. "Very well," he said, with a hint of impatience. "If you really have to."

"Don't worry, sir," said Jenkins. "I'll stay in the corner, out of your way."

Powell now turned to face his guests. "My Lord, ladies and gentlemen," he began, "welcome to this special event.

The unrolling of the mummified remains of an official from Ancient Egypt. After the unrolling, you are invited to join us for refreshments in the room next door. But, back to the business in hand. Many years ago, the official we are about to meet held power in the land of Egypt. Possibly even as a pharaoh. This evening, these remains will see the light of day for the very first time in nearly four-thousand years."

Everyone in the room was already entranced by this presentation, and we hadn't even started yet. Miss Venton looked on, with a severe expression on her face. But soon she too was captivated by the occasion.

"However," continued Powell. "I must warn you. I have received information that this particular burial comes with a curse attached to it. If you believe in such things."

Miss Venton nodded slowly.

"If any of you would like to leave," said Powell, "please do so now. Otherwise, you will remain here entirely at your own risk."

We all remained where we were. Rooted to the spot. Our morbid curiosity now fully aroused.

Powell wandered over to the cupboard, and came back a moment later having exchanged his jacket for a white laboratory coat. He was also carrying a number of modern surgical and medical tools.

The unrolling began. Powell first pulled open the outer rolls of cloth. Dust filled the atmosphere, along with a smell that made us all pull back in disgust. Some of the onlookers had to reach for their handkerchiefs.

The lower part of the corpse appeared first. The legs and torso were withered and blackened with age. The desiccated body had shrivelled so much that the ribs showed through what remained of the skin.

Then, as a climax, Powell unveiled the head. "Behold, the face of the ancient world."

Now we had our first glimpse of the pharaoh himself. The skin again was black, and pulled taut across the skull. But the face had character. Here was somebody who had once lived and breathed just like each one of us. Each person present had their own reaction. The ladies looked horrified, the gentlemen looked on with a more objective eye, and Powell looked satisfied. Lord Elstack appeared overawed by the sight of the mummy. Miss Venton's eyebrows narrowed in horror. And, for myself, I have to admit, I could hardly take my eyes away from that face. It was a sight that might haunt a man's dreams for many years to come. The only person who was unmoved by the experience was the old man, Jenkins. He sat by himself in the corner of the room, and watched the reaction of the others impassively.

Miss Venton spoke up. "This is the pharaoh my father discovered in Upper Egypt."

"How can you tell that?" I asked her.

"You remember the cartouche we found at Dackford's warehouse?"

"Yes."

"Then look." She grasped hold of the charm around the mummy's neck. "This has the same name. Amkotep."

Powell turned towards us. His face twisted into a scowl. "If you're saying you have a claim to this mummy, then you're too late. For the moment, I must ask you to remain quiet."

But Miss Venton would not be silenced. "You rogue," she shouted. "You thief. My father and I spent many years looking for this mummy."

"I know nothing about that," said Powell. "And if you make any trouble in here, young lady, then I shall ask you to leave. If you wish to keep the charm, then you're welcome to it. But don't spoil the evening for the rest of us."

She agreed to accept the necklace, and calmed down.

After several more minutes, we had all had our fill of dust and death.

Powell stepped back, and rubbed his hands. "Now, my Lord, ladies and gentlemen. Refreshments are available for you in the next room. Please make your way through the side-door. And I hope you all manage to stay clear of the pharaoh's curse." He laughed, and opened the door.

Miss Venton and I stayed behind. She was still looking at the remains of the mummy. Transfixed.

I was about to follow the others through the door, when I felt somebody tug at my sleeve. I looked round. It was the man, Jenkins.

"Excuse me, sir," he said. "I have a cab waiting outside. For you and the young lady. I think it would be wise if you left immediately."

Neither Miss Venton nor I were in any mood for light refreshments and inane small-talk. Without hesitation, we both followed the old man out the way we had come, up the stone steps and out through the main entrance. Then we climbed into the cab that was indeed waiting for us at the roadside. To my surprise, the old man climbed in after us. And sat down opposite me.

I looked at him more closely now. He removed his cap, brushed out his hair, and unbuttoned his overalls.

Now I recognised him. "Holmes!"

"You didn't think I'd leave you there on your own, did you?" said Holmes. "I've been investigating our friend back there. It is as I suspected – he is no professor. At least, not of any institution in this country."

The case, it seemed, was now over. Closed. Our client, Miss Venton, was clearly disappointed, but her questions had now been answered. I had assumed we were dealing with a simple case of grave-robbing. But that assumption was about to be proved wrong.

I called round to Baker Street the following morning.

The room was already filled with tobacco smoke, and the seats beside the fireplace were occupied by two men, Inspector Lestrade of Scotland Yard, and Holmes's brother Mycroft. My friend was pacing the carpet, deep in meditation.

As I entered the room, he looked up. "Ah, Watson. About time, too."

I was taken aback by this abrupt welcome. "I thought the case was closed," I said. "Miss Venton found her pharaoh, and now at least she has possession of the mummy's necklace."

"Perhaps," said Holmes, "but things have taken a darker turn." He waved his hand towards the seated men.

I looked towards them. "What's happened?"

It was Lestrade who answered. "Dr. Watson, did you last night attend an event at which an Egyptian mummy was unwrapped?"

"Yes. I went there with Miss Venton."

"Was the event organised by a man who called himself Professor Powell?"

"I think you already know it was."

Mycroft said, "A problem has arisen as a result of that evening."

"Problem? What problem?"

"There were eight people present, I believe."

"That's right."

"This morning, four of those people are seriously ill in hospital. And one man is dead. They were all taken ill shortly after leaving the hospital building."

I was horrified. I looked to Holmes. He shook his head, as though to advise me not to mention his presence there.

"And Powell?"

Lestrade replied, "There's not a sign of him anywhere. We've visited his home. We've searched the hospital. And now we are having all the ports put on alert for him."

"A waste of time," muttered Holmes. "You can be sure the bird will have flown these shores well before dawn."

"As a man of science," I said, "I hesitate to mention it, but Powell did warn us that the pharaoh's tomb had a curse on it. Even Miss Venton found evidence of that. I just wonder if the death have anything to do with that curse."

Mycroft pulled a sour face. "If you believe in such things."

"What do the other victims say?"

"They all seem to agree with you, Dr. Watson," said Lestrade.

"But the symptoms suggest another reason for their illness," said Mycroft. "It seems they are consistent with strychnine poisoning."

"Strychnine?"

"Hardly the work of some four-thousand year old mummy," said Holmes. "I would normally dismiss the story of the curse as superstitious nonsense, and eliminate it as a possibility. But when a man really believes in such things, then a curse has real power. Either way, now we know we are dealing with a poisoning, and we stand on more solid ground."

"But I'm as fit this morning as I was last night," I said. "And I haven't heard that Miss Venton has been taken ill."

"Miss Venton has left town to visit her father," said Lestrade, "so we must assume that she also avoided being poisoned."

Mycroft looked at me. "Why do you imagine that these poor people were affected, when you and Miss Venton were not?"

I made the connection immediately. "They all stayed for refreshments afterwards. That must have been how they were poisoned. Ingestion of contaminated food. Then the symptoms must have come on fairly quickly afterwards. Cramps, stiffness of the joints, agitation, seizures. They would need professional help almost at once. It's a good job they were already in a hospital at the time."

Holmes looked towards me. His eyes flashing. "Once again, it all points to this fellow Powell. Don't you see it?"

I shook my head. "Who was the poor fellow who died?"

"Lord Elstack," said Mycroft. "That's why I'm here. He was a senior member of the government. The P.M. is livid about this. He wants the perpetrator's head on a platter. As soon as ever possible."

"But you can't find him."

Lestrade shook his head sadly.

Holmes strode towards the door. "Then it's up to us to solve the riddle. Come along, Watson. You too, Mycroft. We must visit the scene of the crime."

"The hospital?"

"No. The home of Lord Elstack."

The house was swathed in gloom when we arrived. The curtains were closed. The servants were moving around more quietly than usual. And the man's wife was sitting in the front reception room. She looked deflated, and her eyes were red with crying.

"Good morning, your ladyship. My name is Sherlock Holmes, and this is my friend and colleague, Dr. Watson."

"Welcome, gentlemen," said the lady. "I'm sorry I can't greet you more warmly this morning."

"Indeed. It must be a very difficult time for you."

"I've already given the police a statement, so I don't think I can tell you anything new, Mr. Holmes."

He drew up a chair, and sat down beside the grieving widow. "I'm sure this has come as a great shock to you, Lady Elstack, but I would like you to tell me anything that might be relevant. However odd or peculiar it might seem."

She looked up at him. "My husband was taken ill even before he walked through the door. Oh, it was terrible. His muscles went into spasm. But that was only the start of it. He became agitated. Soon he was sweating like a pig, and his heart was beating rapidly. It only grew worse during the night. Mr. Holmes, my husband was turning blue. I called in the family doctor, but he felt my husband was too ill to move. So I stayed with him. And I didn't leave his side for one moment. Until he finally passed away. In the end, it was his heart that failed."

"All classic signs of acute strychnine poisoning," I said gently.

"And, did he say anything at all?" asked Holmes.

Lady Elstrack pressed a black silk handkerchief to her eyes. "There was something. I think."

"Please, try to remember. Any detail might hold the key to uncovering the mystery behind this terrible event."

"At first, he told me it was the Curse of the Pharaoh. Punishment meted out to anyone who disturbed his ancient bones"

"And then?"

"Then, towards the end, he tried to say something else."

"Yes?"

"His mind was clearly deranged. As far as I could make out, he said '*green the land, red the cliffs and white the sand.*'"

Holmes looked up, as though a great light had shone into a darkened room. "'*These are the colours . . . .*'"

"' . . . . *of Heligoland.*'" Mycroft completed the proverb.

Holmes looked up at me. "Watson. When we visited Powell in his home, what did you see there?"

"Some flowers."

"Yes, but what colours were they?"

"A red rose and a white carnation. Flowers with a message. Both messages of hope and love."

"And lily of the valley. Sweet flowers with green leaves."

"A message of sweetness and happiness."

"And," said Mycroft, "put together, they are the colours which represent the island of Heligoland."

"But there was more," said Holmes. "In the entrance hallway, I noticed a pair of boots. Ingrained in the cleats were small particles of red sandstone. Add to that the fact that our friend Powell was wearing a watch-chain with a fob in the shape of an anchor. Then add the fact that the smoke of German tobacco was hanging in the air."

"I don't follow."

"We have a Germanophile, with a love of the sea, who has recently been walking on red sandstone. There is only one place anywhere near the coast of Germany where red sandstone can be found."

"The island of Heligoland?"

"Precisely."

"And the poisoning?"

"If you wanted to hide a murder by poison, the best way to evade detection is to make it look like an accident. Hide it amongst other poisonings that can be explained."

I rubbed my brow. "I see. So, presumably his Lordship ingested a much larger dose than any of the others, and suffered much more serious effects as a result."

Holmes struck his forehead with the heel of his hand. "Watson, I've been a complete idiot. I should be kicked all the way from here to Charing Cross. This isn't a pharaoh's curse. It isn't even a careless death or a mindless murder. This is a political assassination."

Back at Baker Street, Mycroft sat back in an armchair, and began to explain the situation. "The island of Heligoland lies twenty-eight miles from the North Sea coast of Germany. It was ceded to Britain from Denmark after the Napoleonic Wars. Apart from a roost for thousands of seabirds, it also provides a strategic location for its British garrison. When the Kiel Canal is finally completed, Heligoland will lie like a dagger at the very jugular of German power in the North Sea. Lord Salisbury is currently negotiating to exchange the island for control over certain territories held by Germany in Central and Eastern Africa. The Germans want that island, and intend to have it. The Prime Minister is equally determined to have those territories."

"And where does Lord Elstack fit into the picture?" I asked.

"Isn't it obvious? He has always been opposed to the idea. Bitterly opposed. And he's been making enemies over the issue. The Prime Minister, for one, together with certain powerful figures on both sides of the North Sea."

"So who killed him? Surely not the British government."

"Certainly not. Your see, Elstack had one important supporter. The Queen herself. No, the killer is nobody in the British government."

I was dumbfounded. "Are you saying it's the Germans who've murdered him?"

"I don't think so. This man Powell is English, but he has a genuine love for Germany and for that island. For some reason, he is prepared to stop at nothing to see the island of Heligoland handed over to Germany."

I looked to Holmes. "So, what do we do now?"

"We travel to where the answer must undoubtedly be found. Heligoland."

Mycroft stood up, abruptly. "I shall arrange to have a cruiser waiting for you both in Harwich. The afternoon train should get you there in time to sail this evening."

"You'd better go and pack some personal items then, Watson," said Holmes. "Oh, and don't forget to include your service revolver."

It was early on the second day after leaving Harwich when I staggered out onto the foredeck of the cruiser. We had been sailing east, but had now turned towards the southeast. The dawn was rising red and angry ahead of us. Silhouetted dark against the burning sky stood Sherlock Holmes. His arms were folded across his chest, his coat was billowing out in the gathering breeze, and his eyes were fixed on the sea ahead. He was standing like some conquering hero – perhaps like Washington crossing the Delaware. Full of purpose and intent. Seasickness might lay me low, but never Holmes.

The First Officer joined us on deck, and pointed towards a hunk of land just visible above the horizon. "You'll be pleased to know gentlemen that we are now within sight of Heligoland."

"I shall certainly be glad to set foot of dry land again," I told him.

"However," he continued, "as you'll have noticed, a storm is brewing. So we'll approach the island from the far side. It'll give us shelter from the roughest of the weather."

We stood watching carefully as we approached the island. We saw waves breaking in a cloud of spume against the foot of precipitous cliffs. A sea-stack rose in a tall column of red sandstone, with white seabirds flocking around its treacherous upper reaches.

"Lange Anna," said Holmes. "A landmark in this area."

"And there's a lighthouse flashing farther south along the west coast."

"That's interesting."

We sailed down the east coast of the island and dropped anchor not far from the *Unterland*, a low lying region of reclaimed land on the south and east of the island. Beyond this rose the red cliffs of the *Oberland*.

The cruiser's boat dropped us off on the lea-side of a breakwater. Which was just as well, since the seas were rising alarmingly now. The wind was strengthening and the sky was turning an inky black.

"Have you brought your revolver with you, Watson?"

"You've no need to worry over that score, Holmes," I said.

"Then let's make our way into the town, and make enquiries about our man."

One of the locals directed us to the residence of the Lieutenant Governor. We knocked on the door, and a man opened to us.

"Good afternoon," I said. "This is Mr. Sherlock Holmes, and I am Dr. John Watson. We are here on official business, and we need to introduce ourselves to the Governor.

"I'm sorry, but the Governor is away just at the moment. Visiting Berlin. I'm his secretary. Is there any way I can help you?"

"We're looking for a fugitive from the law," said Holmes. "A man who goes by the name of Professor Powell."

"I know the man very well," said the secretary. "I'm surprised to learn he's done anything wrong. Perhaps you should call in at our local police station."

The police station was more like an ordinary house. The sergeant there seemed interested to learn that he had a villain on the island.

"Yes, I know Professor Powell. And yes, he has only recently returned after a brief visit to England."

"Then perhaps we might have a word with the gentleman," suggested Holmes.

"Certainly. But first, I must give you this. It's a telegram from London. It arrived this morning."

Holmes opened the telegram. "It is as I thought. The matter is now extremely urgent."

"Very well," said the policeman. "Follow me."

The moment he opened his front door to us, Powell recognised who we were. "Ah, Mr. Holmes. And Dr. Watson. What a surprise to see you both here. Won't you please come inside?"

Powell led us in to a small front room, and then turned to face us. He raised one quizzical eyebrow. "How may I help you, gentlemen?"

The darkening sky outside allowed very little daylight to filter in through the two narrow windows. The room was dark and gloomy.

The policeman held up the papers we have given him a few minutes earlier. "These gentlemen have brought a warrant from Scotland Yard. For your arrest, sir."

"Is that so?" Powell now raised both eyebrows in feigned surprise.

"For the murder of Lord Elstack."

"I don't know the man."

"Nonsense," replied Holmes. "He was present at the unwrapping of that mummy in London only a few days ago. Now he is dead. Murdered."

"It's true I have organised the unwrapping of several mummies over recent months. But this is the first time I've ever encountered any trouble. Anyway, you have absolutely no evidence to convict me of any wrongdoing. If the food they ate that evening was contaminated with strychnine, then somebody else must have introduced it to the food when I wasn't looking. If one particular visitor was then greedy enough to eat more than his fair share of the food, then how am I to blame? I repeat, you have no proof of any unlawful activity on my part. If anything is to blame, then it's the curse of the pharaoh. I did warn them about that."

Holmes narrowed his eyebrows, and glared at the man. "Whether it was the curse of the pharaoh, or not, I really don't care, but how did you know it was strychnine poisoning?"

"It was in the newspapers."

"But you had already left the country before the morning papers appeared. And anyway, Scotland Yard withheld the cause of death. Your own mouth condemns you, Powell."

"A slip of the tongue is no proof of guilt. All your evidence against me is purely circumstantial. And anyway, what motive would I possibly have for killing anyone?"

"Mummies were not the only things you were exporting from Africa, were they, Powell?" Holmes shook the telegram in the man's face. "I have discovered that you spent several years living and working in German East Africa. Your love for all things German comes from your time there. Amongst other things, you acted as a middle-man in the export of elephant ivory. I found traces of ivory at Dackford's warehouse. I imagine he's the one who oversees the practical side of your business. I even found him smoking the same German cigarettes you supply him with. When Britain takes over the administration of those African countries, you will be in a position to control of the entire ivory export trade. No wonder you wanted to get rid of anyone who stood in your way. There is your motive for murdering Lord Elstrack. Greed."

"But nothing of my trade is illegal, Mr. Holmes. You still have no proof that I killed anyone."

"Then come back with us, and present your case before a jury."

Powell's eyes darted between the three of us.

The police sergeant stepped forward. "I'm afraid I'm going to have to place you under arrest, Professor."

Powell turned his back on us, opened a drawer in the table, and turned again to face us again.

"Look out, Holmes," I cried. "He's got a gun."

"Now, don't be foolish, Professor," said the police sergeant. "Put that down, and come with me."

Powell hurried towards the door, opened it and turned once more to face the three of us still in the room. "You should have kept your noses out of my business," he yelled. "Now there is no going back. For any of us."

He raised the gun, fired a single shot into the ceiling above our heads and hurried out into the gathering storm.

With my ears ringing from the sound of the gunshot, I ran towards the door. Holmes was already there, watching the dark figure scurry away along a rough track.

"He's making for the lighthouse," said the police sergeant.

"Then we must follow him," said Holmes. "Watson, check your revolver."

"Powell's right, isn't he?" I said. "We have no proof that he is the killer."

"You think not?"

"Well, we don't even know how he managed to kill Lord Elstack, without killing all the other people as well."

"You remember that evening at the unwrapping event?"

"How can I forget it?"

"When Powell collected his medical instruments, he also had with him a hypodermic needle. Now, why would he want one of those to treat a body that had been dead for nearly four thousand years?"

“I can’t imagine.”

“I believe,” said Holmes, ‘that the syringe was loaded with strychnine. Then, just as everyone else in the room was distracted by the gruesome sight of the pharaoh’s body, he plunged the needle into his Lordship’s arm. I am confident that a postmortem examination will reveal a fresh puncture wound.”

“The crafty fellow!”

Rain was already sweeping across the island, soaking everything and everyone in its way. By the time we reached the foot of the lighthouse, we were already drenched. But no matter. We needed to find Powell.

“There he is.” The policeman pointed towards the top of the lighthouse, and the veranda that ran around the outside of the lantern chamber.

We looked up. I could see a figure, standing defiantly against the weather and those who were threatening his freedom.

“Powell!” shouted Holmes. “Come down here, and give yourself up to the law.”

“You come and get me, Mr. Holmes!” The voice carried strongly despite the wind.

Holmes turned to our policeman friend. “You stay down here, Sergeant. I’m the one he wants to see.”

“Be careful, Mr. Holmes.”

The detective pushed open the door, stepped into the lighthouse, and began to climb the steps of the spiral staircase.

I followed, but I must confess that it took me much longer to climb those stairs than it did Holmes.

When I emerged into the lantern chamber, I could see the two men standing outside on the balcony. One was undoubtedly our murderer, and the other was my friend,

Sherlock Holmes. Then the beam of the lighthouse turned on its regular cycle, and caught them both in its intense glare.

When the beam had passed, I stepped outside. Now I could hear their conversation.

"You have nowhere to go, Powell."

"I love this island, Mr. Holmes. I would do anything in my power to secure its future as a part of the German empire."

"And your own wealth, of course."

"Any why not?"

"You stand accused of murder, Powell," said Holmes. "You must face justice."

"Believe me, Mr. Holmes, I would rather die on this windswept island than be hanged in a stinking English prison."

"Then the alternative is in your hands, Powell."

"You mean, jump to my death? Perhaps. But I'd rather take you with me."

As I watched, Powell lifted his gun, and pointed it towards Holmes. Once more, they were both caught in the full glare of the revolving lighthouse beam. It blinded Powell for a moment, and he held his fire.

"No, you don't," I shouted.

Perhaps he hadn't noticed me there, hidden as I was in the shadows. But Powell now turned towards me, and immediately fired his gun. He had no time to aim properly, so the bullet ricocheted off a steel strut and disappeared into the darkness. I already had my revolver in my hand. I took half-a-second longer to prepare myself. Then, aiming to disable rather than to kill, I squeezed the trigger.

At that moment, a flash of lightning cut across the sky, and lit up the man's face. I was horrified. In that instant, the face had changed. It no longer resembled Professor Powell. It was a different face. One I had seen before. One that had been haunting my dreams for the last few nights.

Then, as I watched, Powell fell backwards over the balustrade, and plummeted to the ground.

Holmes and I hurried down the steps, to discover what was left of our adversary. I knelt down beside him, and felt for a pulse. There was none. Then I examined the body. It wasn't my bullet that had killed the man. It was the fifty-foot fall that had broken his neck.

We both looked down at the face, now covered in blood.

"You know, Holmes," I said, "up there, lit by that flash of lightning, I thought I saw another face."

Holmes nodded. "So did I. And I wish I hadn't. It was the face of the mummy. Black and shrivelled."

"Perhaps. Or maybe it was only the harsh shadows cast by the lightning flash. Just a figment of our imaginations."

"I hope you're right, Watson."

The Heligoland-Zanzibar Treaty was signed on the first day of July 1890, and control of the island was handed over to Germany.

An air of despondency settled over Baker Street. Had the pharaoh's curse really been to blame? We had escaped from Heligoland with our lives. Our mission was now over, but with very little to show for it. The murderer, Powell, had escaped facing trial. The remains of the pharaoh had vanished as though into thin air. And we as a nation had lost Heligoland. Of all our cases, this was the most unsatisfactory. And I record the events with a heavy heart.

Sherlock Holmes never referred to the matter again.

Then, one morning in October, I received an unexpected parcel from Egypt. It was a gift from Miss Venton, as a way of thanking me for all the help I'd given her. I felt guilty that we had achieved so little. The parcel contained a stylus, retrieved from the burial chamber of Pharaoh Amkotep shortly before a sandstorm covered the tomb and returned it once more to the oblivion of the desert. The stylus had now been adapted to take a pen-nib. And it is with this pen that I have written, and now conclude, my story of the Pharaoh's Curse.

## The Missing Empress
by Robert V. Stapleton

Glorious weather was not the only delight putting a skip into my step that Sunday morning in June 1887. But, on returning to Baker Street, I found my friend Sherlock Holmes in a much more sombre mood.

He was sitting in front of the unlit fire, glaring at a sheet of paper lying discarded in the grate.

"This is no time to be gloomy, Holmes," I chided him. "The Queen celebrates her Golden Jubilee on Monday, and the nation is already rejoicing."

Without turning to me, he gestured towards the sheet of paper as if it were a warrant to attend the Last Judgement.

I plucked it from the fire-grate and read it through. It turned out to be a note from Scotland Yard. From Inspector Lestrade. An invitation, nay a summons, to attend immediately. To interview a drunk.

"I consider it an insult, Watson," said Holmes, without raising his gaze. "For Lestrade to send for me in this manner is little short of an outrage."

"Look on the bright side," I told him. "It might turn out to be another case."

"To interview a drunk? The fellow probably mistook his way home."

"Or maybe not. At least we should find out what Lestrade considers so important."

"The very reason I didn't destroy the letter the moment I received it." He stood up and reached for his coat, hat, and cane. "I suppose we had better go."

I stepped outside to hail a cab.

"Mrs. Hudson!" Holmes took out his frustration by bellowing at the landlady. "We're going out."

Within ten minutes, we had arrived at Scotland Yard. The inspector was waiting for us.

"You took your time, gentlemen."

Holmes ignored him. I did my best to diffuse the tension between them. "My fault, I think, Lestrade. I was delayed by a visit to a patient this morning. A lady more in need of a friendly face than the tablets I prescribe for her."

"The drunk," said Holmes, turning on Lestrade. "I'd like to see the reason for our being called here this morning."

Lestrade softened his attitude. "Of course. Please follow me, gentlemen."

He took us down a flight of steps to the cells beneath Scotland Yard, secure and safe below ground-level. Our footsteps echoed in the confined passageway as the Detective Inspector led us to a door at the far end. There he opened the viewing port, and looked inside. "An ugly brute, I have to admit," observed Lestrade.

This piqued my colleague's interest. Holmes took his place at the opening and stood for a moment watching the man inside. Then he stood back abruptly. "What does this fellow have to say?"

"You'd better hear him yourself, Mr. Holmes."

"First, tell me what you know."

"His name is Bessington," said Lestrade. "He's well known to the Metropolitan Police as a layabout. He gets drunk whenever he can afford it, but generally he's a harmless cove."

"Until now," said Holmes. "Or why else would you have called upon my services?"

"More a mystery, I would say, Mr. Holmes. I thought you might be interested. You see, in the early hours of this morning, he staggered into a police station in Clerkenwell, ranting about a kidnapping."

Lestrade unlocked the cell door and we followed him inside. The smell of damp clothing and unwashed humanity hung in the air. It was rank enough to turn a tanner's stomach.

Inspector Lestrade left the door open. "Not a pleasant sight, is he, Dr. Watson?"

"I've seen worse," I told him. "But what's all this about a kidnapping?"

From the bench on which he had been lying, the drunk lifted himself into a sitting position and glared up at his visitors. "That's right," he exclaimed. "Kidnap! High Treason! Treachery!" The man seemed to double in size as he spoke, and his eyes shone with an inner passion.

Holmes sat down beside the man, and looked into his bloodshot eyes. "Tell me."

"I'd been drinking."

"Of course."

"To celebrate the Jubilee of the Queen. God bless her. I needed somewhere to sleep. I happened to find myself near the Boar's Head in Clerkenwell. So I slipped 'round the back and climbed down into the basement, like I often do when I'm up that way. It's dry, and out of the night air. It suits me well enough. See? I can be gone again the next morning before anybody knows I've even been there. Nobody knows. Nobody gets hurt."

"Then something happened."

Bessington's eyes flashed again. "Something woke me up. It was late. I heard a church clock strike twelve. Then, I realised I wasn't alone. I could see a light. And people, sharing a meal."

"How many?"

"Four of them. Three men and a woman. They were sitting at a table. I didn't dare move. I knew if they'd seen me, I'd be dead."

"Dead? How did you know that?"

"Because of what they were saying."

"Tell me." Holmes was becoming intrigued.

"They were discussing plans to kidnap somebody."

"Who?"

"Her Majesty."

A tense silence filled the cell.

"The Queen?"

"That's what I heard."

"When was the kidnapping to take place?"

I found myself drawn into the discussion. "On the day of her Jubilee, perhaps?"

"Nah. Not then. The day after."

Now it began to make sense. "Of course," I exclaimed. "Tuesday. There's to be a procession through the streets of London. To Westminster Abbey, for a service of thanksgiving."

Holmes nodded. "Then back to Buckingham Palace."

"But crowds will be lining the streets," I reminded him. "Nobody could possibly kidnap her then."

"That's right, Dr. Watson," said Lestrade. "We'll all be on high alert. If anybody plans to kidnap Her Majesty, it won't be then."

"No," said Bessington. "They'll do it when she gets back to the Palace."

Lestrade leaned closer to Bessington. "Tell us more."

"I didn't hear no more. As soon as they'd gone, I got out of there. In double-quick time, I can tell you."

"You say there were four of them," Holmes reminded him. "Three men and a woman."

"That's right. I saw them."

"Lestrade," said Holmes. "Take me to the Boar's Head, if you please. The place for us to begin is the location of the crime."

"Crime? So, you think there might be something in this fellow's story?"

"It's too early to tell," said Holmes. "I need concrete facts upon which to work."

"I'm beginning to learn your methods, Mr. Holmes," said Lestrade. "I thought you might want to visit the place, so I told them to leave everything exactly as it was."

"Good. And please ask a member of Her Majesty's household to join us there."

The basement of the Boar's Head tavern was a dark and gloomy hole. It reeked of sawdust and stale beer, but it was spacious and private.

Holmes had insisted that we bring Bessington along with us. For the moment, he remained half-hidden in the shadows, with a constable to make sure he didn't slip away. I didn't think there was much chance that he would. He had sobered up by now, and seemed keen to help.

Sir Cuthbert Hollingham joined us a few minutes after we arrived. He seemed loath to climb down into the cellar, but his determination to do his duty outweighed his reluctance. He was a small man, with greying side-whiskers and a balding head, but his presence made up for his lack of height. He introduced himself as a representative of the Queen's household, and complained that he had better things to do at such a significant moment in history.

Holmes ignored his complaints and made his way across the cellar towards a table with four chairs around it. He examined the table. "Is this the way it was last night?"

"Nothing has been touched, Mr. Holmes," said Lestrade.

"Four people." Holmes looked towards Bessington.

The man nodded.

"Might I venture to call them a Council of Four?"

"We need more light," I said. Holmes nodded his consent as I lit the candelabrum in the centre of the table.

He sniffed the air. "They dined on lamb, with a custard dessert." He bent down, and examined each place setting in turn, beginning with the chair facing the doorway. "Hello! What have we here? The man sitting in this place has expensive tastes. A tall man, possibly with connections to Buckingham Palace. Dark haired, with a liking for expensive French wine."

"Guesswork," huffed Sir Cuthbert.

"Not at all," said Holmes. "The imprint of a boot beneath the chair suggests a man about six feet in height. The wine glass contains a small but detectable trace of good quality wine. And a single hair on the table is darkly coloured, with a hint of the sort of Macassar oil favoured by the late Prince Albert.

Sir Cuthbert's eyebrows shot up. Now Holmes had his attention. "It could be the new fellow. Henry Tinderman. He works at the Home Office, but lately he's been helping us prepare for the Jubilee celebrations."

Holmes shifted to the next place around the table. "Ah, here we have the woman in the group. And well dressed, judging by the small feather trapped on the back of the chair. A lady's maid, perhaps. With a perfume that lingers." He looked up at me. "Don't you think so, Watson?"

I leaned closer, and sniffed. "Indeed. Not one that catches in the throat, like so many cheaper scents."

Holmes found the third place very different. "Now, this fellow smells of horse. Undoubtedly the working man of the group, judging by the fragment of sawdust beneath his chair."

"Extraordinary," exclaimed the Palace official.

"Obviously the man to drive the kidnap vehicle."

"Sounds reasonable," muttered Sir Cuthbert.

Holmes turned his attention to the fourth place. "I have to admit, this dark man is not so easy to read." He turned to Bessington. "What can you tell me about him?"

"He had his back towards me the whole time. He wore a cloak, and a top hat he never once took off. His voice was strange, as well. Foreign."

Holmes stood upright. "Here we have the mastermind. A dangerous man. But who is he? The ashtray contains the end of a cigar. Cut, not bitten." He sniffed the tobacco. "Unusual aroma. East European, if I'm not mistaken."

Lestrade broke Holmes's concentration. "Are we to assume, then, that the threat to the kidnap the Queen is real, Mr. Holmes?"

"Oh, yes. Very real."

"Kidnap?" exclaimed Sir Cuthbert. "Then we must put a stop to it at once. I'll have Tinderman put in irons."

"Don't be so hasty, Sir Cuthbert," said Lestrade. "We don't yet know for sure if it's him, or who these other people are, or how they intend to commit the crime."

"Or with what purpose," I pointed out.

Holmes sat down in the mystery man's chair, and looked up to the ceiling. "It has to take place on Tuesday, the day of the public celebrations. We have agreed that the most likely time is after Her Majesty has returned to the palace."

"That's right, Mr. Holmes," came Bessington's voice.

Holmes turned to face Sir Cuthbert. "What will be Her Majesty's itinerary for the rest of that day, Sir Cuthbert?"

The Palace official rubbed his chin thoughtfully. "On returning from the service, she will appear on the balcony of the Palace. Then she will meet officials from around the world, before attending a celebratory banquet."

"And later?"

"A firework display will be held in the grounds of the Palace. Part of the nationwide celebration."

"Hmm. Is Her Majesty to venture out into the grounds?"

"Indeed."

"Then, I suggest that might be the most likely time for these people to make their move."

As we prepared to depart, Bessington called Holmes over and whispered something to him, casting glances toward Lestrade, who was looking elsewhere. Holmes nodded and joined me by the door.

Outside, Holmes suggested he and I should take a cab to the river. We stopped at London Bridge, and wandered along the riverside. We found The Pool of London crowded. With lighters and barges cluttering up the quayside, often several abreast.

"What do you make of this business, Holmes?" I asked.

"It seems as clear as day to me."

"Well, apart from a threat to the Queen, I'm dashed if I can make much of it," I admitted.

"As with all investigations, the successful uncovering of the crime lies in careful preparation on our part."

"What preparation?"

"Well, for example, you notice that ship a hundred yards ahead?"

I saw the vessel. A small steel-hulled steamship, about the length of two Thames barges. The black hull carried a name in rusting white letters: *Drakesian*. Above the white deck-housing rose a tall black funnel. The hold took up the forward third of the ship.

"Did Bessington direct you here?"

Holmes nodded. "He had also overheard the name of the ship, but he felt that Lestrade and the police might bungle it."

"It's like so many others along this stretch of the Thames," I said. "What's so special about this one?"

"Notice the extra-wide gangplank joining it to the quayside."

"Unusual, but is that significant?"

"Perhaps we shall find out."

The moment we reached the steamship, Holmes stepped on deck and examined the covering of the hold. "It has been significantly strengthened," he said. "But why?"

He knocked with his cane on the wheelhouse door. It opened, and a man appeared. He was large and muscular, with narrowed eyes and an aggressive manner. I stepped back in alarm. But he didn't intimidate Holmes for one moment.

"What do you want?"

Holmes returned the man's stare. "I have a proposition for you."

"Who are you?"

"My name is Sherlock Holmes. I am assisting Scotland Yard in a very serious case. And your name?"

"Alfred Dexter." The man spat into the water. "You have a proposition for me, do you, Mr. Holmes? What kind of proposition?"

"Your boss has hired you to undertake a singular task."

"Says who?"

"Don't deny it."

The man shrugged, but looked suddenly wary.

"I want you to tell your boss that you have changed your mind. You will allow him to use your vessel and crew, but not with you in command."

Dexter laughed. "He'll kill me. Nemirov doesn't like traitors."

Holmes smiled. At least we now had a name for the mystery man. "Then I suggest you make yourself scarce."

"And if I don't?"

"I will see that you are hanged for treason."

Dexter looked alarmed. "Now, look here, Mr. Holmes. I went along with this business at first, but kidnapping the Queen was never my idea."

More of the plot was confirmed. "Then pull out while you still can."

"How can I do that, and stay alive?"

"Take the next train for the West Country, and lose yourself there."

"But they'll come looking for me."

"I think not. They have only two days before they have to flee the country."

"Look, I'm no supporter of the British Establishment, but I have to admit, I never was keen on this business. I prefer Mr. Marx to Mr. Nemirov."

"Then go. But first, tell me everything you know about these people. This Council of Four."

"That's a good name for them, Mr. Holmes. Although Nemirov doesn't like titles and names. The crew are mostly Dutch, but they understand English, and they were hired by Nemirov, so you'd better come down to my cabin. Then I'll tell you all I know."

We all squeezed into the captain's cabin, which was more a cubbyhole than a place to sleep. Holmes and I remained standing, as Dexter slumped onto the bunk.

"Let's begin with this man you called Nemirov," said Holmes. "What can you tell us about him?"

"He's a refugee from the Russian Tsar. I don't know what they want him for, but he seems to be on the run, so to speak. He has a passionate dislike for authority of any kind."

"Hmm. A man with a chip on his shoulder."

"He plans to build a bright new world, and he's prepared to move heaven and earth to achieve it."

Holmes nodded. "I understand a man called Henry Tinderman may be involved in this business too."

"A man high up at the Home Office," Dexter agreed. "That's him, all right. But he spends a lot of time at Buckingham Palace."

"Helping prepare for the Jubilee," said Holmes.

"That's right. He used to be a loyal servant of the Queen."

"But not now?"

"No."

"Why not?"

"A certain personage at the Palace took some friends to spend a week with him. I don't know what happened, but it plunged the household into financial ruin. Tinderman is now a very angry man, Mr. Holmes."

"And a dangerous one."

Dexter nodded.

"And the woman?"

"Angelique Pellier. She comes from a humble French family, but she wanted to make something of herself. She fell out and fled to England. Now she's in service at the Palace."

"And the other man?"

"Benjamin Sligo. Like his name, he's Irish. He wants to see the liberation of his country from the British crown."

"Like so many."

"He served in the army until he was injured and was forced to make the best he could of life as a civilian. His skill with horses helped him find work as a groom. And now he's a valued member of Nemirov's conspiracy."

Holmes glared down at Dexter. "That information is extremely useful. But before we go, tell me one thing. Is there to be another meeting?"

"Yes. A full gathering of their supporters."

"Where?"

"The Boar's Head in Clerkenwell. This evening."

"Of course. And the password to get in?"

"'Jubilee'."

"Naturally. Well, thank you, Mr. Dexter. Now I suggest you leave at once. London is no longer a safe place for you. I shall send a telegram in your name, informing the meeting that you no longer wish to be a part of their scheme, and that you will not be at the gathering tonight."

"Thank you, Mr. Holmes. You'd better send it to Tinderman, at the Home Office."

"I shall do that. But, for the sake of your life, you must disappear before he receives it."

Upon our return to Baker Street, Holmes immediately set about combing through his filing system. I could detect a frenzy in his search, which meant he would resent any interruption until he had found whatever he was looking for.

I sat down beside the hearth, and waited.

After several minutes, he stood up. "A-ha!"

"What have you found, Holmes?"

He held up a newspaper cutting. "Nemirov. I thought the name rang a bell."

"Sounds East European."

"A known anarchist by the name of Anton Leonid Nemirov. Born in Kiev in 1839."

"An anarchist? You mean, he hates everyone."

"He is a man with a vision, Watson. This is a report of a public speech he gave a few months ago in Hyde Park. He blames the Russian Empire for persecuting his family and murdering his parents. He now calls upon everyone who has been treated badly by the authorities in any country to join him in forming a new state, a nation where everyone is free to live out their own lives without fear of persecution."

"A Utopian dream," I replied. "But to kidnap the Queen is a capital crime."

"Then we need to know what happens at that meeting tonight. We have to find out exactly what they are planning."

"Will you go, Holmes?"

"I would like for you to go instead, Watson." He looked towards me. "Take Bessington with you. Lestrade will have finished with him by now."

"Good idea, Holmes."

"And see if you can persuade Sir Cuthbert to go with you as well. He might not like it, but his presence there could prove useful."

"Won't the landlord have warned Nemirov in advance?"

"No. Scotland Yard have sworn him to secrecy."

"And how do we gain entrance without alarming the guests?"

"That is why you are taking our friend Bessington with you."

"And what will you be doing, Holmes?"

"Making plans," he replied, as he sat back and lit his favourite briar pipe.

I arrived with Bessington at the Boar's Head early in the evening. Sir Cuthbert had agreed to accompany us. He felt it his responsibility to help deal with this threat to the Queen's safety.

The sound of voices, together with the smell of alcohol, told us the Public Bar and the lounge were busy with customers. Bessington led us to the rear of the building, and lifted a metal grille. "This is the tradesman's entrance," he told us with a chuckle. "I usually get in this way. And not just at this place, neither."

In the evening light, Sir Cuthbert's face showed his annoyance. Only his sense of duty prevented him from hurrying back to the Palace.

Following Bessington, we climbed down through the opening and into the cellar we had visited only a few hours earlier.

Again, the air in that underground room smelt musty, and I could feel the cold seeping out of the stone walls.

I lit the lantern I had brought with me, and looked around. The place appeared to be empty. We found a corner at the dirtiest end of the cellar, doused the flame, and sat hidden in the darkness.

I had dressed suitable to the occasion in a tweed suit and a flat cap. Against my advice, Sir Cuthbert had tried to maintain his dignity by wearing his usual black suit and top hat. "I hope we won't have to stay here long," he muttered.

"I think we might," I told him, "so you'd better make yourself comfortable."

At the far end of the cellar, the door at the top of the stairs opened and light flooded in, while we sat hidden among the shadows. I heard somebody climbing down the steps and, peering from the darkness, I saw a man that I didn't recognise. He hung a lighted lantern on a joist in the centre of the cellar. Only now could I see properly how the room had been set out. Several rows of chairs faced towards the front, where four seats stood facing the other way. Some event was planned to take place there that evening – the meeting we had come to observe.

Another man remained at the top of the stairs. We heard him ask the next person for the password. The fellow muttered "Jubilee", and was allowed to descend. Other people followed, until the gathering had amounted to about thirty individuals.

I noticed another man arrive who looked particularly suspicious. He was dressed like a fisherman in a navy blue jersey, corduroy trousers, and a peaked cap. The seating area filled rapidly, and soon a cloud of blue tobacco smoke hung over the gathering. Somebody slammed the entrance door shut. At the front of the gathering, the four chairs were now occupied. One of the men seated there stood up and called for order. He was tall and had an air of authority about him.

"Tinderman," hissed Sir Cuthbert into my right ear.

I nodded. The man from the Home Office.

"Ladies and gentlemen," said Tinderman, "the time is drawing near when we shall see the fulfilment of our grand design." All around the room, people nodded and whispered to one another. "We are a select few. Each of us has a unique reason for being at this gathering. The fact that you knew the password secures your right to be here this evening, and guarantees the distinction of our gathering. This pleased the crowd. Tinderman continued. "I shall now hand you over to the man who had masterminded this whole affair." He sat down, and another man stood up.

This man was less tall, but stood ram-rod straight. A shock of blond hair stood out from his head, giving him an eccentric appearance. His eyes panned around the room. Then he bowed towards the gathering. "Welcome to this meeting," he said, in an accent which placed him firmly from Eastern Europe. This had to be the Ukrainian. Nemirov. "This will be our final meeting before Tuesday, when our purpose is achieved." A rumble of conversation rolled around the gathering, but faded away again as Nemirov continued. "Thanks to the support of each one of you, everything is now ready. You each know your particular roles. But a problem has developed."

Some people sat upright, and many leaned forward, all intent on learning about this new threat to their plans.

"Dexter." He spat the name. "The captain of the steamer has absconded." Angry words emanated from the gathering. "He has run out on us. But we still have the ship itself, and her crew. Now we need a new pilot for the *Drakesian*."

It was at this point that the fisherman stood up and pushed his way to the front. "I'll do it," he said. "I'll skipper that ship for you."

"And who are you?"

The fisherman took off his cap respectfully. "Name's Craster. An honest seaman who has spent twenty years before the mast, and has now fallen on hard times, all because of those ship owners – faceless businessmen who want to wring out every last penny from the poor, and take no thought for the honest working man."

"And do you share our goals?"

"Freedom for all men," said Craster. "That's good enough for me."

"Then you must be ready to sail on Tuesday evening – the very moment we appear with our precious load."

Craster looked up at him. "And what or who might that be, sir?"

"If you don't know by now, then it is better you don't know at all."

"You mean, Her Majesty?"

Nemirov's face broke into a mirthless smile.

"May a humble man like myself ask the purpose of this action? I can see it as a blow against authority, but what will we do with Her Majesty?"

The Ukrainian stood straight and proud. "We will hold her in comfortable seclusion. In Rotterdam. And negotiate a ransom." A rumble of approval ran around the gathering. "We will force them to take us seriously."

"May I be so bold as to ask the price of an Empress's ransom?"

Tinderman stood up again. "Simple. The complete abolition of the monarchy." Everyone cheered.

I felt Sir Cuthbert stir beside me. "The bounder!"

Faces turned towards where we were sitting. "Who's there?" demanded Nemirov.

Bessington turned towards us. "That's blown it. They'll be after us now." He pointed towards the grille where we had entered. "Go!"

I pushed Sir Cuthbert back towards the steps that had brought us down into the cellar. Behind us, I heard Bessington call out, mimicking his drunken drawl. "No need to worry, gents and ladies. It's only me."

Masked by the sounds of shouts and scuffling, I pushed Sir Cuthbert up through the grille and into the night air.

Clutching his cane and top hat, Sir Cuthbert followed me, as we ran for our lives.

The next morning, Monday, Holmes seemed more interested in the newspaper than in listening to my story.

"Today," he told me, "Her Majesty will travel from Frogmore, and this evening will attend a dinner to be held in her honour."

My eye was drawn to the back page of his paper, and to an article in the *Stop Press* column. "Look at this, Holmes."

He turned the paper over, and read the article.

"Early today, police pulled the body of a man from the River Thames. Inspector Lestrade of Scotland Yard identified the man as one Josiah Bessington, a vagrant of no fixed abode."

I gasped. "Bessington. Drowned."

"I very much doubt if that was how he met his end, Watson."

"I agree, Holmes. The poor man must have given his life so that Sir Cuthbert and I could escape. If it hadn't been for him, the police would be dealing with three corpses by now."

Holmes folded his newspaper, and dropped it onto the table. "Today, we must wait, Watson. Prepare. But tomorrow, we shall see what will happen."

Holmes was absent for much of that day, and when I later asked him how his day had gone, he merely smiled and said it had gone as expected.

On the following day, June twenty-first, 1887, Victoria, Queen of the United Kingdom of Great Britain and Ireland, and Empress of India, rode in an open carriage to celebrate her Golden Jubilee at Westminster Abbey. She was escorted by Indian Princes and other dignitaries. Crowds thronged the streets, and people gathered to see the pageantry and to celebrate the Queen's fifty years on the throne. The Queen later waved to the cheering crowds from the balcony of Buckingham Palace. After receiving various dignitaries, she celebrated with yet another banquet.

As I sat with Holmes over afternoon tea, he gave me my instructions. "Your part in this evening's events is crucial, Watson."

"My part?"

He explained what would happen. "Naturally," he continued, "you must liaise directly with Sir Cuthbert. He has been told exactly what to do. Officially, the Queen will be wheeled outside to enjoy a display of fireworks."

"Officially?"

"In reality, she will be travelling by closed carriage, for an evening of peace and quiet at St James's Palace."

"But where will you be?"

"Unfortunately, I have other matters to deal with. But I trust you to do the right thing."

"Which is?"

"To keep Her Majesty safe. Oh, and don't forget to take your service revolver along with you."

Dusk was falling when I reached Buckingham Palace, and joined Sir Cuthbert at one of the side entrances near a coach house. He seemed agitated. "I really do not like the idea of putting Her Majesty in any kind of danger."

I took out my revolver. "Don't worry, Sir Cuthbert. I won't let anything happen to her."

"Well, for better or worse, the time has come to put into operation Sherlock Holmes's plan." He disappeared inside.

The clopping of horses' hooves made me turn and hurry towards the inner courtyard. There I saw an enclosed four-wheeled clarence waiting. The two horses seemed anxious to be off.

I slid into a dark corner beside the building as three shadowy figures boarded the clarence. A figure I recognised as the French woman, Angelique, climbed in. The groom, Benjamin Sligo, climbed onto the box seat at the front, and took the reins. Then Henry Tinderman, dressed in his finest attire, appeared and took his place beside the driver.

Once more the door opened, and Sir Cuthbert emerged, escorting a small woman. She was dressed in black and held a veil across her face. Sir Cuthbert helped the woman climb up into the clarence and then closed the door. I recognised the figure at once. "The Queen," I murmured as Sir Cuthbert joined me.

The driver shook the reins and the horses trotted slowly out of the courtyard, heading towards one of the side gates of the Palace grounds. I began to panic. The very people who had been plotting the kidnap of the Queen had now taken her into their own hands, and away from my own care. Would our plan work? Why had we let things go this far? Was this truly what Holmes wanted? Undoubtedly, it had to be part of his scheme, but I hoped with all my heart he knew what he was doing.

As soon as the vehicle had rounded the corner of the building and was out of my sight, I felt Sir Cuthbert take me by the arm. "Quickly, Dr. Watson. We must leave at once." I calmed myself – this was what we had planned.

I followed him around the corner of the coach house and towards a hansom cab standing in the shadows. It was ready to leave at once. We climbed on board, and immediately drove off at a brisk trot.

"Make sure that you stay out of sight," Sir Cuthbert called to the cabbie. Then to me. "He's a man we can trust – the best in the whole of London." We sat back, as there was nothing more that we could do at the moment. Our fate, and the fate of our Queen, remained at that moment in the hands of our skilled and determined cab driver.

Surrounded by the sound of fireworks and the voices of exhausted and drunken members of the populace, we rattled along at a fair old lick, following the clarence through the streets of London until it reached the north bank of the river. Not far, but far enough for my fraying nerves.

I could see the clarence now, in the distance and almost out of sight. It had already reached the *Drakesian.* I could now see the purpose of the extra wide gangplank, as the horses and carriage had driven straight onto the deck of the steamer and had drawn to a halt there. Several of the ship's crew were now busy tying the clarence down, whilst others cast off the ship's mooring lines from the quayside.

I could see all this happening, but I was too late to prevent the steamer from pulling away. Sir Cuthbert leaned out of the window, and called to the driver. "Slow down."

I noticed a man stepped out from the shadows. It took a moment before I realised that it was Lestrade.

"Dr. Watson," he called, "our water transport is ready and waiting."

Sir Cuthbert and I climbed down from the hansom and followed Lestrade towards where two stream launches lay at the quayside, smoke already rising from their funnels. We boarded the nearer of the vessels. The engines rumbled and belched out smoke and sparks into the night air, and the propellers churned up the water behind us into a maelstrom of furious foam – fury which reflected my inner anxiety that the kidnappers might get away.

I gazed ahead into the darkness, looking for any sign of the steamer. Then I saw it. Already well downstream of London Bridge, it was steadily pulling ahead of us. The light air was heavy with coal smoke billowing from the vessel ahead. Their ship's lights showed them to be making rapid progress.

"Look at their speed!" I cried. "They're getting away!"

"They're certainly making a run for it," said Lestrade. "In this river, at night, such speed is utter madness."

We weren't getting any closer. It would take a miracle if we were going to catch up with that speeding vessel now.

But then, the miracle happened. The ship turned abruptly towards the north bank of the river. It struck something below the water, and came to a shuddering halt. As we drew closer, I could see the carriage we had pursued through the streets, still tied securely to the rail stanchions, and presumably still holding the person of the Queen. We heard loud and heated voices coming to us across the water as men shouted at one another and quickly turned their anger upon us.

Drawing level with the stranded steamer, I leapt on board and took out my revolver. I could see three men standing in the bows of the ship. Nemirov stood farthest away from me. Although I couldn't see his face, I could tell that he was angry at having been stopped. Benjamin Sligo, the Irishman, stood between the two horses still harnessed to the clarence. He was struggling to keep the animals calm. Henry Tinderman stood nearest to me. In the darkness, I observed that he was holding a boathook, which he held out towards me in a threatening manner. I remained where I stood, while members of the Metropolitan police swarmed onto the deck.

With his eyes fixed only upon me, Tinderman failed to notice another, smaller man who jumped up onto the deck beside him. He turned too late to avoid Sir Cuthbert's swinging fist. It caught the traitor's jaw with a sickening thump, and sent him sprawling to the deck.

"You swine!" growled Sir Cuthbert.

At the sound of confusion around them, the horses began to panic. When the second launch coming up behind us sounded its steam-whistle, both animals reared up, and one of them landed on Sligo. The Irishman screamed as the terrified horse trampled him to death.

Another man hurried forward, took hold of the reins, and calmed the animals down. I recognised this man as the replacement pilot, Craster.

I dragged Sligo's body away from the horses, but there was nothing that I could do save him. The pilot turned towards me. "I'm glad to see you are unharmed, Watson."

"Holmes? What on earth are you doing here?"

"I had to make sure these rogues didn't get away."

"You mean, you deliberately ran the ship aground."

"Indeed."

I looked around. "But where's Nemirov?"

"I saw him drop over the side of the ship," said Holmes. "Lestrade is organising a search party at this moment."

"How can I help?"

"Check on the carriage."

"Of course. The Queen."

I hurried to the clarence, opened the door and looked in at the black figure sitting in the rear seat.

"Your Majesty," I said. But then I noticed another figure. Sitting facing her was the final member of the Council of Four, Angelique Pellier. She was holding a small, single-shot pistol, and was pointing it towards the figure in black. The young woman gave me a cutting stare, saying, "Step back."

"Your conspiracy has failed," I told her, raising my revolver. "Drop your weapon."

"You can kill me," she hissed, "but first I shall kill the most powerful woman in the world."

The woman in black removed the veil from her face. "I don't think so, my dear," she said.

I recognised both the voice, and now the face. "Mrs. Hudson?"

"Hello, Dr. Watson," she said. "I've never in my life impersonated the Queen before."

Even in the darkness, Angelique Pellier looked as confused as I felt.

My landlady again turned to the Frenchwoman. "If you kill me, nobody will miss me very much. Your plans were always doomed to fail. You see, you were up against Mr. Sherlock Holmes."

In desperation, Angelique Pellier cried out for her co-conspirator. "Anton!"

When she received no reply, she pressed the gun against her own head and blew out her own brains.

It was nearly dawn by the time Holmes and I returned to Baker Street. Having made Mrs. Hudson feel like genuine royalty and then delivered her to her own rooms, we stood at the foot of the stairs leading up to the sitting room. I started to question Holmes as to how he could place our landlady in such jeopardy, but he held up a hand. "There was still too much that was uncertain, Watson," he said. "We had to give them rope to make absolutely certain they were committed to the plan, so that they couldn't wiggle out of the charges. We needed someone to take the place of the Queen. There was no one else that I trusted more than Mrs. Hudson, and she was willing. And if we had told you, you would have objected."

I could see that he didn't want to discuss it further right then, but I would have a few more things to say in the future, both about the lady's safety, and my ignorance of his plan. Leaving it at that, we finally retired to our rooms.

I opened the door and immediately stood stock still. In the thin light of the early morning sun, I could see a man sitting in a chair beside the fireplace. I recognised him at once. Nemirov. He was holding a revolver.

Holmes did not seem the least bit surprised to see him, but sat down in a chair facing the Ukrainian.

Nemirov waved the gun to indicate that I should close the door and take another chair.

Holmes broke the tense silence. "Your plot to kidnap the Queen has failed, Nemirov. Sligo and Angelique Pellier are both dead. Tinderman is under close arrest. And the crew of your steamer are in the hands of Scotland Yard. Nothing remains for you except the hangman's rope."

"Nemesis," I breathed.

"Precisely, Watson."

The Ukrainian smiled. "In reality, we did nothing more than kidnap your landlady – if you can call it kidnapping. She came with us willingly enough."

"You still have to answer for sedition and murder."

"We are all driven by our dreams, Mr. Holmes," said Nemirov. "Mine is to see a world of freedom and equality."

"But not for people like Bessington."

"Who?"

"The drunk that you murdered."

"A nobody."

"On the contrary, a man with the right to the very things that you claim to stand for."

"But his death hardly affords the publicity I seek. On the other hand, the murder of the famous Sherlock Holmes would bring the attention of the entire world to my cause."

A carriage drew to a halt in the street outside. In silence, we listened as somebody climbed the stairs, and stopped on the landing outside our rooms.

Nemirov scowled at the door, and gripped his revolver more tightly.

The door opened, and a man stood framed in the doorway. I recognized him. His waxed moustaches gave him an imperial demeanour. Dressed in black, with his left hand in his pocket, he held a gun in his right hand.

I watched as the expression on Nemirov's face transformed. He looked as if he were facing the devil himself. The Ukrainian stood up, and raised his revolver with a shaking hand. The crack of two gunshots assailed our eardrums, and shattered the early morning calm.

Nemirov collapsed onto the hearthrug, with a single bullet-hole in the centre of his forehead. I later discovered the Ukrainian's bullet buried deep within the wooden door-frame. It remains there to this day.

The man in the doorway lowered his weapon. "I am indebted to you, Mr. Holmes, for giving me the chance to deal with this scoundrel myself." The man spoke with a slight but detectable German accent. "I consider Her Majesty's honour now restored. Her Majesty would like you to accept a small gift in recognition of your services last night." He held out a small box, which Holmes took and opened. Inside lay a miniature: A small painting on mother-of-pearl of the late Prince Albert.

"Please convey my thanks to Her Majesty," said Holmes, "but I cannot possibly accept this gift."

I was shocked. "But Holmes, you cannot refuse the Queen."

"Indeed not. But the gift should go instead to our landlady, Mrs. Hudson. After all, she proved more courageous last night than any of us."

I nodded. "She will be delighted."

Now satisfied, the man in the doorway gave a sharp bow, clicked his heels, and left.

Holmes breathed a deep sigh. "I do believe that this case is now at an end." He waved vaguely towards the body of Nemirov. "Lestrade can tidy up, and take the credit, if he likes."

Later that morning, I sat in our rooms, reading the newspaper reports of the Jubilee celebrations. Holmes stood in the open window, violin in hand, playing a romantic melody. His face showed a look of sublime happiness. Summer had finally come to Baker Street.

# Dr. Agar and the Dinosaur
by Robert V. Stapleton

When relating "The Adventure of the Devil's Foot", I promised to tell the story of how my friend, Sherlock Holmes, first made the acquaintance of Harley Street physician, Dr. Moore Agar. It is a story I have described as dramatic. And so it proved, as it nearly resulted in the deaths of all three of us. With my notes open before me, I now take up my pen to fulfil my promise to give the story in full.

Following the loss of my dear wife and the sale of my medical practice, my world once more revolved around 221B, and the eccentric man with whom I shared rooms there. The years following the return of Sherlock Holmes, as though from the dead, turned out to be busy and demanding on both of us, and the summer of 1895 proved no exception.

From his place in the armchair beside the empty grate in our sitting room, Holmes looked up from his reading of the morning newspaper. "Now, there is a singular matter, Watson."

"You have the advantage of me, Holmes," I replied.

"Why, the theft of a skull."

I failed to share his enthusiasm. "You are telling me somebody likes old bones. Why is that so remarkable?"

"Because, Watson, the skull belonged to a long extinct species of dinosaur."

I returned his gaze, with surprise. "Here in London?"

"Precisely. According to the article, it had been sent to this country on temporary loan from a museum in Washington, D.C."

"And now it has gone missing."

"And the police have drawn a blank in their investigations of the matter."

I chuckled. "I can imagine Lestrade scratching his head over this business."

Holmes sat back, and stretched out his legs. "I expect we shall find out presently."

Almost at once, we heard a vehicle draw to a halt in the roadway outside. Holmes, still in his purple dressing gown, took his stand beside the hearth, facing the doorway. And waited.

The door opened, and Mrs. Hudson stepped inside.

"Excuse me, Mr. Holmes," she began. "But you have a visitor. A very important man, sir." She passed a visiting card to Holmes, and waited.

Holmes read it, and looked up. "Thank you, Mrs. Hudson. Please show Dr. Agar in."

I expressed my surprised. "Not a visit from Scotland Yard, then."

"Apparently not," returned Holmes. "At least, not directly."

A man walked in. He was in mid-life, of medium height and weight, with thinning gray hair and bushy side-whiskers. He carried himself with a slight stoop, and his sad brown eyes betrayed a troubled mind. Even in the middle of the morning, he presented a less-than-perfect appearance.

"You are Dr. Moore Agar, of Harley Street," noted Holmes.

"The same," replied our visitor. "And you, I hope, are Mr. Sherlock Holmes."

"I have that honor. And this is my colleague, Dr. Watson."

The visitor and I exchanged nods.

"Please take a seat," said Holmes, indicating a chair he had conveniently placed opposite his own beside the fireplace. "I see you are a man preoccupied with antiquities," Holmes continued. "More so perhaps than with the care of your more general appearance. Cuff-links of carved bone faded with age, and a watch-chain fob fashioned from an ancient Greek coin. You had time to attend to those items this morning, yet you have not found occasion to brush down your coat or polish your boots."

Dr. Agar appeared embarrassed by the comments.

"Forgive me, Dr. Agar," continued Holmes. "I merely voice my observations."

"But I do not neglect my patients, Mr. Holmes."

"Indeed not," replied Holmes, affably. "Come now, tell us about your missing dinosaur skull." I noticed a hint of mirth play about my friend's countenance. "For that is the purpose of your visit here, is it not?"

Dr. Agar leaned forward in his seat, and fixed Holmes with a penetrating stare. "A few months ago, I accepted an invitation from a colleague in the United States to present a series of lectures there on recent developments in Medicine and Surgery in this country."

Holmes nodded.

"He knew of my interest in ancient history, so whilst I was in his country, my associate took me to visit a number of museums. One I found particularly fascinating. The place was filled with the most amazing skeletons of long-extinct creatures. We have our own exhibits in this country, but I had never seen anything remotely like this. A member of the museum staff told me about the discoveries made in recent years in Colorado and Wyoming, of the remains of huge creatures from the Cretaceous period of pre-history. He told me of men in the United States who set great store by collecting and exhibiting such things. These men expend huge sums of money on securing the remains of these ancient creatures."

"An object of such curiosity might well attract the interest of people in this country as well," said Holmes, soberly.

"Precisely my thinking, Mr. Holmes. I wanted to learn more, so he introduced me to an official at the Smithsonian Institution in Washington, D.C. This gentleman took me to see some of the latest fossil remains they had uncovered, and are even now in the process of restoring. Among these remains, I discovered the huge skull of a horned dinosaur. A creature they are now calling *Triceratops*." Dr. Agar's eyes glittered with animation. "Each has two genuine horns. Huge, deadly things. In 1842, Sir Richard Owen proposed the name *Dinosaur*, meaning 'terrible lizard'. The moment I first cast my eyes on this monster, I understood how apt the name was. The sight of it filled me with awe, Mr. Holmes. At that moment, I knew I had to have this very skull for exhibition here in London."

Dr. Agar paused in his telling of the tale. With the warm summer weather, and the enthusiasm with which he spoke, Dr. Agar took out a white handkerchief and wiped his moist forehead.

All this time, Holmes had been listening with rapt attention. "Pray, continue with your story, Dr. Agar."

"Before I left," continued Dr. Agar, "I had a meal with my new acquaintance at the Smithsonian. The drinks flowed, and before the end of the evening, he had signed an agreement allowing me to borrow one of these skulls. He also undertook to ship it across the Atlantic as soon as I had found a suitable venue for the exhibition."

Dr. Agar turned his gaze upon me. "I had been planning to organize an exhibition of my own inadequate collection, and I realized this dinosaur would be the highlight of the event. The focus of publicity."

"I have seen the model dinosaurs at the Crystal Palace gardens in Sydenham," I told him.

"An imaginative attempt by Waterhouse Hawkins to popularize and set in concrete the extent of Sir Richard's limited research at that time," he retorted with a smile. "But I am talking about the real thing – genuine fossilized bones of gigantic creatures."

"And you managed to arrange a suitable venue," noted Holmes, returning to the subject in hand.

"I was lucky," said Dr. Agar. "I managed to hire a room at the Museum of Practical Geology, here in London. The Museum agreed to receive the crate containing the skull and have it ready for me to inspect the moment I was free from my medical commitments."

"And this dinosaur duly arrived," I concluded.

"Two days ago, the crate was unloaded at the Port of London docks, exactly as agreed. The Geology Museum's own contractors collected it that afternoon, and delivered it to the room assigned to me. The American museum had also sent a courier to accompany the skull. He took a room at a local hotel. All seemed well. When I received the news that the crate had arrived, I was delighted. I was delayed by my work, and arrived first thing the following morning. Then I opened the crate." Dr. Agar's expression fell. "To my horror, I discovered that it contained nothing more than a shapeless lump of rock. But of the skull, I could find absolutely no trace whatsoever."

"And what did the courier have to say?" asked Holmes.

"He assured us the Triceratops skull had been packed, and that the crate had not been tampered with in any way since the moment it left Washington."

"To summarize," said Holmes, leaning back in his chair, and cupping his hands behind his head. "At some point between the crate leaving America and your inspecting it, the skull vanished."

Dr. Agar took a deep breath, and let it out slowly. "So it seems, Mr. Holmes. But how could something that big simply disappear into thin air? And, if somebody stole it, what reason might they have had?"

"The reason for such a theft, you mentioned yourself, Dr. Agar. The skull must be worth a great deal of money to whoever took it. To collectors in America, and other museums across the world."

"The biggest mystery of all is how the thief managed to accomplish such a feat. The skull itself weighs more than a ton."

Holmes pursed his lips in thought. "That remains to be seen," he said. "But whatever can be delivered can just as easily be removed."

Dr. Agar looked pleadingly at Holmes. "Neither the Museum nor Scotland Yard seems able to trace the skull. I'm at my wits end about this matter, Mr. Holmes. You're my final hope."

"I can promise nothing," said Holmes, smiling modestly. "I merely make deductions based upon the facts presented to me."

"Then allow me to present you with the starkest of facts, Mr. Holmes. Come with me to the Geology Museum, and see what deductions you can make of this matter."

Dr. Moore Agar's four-wheeler took us to Piccadilly, and then round the corner into Jermyn Street, where it dropped us off at the entrance to the Museum of Practical Geology.

In the doorway, we encountered a familiar figure waiting for us.

"I'm surprised you consider this business merits your attention, Mr. Holmes," said Inspector Lestrade.

"On the contrary, Lestrade," replied Holmes. "Any case considered too demanding for Scotland Yard is something I am always willing to consider. And, as for this present matter, I find it curiously compelling."

We followed Dr. Agar along echoing corridors to a room empty of all but a small desk and table set beside the wall, and a single wooden crate standing alone in the centre of the floor-space.

The crate measured approximately seven feet in length by five feet in both width and height. The lid had been removed and stood on the floor, propped up against one side of the crate. Holmes and I looked inside, and discovered a rough-hewn boulder of white rock.

"Hmm," mused Holmes. "My knowledge of Geology suggests that this stone comes from no farther away than northern France."

"Instead of a skull recently transported from America," said Lestrade.

Holmes turned to Dr. Agar. "Can you show us what it ought to look like?"

"Certainly," replied Dr. Agar, collecting a line drawing from a folder on the adjacent desk, and spreading it out upon the table top.

We all looked down at the image of a skeleton – a huge horned dinosaur. "An intimidating monster," I said.

"Even more in the flesh, so to speak," said Dr. Agar.

"And when exactly was this delivery made?" asked Holmes.

"As I said, I called in yesterday morning, and discovered what you now see."

"You say the Museum's own contractors delivered it," said Holmes.

"That's correct," said Lestrade. "The Museum is occasionally obliged to receive and dispatch items of great size and weight. The contractors collected it from the docks, and brought it here late in the afternoon."

"And what about the other crate?" Holmes asked, with eyebrows raised in enquiry.

Lestrade looked at Holmes, with furrowed brow. "What other crate are you talking about, Mr. Holmes?"

"An elementary matter," replied Holmes. "If the crate was delivered in the same condition in which it was sealed, then it follows that there must have been a second crate delivered to the Museum." He knelt on the floor, and examined the floorboards on all sides of the crate. "Although the floor naturally shows a great deal of wear, it is quite evident that another crate stood here in the recent past. Within a matter of days, in fact."

"In that case," said Lestrade, looking intrigued, "I suggest we speak with the delivery staff."

"Yes," said one of the Museum's workmen. "We placed a heavy crate on the floor here two days ago."

"Did you find anything else in the room?" asked Holmes.

"No, sir. The room looked exactly as it appears now."

"No other crate?"

"No, just the one."

"And yet, another crate was here, either before or after you undertook your delivery," said Holmes. "The indentations in the floorboards, together with minute specks of wood shavings, settle the matter."

Dr. Agar shook his head in dismay. "I can hardly imagine a thief coming in here and walking out with something so heavy."

"Maybe not on his own," replied Holmes, "but I can imagine a legitimate firm being employed to come in and remove it." He turned to Lestrade. "I suggest that he pay another visit to the Museum office. They might have a record showing who came to remove a heavy item between the delivery of the crate and Dr. Agar's arrival here the following morning."

We made our way to the Secretary's office.

"We keep a record of everything that comes in and goes out," said the Secretary, consulting the day-book. "At five o'clock that evening, our contracted workmen delivered a crate they had collected from the docks."

"That confirms what we already know," said Holmes. "A crate was delivered. And then?"

"Only two hours later, another wagon arrived, to deliver a second wooden crate."

"Now we are getting somewhere," said Holmes.

"They had paperwork which appeared to be legitimate."

Holmes nodded. "And did they leave a name and address?"

"Indeed they did," replied the Secretary. "We insist upon it. They gave their name as Jenitsen and Nephew, and gave an address we can only assume to be authentic."

Holmes turned to Lestrade. "We need to find these people, Lestrade, and I suggest this is a job for the Metropolitan Police."

"Leave it to us, Mr. Holmes," replied Lestrade. "We'll find this man, Jenitsen, and bring him along to Baker Street so you can see what you make of him."

Dr. Agar turned to the door. "In the meantime, gentlemen, I must return to Harley Street. I have patients waiting for me."

"Of course," said Holmes. "And yet, judging by the way this matter is shaping, it might be wise for you to clear your diary for the next few days."

By the middle of the afternoon, Holmes was ready to interview the owner of the removal firm.

"Now, Mr. Jenitsen," he began, standing once more in front of the empty hearth in Baker Street. "You admit it was you who came to the Geology Museum two nights ago."

"That's right, Mr. Holmes," said the little man standing before him. "I have neither wish nor need to deny the fact." Jenitsen was not a tall man, but what he lacked in height he made up for in muscular strength. Even so, with two burly constables flanking him, he looked like a man who had come to meet his doom.

"Then, kindly furnish us with the details of your purpose in being there."

"Well, Mr. Holmes," he began. "It all started when this bloke came into our office a week ago."

"Can you describe the man?"

"Foreign. In expression, language, and clothing."

"European?"

"No."

"American?"

"Not like any I've ever met."

"Please continue."

"Well, this bloke told me he had a job for me. He would pay me up-front. Handsomely, like. I wasn't going to turn down a job like that now, was I?"

Holmes was becoming impatient. "Of course not. Now, please tell us about the job he wanted you to undertake for him."

"That's what I'm coming to, Mr. Holmes. He wanted me and my brother's lad to collect a heavy wooden crate from a train due to arrive at Charing Cross from Paris. We were to take the box direct to the Museum of Practical Geology, in Jermyn Street. He gave us the time and place for both collecting and delivering."

"And you did that."

"Of course. Mind you, with the crate being so heavy, we needed to hire in a few other lads to help. But we got the job done. We collected the crate, and took it to the Museum at exactly seven o'clock that same evening. Just like the fellow told us. Odd that, weren't it, him being so precise about the time?"

"Where did you leave the crate?"

"We wheeled it to a room along one wing of the building. It was a heavy job, I can tell you. But we got it there, and signed that it had been delivered."

"And the other crate?"

"Ah, yes," Mr. Jenitsen rubbed his chin thoughtfully. "That was the other part of the job. We put the crate down on the floor, directly beside another wooden box that was already there. Same size. Same shape. And the same weight, as we found out when we carried the blooming thing out to the wagon."

"And what happened to this other crate?"

"We took it all the way back to Charing Cross station, and put it back on the very same train we'd taken the other one off."

"Did the crate carry any identification?"

"Only what I fastened onto it. The bloke who hired us gave me a luggage label to fix on."

"Do you remember what it said?"

"It's my job to make sure everything gets to where it should be. It said, '*The Gare du Nord, Paris. To be collected*'. That's all I can tell you, Mr. Holmes, and that's the truth of it."

"Nothing more?"

"Oh, wait a minute. The back of the label had a picture."

"Of what?"

"Of a spider."

Holmes turned, and rummaged through his collection of newspaper cuttings. For several minutes, he paid no attention to anyone else in the room. Then, as Lestrade was about to turn and leave, Holmes stood up, holding a sheet of newsprint in his hand.

“Mr. Jenitsen,” said Holmes. “You said this man gave you a label bearing the image of a spider.”

“That’s right, Mr. Holmes.”

Holmes passed him the cutting. “Then kindly look at this picture.”

Jenitsen studied it for a moment, and then looked up again, wide eyed with amazement. “Yes, Mr. Holmes. That’s the exact one I saw on the label.”

Holmes took back the cutting and looked around triumphantly. “This is an advertisement from a couple of years ago. It invites collectors of antiquities to gather for a private auction, in Paris.”

“Does it give an address?” asked Lestrade.

“It asks anyone interested to contact the Proprietor, Rue St. Martinot, Paris.”

“And is this relevant to the present business?”

“A picture of a spider links this advertisement with our present case. I think that makes it of enormous interest. Our search for the dinosaur skull must now take us across the Channel to Paris.”

I consulted our Bradshaw. “A train is due to leave Charing Cross for Paris by way of Calais first thing in the morning,” I told him.

“Then we should be in Paris by the late afternoon, in time to reach the Rue St. Martinot before the end of the day.”

“I’ll get in touch with the Paris Police,” said Lestrade, “and warn them that you’re on your way.”

“Watson,” continued Holmes, “get our things packed, and tell Dr. Agar to be at Charing Cross in time to catch that train. In the meantime, I need to think.” So saying, Holmes took his seat beside the window, and lit up his old and oily clay pipe.

Dressed in his gray traveling cloak, Holmes set his face with determination as we journeyed to Paris the following day. He said nothing for most of the time, whilst Dr. Agar and I shared tales of our various experiences in the medical profession. We had more than enough stories to last the whole journey.

When we alighted from the train at the Gare du Nord, Holmes made immediate enquiries about the crate labelled "*To be collected*".

It had indeed been collected, but the station officials could tell us no more, other than that the man who collected it had been neither French nor European.

"Sounds like the same fellow Jenitsen described," I told Holmes.

"I am sure you are right," he replied.

"The only address we have is Rue St. Martinot," I added. "It might be busy at this time of day, but it should be easy enough to find.

"Then it is there we must extend our search. I fancy the game is now afoot, Watson."

We took a cab through the rush-hour streets of the French capital city, and ten minutes later, our cab dismissed, the three of us were standing at the end of a narrow street, which matched our expectations only in its nameplate.

Holmes wandered slowly along the lonely street, looking carefully at each and every entrance in turn. When he reached the far end, he stopped, looked back at us, and beckoned for us to join him there. Carrying our bags, I made heavier weather of it than either of my companions.

I soon found myself standing before a forbidding front door with a mixture of curiosity and trepidation. What was this place? What secrets lay concealed beyond its gloomy entrance?

"I'll wager this is what we want," said Holmes as he stepped up to the door and pressed the bell-button. A sharp jangling sound deep inside the property was followed a few seconds later by the door opening. An elderly woman stood in the doorway, a creature shrivelled and bent with age. Her skin looked as yellow as parchment and her mouth displayed a scattering of broken teeth, but her expression looked as sharp as the doorbell itself. The old woman reminded me of Madame Defarge, whom Dickens describes in his novel *A Tale of Two Cities* as sitting, knitting, beside the guillotine, with a vengeful eye which showed no hint of pity.

Madame Defarge grunted something in deep guttural French.

"We have come to speak to the proprietor," explained Holmes. "So I suggest that you invite us inside."

The woman in the doorway nodded slowly but remained where she stood.

"I know all about the spider," added Holmes, fixing her with a penetrating stare.

"Do you, indeed?" She sounded mildly impressed.

Slowly, the woman stepped aside, and Dr. Agar and I followed Holmes into the entrance hall. Madame Defarge closed the door and led us along a dark passageway, towards a closed door at the far end.

"Leave your bags out here," croaked the old woman, opening the door.

I pushed them into one corner of the passageway and followed Holmes, Dr. Agar, and the woman in through the door.

At first glance, the room appeared empty. But as we watched, a man emerged from the shadows at the far end of the room, tall in stature, dark in countenance and hair colouring, and with angular facial features.

The man grinned. "Welcome to my parlour, said the spider to the flies. Permit me to introduce myself, gentlemen. *I* am the spider."

But I recognized the man by a different name.

"Khan!"

"Dr. John Watson," the man said, with a sneer in his voice. "The famous companion of Mr. Sherlock Holmes, here."

"And now a colleague also of Dr. Moore Agar of Harley Street," I said, indicating my other companion.

"It is indeed fortuitous that we meet again after so long, Dr. Watson."

"Do you know this man?" enquired Holmes.

"Sadly, I have to admit that I do," I told him. "Although he looks older than the last time we met."

"The years have changed us both," said Khan. "But perhaps not on the inside."

I half-turned towards Holmes. "I came to know this man during my time with the Army in Afghanistan. We all knew him then as 'Khan of the Mountains'. He was one of the bandits who waged blood-soaked war upon our soldiers. He is personally responsible for the deaths of many fine young men. I'll wager a pretty penny that the revolver he is now holding was taken from the hand of one of our soldiers as he lay dying, or perhaps suffering terrible torture."

Khan gave a nasty grin. "Tell them about the last time we met."

"I was on patrol with a party of soldiers. We had made camp for the night when, out of the darkness, a band of these villains descended with deadly ferocity. Half of our men were dead before they could take up their firearms. It was a massacre. I fled, together with three other men, leaving the dead behind, but with Khan and his ruffians in hot pursuit. We reached a ravine, with only one way across: A rope bridge so flimsy that we hesitated before committing our lives to such a contraption. But we had no choice. As the others crossed, I kept our attackers at bay with my revolver. Eventually, despite Khan's threats and insults, I also crossed the ravine. Had it not been for the darkness, I have no doubt this fellow would have shot me dead. The moment I reached the far side, I cut the rope securing the bridge, and allowed it to plummet into the gorge below."

Khan added, "I predicted that we would meet again one day. And, on that day, one of us would surely die."

"You were always prolific with your threats, Khan," I told him.

Khan laughed. "But first, to business. It is no doubt your search for that skull that brings you to my doorstep."

"Indeed," said Holmes. "I am working with Scotland Yard to find that stolen skull and bring the thief to justice."

"Scotland Yard has no jurisdiction here," said Khan.

"No, but the Paris Sûreté certainly does."

"In that case, I have to disappoint you, gentlemen," said Khan. "I do indeed have the item you seek, but it is not here."

"Then what have you done with my Triceratops?" demanded Dr. Agar, stepping forward to confront Khan.

"It is somewhere safe," returned Khan, standing firm. He turned to Holmes. "I can only assume, Mr. Holmes, that your skills of detection brought you here this evening."

"Together with your advertisement," said Holmes, holding up the newspaper cutting.

"Ah, yes. The advertisement. I initially needed to go public in order to build up my web of purchasers, dealers, and agents. Since then, it has grown by word of mouth."

"If nothing else, I have to admire your organizational skills," said Holmes.

"My genius," replied Khan, "is to persuade people across the world to do little jobs for me, not realizing they are part of a greater web of deception. An American contact of mine told me about the skull several months ago. I organized the construction of an identical crate, then traveled to England to organize its exchange of the other. As I told you, I am the spider."

"I wish you had remained in Afghanistan," I told him.

"I left because I considered my talents wasted there. Fighting the invaders was a laudable occupation, but it hardly made me a wealthy man. I quickly became involved in the selling of antiquities. Whether legitimate or stolen, I chose not to ask. I now provide a service to people who wish both to sell and purchase such objects. I decided to go worldwide. Hence my advertisement, which was placed in newspapers across the globe."

"And why do you dare to tell us all this now?" asked Holmes.

"Because you will not live long enough to share it with anyone else," said Khan.

"When do you plan to sell the skull?" demanded Dr. Agar.

"Tonight. Within the next few hours, men from across the world will gather to bid for it. To the right people, it is worth a fortune. And since I am the one who has now acquired the thing, I shall be a very rich man before dawn tomorrow."

"You fiend!" cried Dr. Agar, once more advancing towards Khan.

"Stay where you are!" growled Khan, raising the revolver. "Time is going on, and I must deal with you three before I leave."

He looked to me. "Dr. Watson, remove your gun, and drop it into the left-hand drawer of the table in the corner of the room."

I removed the revolver from my pocket, and pushed it into the indicated drawer. Now we were without any form of protection.

"Turn round," said Khan, "and go out through the door by which you came entered. Then turn left, and follow the flight of steps down."

We turned, and noticed the woman we had first met at the doorway. Holding a lighted lantern, she led the way down into the depths of the building's foundations.

Behind me, Holmes remained silent as he descended the steps. Only the tapping of his cane upon the stone stairs told me he was there.

We finally came to a halt outside a closed wooden door.

"Dr. Agar," came Khan's voice from the rear of this bizarre procession. "Kindly open the door, and lead the way inside."

By the light of the lantern, we saw that the room was unlit, and roofed with a vaulted stone ceiling. The place smelled of mildew – clearly a place of some antiquity. Worst of all, as we stepped down into the room, we discovered the place was flooded, with water submerging us to waist height.

"What is this place?" I demanded.

"The place of your demise, Dr. Watson," came Khan's voice from the doorway. "You will live only so long as you can remain awake. The moment you submit to sleep, you will drown. Nobody will ever find your bodies down here. Now, I wish you all *adieu*."

Khan laughed and closed the door, plunging the flooded room into the most profound darkness.

Dr. Agar gave a deep sigh. "I must apologize to you, gentlemen, for leading you into such a dreadful predicament."

"It is hardly your fault," I told him.

"But we will all be dead within a couple of hours, either from drowning or from hypothermia."

I felt something bump against me. A bulky object, floating in the water. "Holmes," I said. "I have found a body."

Dr. Agar took out a matchbox and struck a match. It flared in the darkness, and we looked down at the corpse as Holmes turned it over onto its back.

"Poor fellow," he breathed.

"I recognize him," said Dr. Agar, grimly. "It's the American courier. But what is he doing here?"

In the light of a second match, Holmes searched the man's pockets, and brought out a card. "This declares him to be a Pinkerton agent. Now it makes sense."

"How?"

"The Americans must already have known about Khan's network, and decided to take the opportunity to send their agent to investigate. We can only assume he walked into a trap."

"Just as we did."

"There is nothing we can do for him now," said Homes, "so let us consider our situation. I suggest we return to the doorway."

In the light of another match, Holmes examined the stone steps down which we had so recently entered this accursed room.

"I would draw your attention," said Holmes, "to the fact that the steps above the level of the water are dry." Holmes allowed the match to burn itself out. "Before entering this building, I noticed the river close by. It seems reasonable to conclude that the level of water in here it the same as that of the river outside. And therefore that the quantity of water coming into the room is balanced precisely by the quantity of water leaving it."

"How is that significant?" I asked.

"If you listen carefully, you can detect the sound of water running in, no doubt from some freshwater spring the builders broke into during the construction of the foundations. The water is also finding some way of escaping from the room, and flowing into the river. Presumably through a gap between the stone blocks making up the wall."

Our wet clothing was already draining the warmth from our bodies, and I wondered how long we could last. But I said nothing as Holmes began to rap the stonework of the walls with the top of his cane. After a few minutes, he paused in his work.

"A-ha!" he cried. "Here we have a different sound. Behind this stone, I detect a space. Dr. Agar, another match, if you please."

In the brief, flickering light of the match, Holmes handed me his cane, took out his pocket knife, and began to chip away at the mortar surrounding one of the blocks. "We shall have to pull it out together," he said.

Our three pairs of hands fought for purchase along the edges of the stone, a few inches below the waterline, and pulled. In the darkness, I could feel the wet, rough stonework chafing my fingers. But a grating sound of stone against stone suggested we were making progress. As soon as the block had moved out sufficiently, we placed our hands beneath it and lifted. In this way, we eased the stone away from its resting place until it was free, and allowed it to sink to the floor of the flooded room.

Looking through the gap in the wall, I could see a half-submerged water-channel, leading off into the distance, with subdued light now filtering in along its length. The gap allowed sufficient room for Holmes to climb through. He stopped, and looked up. "This must be the bottom of some inspection shaft," he called back, "although it has not been visited for many years."

"Can you find any way of climbing out?" I enquired.

"Indeed I can. A series of corroded iron rungs are fixed into the wall directly above me. They lead up perhaps twenty feet to floor level, judging by the number of steps we took coming down here. You wait here with Dr. Agar."

Ignoring the scurrying of rats, disturbed by our unexpected disturbance of their world, I watched Holmes climb up until he disappeared into deeper darkness.

A few minutes later, we heard a sound from the other side of the door. We stood back as it burst open, flooding light into the underground room.

"Are you alright, Watson?" came Holmes's voice.

"Yes. How about you?"

"Encouraged. And how is Dr. Agar?"

"Cold," the Harley Street doctor replied.

"In that case, come up and meet Inspector Albert of the Paris Sûreté. It seems Lestrade remembered to tell the Paris police that we were coming."

The French policeman greeted us warmly and insisted we change out of our soaking wet clothes. "We have your luggage," he told us, "and I am sure we can supply anything else you might need."

As we changed into dry clothing, Holmes explained to Inspector Albert about Khan and the stolen dinosaur.

"Inspector Lestrade appeared confused," said Albert, "but I followed you here and now that I have the full story, I am ready to help in any way I can."

"But where has Khan gone?" Dr. Agar sounded exasperated. "He is planning to sell the dinosaur skull tonight, presumably by auction to the highest international bidder. If he does that, we might never find it. Our American cousins will never trust us again."

"As we were climbing down to the cellar," said Holmes, "I happened to notice a detectable smell about Khan's clothing. Tobacco. I am willing to hazard a guess that he had been in a tobacco warehouse not long before we met him."

I turned to Albert. "Do you know of such a place, Inspector?"

"I know of several, all within a short distance of each other," said the French policeman.

"But we can narrow down the search," Holmes stated. He turned to a figure standing almost unnoticed in the shadows, the woman that I had called "Madame Defarge". "Can you tell us where Khan has gone?"

The old woman sneered back, "I will never tell you, *Monsieur*."

As she turned away, the old woman cast a glance toward a bureau standing at the far side of the room. Holmes immediately strode over to the bureau, opened it up, and began to rummage through the contents of its drawers and alcoves. A moment later, he stood back, holding a carved wooden printing block, nearly six inches in length, and a pad of black ink.

"I suggest that here we have the answer to our problem," he said. "But we shall see. Watson? Paper, if you please."

From the same bureau, I took out a blank sheet of paper and spread it out upon the table in front of Holmes. He inked the block and pressed it to the paper. The image of a spider lay before us, the exact replica of the one on the advertisement, only somewhat larger.

Holmes turned to Albert. "Inspector, I suggest your men search for a warehouse displaying this image of a spider. We may also assume the road outside will be congested with parked vehicles."

Inspector Albert turned and gave a few instructions to his assistant, who turned and hurried away. "That should be easy enough to find, *Monsieur* Holmes. I have a coach waiting outside. Shall we go?"

The coachman took us to an area of the city lined with warehouses and stopped when a man in uniform waved us down. After Inspector Albert had received the man's report, we turned another corner and drew up outside one building that looked no different from any other.

"See," said the inspector. "The poster on the door. The spider, *Monsieur* Holmes. This has to be the right place."

"And, judging by the number of other conveyances parked outside, I would tend to agree," replied Holmes.

Albert looked around as three other vehicles arrived, and uniformed officers spilled out into the street. "While you were changing, I called in some more of our men."

This time, we entered the building without knocking, and soon found ourselves in a large interior room. The air held an all-pervasive smell of raw tobacco leaf. I became aware of people all around me who pulled back into the shadows as we entered. If I hadn't already been assured by Holmes, I would now be certain we had reached the correct place.

In the centre of the room, I saw Khan. And, next to him, a thing which at the same time both echoed my darkest nightmares and thrilled me to the core. A massive skull, approximately six feet in length, with a frill behind the head, and the bony cores of two lethal-looking spiked horns. The jaws held a multitude of grinding teeth, and the face ended in a vicious beak, with a smaller horn on the snout.

"Isn't she magnificent, Dr. Watson?" gushed Dr. Agar. "A Triceratops, in all her splendour!"

Khan stepped towards us. "This is a private gathering," he shouted. "I demand that you remove yourselves forthwith."

Inspector Albert, flanked by two uniformed policemen, confronted Khan. "You must come with me, *Monsieur*. You must answer questions about the theft of this skull. And murder."

With a sneer distorting his severe expression, Khan pulled his revolver from beneath his coat, and leveled it at me. At the very moment he pulled the trigger, one of Albert's men threw himself toward the gunman, and caught the full force of the gun's discharge.

I reached for my own gun, but remembered I had forgotten to collect it from the drawer at the Rue St. Martinot. Instead, I heard another revolver fire from close beside me. I saw Khan stagger back, with pain and shock showing on his face, and blood staining the right shoulder of his jacket.

As Khan retreated another step, I watched him trip, and fall heavily against the skull of the Triceratops. Hardly believing what I was witnessing, I watched as one horn of the dinosaur emerged, covered in blood, through the centre of Khan's chest.

The grotesque and blood-soaked scene reminded me of a gargantuan beetle mounted in the collection of some eccentric entomologist.

I broke off my attention, looked around, and saw Dr. Agar standing behind me, holding my own gun.

"You left it behind," he told me, "so I brought it along in case it turned out to be useful."

As I bent down to care for the fallen policeman, and call for his colleagues to consign the badly injured officer to hospital, Dr. Agar examined the man he had shot. None of us had any doubt that the man who had stolen the dinosaur now lay dead, impaled by the very object of his criminality.

Inspector Albert immediately took charge of the situation, and arranged for each person present to account, in writing, for his presence there that night.

At least one newspaper headline the following day read, "*Man Killed by Dinosaur in Paris*".

With such publicity, Dr. Agar's exhibition at the Museum of Practical Geology in London proved a tremendous success. Private donations flooded in, and fully paid the costs of transporting and exhibiting the dinosaur skull.

Sherlock Holmes turned down the invitation to be guest of honor at the opening. But despite his protestations, and out of respect for Dr. Agar, he did agree to stand beside the dinosaur for a photograph. I have it before me now, and slip it once more between the pages of my notebook, as I finally conclude my story of Dr. Agar and the Dinosaur.

> *. . . Dr. Moore Agar, of Harley Street, whose dramatic introduction to Holmes I may some day recount . . . .*
>
> Dr. John H. Watson – "The Devil's Foot"

# The Mystery of the Green Room
by Robert V. Stapleton

"How is the girl, Watson?" Sherlock Holmes posed the question the moment I stepped through the door of our sitting room in Baker Street and sat down heavily in my customary easy chair.

Our acquaintance was still in its early days, and I had been too preoccupied with my patients to take a great deal of interest in Holmes's latest activities. "The girl is not at all well, Holmes."

"I am sorry to hear you confirm the fact."

"But how do you come to know about my young patient?" Now, in that summer of 1882, I was accustomed to the singular skill of my friend to make deductions based upon even the most sparing of facts, but this turn of events made me look up at him with renewed awe.

From his seat beside the laid but unlit fire, Holmes smiled, and studied me through steepled fingers. "You have been out visiting the sick. That is evident from the fact that your medical bag now lies on the floor beside you."

"I'll admit that appears obvious."

"And the expression on your face suggests that the condition of your patient is a cause for concern."

I nodded. "True enough."

"The bulge in your coat pocket could be made by nothing other than a bag of sweets. That, together with the fact that the bag appears to be full, suggests that the child was in no mood or condition to enjoy them."

"Surely you are now taking your skills of deduction into the realms of speculation?" I retorted.

"Not at all. It is merely a matter of observation and deduction."

"Very well. I have to admit to the truth of it. But how could you tell that the child was a girl?"

"Now there I have to admit to a certain amount of duplicity. You see, I was in the public gardens at the center of Morpeth Square when you approached the front door of Number Eighteen."

I stared back at him in amazement. "You were there? I have to admit, I was complete unaware of your presence anywhere near the place."

"I am glad to hear it. Otherwise my disguise would have been entirely without value."

"The only person I saw was the gardener." Then it occurred to me. "*You* were that gardener."

"Correct."

I remembered the scruffily clad figure, employed upon pruning a bed of roses. "I would never have guessed."

"That was my intention."

"But what were you doing there in such a disguise?"

"I was watching the very house you called upon this afternoon. As you will already know, it belongs to a certain Jeremiah Edlingholm, the manager of the branch of the London and South Coast Bank situated in Horsegate Road. I know that Mr. Edlingholm is married and has a young daughter of eight years."

"The girl's name is Amy," I explained, in an attempt to regain a measure of dignity in the face of this surge of revelations.

"I also know that he and his family moved in there no more than three months ago."

"I believe that is true.'

Holmes laughed at the discomfort evident in my expression. "Please do not be offended, Watson. It was not you I was there to observe. And anyway, I left shortly after your arrival. It was a matter of balance. If I had spent too little time there, my time would have been wasted, but if I had spent too long there, I might have risked drawing undue attention to myself. I arrived back here shortly before you did – with just sufficient time to change out of my work clothes."

I nodded. "You are quite right in saying that I am worried about the girl. The parents called me in because nobody else was able to provide them with any hope of recovery. And, quite frankly, at first I was not sure I could either. One physician had pronounced that the constriction in the girl's throat meant she was suffering from diphtheria. Another suggested cholera."

"Dear me!" said Holmes. "That is yet another blow to a man who has faced a great deal of trouble during the last few months."

"How do you mean?"

"Mr. Edlingholm's bank suffered a robbery at the end of May," he elucidated. "Banknotes were taken, to a considerable value. Although the numbers printed on them are known, Scotland Yard has had little success in tracing any of them. The crime has left them completely baffled."

"And for that reason, they called in yourself," I concluded.

"As you will remember, I was otherwise preoccupied at the time. There had been one definite attempt to assassinate Her Majesty, and at least one other had been contemplated. Scotland Yard were busy arresting every suspect they could lay their hands on, whether sane or insane."

"I remember they called you in, but I know nothing of the details."

"It continues to be an extremely delicate matter," said Holmes as he stood up and moved across the room to the window, where he remained looking out upon the busy street below.

"But you decided to assist them with their enquiries into the crime."

"Indeed, and the more I have looked into this matter, the more intriguing I have found it to be. And baffling. I have to admit, I am as perplexed as the police. The matter appears simple enough, but I am at a loss to find any way forward with the investigation. I can cope with facts, information, and evidence, but in this case there seems to be nothing for me to work with. What we do know is that when the bank's strong-room was locked on the Saturday afternoon, nothing was amiss. Then, when it was opened again on the Monday morning, a large amount of money was discovered to have gone missing. And the strong-room door was found to be still locked."

"Somebody must have used a key to gain entrance."

Holmes turned to face me again. "In the absence of any other indications, that had to be the assumption at which we arrived. The same was true of both the front door of the bank and the door to the staircase leading down into the vaults. The inevitable conclusion was that a complete set of keys had been used. But the only two sets were in the possession of the two most significant men at the bank: The manager himself, Mr. Edlingholm, and the Chief Cashier, Mr. Obadiah Mitchelson."

"I suppose you are going to tell me they both still had their keys in their possession on the Monday morning."

"That is exactly the situation, Watson. When Scotland Yard was brought in to investigate the theft, they took both men in for detailed questioning. It turned out that both sets of keys had remained securely in their possession throughout the whole of the weekend. Both were able to give detailed accounts of their activities since the Saturday afternoon. Mr. Mitchelson and his family had been away from home, staying with his wife's parents at their home in Kent. Mr.

Edlingholm was busy preparing to move house, and had been busy packing the family's possessions into tea-chests, under the careful scrutiny of his wife."

"I do remember you being somewhat preoccupied at the time," I told him, "but you felt unable to share any of the details with me."

"Beyond what I have just told you, there were no details."

I nodded. "Are you suggesting, Holmes, that a *third* set of keys had been employed for this robbery?"

"That had to be the only solution. I carefully examined both sets of keys, and discovered that those held by the Chief Cashier had traces of wax adhering to the teeth of some of the keys, with none at all on those belonging to the Manager."

"And yet neither man could account for this."

"Obviously somebody had borrowed Mr. Mitchelson's set of keys and had made wax impressions of them without his knowledge. When it became clear that Mr. Mitchelson could shed no further light on the matter, we realized we had come to the end of our investigation, and could see no way forward. The suspicion still remained that either man could have been responsible for the theft, as no evidence could be found to link the crime to anyone else."

"That was why you were watching the house. On the lookout for anything unusual in the bank manager's behaviour."

"Quite right."

"And then I came along."

"Indeed. I have been watching surgeons and medical men come and go at that house for much of the week, but your appearance proved the most hopeful event to have taken place since the girl was taken ill."

"That is kind of you to say so, Holmes."

"Think nothing of it, Watson. It is merely my personal observation."

"Although, it is my professional opinion that the illness is more likely to have been caused by poisoning."

"What makes you say that?"

"Observation and deduction," I replied. "Elementary, Holmes."

"Hmm." He smiled, and inclined his head slightly.

"The symptoms, including headaches, stomach pains, vomiting, and diarrhea, might just as easily have resulted from poisoning by a salt of some heavy metal."

"And you have one particular culprit in mind?"

"Precisely. But I am not prepared to name it at this time. Not until I am sure."

"I have a certain expertise when it comes to the detection of poisons," said Holmes modestly. "I would be more than happy to accompany you on your next visit to that house. My opinion might prove useful to you."

The following morning, I paid another visit to Number Eighteen Morpeth Square. And this time I was accompanied by Sherlock Holmes.

Here was a district of the capital city which displayed affluence and privilege. Simple and secluded, yet with an air of quality and self-confidence. The houses had been built in terraces along three sides of a rectangle, with the entrance at the far end of the square. Separated from the road by a row of iron railings, with a front door approached by a flight of stone steps, each house looked out onto a small public garden occupying the center of the square. A couple of elderly men were wandering among the shrubs, bushes, and flowerbeds. Others were sitting on the benches set out along the footpaths. I found it difficult to envisage Sherlock Holmes spending several hours here acting – and indeed working – as the gardener in that place.

The maid opened the door to Holmes's knock, and invited us both to step inside. We waited in the morning room until the door opened and Mr. Edlingholm himself stood in the entrance. He was a big man, with auburn side-whiskers and the appearance of one who has achieved comfortable success in life. At this moment, however, his face exhibited signs of considerable mental strain.

"Mr. Holmes," said he. "It is good to see you again." The two men shook hands. "Have you made any progress with that terrible business at the bank?"

"Not yet, Mr. Edlingholm," replied Holmes. "But I am sure that Scotland Yard is making every effort at this moment to locate your money and to bring the thief to justice. Today, however, I am here to assist my colleague, Dr. Watson."

The bank manager turned to me, and raised his eyebrows as though enquiring as to the purpose of our visit.

"I should like to examine your daughter again, Mr. Edlingholm," I told the man.

"Amy? Yes. She has shown no signs of improvement since your visit yesterday, Dr. Watson. As we told you, the previous physician indicated cholera. You yourself examined her and said nothing to contradict his opinion."

"Having given the matter my full consideration since I was last here, I am prepared to do so now," I replied. "I am hoping to explore another possible cause of your daughter's illness. May we have your permission to revisit the sick-room?"

"Certainly. My wife is sitting at the bedside."

The air in the little girl's bedroom felt stuffy and oppressive. The heavy drapes covering much of the closed window made the room appear dark and dismal. On one side of the room stood a dark-brown wardrobe. On the other side stood a simple washstand. The ambient color of the room was green. Woodwork throughout the room had been painted green. The walls of the bedroom were covered with an expensive paper, thick in texture, with raised decorations of flowers in bright green. A green coverlet lay across the sickbed, wherein lay the little girl, looking pale and sickly.

"Amy loves that wallpaper," said Mr. Edlingholm as he noticed my interest in it. "She finds the texture comforting, and she strokes it lovingly every night."

Holmes looked at the wallpaper, and then toward me.

I nodded. The very same thought was evidently occupying both our minds.

The child's mother rose from her chair beside the bed, and greeted us. "Dr. Watson. It is good of you to come again so soon."

"I have brought a friend with me this time," I told her. "Mr. Sherlock Holmes."

"The detective?"

"On this occasion, here as a colleague."

She turned to face Holmes. "But what about the theft from my husband's bank? Are you not helping out with that investigation, Mr. Holmes?"

"That is another matter entirely, Mrs. Edlingholm," said Holmes. "Today, I am concerned with Amy's health."

Leaving Holmes to inspect the wallpaper, I took a second the chair and examined the little girl. "Good morning, Amy."

"Good morning, Dr. Watson."

"How do you feel today?"

With her eyes fixed upon Sherlock Holmes, she tried to smile. "Still sick."

I proceeded to give the child a thorough physical examination.

"She still has moments when her mind is disturbed," said Mrs. Edlingholm.

"That is understandable," I told her.

"She keeps imagining somebody coming into the bedroom during the night."

"Her father, perhaps?"

"No. Someone she doesn't recognize."

"The sick mind can play the most amazing tricks upon us," I explained, soothingly.

After several minutes, I stood up, looked down at the child, and announced my diagnosis. "I am convinced that Amy is not suffering from cholera, or any other contagious disease."

Her mother appeared relieved by this news.

"I believe, however, that something else is making her ill," I continued. "I feel that I know what it is, but I'm not prepared to commit myself until I'm certain. Whether I am correct or not, I would like you to remove Amy from this room."

"Remove her from the bedroom?" Her mother sounded shocked. "But she is far too sick to move, Dr. Watson."

"Nevertheless," I returned, "I believe it is essential for the recovery of her health."

The mother nodded. "In that case, I shall arrange the matter when you have gone."

"Arrange the matter now," I told her.

After a moment's pause, Mrs. Edlingholm opened the bedroom door and called out, "Molly."

The housemaid appeared in the doorway almost at once. "Ma'am?"

"Arrange the settee in the lounge. We're going to transfer Amy to sleep down there for a while."

Still examining the wallpaper, but being careful not to touch it, Holmes took out his pocket-knife, scraped away a sample of the green decoration, and proceeded to drop it onto a sheet of paper torn from his pocket-book. He then folded it up and tucked away beneath his coat. He next scraped away some of the paintwork, and added a small sample of this to his inner pocket. Holmes turned to the girl's father. "How long have you had this wallpaper, Mr. Edlingholm?"

"We had it hung just before we moved in here."

"That must be no more than three months ago," Holmes determined.

"That's about right, Mr. Holmes."

"And the paintwork?"

"A similar length of time."

"And Amy has been sleeping in this room all that time?"

"Indeed. And becoming frailer by the day."

"I agree with Dr. Watson," said Holmes. "I believe it is imperative that we remove the girl to a more secure environment as soon as possible."

Whilst I opened the window, allowing the outside air to refresh the heavy atmosphere of the sick-room, Mr. Edlingholm picked up the little girl, together with her bedclothes, and carried her from the bedroom.

"I need to undertake some investigation," I told the parents once I was sure the girl was comfortably settled, "but I'll return later in the day."

On our return to 221B Baker Street, I went immediately in search of my medical books, and returned to the sitting room a few minutes later with an armful of learned tomes.

"Well, Watson," said Holmes. "What says your professional opinion?"

"I am increasingly convinced of my medical diagnosis," I told him. "But I await to hear your opinion first, Holmes."

"Then you shall have it," said he, gathering together some of his scientific equipment and arranging it upon the dining table. "You have no doubt heard of the Marsh Test."

"I have certainly heard of it," I told him. "But, if you intend to carry out such a procedure here, it would undoubtedly be safer to let in the fresh air before we start." I opened the window and allowed the warm summer air, together with the raucous noise of the Baker Street traffic, to invade the quiet stillness of our room. It seemed strange to me that the ordinary world should continue to turn whilst we delved into the mysterious chemistry of poison.

Holmes turned his attention to the apparatus now assembled on the table. "As you can see, Watson, I have set up an asymmetrical U-tube, held in place by a wooden clamp."

"Indeed."

"The longer end of the tube remains open, whilst the shorter end is fitted with a narrow glass tube secured by a simple cork bung. This glass tube tapers to a narrow aperture at the end, and is fitted with a tap halfway along its length, allowing gas to flow from the tube toward the end of the opening."

"I am following you," I told him.

"Before closing the tap, I admit into the bottom of the tube a small amount of diluted hydrochloric acid, together with several small pieces of zinc."

"Producing an immediate chemical reaction," I observed. "Bubbles of hydrogen gas."

"Then, in order to prove that we have no contaminants in the tube, I close the tap, and wait for the hydrogen gas to build up inside the U-tube. When the pressure inside the tube has built up sufficiently to push the acid up the open end, I turn the tap, and allow some of the gas to escape through the narrow aperture. I then apply a lighted match to the resulting gas."

I watched carefully as the experiment proceeded. "Which burns with an almost invisible flame."

Holmes took up a white, glazed saucer, and held it against the flame. "See, Watson, the flame leaves the white surface unmarked. This verifies the purity of the ingredients," he explained. "Now, I extinguish the flame, close the tap, and repeat the experiment, but this time adding to the U-tube the scraping I took from the sickroom wallpaper earlier today."

I watched with keen interest as Holmes opened the folded paper, and poured the green powder into the U-tube. For several few minutes, we both stood watching the chemical reaction.

"Once again," continued Holmes, "the gas in the closed end of the tube has built up sufficiently to cause the liquid in the open end to rise."

I nodded. "Just as on the previous occasion."

"Now, I open the tap, and apply a flame to the resulting gas."

"Which now burns with a very slight mauve-tinged flame."

"This time, when I apply the flame to the white saucer, it leaves a dark, silver-gray deposit. Indicating the presence of a metal."

"Which might turn out to be antimony."

"Then allow us to remove any doubt. I apply a small quantity of sodium hypochlorite solution to the deposit."

He picked up a bottle from the table beside him, and allowed a few drops to mix with the dark deposit. The silver-gray deposit rapidly dissolved.

"Now we must clean the equipment," announced Holmes, "and repeat the experiment using the scraping I took from the paint."

The result turned out to be similar to the previous sample.

"Once again, we take a further sample. This time of the girl's bodily fluids. I notice you have such a sample with you, Watson."

"Indeed. What sort of a doctor would I be without having collected a sample from my patient?"

This time, at the very moment that the silvery deposit dissolved, we looked at each other in triumph.

"Proof positive, Watson," declared Sherlock Holmes.

"The little girl is suffering from arsenic poisoning, absorbed from contact with her bedroom environment," I concluded. "Science confirming my own medical opinion."

On our return to Morpeth Square, we discovered that Mr. Edlingholm had returned to his place of business, and Amy was asleep in the front sitting room.

"It is a little too early to say," said her mother, "but Amy does appear to be calmer now that her bed has been made up downstairs."

I looked down at the sleeping child. "Mrs. Edlingholm, my colleague and I are now of the same opinion, that your daughter's illness has been caused not by any contagious disease, but by arsenic poisoning."

"Oh, dear!" The child's mother held her hand to her mouth, looking deeply disturbed by this news. "We've always tried to be so careful about what we feed to our daughter, Doctor."

"We are also agreed that the poison is coming from various items in her bedroom – particularly the wallpaper. The coloring is heavily contaminated with arsenic."

"The green?"

"Indeed. Scheele's Green. Not only is it present in the wallpaper, but also in the paint work. I suspect also that it might also be present in some of the textiles in the room. The arsenic is being transmitted to Amy by small particles in the air, and through physical contact with the wallpaper and other contaminated items."

Mrs. Edlingholm looked even more shocked. "Poor Amy. What can we do to make her better, Dr. Watson?"

"You have already done the first thing necessary, which is to remove her from the source of the contamination – her bedroom. Down here, she can at least begin the process of recovery. I would suggest that you also open the windows, so that the fresh air can dilute the arsenic-filled air which has undoubtedly contaminated the entire house. After all, this is the middle of summer."

"If you consider it important, then we can certainly do that."

"Then we must cleanse her of all traces of the poison. To begin with, you must wash her down, from head to foot, to make sure none of the poison remains on her skin, threatening to enter her system. And wash all her clothing. Next, you must give her plenty of water to drink. This should help clear her stomach of any poison that she might have ingested. Then we need to cleanse her bloodstream. The inclusion of garlic in her diet would be one good way of helping with that."

"Garlic?"

"Indeed, if you can find a ready supply – even if only for a few days."

"Don't worry, Dr. Watson. If our daughter needs it, we can certainly get hold of it for her. Is there anything else?"

"Oh, certainly. You must try to persuade her to drink plenty of milk." I reached into my bag and drew out a sheet of paper. "Here is a list of the kind of foods that will help. I shall leave it with you."

"I'm still concerned about that bedroom," said Holmes, who had been sitting quietly in the corner of the room. "Has the girl repeated her assertion that a man entered her bedroom?"

"Indeed, she has," replied Mrs. Edlingholm. "She insists that a man used to come into her room during the night."

"How often was that?"

"On a number of occasions during the last few weeks, Mr. Holmes."

"Hmm. Interesting. With your permission, I should like to make another inspection of the sickroom."

"Please, feel free to help yourself."

I stood in the doorway of the now-empty bedroom, whilst Holmes once more examined the wallpaper.

"What are you looking for now?" I enquired. "You have already tested samples of the pigment."

Holmes was holding a magnifying lens in his hand as he now examined the surface of the paper. "Somebody has been making holes in this paper. Extremely carefully. Whoever was here has cut thin vertical slits, as though with a sharp razor."

"How extraordinary! Are you sure?"

"Oh, the matter is beyond doubt. I can only conjecture that whoever it was had been looking for something hidden beneath the surface layer. See how thick and bulky the paper appears."

"It might simply be the high quality of the paper they used."

Holmes opened up his pocket-knife and slid the blade beneath the wallpaper. "Watson, would you please ask the maid to bring me a bowl of warm water and a sponge?"

I watched carefully as, a few minutes later, Holmes applied water to the edges of the wallpaper roll, and eased the edge of the paper away from the wall. "There is definitely a gap under here," said Holmes. "Only the edges of the paper have been properly secured to the wall."

Intrigued, I watched him carefully. "Is anything hidden underneath?"

"I am sure of it. Do you happen to have a pair of forceps with you?"

I opened my medical bag, drew out a pair of forceps, and handed them to Holmes.

"Now we shall see," he said as he pushed the forceps between the paper and the plaster behind.

I watched with growing astonishment as my friend slowly withdrew the forceps, together with a sheet of white paper. "What have you found?" I asked.

He held the paper up to the light, and examined it carefully. "A Bank of England banknote," he declared, handing it to me.

Holmes repeated the operation, and had soon retrieved a further two banknotes from behind the wallpaper, which he handed to me.

I examined the notes now in my hands. One was to the value of twenty pounds, whereas the other two were valued at fifty pounds each. "Could this be Edlingholm's own personal bank deposit?" I submitted.

"I am sorry to say, Watson, that we may well have uncovered some of the money stolen from his bank earlier this year. Scotland Yard are bound to come to the conclusion that Edlingholm concealed the money here himself."

That was indeed the conclusion that Inspector Lestrade reached when we visited him at Scotland Yard later that afternoon. This shrewd, rodent-faced policeman had already proved himself to be a good detective, and he was already developing a guarded respect for the skills Sherlock Holmes had exhibited on more than one occasion.

"I have to admit, Mr. Holmes, you have done an exceptionally good job in finding these banknotes," said the inspector. "The numbers tally precisely with some of those missing from the bank. Although, it has to be admitted, these are not the first we have come across."

"Really?" Holmes's ears pricked up. "Have others surfaced?"

"Only the occasional one or two, and all within the last couple of days. They were paid in at large stores across London – and one at the Dorchester Hotel for a meal. Another was furnished in payment for a bank loan. But by the time we were able to respond to both occasions, the person in possession of the banknotes was long-gone, leaving no trace whatsoever of his identity."

"What do you intend to do next, Lestrade?" asked Holmes.

"You need hardly ask a question like that, Mr Holmes. We have no choice but to arrest Mr. Edlingholm on suspicion of stealing that money from his own bank and concealing it upon his own premises."

"And why do you imagine he would have taken such a risk?"

"That is one of the questions he will need to answer. Both here, and in a court of law."

"If you intend to arrest Mr. Edlingholm, then I would ask you to refrain from passing this information on to the gentlemen of the Press – at least for the next forty-eight hours."

Lestrade rubbed his chin thoughtfully. "I suppose you have been helpful with this case, Mr. Holmes, so I think I can allow you twenty-four hours. But then I shall need to bring my suspect before the magistrate, in open session. The Press will inevitably be there."

"Then we have just one day," said Holmes, turning to me. "Let us make sure we use our time in the best possible manner."

We returned to Baker Street in a dejected frame of mind, myself thoughtful of my patient, my colleague brooding over the unenviable task before him. Holmes filled the bowl of his churchwarden with a plug of shag, and was soon enveloped in a thick cloud of smoke. We both sat silently staring into space.

Holmes eventually broke the silence. "On the surface, Edlingholm's guilt appears to be sealed. But can we really believe that he would steal the money from his own bank and then hide it in his own daughter's bedroom?"

"The idea seems preposterous," I replied. "It's hardly the sort of devious trick in which a doting father would involve his only daughter."

"And yet, Lestrade was right. The questions need to be asked, and answered."

I was distracted from my thoughts by the sound of two pairs of footsteps on the stairs outside our rooms. The door opened to reveal Mrs. Hudson.

"Mr. Holmes. There is a lady here to see you."

"Very well, Mrs. Hudson. Please show her in."

With all the fluster of a whirlwind, in stormed Mrs. Edlingholm. "Mr. Holmes," she roared. "What have you been doing? No doubt you are aware that the police have arrested my husband, on suspicion of stealing the bank's money. They tell me that you discovered it hidden behind the wallpaper in my daughter's bedroom."

Without rising from his seat by the window, Holmes nodded. "That is true."

"And you never thought to tell *me* about this?"

"With so many other problems besetting you, Mrs. Edlingholm, I did not wish to add to your worries."

"Not wish to add to my worries? How dare you! Anything that brings my husband into disrepute, and threatens to send his wife and child into the workhouse, has everything to do with me!"

"I do not think it will come to that."

"Really? Are you planning to come up with some amazing new piece of evidence to completely reverse the opinion of Scotland Yard?"

"It would not be the first time," replied Holmes.

"Or do you intend to wave a magic wand and set my husband free again?"

Holmes arose abruptly from his seat, clearly agitated, and wishing to calm this difficult state of affairs. "Maybe not a magic wand," said he, "but perhaps some information which you alone can provide."

"Me?" Mrs. Edlingholm scowled. "I don't see what more I can do to help you."

He fixed her with his steely stare. "Tell me about that wallpaper. The paper covering the walls in your daughter's bedroom."

For a moment, she turned her gaze away from him. "Until Dr. Watson informed me, I was totally unaware that it carried poison." Then she once more riveted him with her glare, "I would never knowingly have placed my daughter in any kind of peril."

"So I would imagine. And you have only been living in that house for the last three months."

"That is correct."

"Then I assume you had the place decorated before you moved in."

"That is also true. We were fortunate enough to be able to afford a professional decorator to come in and apply fresh paint and wallpaper to all the rooms."

"Then I need to know the name of the firm you employed to do the work."

"We were recommended a firm with offices in the West End – a firm called Paradise Home Adornment. A man called Wallace Goodwell is the proprietor there. He proved to be extremely helpful, and had the work completed in good time for our removal."

"Who recommended this firm to you?"

"My husband's Chief Cashier. Mr. Obadiah Mitchelson."

An expression of enlightenment lit up Holmes's face. "And did Mr. Mitchelson also employ this firm to decorate his own house?"

"That is what he told us, Mr. Holmes. Indeed, he invited us round to his house to see the quality of the work they had carried out for him. We went, and were so satisfied with the results that we decided to book Mr. Goodwell's firm to complete the decorations in our own new home."

"Which he proceeded to do."

"Indeed. I think he valued our business, and considered us priority customers."

"In that case, I think we ought to pay Goodwell a visit. What think you, Watson?"

"Indeed, I heartily concur."

"And I would like you to come along with us, Mrs. Edlingholm."

"You think my presence might be of value on this occasion?"

Holmes gave her a wry smile. "We need to reach the bottom of this business, and our visit to Paradise Home Adornment is where we have to now extend our search."

The moment we stepped outside into the scurry of Baker Street, Holmes hailed a cab which brought us presently to the entrance of a smart, glass-fronted shop bearing the name Paradise Home Adornment.

Holmes inspected the front of the premises. “Is this the place, Mrs. Edlingholm?”

“Yes. It doesn’t appear to have changed in any way since I last visited the establishment.”

Holmes opened the door, and led the way inside.

A smartly dressed man approached us. “Good afternoon.”

“Good afternoon,” returned Holmes. “Mr. Goodwell, I presume.”

The man gave a slight bow of acknowledgment.

“I am Sherlock Holmes, and this is my colleague, Dr. Watson. And I believe you already know Mrs. Edlingholm.”

“Certainly. Good afternoon.” Turning back to Holmes, he continued, “How may I be of assistance?”

“I am interested in the work you recently carried out at the home of Mr. and Mrs. Edlingholm.”

“I hope all is well.”

“Sadly,” said Holmes, “it turns out that the wallpaper put up in their little girl’s bedroom is impregnated with arsenic, and it has been poisoning the child.”

“Are you certain?”

“The matter is beyond doubt,” I responded. “Along with some of the paint employed.”

“Dear me,” said the man. “I had no idea it would put anybody’s life in danger. Believe me, we do our best to provide the public with the materials they require, making sure they are of the very highest quality. Those new colors are extremely popular nowadays. So vibrant. So lively. They bring light and brightness to rooms which have always been shaded in darkness.”

“An admirable ambition,” said Holmes. “But I would urge you to be more circumspect in your choice of the materials you employ.”

The man appeared suitably humbled.

"However, that is not the matter which brings us here today."

"Then perhaps you'd better come with me to my office at the back of our store," said Goodwell, looking around him at the other staff and customers. "We can speak there freely and without the danger of being interrupted."

Once seated in the office, Holmes leaned forward, stared at the proprietor, and came to the point of our visit. "I need to know from you, Mr. Goodwell, who it was who carried out the decorating work at the Edlingholm property. You must be able to provide me with that information."

Mr. Goodwell stood up, reached to the shelving above him, and brought down a large, leather-bound ledger. "We employ teams of workers to carry out the decorations, Mr. Holmes. Groups of two or three men, each detailed to a separate district of the city. It is an efficient method of working, and has resulted in nothing but approbation from our clients. Until now."

"Are you able to give me the names of those who worked on this particular project?"

Goodwell searched through his records. "Ah, yes, here we are. Two of our men worked on the property. William Ardley was the foreman. And a man called Harris Greep helped him with the work."

"What do you know of them?"

"Ardley is a responsible and trustworthy employee, who has been with our firm for many years. Of the other man, I know very little. He has been carrying out some casual work for us during the last year – learning the trade as he went along, is what he told us. Which was just as well, because, sadly, Bill Ardley's usual assistant was killed in a tragic accident shortly before work began on one particularly important job."

"Where was that piece of work carried out?"

"At the home of Mr. Mitchelson, Mr. Edlingholm's Chief Cashier. We were delighted when Mr. Greep stepped in at extremely short notice to help complete the assignment. A very nice job of work he made of it, as well."

"You say the man who was supposed to help with the work was killed."

"That is correct. A very nasty accident. You might remember it. He was standing among the bustling crowd on the platform of the underground railway at Paddington Station when he slipped and fell beneath the wheels of an approaching train."

"Yes, I remember reading about it," I told him. "A nasty business."

"Are you sure it was an accident?" Holmes asked him.

Mr. Goodwell appeared shocked. "Dear me, Mr. Holmes, are you suggesting he might have been pushed to his death? That really is a thought too terrible to contemplate."

"It is merely one line of enquiry," admitted Holmes.

"The police have always considered his death to be an accident."

Holmes nodded. "Of course."

Sherlock Holmes and I returned with Mrs. Edlingholm to her home in Morpeth Square, and she invited us inside. Little Amy, still lying in the front room, was giving every appearance of recovering slowly but steadily from her illness.

"I should like to pay another visit to the upper part of this house, Mrs. Edlingholm," said Holmes. "I believe there's something more to be discovered there."

"Certainly," she told him, "but I can't imagine what you have in mind."

"First, can you tell me what lies above? Is there an attic of some kind up there?"

"If there is, I have to admit, I've never been there to find out."

"Do you know of any trapdoor which might give access to a space above?"

"No. I can't recall ever having seen anything of the sort."

"And yet, there must be some such access," mused Holmes. "Do you happen to have a pair of kitchen steps?"

"Yes."

"May I borrow them for a few minutes?"

"Certainly, if you think they can be of any help."

I followed Holmes up to the landing immediately outside the green bedroom door, while Mrs. Edlingholm waited downstairs. I was keenly interested to discover his intention.

The landing area gave access to the master bedroom, and to other rooms on that upper level of the house. It also gave access to the rear of the house, and to the bedroom set aside for the use of the housemaid.

Holmes now stood on the landing, looking up at the ceiling. In the shadows, it appeared to be as professionally papered as the rest of the house.

"A-ha!" said he, setting the steps close to the rear side of the landing. Then he climbed them and pushed against the ceiling above him. I was amazed to see a section of the papered ceiling push upward on a hinge, and fall over softly onto the ceiling joists somewhere in the darkness.

Holmes heaved himself up to the opening and peered through. "Now, this is very interesting," came his report, as he allowed a coil of rope to drop through the gap. A length of knotted rope now reached from the floor to the opening above.

"Do you need a light?" I called up to him.

"Not at the moment," he replied. "There appears to be plenty of illumination provided by a skylight in the roof above my head – and a number of others along the full length of this terrace. This is undoubtedly the means of ingress and egress for Amy's night-time visitor."

I watched Holmes disappear up into the attic space and decided to follow. I climbed the steps until I could see over the lip of the trapdoor, looking along the entire length of the highest part of the entire row of houses. Weaving its way between buttress walls and chimney stacks, a passageway led as far as I could see. Rough-hewn planks of wood had been laid down along its length, to establish a secure passageway. I could see Holmes in the distance, kneeling down and examining the wooden surface.

"What have you found now?" I called.

"A skylight above each of the houses illuminates a trapdoor leading down into the dwelling. Most show no signs of recent use, but one or two have rope handles attached to them for easy raising."

"Can you see any trace of the intruder?"

Holmes returned and followed me down the steps until we were once more standing on the landing directly outside the girl's bedroom. There Holmes took out his pocketbook and showed me a few scraps of wool. "The intruder had to make his way along that passage at night, and as silently as possible, in order to avoid being detected from below. In order to accomplish that, he had to make his way in stockinged feet. As a result, he has left traces of wool caught on splinters attached to the boards."

"Is that significant?"

"In itself, maybe not. It merely proves that somebody has been up there in the fairly recent past, attempting to move as silently as possible."

Holmes thanked Mrs. Edlingholm for allowing him to investigate and led the way outside. There, we stood in the roadway and looked up at the top of the terrace buildings.

"You can see the skylights from here, Watson. But where does that passageway lead?"

I looked along the street. "To the left, it ends at a blank gable-end."

"No, no," said Holmes. "The wool from his stockinged feet lay in the other direction."

We made our way to the far end of the terrace. "Now what do you see, Watson?"

"By George! It's a tobacconist's shop, adjoined to the end of the terrace – a place that might well remain unoccupied during the night. But how would our intruder make his way in there at will?"

We made our way round to the back of the shop. "There you are, Watson," cried Holmes triumphantly. "A side-entrance, leading directly from the access lane and into the back yard."

"Harry Greep?" said Inspector Lestrade, when we informed him of our progress in the case. "Now there's a name that rings a bell, as loud and clear as Big Ben himself."

"I remember the name from our initial investigation into the bank robbery." said Holmes.

"Indeed, you would, Mr. Holmes," said the detective. "He was one of our strongest suspects at first. But when we made our investigations, he came out cleaner than a shirt fresh back from the laundry. He even demanded that we search his house from top to bottom."

"Always a suspicious thing for a criminal to do," I replied.

"Naturally, you found nothing," said Holmes.

"Not only did he have none of those missing banknotes on the premises, but he appeared to be more in debt than in credit with the local commercial traders."

"I seem to remember he had been in trouble before."

"He has quite a record, has our Harry," said Lestrade, "but he told me he was now a reformed character. Said he had turned over a new leaf and was learning a new trade."

"That is certainly true," said Holmes. "He seems to have become an expert in wallpaper-hanging."

"That doesn't sound like Harry Greep. The fellow's as bent as a hairpin – one of a network of villains who make a habit of targeting the vulnerable across London."

Holmes nodded. "And since then, you have made no progress at all with the case."

"And neither have you, Mr. Holmes."

"But now we have a connection between an employee of the London and South Coast Bank, and a member of the criminal fraternity – a connection through the Chief Cashier."

"And not a scrap of evidence to be used against him."

"But enough to cast doubt on your accusation that Mr. Edlingholm was responsible for the theft."

"That remains to be seen."

Holmes returned a knowing smile. "I'm certain the Chief Cashier is not our man. But if we can catch this fellow, Greep, in the act of retrieving some of his stolen banknotes, would that be sufficient to allow you to release the Bank Manager?"

"It would unquestionably cast the case in an entirely new and very different light, Mr. Holmes."

"Capital! Then allow me to place an article in the local evening papers, warning people of the dangers of arsenic poisoning in wallpaper, and suggesting they redecorate their houses immediately. I shall make no mention of the Edlingholm's home, but the thief, whoever it turns out to be, will want to remove the evidence before the walls can be stripped and the money uncovered."

"Very well. When do you anticipate he might come to collect those notes?"

"As soon as ever possible, I should imagine. Perhaps as early as tonight "

"Then we must be ready for him."

We gathered at the Edlingholm home late that evening. The shorter nights of summer meant that our time would be limited, but we still had to be prepared to remain there all night if necessary. Holmes asked to borrow my service revolver, a request to which I readily acceded.

Lestrade had come with five of his most reliable constables. "I'll take my place in the green bedroom," he announced.

"In that case," said Holmes, "I elect to remain at the rear of the tobacconist's shop, ready to apprehend our man if he manages to escape your clutches. However, I would value the use of two of your constables, Lestrade. Perhaps Rand and Murcher, by choice."

"You may have them, although I doubt that you will need them."

"And I shall leave Watson with you."

As the darkness deepened and, as a local church clock chimed off the early hours, I stood with Inspector Lestrade in the darkest corner of the bedroom. The door stood open so we could see the landing. The three remaining constables waited in a room on the other side of the landing, ready to emerge when summoned. Lestrade had a lantern on the floor beside him, closed on all sides, and turned down low.

At what must have been the darkest hour of the night, we were disturbed by a scuffling sound coming from the roof-space above us. The trapdoor, which I had seen opened from below by Sherlock Holmes, now hinged upward, and the knotted rope dropped abruptly but noiselessly down into the landing.

In the light of the moon shining through the window, I observed a dark figure climb down the rope as nimbly as a monkey and step silently into the green bedroom, only feet away from where we stood. The man seemed to know his way around in the darkness, and I half-expected him to see us and make his immediate escape. Instead, he turned his attention to the wallpaper directly opposite the window and ran his hand along the paper. The steel of a cutthroat razor flashed as the man proceeded to make a slit down the paper.

I would have pounced upon the man at once, but Lestrade held me back, and shook his head.

Even with the man's back against the outside light, I could see him extract something from behind the wallpaper. Now we had the man in possession of the stolen money, Lestrade opened the lantern, and held it high. "Hello, Harry."

The intruder turned abruptly to face the policeman, and the constables as they entered from the landing. His face showed both surprise and terror.

In the ensuing confusion, Greep threw himself toward the rope and climbed up it at a remarkable speed.

When two of the constables set off in pursuit, I realized they had little chance of catching up with the man. Our only hope now lay with Holmes at the tobacconist's shop. Lestrade had come to the same conclusion, and followed me as I hurried down the stairs, and ran out through the front door and down the street.

We arrived at the rear of the shop, to find Sherlock Holmes holding my revolver and facing the intruder, now securely in the hands of the two constables assigned to accompany him.

"Harris Greep," said Lestrade, "I am arresting you on suspicion of theft and murder."

Greep glared back. "I went to great lengths to keep my business secret. How did you manage to find out what I was doing?"

"We had a little help from Mr. Sherlock Holmes here."

Greep glared at Holmes. "Life for us criminals is bad enough without amateurs like you getting involved in crime detection. Why couldn't you keep your nose out of my business?"

"Your business has gone on long enough, Greep," returned Holmes. "This has been the result of long-term planning on your part. You decided to concentrate upon the inhabitants of wealthier streets, such as Morpeth Square, and the sort of people who could afford to pay for the professional decoration of their homes. You inveigled your way into working for a decorating firm, and became proficient at wallpaper-hanging. You waited for the right chance to come along, which it surely would.

"When you heard that the Chief Cashier at the London and South Coast Bank wanted his house redecorating, you went along to act as another hand, and you took the opportunity to make wax impressions of his bank keys. Then you waited. But your waiting proved short-term, because you heard that Mr. Edlingholm wanted his house decorating in view of his imminent removal there."

"This is all speculation," cried Greep.

"Not at all," replied Holmes. "It is merely deduction based upon the facts. I might even be able to place you at the scene of the death of the firm's previous wallpaper-hanger. You pushed him to his death beneath the wheels of an underground train, so you could step in and take his place with the decorating firm."

"You have no proof of any of this."

"Perhaps, but then you undertook the robbery and immediately set about hiding the stolen banknotes behind the paper on upper floor bedroom in several of the houses you were working on, both in Morpeth Square and other streets in that part of London."

"Which streets?" Greep challenged him.

"We'll find them easily enough," replied Lestrade bluntly.

"Now," continued Holmes, "with the stolen banknotes hidden, and with no way of linking them to yourself, you were able to enter the rooms from above whenever you needed to draw upon your stolen plunder. However, your luck ran out when you targeted the room of Mr. Edlingholm's daughter and the poisonous nature of the wallpaper was discovered. The Edlingholms will have to arrange for their child's bedroom to be redecorated. But I suspect they might select a different firm to undertake the work next time."

A few days later, as we traveled by cab along the side of Hyde Park on our way to Baker Street, we happened to notice the Edlingholm family standing together in the late summer sunshine, listening to a brass band concert.

"They look intensely happy together, do you not think?" I asked.

"Indeed, considering all they have gone through together in the last few months."

"And yet, about the case, I realize I am not yet in possession of all the facts."

"Are you not? What do you still wish to know?"

"I find it difficult to imagine that this fellow Greep has been working alone."

Holmes nodded sagely.

"Lestrade described him as part of a network of criminals working in the city. Who else was involved with him in this particular project? Was the decorating firm involved? Was Goodwell involved? And what about Ardley? Was he working with Greep in his nefarious scheme?"

"I think none of those," replied Holmes, as he sighed and stretched out his legs as far as they would go in the confined space of the cab. "Consider the tobacconist's shop."

"The tobacconist's? Do you mean the one at the corner of Morpeth Square?"

"Of course. If you wish to find a den of thieves, then I would suggest that shop, Watson. The time I spent watching the square was not confined to simply observing the Edlingholm household. I also paid close attention to those who frequented the tobacconist's shop, and I recognized among them several of the most notorious criminals in the city."

"I can hardly believe such a thing of a small shop in a prosperous and upmarket area of London. The place looks so innocent."

"And yet, it is true. I happened, on one occasion, to enter the shop, purporting to be in search of a particular brand of pipe tobacco. I recognized the man behind the counter as one who is high up on the wanted list of Scotland Yard."

"Did he recognize you?"

"Hardly. You yourself failed to see through my disguise as a common workman."

"Lestrade will want to make a number of arrests now," I ventured.

"When we sprung the trap and caught our thief, I fear the rest of the birds flew to other bushes."

"To be taken another day."

"Let us hope so, Watson."

"This completes another case for my journal," I cried. "The public shall learn the true story of the Green Room."

"And yet, just for the moment, we must allow Scotland Yard to enjoy the limelight of publicity."

"Even though the solving of this entire investigation was down to you, Holmes."

"It was a mere matter of observation and deduction," he said smiling genially. "The entire process was quite elementary, Watson."

# The Turk's Head
by Robert V. Stapleton

The investigative powers of my friend Sherlock Holmes were matched only by his skill with the violin. Both these areas of his life were the subject of constant and focused development during the many years of our acquaintance.

My notes from those days remind me that it was on a sunny September morning in 1899, as I returned to our rooms in Baker Street bearing the morning mail, that I discovered Holmes, standing at the open window, striving to master a particular stanza from a Bach concerto.

"No! No! No!" he yelled as he turned from the window, with frustration evident in his voice. "This will not do, Watson. I fear old Johann has the better of me today."

I sorted through the correspondence, placing a handful unopened upon the table, but retaining another letter for closer inspection.

"Is that for me?" asked Holmes, returning his instrument to its case.

"That is indeed how it is addressed," said I, turning the sealed envelope over in my hands. "But what attracted my specific attention was the postmark: Penzance, Cornwall."

"An area of the world we visited on a previous occasion," he observed.

"I recall it well," I replied coldly. The incident known as the Cornish Horror was still too recent in my memory to allow me much ease at the prospect of revisiting that area of the country.

"Then kindly read the letter for me, my dear fellow."

I took hold of my letter-opener, a souvenir I had purchased a few years previously on a visit to the Crystal Palace, and slit open the envelope. I began to read.

*Dear Mr. Holmes,*

*We are in a desperate plight down here. One innocent man is dead, and another is due to stand trial for his murder. We urgently need your assistance, and hope you will be willing to visit this corner of the realm before it is too late.*

"Succinct," observed Holmes.

"The letter is from a Miss Merryn Penrose, who gives her address as the village of Port Caer."

I handed the letter to Holmes and took down from our book shelving an atlas of Great Britain. This I placed upon the table, and found it readily fell open at the section dealing with the Cornish Peninsula. "Here it is. With a name like that, it had to be on the coast."

Holmes proceeded to examine the letter.

"An educated lady, I see," he said, "judging by the fastidious copperplate handwriting. Also, a lady with passion in her heart. See how strongly she forms her letters. Especially that last line. All in thick black ink, which had hardly dried before she sealed it."

I could see from his expression that Holmes was already intrigued.

He looked up at me. "What think you, Watson?"

"Although I have no wish to visit that area again in a hurry, I feel we must definitely respond to the lady's *Cri de Coeur*, even though she tells us absolutely nothing about the matter."

"On the contrary," said he. "This letter tells us a great deal. We know a murder has been committed there, and we know that the local police are involved, having possibly made one of their customary errors of judgment. We also know that the accused is a man for whom the lady holds strong feelings."

Having made further study of our atlas, Holmes turned his attention to our dog-eared Bradshaw.

"Watson," he cried, "would you be kind enough to arrange for two berths on the overnight train from Paddington Station to Penzance? From there, a carriage should bring us Port Caer soon after midday tomorrow."

For the final few miles of our rail journey, I looked out at the rugged coastal scenery passing by our carriage window. The sight of the ocean, which likely thrills the heart of every Englishman, had a sinister look about it that day.

Holmes stepped down onto the platform at Penzance, rested by his night in the sleeper carriage. He drew a deep breath. "Is that sea air not refreshing, Watson?"

"It certainly blows away the cobwebs," I replied, not having enjoyed the same soundness of slumber.

We found a horse and trap which took us along a dusty coastal road towards our destination. We rolled through open moorland, strewn with russet bracken and decaying foliage lying beneath a cold and oppressive sky.

"Port Caer," announced the driver as we swayed into the main street at the top of the village. "The very last place on Earth the Good Lord made. And that's a fact."

"Why do you say that?" I enquired.

"Begging your pardons, gentlemen, but not many people come to this place. And them as do will just as soon make a speedy return to civilization."

After we had paid him off, the driver left with greater alacrity than that with which he had arrived.

Holmes and I stood at the top of the main street, with our luggage on the ground around us. The smell of the sea wafted towards us on the breeze, with the mewing and squawking of gulls filling the air around us.

"What now?" I asked.

Holmes brightened. "I see the village inn, beneath the sign of the Seven Stars. Come, Watson, we must make our reservations for the night."

The landlord, who introduced himself as Henry Rowe, appeared not the least bit surprised to see us. "Good afternoon, gentlemen," said he. "How may I help you?"

"We need two rooms for the night," I told him.

"With views overlooking the sea," added Holmes.

We signed the visitors book beneath the landlord's careful scrutiny. "You gentlemen up from London?"

"Indeed we are," I told him.

"Then Mr. Holmes here must be the detective Miss Penrose wrote to."

"You know about that business?"

The landlord chuckled. "There are very few secrets in a place as small as this, Dr. Watson. But I would counsel you both to conclude your business here quickly, and then leave as soon as you can."

"That sounds like a threat."

"Oh, my goodness me, no. Merely a word of friendly advice."

"Then we must begin at once by visiting Miss Penrose," announced Holmes. "She gives her address as 20 High Street."

I glanced at Rowe. "Where is that?"

"You go out of the door here," said Rowe, "turn right, and follow the road downhill. You'll find her house along the terrace towards the bottom of the hill."

We thanked him, deposited our bags up to our rooms, and immediately set off in search of the lady who had summoned us to Cornwall.

The village looked to be a typical workaday Cornish fishing community. A small harbor lay between protective stone jetties, with precipitous cliffs rising on both sides. Behind the village, two roads led across wild moorland – one leading back the way we had come, and the other trailing away towards the north.

The sight made me shiver. "This is a bleak place, Holmes."

"Bleak in many ways, Watson," he replied. "These small communities can often hold great darkness. The hearts of the men and women in such places are liable to harbor as much evil as you will find in the darkest backstreets of London."

Miss Penrose answered our knock and we found ourselves facing a proud lady in her thirties, with sharp facial features and dark hair tied back in a severe bun.

"Mr. Holmes?"

"Indeed," he replied. "And this is my colleague, Dr. Watson."

"Please step inside, gentlemen," said Miss Penrose. "I am glad you felt able to come all this way at such short notice. And thank you for your telegram, Mr. Holmes. It made me quite a celebrity in the village. Not many people receive such things around here."

She led us into the parlor and invited us to sit on either side of the fireplace.

"I imagine you will be tired after your long journey," said Miss Penrose. "May I offer you a cup of tea?"

I readily accepted the offer. Holmes declined, and sat with his attention riveted upon our hostess who, a few minutes later, took an upright chair facing Holmes.

"Let me begin by repeating what I told you in my letter. One man is dead, and the other is to stand trial for his murder."

"Dear me! And both innocent men, you say."

"That is the tragedy of the matter."

"And what exactly do you wish me to do?"

Miss Penrose looked down at her hands, now folded in her lap. "I had been entertaining hopes that you might rescue the one accused of murder."

"Who exactly is he?"

"A local man, by the name of Jowan Marrack. The accusation is that he pushed the victim from the top of the high cliff just to the east of here. A place called the Turk's Head."

"Marrack is a man for whom you hold some affection."

She blushed. "Is it so obvious?"

"He certainly has a place in your heart."

"He is a married man, Mr. Holmes."

"Nevertheless, you have feelings for him."

"I have known Jowan ever since I came to this village, some ten years ago, and I am certain he would never kill anybody. I came to work as a teacher at the school here in Port Caer. I still teach the little ones – the infants. Jowan was the first person to show me any kindness when I came here as a stranger – which is more than can be said for his wife. A nasty piece of work she is. Why Jowan married her, I really cannot imagine. And I don't think he could tell you either. Their relationship has been difficult for many years now, but divorce, even if they could afford it, would cause a scandal in the village. So they stay together out of convenience. They have no children, which is perhaps the greatest blessing."

"And the man who was killed?"

"His name was Michael Warrington. It seems he was a police detective, on assignment from Truro. Although nothing official was told us, everyone in the village imagined he was here to investigate allegations of smuggling."

"Are there grounds for such an investigation?"

“Smuggling is nowhere near as bad as it was a century ago.”

“But smuggling does go on here.”

“That is beside the point, Mr. Holmes.” She looked up at us, glancing from one to the other. “Whatever my personal feelings, the point is that an injustice is being perpetrated here, and somebody needs to put an end to such a terrible state of affairs.”

Holmes leaned forward. “Miss Penrose, I need to know all the facts if I am to make any progress with this matter.”

“I have told you everything that I know.”

“Perhaps.”

“Then I suggest you pay a visit to our local policeman, Constable Evans. He understands the situation better than I. The Police House is on the waterfront down beside the harbor. Between the chapel and the village Post Office. You will recognize it by the public notices exhibited in the window.”

“Then let us waste no time in calling upon the man.” Holmes stood up, turned, and strode from the house.

I thanked Miss Penrose for her hospitality and followed in his wake.

We found Police Constable Evans at home when we knocked upon his front door and introduced ourselves.

“Do please come inside, gentlemen,” said the upholder of the law. “I’ve been expecting you.”

As Evans led us into the front room, his attitude felt cold and formal. He glared towards Holmes. “I imagine you are here to investigate the murder of Michael Warrington.”

“Merely at the request of one of the locals,” replied Holmes.

“Miss Penrose, no doubt.”

“We have just this minute come away from visiting the lady.”

"This is all highly irregular," said Evans, "but how may I help you?"

"I should like to examine the scene of the crime," said Holmes. "Miss Penrose tells us the victim fell from a place known locally as the Turk's Head."

"He was pushed, Mr. Holmes. The Turk's Head lies on the highest point of the east cliff. The locals keep it whitewashed, resembling an Arab turban, to act as a landmark warning shipping of the dangerous rocks along that stretch of the coastline."

"Then please lead on."

The policeman pulled on his coat and led us along a footpath which took up to where stood the great white rock, a position which commanded a wide view of the ocean and the jagged rocks which projected from its surface.

Holmes stood looking out at the scene, his cloak billowing in the breeze. "Is this the place?"

"The exact spot, Mr. Holmes. Warrington died from injuries sustained by falling from this cliff onto the small beach more than a hundred feet below."

Holmes knelt down to examine the earth closest to the clifftop edge. "Too many people have visited this spot to leave much in the way of evidence," said he. "Hello, what's this?"

"What is it, Holmes?"

"The prints of a man's boots, scraping the turf on the very edge of the cliff. Perhaps the last trace of a man losing his footing. And the footprints are facing out to sea. I commend that to you for further consideration."

Evans shook his head. "Purely incidental. We know he fell from here."

Holmes stood up again. "And what motive might there have been for the murder?"

"The motive is clear as day," said Evans. "Michael Warrington came here from our Police Headquarters in Truro to investigate rumors of smuggling."

"Accusations which focused on the accused?"

"Jowan Marrack. Indeed."

"And were the rumors well founded?"

"The issue of smuggling became a secondary matter when Warrington was killed."

"And suspicion of both fell upon Marrack."

"It seems he had been involved in some recent smuggling. So he had a motive."

"Really?"

"I am sure Miss Penrose would have you believe the man to be innocent. But Jowan Marrack is a fisherman, Mr. Holmes – a member of the crew of a local fishing boat. The skipper, a man called Jago Stark, has given evidence in the Magistrates' Court that he heard Marrack whisper dark threats against Warrington. He even threatened to kill him if he began to make trouble."

"The suggestion being that he then carried out those threats."

"More than a suggestion, Mr. Holmes. Considering the circumstances, I can see no other reasonable explanation."

"And can you place Marrack at the scene?"

"A button, identified by his wife as belonging to her husband's jacket, was found here, beside the Turk's Head rock. Marrack must have invited Warrington up here to discuss the problem of smuggling. They had an altercation, during which Warrington ripped the button from his killer's jacket before plunging to his death."

"A neat story," said Holmes doubtfully. "But you cannot prove the matter beyond all shadow of doubt, can you?"

"I placed the facts before the local Magistrate, who decided there was sufficient evidence to send the accused for trial at the Assizes in Truro."

"Who is the local Magistrate?"

"Major Ebenezer Rosdew. He has a large house along the road to Truro, with magnificent views of the harbor and the village."

"Does he live alone?"

"He has never married, but he does have a faithful housekeeper."

"Then it seems we must call upon the major."

"You are welcome to try, Mr. Holmes, but he is unshakable in his judgment."

"I am sure of it," said Holmes. "So, the death of Warrington benefited Marrack. Hence the accusation."

"Correct."

"But who stands to benefit from the execution of Marrack?"

Constable Evans rubbed his chin thoughtfully. "Justice will benefit, Mr. Holmes."

"No other person?"

"There is, of course, his wife."

"Indeed?"

"Talwyn."

"I have heard that their marriage is not a happy one, but how might she benefit by the death of her husband?"

Evans took a deep breath. "I suppose you are bound to find out sooner or later, Mr. Holmes. It's an open secret here in the village that Talwyn Marrack and Major Rosdew are friends, and frequently enjoy each other's company."

"And if Marrack is hanged for the murder of Warrington, she would be free to marry the major."

"I suppose that is true."

"Do you not think that suspicious?"

"If you are suggesting that Major Rosdew is unjustly accusing Marrack of Warrington's murder simply so he can marry the man's widow, then you are venturing onto dangerous territory, Mr. Holmes."

"It is too early to make such an accusation," said Holmes. "I merely commend the idea to you for consideration."

On our return to the Police House, Sherlock Holmes asked to see a sample of the major's handwriting. Puzzled, Evans handed him a sheet of paper. "Here is a letter, in the major's own hand, informing me of the date set for Marrack's trial at the next Assizes."

Holmes took the letter. "May I retain this document for the moment?"

"You will have to sign for it," said Evans.

Holmes and I repaired to the bar of the Seven Stars and ordered food and drinks. "I see you are a musical man," Holmes told the landlord.

Rowe looked surprised.

"The way you draw the ale suggests you play the violin."

"In a very amateurish way, Mr. Holmes," said Rowe. "The instrument has remained untouched in my living room for several months now."

We took our seats in the inglenook and looked around. A group of men stood at the far end of the room, casting furtive glances in our direction.

"I see we have attracted the attention of the locals," observed Holmes.

One of the men detached himself from the gathering and sauntered across the room to stand directly in front of us. His face displayed defiance.

"You must be Jago Stark," said Holmes.

"And you must be Sherlock Holmes," replied the man, with a sneer. "As unwelcome in this village as the plague."

"And you are the skipper of the fishing boat, *The Merry Maid*."

Stark raised his eyebrows in surprise. "How do you know so much about me?"

"I observe, and I listen," replied Holmes. "Tell me, Mr. Stark, is it true that your crewman, Jowan Marrack, stands accused of murder almost entirely upon your own evidence?"

The man leaned his knuckles upon the table, and brought his face to within a few inches of my colleague's withering gaze. "What are you saying, Mr. Holmes?"

"Merely that any man in the village might be guilty of killing that policeman."

Stark stood upright. "Are you accusing me of lying?"

"I am accusing nobody of anything. But, remember this: If it is discovered that you gave false evidence in a court of law, then you will find yourself in serious trouble."

"I don't like what you're saying," growled Stark. "And I don't like you being here in this village. Asking questions. Go back to where you came from, or you might find yourself in deep trouble."

Holmes stood up, removed his hat and cloak, and stepped forward to confront Stark.

In his turn, Stark stood back, the more carefully to survey his opponent.

"I need your cooperation, Stark," said Holmes.

"Well, I'm not going to help the likes of you."

Stark threw a punch towards Sherlock Holmes, who dodged to one side and easily avoided contact with the fisherman's fist.

After being caught momentarily off balance, Stark recovered himself and threw another punch. Again, it missed the mark.

Holmes stepped forward and landed a solid blow in the center of the other man's face.

Stark staggered backward, creating chaos among his friends, and collapsed onto the floor. The man's fellow drinkers picked him up, dusted him down, and led him out of the public bar.

Holmes collected his garments, and returned to his seat.

From somewhere in the shadows, I heard somebody chuckling. I looked around, and found an elderly man sitting a few feet away. So well was he hidden in the shadows that I had failed to notice him at first. His gnarled hands and weather-beaten face gave every impression that he had worked for most of his life as a fisherman.

"He's always ready from a scrap, is that one," the septuagenarian told us.

"Then he needs to learn to take less drink before he picks a fight," said Holmes.

The old man beckoned us into conspiratorial closeness. "My name is Enoch," he told us. "I spend so much time in this place that most people forget I'm here at all. Believe me, I know what's going on, both in this inn, and in the community as a whole. Like you, I keep my ears alert and my eyes open."

"And what do you have to tell us?" Holmes asked him.

"You need to be careful of Stark," said Enoch. He took another deep gulp of his ale. "He is Major Rosdew's man."

"How do you mean?"

"With the major being the principal person in authority, both in this village and for several miles around, and with him living outside the village, he needs somebody to represent him within the local community. Stark is the man who provides him with that information. There's nobody who knows the community better than Stark – except, through his communication, the major himself."

Holmes called for another drink for the old man. "Then the major will be aware that we are in the village."

"Undoubtedly. Especially after what just happened here in the bar."

"In what else is Stark involved?"

"Anything that's doubtful. He organizes some small-scale smuggling. And, with his influence over the major, he can make life very difficult for anyone in the village and surrounding area whom Stark imagines threatens his interests."

"And the accused man's wife?"

Enoch lit up his pipe and began to blow clouds of tobacco smoke across the table. "Talwyn Marrack. Yes, she knows what's going on here as well. She's a good friend of the major. Has been for several years now. She'll be glad when they put her husband's neck in that noose. Can't come soon enough for her. And the major."

Holmes took out his own pipe, lit a bowl of shag tobacco, and sat deep in thought. For several minutes, the two men sat side by side, enveloped in a cloud of smoke. They reminded me of a pair of Toby jugs, steaming with hot punch.

Eventually, Holmes broke the silence. "I cannot understand why a detective from the county force should come here merely to investigate a minor case of smuggling."

Enoch nodded. "Curious."

"Something else is going on here," continued Holmes. "Some matter dark enough to justify the killing of a policeman, and the execution of an innocent man."

Enoch removed his pipe. "You will find this a law-abiding community, Mr. Holmes. Anyone who causes trouble here is removed from the village. And they never return."

"Removed? By whom?"

"By the magistrate, of course."

“A good friend of Talwyn Marrack.”

The old man nodded.

Holmes stood up. “In that case, we need to call upon the lady. Come along, Watson.”

I followed my companion outside, conscious that all eyes were trained upon us, not least those of our new friend, Enoch.

Mrs. Marrack lived at a fisherman’s cottage down beside the harbor, at the very heart of village life. To Holmes’s knock, Mrs. Marrack answered by opening the door and glaring out at us.

“Mrs. Marrack?” said Holmes pleasantly. “My name is Sherlock Holmes, and this is my associate, Dr. John Watson.”

“You’ll be the man who attacked poor Mr. Stark.” It was a statement of fact. “I do not approve of men brawling in public, Mr. Holmes.”

Holmes bristled. “We have plenty of witnesses who will testify that he threw the first punch. And the second. Striking him was the only way I could bring him to his senses.”

“I’ll admit he can be a hot-head at times.”

“May we come inside?”

Mrs. Marrack stood aside, and allowed us to enter the parlor. I detected the scent of lavender in the air.

Seated in a chair in the middle of the room, we found Jago Stark.

“Come to gloat, have you?” he asked.

“Not at all,” returned Holmes. “I am merely in search of a few honest answers.”

Stark and the lady of the house looked at each other, seemingly uncertain as to how to respond.

Holmes turned his attention to the whitewashed wall on the far side of the parlor. His eyes fixed upon a pair of black wooden objects resting on a series of metal brackets fastened to the wall.

"Those look like Polynesian war-clubs," said Holmes.

"That's right," said Mrs. Marrack. "My father was a sea captain for many years. He sailed the world, saw plenty of places, and met a great many people. He brought those back to this country maybe fifty years ago. They have remained in the family ever since, and have been in this house since my husband and I moved in here."

"Very interesting."

"May I get you gentlemen a cup of tea?" asked Mrs. Marrack, evidently trying to distract our attention from the war-clubs.

"That would be a good idea," replied Holmes. "Meanwhile, my companion here will give Mr. Stark a thorough medical examination."

So, as Mrs. Marrack left the room, while casting a suspicious glance towards Holmes, I bent to my task of examining my patient. "The swelling around the eyes appears to be coming out already." I announced. "You'll have a real shiner by the morning."

Stark chuckled. "It won't be the first time."

"Your nose has been bleeding, but I'm fairly sure it hasn't been broken."

"Nor should it be," replied Holmes. "When I strike a man, it is with the precision of a surgeon."

With Stark facing me, and with Mrs. Marrack busy in the kitchen, I watched Holmes take out his magnifying glass and study the two war clubs. By the time I had reassured my patient that he would survive to see another day, Holmes appeared satisfied and sat down beside us.

Mrs. Marrack returned to the parlor and handed us each a cup of tea. "Now, how may I help you, Mr. Holmes?" she asked as she sat down beside Stark.

"I am interested in Major Rosdew," said Holmes. "Can you tell me anything about him, Mrs. Marrack?"

"You have no doubt heard that he and I are friends."

"That in itself is no crime."

"Then allow me to tell you, Mr. Holmes, that the major is a wonderful man. He is kind-hearted and generous."

"He is also the local magistrate."

"Indeed he is. Many in this village, and for miles around, will tell you that he is a good and thoughtful man. Young men have a tendency to get themselves into trouble. Often they are either misguided, or struggling to find their feet in the world. Most are not bad people, Mr. Holmes, and the major recognizes the fact. But he has to be hard on anyone who commits a crime. So whenever one of these young men appears before him to answer for his misdemeanor, rather than sending him for trial and possible imprisonment, the major will impose a fine. The amount will be high enough to deter any other would-be criminals, but far too high for any of the young men to pay. The major gives them an alternative: To pay off their fines by installments, by leaving the village and taking on various laboring jobs."

Holmes turned to the man sitting beside Mrs. Marrack. "Do you know about this, Stark?"

He shrugged. "I know it happens."

"You know more than that. Now tell me."

"I see no reason why I should wash somebody else's laundry in your presence, Mr. Holmes."

"Are you afraid of what the major might do to you?"

"He is a powerful and influential man, Mr. Holmes."

"I also have influence," said Holmes. "And let me tell you, Stark, that unless you give me every assistance in this matter, I shall make sure you face the full weight of legal wrath."

Stark returned a dark look. "What do you want to know?"

"Those young men – the ones the major sends away from the village. Where do they go?"

Stark took a deep breath and looked down at his hands, as though embarrassed by what he was about to tell us. "Major Rosdew has a number of places across the county that house these men. They stay overnight at some farm or outbuilding far from civilization, and travel each day to undertake laboring work."

"Such as?"

"Some work on the land, or care for animals. Others are set to work in factories."

"And the money they earn?"

"It pays for their accommodation, and the employment of those who organize this work."

"And the rest of the money?"

"Any remaining is returned to the major."

"To pay off their fines?"

"I'm not privy to the details, Mr. Holmes."

I could see Holmes's expression growing ever darker. "May we conjecture then that, however hard and long these young men work, they will never pay off the entire fine they owe?"

Stark remained silent. He obviously felt he had spoken too hastily.

"Let us call this business exactly as it appears," said Holmes. "Men working for the enrichment of others. We are talking about slavery."

"That's not how it is." Mrs. Marrack's voice rose to a crescendo. "You cannot say that about such a good man. This is not slavery, Mr. Holmes. How dare you even suggest it!"

She turned to Stark. "Tell him, Jago. Tell him he's got it all wrong."

Stark shrugged. "It depends how you look at the matter."

Holmes leaned closer. "Take me to see one of these farms, Stark. Show me. And allow me to judge for myself."

"When?"

"Now."

"But the hour is late, Mr. Holmes. It will be midnight before we can reach even the nearest one."

"Then let us delay no further." Holmes stood up. "Arrange a carriage to collect us outside the Seven Stars, and take us to this farmstead. As soon as possible."

The carriage driver, a local man, let us know by a torrent of colloquial invective that he objected to being called out so late in the evening. Holmes placated the man by promising him a handsome fee when he brought us safely back again at whatever hour our business was concluded.

Holmes and I sat opposite Stark in the enclosed carriage as the driver whipped up the horses and we drove briskly away.

With night already creeping across the Cornish countryside, I looked out at the shadowy fields as they moved by our window at a steady pace. We passed the occasional windswept tree, and lights shining from the windows of dwellings out across the moor. I had no idea where we were heading, but Holmes looked to be taking the entire business in his stride. He plied Stark with questions about village life and the Cornish language.

Almost an hour after leaving Port Caer, I saw the cold light of the moon casting its rays across the buildings of a lonely farmstead, set in a landscape devoid of interesting features.

A low, barn-like structure lay to one side of the farmyard.

Somewhere, a dog was barking.

"Did you bring your revolver with you, Watson?" asked Holmes.

"I have it here," I replied, checking that the weapon was loaded and ready in the pocket of my coat.

Holmes looked around. "There's no knowing what dangers might lie out there in the night."

Immediately the carriage drew to a halt, Holmes opened the door and jumped down onto the ground. "Keep them talking for as long as you can, Watson," he told me, as he disappeared into the darkness.

I followed Jago Stark out into the cool night air. A door in the farmhouse opened and a man appeared. In one hand he carried a lantern, and in the other he held a leash attached to a ferocious looking dog which appeared determined to sink its teeth into us given the chance.

We stepped closer.

The farmer, a thickset, squat fellow, demanded to know who we were. He looked at Stark. "I recognize you, but I don't know the other man."

"My name is Dr. John Watson," I explained.

"And your business here, Dr. Watson?"

"I have come from Port Caer to check on the physical health of the young men laborers you have living here."

"Have you, indeed?" he replied, doubtfully.

"The major is concerned about their welfare."

"Then this is the first time he's ever shown it."

"May I have your permission to examine them?"

"Certainly not," he thundered. "If any of them need medical care, then it's my job to provide it. I send a fair slice of their wages back to Major Rosdew every month, so he ought to be satisfied with that."

"He merely wanted me to check on their condition."

"If you failed to understand my meaning the first time," said the farmer, "then allow me to repeat myself. You are not going to see those men. They need their sleep if they're to put in a proper day's work tomorrow. You should leave now."

When we hesitated, four more men emerged from the house. All large and bulky, with a couple of them carrying pick-ax handles.

"It really is time for us to leave, Dr. Watson," came Stark's voice from close beside me.

The moment we climbed back into the carriage, I found myself sitting opposite a dark figure.

"Ah, there you are, Holmes," said I. "I kept them talking for as long as I felt it safe."

"You did an admirable job, my dear fellow," said Holmes. "It allowed me time to interview a couple of the men inside that building." He nodded toward the barn.

"How did you gain entrance?"

"That will remain my secret," he replied.

"And what did you discover?"

"It merely confirms what we already knew. Those men are sent to provide casual labor wherever they are needed. Some in fields, others in factories or warehouses. They believe they are here to pay off their fines, but they are being held under threat of harsh treatment if they step out of line."

On our return to the Seven Stars, Holmes paid off the driver, asking him to collect us again first thing the following morning.

"Where to now?" I asked Holmes, as we sat together at breakfast.

"This matter is rapidly coming to a head," replied Holmes.

"Well, I'm dashed if I can see it," I admitted.

"I have sent a note to Constable Evans, asking him to accompany us this morning. I think it is time to involve the County Constabulary."

At the sound of horses' hooves and carriage wheels outside, we emerged into the open air to find our transport awaiting us – and Constable Evans standing beside the same carriage we had employed on the previous evening. We all climbed on board.

"I hope this will be worth the loss of an entire morning," said Constable Evans. "I have work to do here."

"As do I," said Holmes. "First, it is time for us to interview the magistrate, Major Rosdew. I think it would be wise to have you with us."

"In your note, you mentioned visiting Truro."

"Indeed," said Holmes. "Once we reach Truro, I hope you will arrange matters so that I can view both the body and the accused."

Evans drew a deep breath. "Very well, Mr. Holmes."

"But let us deal with one matter at a time, shall we?"

The house occupied by Major Rosdew stood at the end of a long drive, leading up from the main road to Truro.

The housekeeper opened the door and invited us to step inside. Our reception was made easier by the presence of the policeman, and we were asked to wait in the library for the major to complete his morning ablutions.

The moment the major entered the room, I could see why people held him in such high respect. He stood over six feet in height, with a mop of black hair topping a face with a firm nose and thick lips.

"We are sorry to arrive so early," said the policeman effusively. "Mr. Sherlock Holmes here is trying to tie up a few loose ends regarding the recent murder."

Major Rosdew smiled and held out his hand to each of us in turn.

"Please tell me, Major," Holmes began. "Why do you consider the evidence against Jowan Marrack sufficient to send him to stand trial for murder?"

Rosdew's face broke into the sort of smile normally reserved for small children or recalcitrant domestic animals.

"You are a stranger here, Mr. Holmes," said he. "You need to have lived in this community a long time to understand both domestic and community life here. I consider the evidence against Marrack to be complete."

"Even though circumstantial."

"His button was discovered at the scene of the crime."

"Perhaps planted."

"There is also his expressed antipathy towards the detective who was killed."

"In haste, we all say things that might incriminate us in the eyes of others."

"And then there is his personal confession."

"His confession?"

"You didn't know about that, did you? Yes, his freely made a written and signed admission of guilt. You see, Mr. Holmes, I am not the unjust and uncaring man that some in the village would have you believe."

"Like the families of the young men you send to pay off their fines by the sweat of their brows?"

"They would find life in the army or navy a great deal more brutal, Mr. Holmes. They are well-fed, and comfortably provided for. So, as you can see, there is no reason for you to remain here any longer."

"Are you trying to be rid of me, Major?"

"Merely preventing you from wasting any more of your valuable time, Mr. Holmes."

Once more in our carriage, and on our way down the long driveway, Constable Evans glared at Holmes. "Does that satisfy your curiosity, Mr. Holmes?"

"Not in the least," replied my companion. "And that man knows it."

"Do you still wish to visit Truro?"

"Oh, most certainly."

We arrived at the cathedral city of Truro within a couple of hours. All that time, Holmes had remained quiet, lost in gloomy speculation.

As we drew to a halt outside the Police Headquarters, Holmes announced, "First, I wish to see the body. Then, I should like to interview Jowan Marrack. I think, given the developing intelligence surrounding this case, that would be the most important business of the morning."

"Very well," said Evans, as he climbed out of the vehicle. "I shall make the necessary arrangements."

Detective Chief Inspector Branwell emerged to greet us at the door. "Good morning, gentlemen," said he. "I understand you are investigating the murder of Sergeant Warrington."

"That is correct," replied Holmes.

"Frankly, I don't see any reason for your being here, Mr. Holmes. We have a man due to stand trial for that murder."

"We can deal with that matter later," said Holmes. "But first, I should like to examine the body."

"As you wish. But I don't see what you can gain other than confirming our own conclusions."

"Nevertheless."

"You are fortunate that we still have the body. It has been released to the family, and they are due to remove his remains later today."

The stench of death always reminds me of my time in Afghanistan. Even now, after many years, those memories continue to haunt me.

In the mortuary, the police surgeon led us to where Warrington's body lay on a slab of cold marble, covered by a white shroud. The surgeon removed the covering.

Now, several days after the murder, the corpse showed signs of decomposition.

Holmes stepped forward. "Would you please help me turn him over, Doctor?"

Together, the two men turned the corpse onto its front, giving a clear view of the back of the head.

Holmes took out his magnifying glass and examined the skull.

"How did he die?"

"That is a matter for the coroner, sir," replied the medical man.

"Come, come," said Holmes petulantly. "Just tell me."

"The evidence suggests he died of multiple injuries consistent with having fallen from a great height, and having collided with rocks on the way down. His broken neck suggests he landed on solid ground with considerable force."

Holmes stood back. "What is your professional opinion, Watson?"

I stepped forward, and examined the corpse. "I concur," I told him. "But I would suggest that the man was dead before he fell. That heavy blow to the back of the head must surely have been the fatal injury."

"Those are my own conclusions," said Holmes. "I have seen all I need to see."

As the surgeon covered the corpse, Holmes looked at those gathered around him. "Thank you, gentlemen, for your time and patience. Now, we need not prolong our visit, but I must speak with the man accused of this crime. Jowan Marrack."

As we followed the Chief Inspector towards the cells, Holmes sighed. "Things look dark for our friend Marrack. Don't you think so, Watson?"

"How much darker can they possibly become?"

"That blow to the head."

"Clearly inflicted by some heavy blunt object."

"Such as a Polynesian war-club?"

"Exactly so."

"I examined those clubs when we visited Marrack's home. On one of them I discovered a minute spot of blood, and traces of skin."

"Then his guilt appears more certain by the minute," said I.

"Indeed. We have the accused, in possession of the murder weapon, together with incriminating evidence and a possible motive. And, if the major is to be believed, a confession of guilt."

We found Jowan Marrack sitting in his cell, his blanched face displaying the horror he now faced: Trial for murder.

"I didn't kill him, Mr. Holmes," the accused man insisted. "I have no idea who did it, but it certainly wasn't me."

Holmes stood over him. "Despite your denial, Marrack, things look bad for you."

"I blame that Jago Stark," said Marrack. "We've been friends all our lives, and I've helped crew his boat for the past fifteen years, but those things he told the magistrate were pure fantasy. Lies."

"Tell me about those war-clubs hanging in your house."

"What about them? I never touch them. Horrible things. I don't know why you want to talk about them. That detective died after being pushed from the Turk's Head, didn't he?"

"Allow me to put one question to you, Marrack," said Holmes. "Did you ever sign a statement of confession?"

"A confession? Certainly not, Mr. Holmes. I never signed any such thing. If such a document exists at all, then it has to be a forgery. Yes, Major Rosdew did try to pressure me into admitting guilt. But I would never do such a thing."

"That is all I needed to know," said Holmes. "Rest assured, Mr. Marrack, I shall do everything in my power to have you released at soon as ever possible."

Outside the cell, I gasped. "Then it must have been Stark. Or even the major."

"We shall see."

As we took our leave of the Police Headquarters, Holmes paused and turned to face Branwell. "What about the other matter, Chief Inspector?"

"You mean the business concerning Major Rosdew?"

"Indeed."

"A delicate matter. But we have no solid evidence to warrant further investigation."

"Then, perhaps I can provide some for you."

The moment we alighted from our carriage, and again entered the Seven Stars, we were met by the landlord.

"I'm glad I've found you, Mr. Holmes," said he, handing over a folded sheet of paper. "I have a message for you."

Holmes read the note. "It appears to be a request by Major Rosdew that we meet him at the place where the body was discovered."

"The beach directly below the Turk's Head?"

"The note makes that clear."

"At what time?"

"At four o'clock this afternoon, according to the note."

"Less than an hour from now."

Holmes had a sparkle in his eye. "Watson, come with me to the laundry room at the rear of this building. And bring a bowl of water with you."

I found Holmes standing beside a draining board, and placed the bowl of water in front of him.

"Excellent," he declared. "I have here three pieces of correspondence: The initial invitation letter that we received from Miss Penrose, the note we have just been handed, and the letter written by Major Rosdew to Constable Evans." He laid out the documents side by side.

"Now, watch as I allow a drop of water to soak a small portion of each sample of script."

I watched as he dropped a small amount of water onto the final word of the first document, and saw the ink dissolve. Holmes held the paper at an angle so that the drop of dissolved ink ran down the page. After setting this aside to dry, Holmes did the same with the other two items of correspondence. Finally, we had three pieces of paper, with ink stains trailing from the script.

Holmes took out his magnifying lens, and closely studied the three items. "See, Watson," he told me. "In each case, the water has separated out the constituent elements of the ink."

He picked up the first letter. "This clearly shows that Miss Penrose used one kind of ink, almost certainly a commercially used brand. The second letter, the invitation we received this afternoon to meet at the beach, is written with the same ink used by Miss Penrose."

"Did she write that one as well?"

"I think not. I would hazard a guess that the ink used for both letters is available at the local Post Office for anyone in the village to use. Also, although the note has been written in upper case characters, no doubt to obscure the writer's identity, the hand is different. See how Miss Penrose forms her capital letters."

"A woman's hand, then."

"Undoubtedly. The merest hint of lavender still clings to the paper. But the writing on the invitation matches Mrs.

Marrack's hand. I studied a sample of her writing whilst you were caring for Stark."

"And the third letter?"

"The letter Evans received from the major – the ink is distinctly different. Possibly made to his own recipe."

"What do you conclude then, Holmes?"

"That this afternoon's invitation came not from the major, but from Mrs. Marrack."

"To what intent?"

"We shall soon find out."

Our descent to the small patch of sand at the foot of the cliff was by way of a rough and steep pathway. Sea pinks and other hardy flowering plants clung to the rocks as though for dear life.

"The tide is rising," I told Holmes. "What do you suppose Mrs. Marrack has to show us down here?"

"Nothing at all, Watson. In fact, I very much doubt that either she or the major will make a personal appearance on the beach."

"So, why did we come?"

"There are important facts yet to be revealed in this case, Watson. If Mrs. Marrack has asked us to come here, then we need to at least accede to her request."

As we stood on the rapidly reducing stretch of sand, I felt something fall upon my head. A pebble bounced from my hat, and landed in the water. I looked up in time to notice a rock descending toward us.

"Holmes!" I cried, pushing my companion aside. "Watch out!"

The gray rock landed at our feet, and buried itself in the sand.

I looked up, and saw a figure, standing at the top of the cliff, silhouetted against the sky.

By the time I had brushed myself down and looked up again, the figure had gone.

"Somebody tried to kill us."

"So it would seem, Watson."

"And our way back is now cut off by the rising tide."

"And the sea is too rough for us to swim to safety."

At that moment, we both heard the sound of a maroon rocket exploding above the village.

"I think we shall not die today, though, Watson," said Holmes as the local lifeboat approach us from the direction of the harbor. The boat, powered by a dozen oarsmen, rounded the promontory of hard granite rock, and drew towards us from the sea. A man stood in the prow.

"There you are, Mr. Holmes and Dr. Watson!"

I recognized the voice. "Enoch!" I shouted back against the growing wind. "What a surprise. It is extremely good to see you."

"We got your note, Mr. Holmes," came the old man's voice. "It seems you were expecting to become trapped down here."

When the men had brought the lifeboat to within a few yards of the beach, one of their number threw a life-line in our direction.

Within a couple of minutes, soaked to the skin by flying spray and momentary immersion in the sea, we were safely on board the boat.

As we drove through the waves, on our way back to the harbor, I looked back at the cliff, and at the Turk's Head high above. If anybody had been there, they were long gone now.

I noticed Holmes's face light up. "Now I have all the evidence I need," said he. "My case is complete."

After changing into dry clothing, and having paid for drinks for the entire crew of the lifeboat, Holmes and I made our way once more to the house of Miss Penrose. The lady was keen to hear of our progress in the case. Night was falling, and the wind was blowing in from a dark and brooding ocean. We were both glad to be in the warmth of her parlor.

"Are you now convinced that Jowan is innocent, Mr. Holmes?" asked Miss Penrose.

"The evidence forces me to conclude that he is indeed innocent of the murder of the police detective," said Holmes. "And, following our adventure down on the beach this afternoon, the identity of the murderer is now clear to me."

"Can you tell me who it is, Mr. Holmes?"

"Not yet. Let us just say that there is more going on here than merely the one murder."

"What more?"

Our discussion was interrupted by a heavy knock at the front door. Miss Penrose answered, and found Constable Evans standing in the entrance.

"I'm sorry to disturb you, Miss Penrose," said the policeman. "But I'm looking for Mr. Holmes."

"Well, he is here," she replied. "Please step inside."

The policeman made his way into the parlor. "Mr. Holmes. Come quickly. Major Rosdew has climbed up to the Turk's Head. And the people of the village are following after him. Somehow, they heard that he is to be investigated for corruption and malpractice. They are all extremely angry."

I gasped as I followed Holmes to the doorway, and we both looked out towards the cliff, and to the Turk's Head rock, standing prominently against the darkening skyline. In the darkness, we could see lights moving – a procession of burning torches, indicating the presence of a great many people, all converging upon the rock itself.

"Come, Watson," said Holmes. "I believe this is a crucial moment for our investigation. And far more so for Jowan Marrack."

We made our way as fast as we could to the highest point of the cliff, and found almost the entire village gathered beneath the white rock of the Turk's Head. The people were shouting a variety of taunts towards a man on the very brink of the cliff – a man standing lonely but defiant, challenging the entire world by his stance: Major Rosdew.

Holmes and I pushed our way through the throng, until we stood facing the major.

His face lit up as he recognized us. "Well, Mr. Holmes, what conclusions have you come to following your investigations? Have you identified the murderer?"

"I believe that I have," called Holmes. "I've heard the tales people have told me, and I've spoken with the police at Truro. I've interviewed the suspected man himself, and I've seen, in his own house, the murder implement – the Polynesian war-club hanging on the wall above his fireplace. I examined the head of both clubs, and discovered that one of them carried traces of skin and blood."

"And your conclusion, Mr. Holmes?"

"From my initial examination of the facts, I concluded that Mr. Marrack was indeed the murderer. But I held that opinion for only a short time. This afternoon, Dr. Watson and I were asked to meet you down at the foot of this cliff. The result was that we very nearly lost our lives. Not once, but twice. A rock fell from up here, and narrowly missed us both. On looking up, I noticed a figure. Then we were left at the mercy of the tide, with no way of escaping from that beach. Having examined the letter inviting us there, the truth became undeniable when I noticed that the figure on the clifftop was a woman."

He turned to face the person standing closest to the major. "It was you, Mrs. Marrack. You tried to kill us earlier today. It was when I saw you, standing high above us, that everything finally fell into place. When I examined the body of the dead man, I noticed that the back of his head had been struck with a blunt instrument, the dimensions of which matched the war-club in your house. He died, not from landing upon the shoreline, nor from striking the rocks on the way down. The man died from a heavy blow to the back of his head. A war-club was indeed the murder weapon, but the hand that wielded it was *yours*, Mrs. Marrack."

"But Holmes," I exclaimed, very much puzzled, "whoever delivered that blow did so with considerable force."

"That is indeed true," replied Holmes, his gaze still fixed upon Mrs. Marrack. "But fishermen's wives are a tough and hardy breed. Sturdy of arm and strong of will. Such a woman, with passion in her heart, could easily have delivered that killer blow."

"But how would she have carried the club all the way up here without it being seen?"

"It takes but a moment's thought to imagine that she hid it beneath a voluptuous coat, like the one I saw hanging in the entrance to her house."

With all eyes now fasten upon her, Mrs. Marrack clutched the major's arm, her eyes showing terror. "You seem to know everything, Mr. Holmes."

"I believe I know enough to have you tried for the murder of that policeman, rather than your husband."

She looked up into the face of the major, as they stood together, swaying against the strengthening wind.

"It was the motive for the killing that had me baffled," said Sherlock Holmes. "Why would the police send a detective to investigate a minor incident of smuggling? Then again, why would anyone choose to lure the man up here and then push him to his death? There had to be more to this business."

Holmes turned once more to the major. "The detective from Truro was not interested in smuggling, was he, Major? He was sent here to investigate *you*, and your disgusting arrangement of selling young men into slavery."

"You don't know what you're talking about!" spluttered the major.

"Why would the detective from Truro come all the way up here, to the Turk's Head rock, unless he had been lured by the promise of incriminating information about you, Major? From the person who knew you best of all – Mrs. Marrack."

"So," he growled, "you intend to have me broken, and Talwyn hanged for murder. Is that your game?"

"That would be a matter for the law."

"I am still the magistrate in Port Caer, Mr. Holmes!" roared Major Rosdew. "I shall deal with this matter in my own way."

"Then permit the truth to prevail. Admit that you forged the confession that now threatens to convict Jowan Marrack of murder."

Rosdew nodded. "It is as you say."

The major then turned to face the open sea.

Standing beside him, Talwyn Marrack also turned.

Without saying anything further, the two grasped each other by the hand, and launched themselves into the abyss, together tumbling into the darkness below. No sound came up to us other than the howling of the wind, and the crashing of relentless waves against ageless rocks. Nothing more was ever heard of the two who jumped, and no trace of their bodies was ever found.

After a moment of stunned silence, Constable Evans turned to face the crowd. "I shall take steps immediately to have Jowan Marrack released from prison, and all those young men returned to their families."

The crowd gave a cheer, and gathered around their local policeman.

"Let him receive their plaudits," said Holmes, as we turned away. "People need their local heroes."

The following morning, as the villagers set about their daily work, Sherlock Holmes stood in the open window of his room at the Seven Stars, picked up the violin he had borrowed from the landlord, and began to play. Across the rooftops of the village, and the boats in the crowded little harbor, the sounds of Bach's violin concert spread as a healing balm, bringing sweetness and harmony to this stunned but now liberated community.

When he had finished playing, he looked round at me. "Watson, this instrument may not be up to the standard of my Stradivarius, but at least I have finally matched the master himself."

It seemed to me that Holmes had accomplished something even more amazing: He had exorcised from our minds something of the horror of our previous visit to Cornwall.

A few weeks later, back in Baker Street, we received an invitation to attend the marriage of Miss Merryn Penrose and Mr. Jowan Marrack. Of course, Holmes would never have accepted the invitation, but he did consent to write a letter of congratulations to the happy couple – which, for him, was a substantial demonstration of his esteem.

## You Only Live Thrice
by Robert V. Stapleton

The streets of Guildford felt cold and depressing. The chill January wind cut through even my corpulent frame, whilst the strident voices of newspaper vendors broadcast news of Queen Victoria's latest illness.

The moment I reached the comparative warmth of the Surrey County Police Headquarters that morning, the Superintendent called me in to his office.

"How do you like this weather, Baynes?" he asked me, as he sat back in the luxury of his upholstered leather chair.

I contemplated the smart new calendar for 1901, standing between us on the desk. "I shall be much happier when the summer comes, sir."

"In that case, how would a trip to the West Indies suit you?" He smiled as he watched my expression brighten.

I knew from years of experience that far more lay behind that question than initially met the ear. I replied cautiously, "It would be a refreshing change, sir. Where exactly do you have in mind?"

"Barbados," he replied. "I understand the climate there can be more agreeable than even Guildford at this time of the year."

"I should hope so, sir." I wondered what was coming next.

"You are to go there and arrest a man going by the name of Jason Fairworthy-Smith. Though what his real name might be is beyond both myself and Scotland Yard."

"Fairworthy-Smith, the swindler?" I replied. "That fellow from the village of Greenford Steeple, who makes himself out to be a gentleman? The last time I came across him, he was making a fortune out of selling shares in some bogus Australian goldmine – amongst other dubious projects."

The Superintendent nodded. "He targeted mostly rich people, but some other investors lost everything they owned. In his determination to make himself a rich man, Fairworthy-Smith also made a number of powerful enemies among the criminal underworld."

"No wonder he wanted to make himself scarce," I added, "and head to sunnier climes."

My superior consulted a paper lying before him. "Mr. Sherlock Holmes has recommended you for this particular job." He looked up at me again. "You have had dealings with this gentleman on a previous occasion, I believe."

"But that was several years ago now, sir," I replied, taken aback by this unexpected revelation. "I have no idea why he might have considered me suitable for such an assignment."

"Nevertheless, his recommendation is good enough for me," said the Super, looking me squarely in the face. "You are to travel by Royal Mail steamer to Bridgetown, secure Fairworthy-Smith's arrest, and return with him as soon as possible. And remember, Baynes, this is constabulary business, and not some holiday jaunt for indolent police officers."

"I shall try to remember that, sir."

"Fairworthy-Smith absconded before we could complete our case against him. But the documentation is now prepared." The Super pushed a bundle of papers across the desk. "Your ship leaves on Friday."

I picked up the documents, and examined the travel warrant and arrest authorization.

"That gives you three days to prepare."

I hesitated. "It occurs to me, sir, that if our man is desperate enough to travel so far away in order to avoid apprehension, he might turn out to be particularly dangerous when threatened with arrest."

The Superintendent pondered the matter. "You have a good point, Baynes. In that case, you'd better take your revolver with you."

The voyage to Bridgetown lasted a week, much of which time I spent in utter misery, as *mâl de mer* seized me with a grip of iron, and confined me to my cabin.

On the morning I was feeling better, I descended to the saloon for breakfast.

I collected my choice of food, approached an empty table, and sat down.

As I picked up my knife and fork, another man approached. He had dark hair, a sallow complexion, and was wearing a brown suit over a thin but wiry frame.

"Do you mind if I join you?" he asked.

Not wishing to appear rude, and in need of some company for a change, I replied that I had no objection.

The man sat down.

"My name is Mordred Scarrington," he began, fixing me with his steely gaze.

I wondered if I had heard the name somewhere before.

"And I am Inspector Baynes," I replied plainly, not feeling in the mood to play games of guess-what-I-am.

"A policeman," observed Scarrington. He seemed taken aback by this revelation.

"On police business."

"Metropolitan Force?"

"Surrey County Constabulary."

He relaxed somewhat. "With business in Barbados?"

"Indeed. And yourself?"

"I am also traveling to the island on business," replied Scarrington. "On behalf of an important client in London."

Being a naturally suspicious policeman, I wondered if perhaps we were both after the same man. "I understand Barbados is a small island."

"Then perhaps our paths might cross again."

The remaining days of that transatlantic voyage were distinguished by only two notable events. One evening, as the weather was becoming warmer, I ventured out on deck. The sea was calmer than it had been farther north, and the clear air made the stars shine with a brilliance I had rarely seen in Surrey.

As I stood beside the safety rail, smoking my final cigarette of the day, I had the distinct impression that somebody was approaching me from behind.

I stepped adroitly to one side, and turned to face whoever was there. A shadowy figure, with hands outstretched toward me, immediately turned and slipped away into the shadows, leaving me with the unpleasant impression that I had escaped death by only a few seconds. I also had the impression that the figure I had seen was my recent acquaintance, Scarrington.

The second occasion was the night before we were due to arrive at Bridgetown. I was lying on my bunk, trying in vain to remain cool, when I heard the door to my cabin unlock and open. The sound was slight, but distinctive. In the darkness, I became aware of another presence in my cabin. Moonlight, filtering in through the porthole, glinted on a fragment of steel. A knife. That was enough for me. I stood up, shouted my defiance, and threw one of my boots at the approaching figure. Instead of leaving, the intruder drew closer. It was at times such as this that I cursed by bulky size. I had no wish to make a fight of it, since I would be at a disadvantage on almost every count: Fat, slow, middle-aged, and, at that moment, unarmed. But my size and muscular strength gave me one advantage in the darkness. I threw myself at the intruder, knocking him off balance. Then I grasped the hand holding the knife, and twisted it until the weapon clattered to the floor. Now disarmed, the figure cursed me, turned, and fled.

Having secured the cabin door with a chair against the handle, I slept fitfully for the rest of the night, and awoke in the morning, alert to the fact that the ship had stopped moving, and the engines were no longer running.

I looked outside, and saw land.

*Barbados.*

After a hurried breakfast, during which time I noticed that Scarrington was keeping his distance from me, with his right wrist strapped up and resting in a sling, I ventured out on deck, and looked around. The steamer was now moored to a buoy, stationary in a turquoise sea. Across the water, beyond a flotilla of other harbored vessels, the island looked magnificent in the light of the early dawn. The shore was lined with trees, behind which houses with whitewashed walls and red tiled roofs lay partially hidden, as though nervous of too impulsive an encounter with their foreign visitors. A gentle off-shore breeze carried the smell of earth and humanity. Above the horizon, beyond flat farmland and green rolling moors, the rays of the rising sun reached up into a blue sky, promising a warm and glorious day.

One of the ship's officers approached me.

"Is this your first time in the West Indies, sir?" he asked.

"It is indeed," I replied. "I assume we have now reached our destination."

"Quite correct. We are now lying in Carlisle Bay, awaiting transfer to the dockside at Bridgetown. It shouldn't be long now, sir. You will find Barbados a delightful place. I hope you have an enjoyable stay."

I hoped so too.

The moment I set foot on the quayside, I was greeted by a young man, dressed in a khaki uniform, and displaying a distinctly military bearing. He gave me a broad grin, white teeth lighting up his dark face. "Good morning, sir," he said. "You must be Inspector Baynes."

I took out a handkerchief, mopped my brow, and nodded.

"I am Sergeant McAdam, sir, of the Royal Barbados Police Force, Central Station Guard. I have been sent to welcome you to Bridgetown, and to take you to meet the officer in charge."

"I also need to check in to my hotel," I told him.

"You have no need to worry about that, sir. I have already arranged for your luggage to be taken there directly."

"Very well, Sergeant. Lead the way."

He took me through the city center, past sellers of yams and sweet potatoes, to the impressive Police Headquarters building. I was looking forward to meeting the man in charge, hoping that he might exert his utmost effort in helping me complete my mission to the island.

The officer in charge, an Englishman with a cut-glass accent, greeted me warmly and invited me to sit down in a wicker chair. After a few polite inquiries about the voyage, he clasped his hands together, and leaned over his mahogany desk. "News has come through from England, via the miracle of undersea telegraphy, that Her Majesty the Queen has sadly passed away. She died on the twenty-second, surrounded by her family."

"That is very sad news, sir, even if it was to be expected," I replied. "Long live King Edward."

"Indeed. *God Save the King!* I am sure that we now stand on the very brink of a new era, as well as a new century."

I nodded.

"Now, to the reason for your visit here, Baynes. This business of yours shouldn't take very long to complete. I should think that you'll be on your way home by the very next steamer."

"I hope so, sir," I replied. "I am here with the single purpose of arresting that fellow, Fairworthy-Smith. I only need to know where I can find him, and then I can prepare to be on my way."

"Yes, we know about Fairworthy-Smith," he replied guardedly. "A slippery customer. If we'd had the paperwork earlier, we might have had him arrested before you arrived."

"Of course, sir." I passed across to him the documents concerning the case, which I had been given in Guildford.

He glanced at them, nodded, and put them to one side. "I can safely leave you in the capable hands of Sergeant McAdam."

"Thank you, sir. He seems a keen and personable young fellow."

"He will be able to supply you with anything else you might require."

"I am sure he will prove to be a most useful companion, sir."

"Splendid. Well, don't let me delay you."

I left, feeling slightly disappointed by my interview, and found Sergeant McAdam waiting for me outside, standing beside a horse and trap. The animal seemed as anxious to be on its way as did the policeman.

I climbed aboard. "What do you have planned for me, McAdam?"

A broad grin once more lit up his face. "If it's all right with you, sir, I shall give you a guided tour of the city, show you the sights, and then drop you off at your hotel, in time for your midday meal."

"That sounds extremely civilized," I told him. "Then I shall need you to find out for me as much as you can about the present whereabouts of our fugitive, Jason Fairworthy-Smith."

As promised, McAdam made sure I reached my hotel room around midday, allowing me time to change out of my traveling clothes before luncheon.

The moment I stepped through the door of my hotel room, I had a feeling that I was not alone there.

I was trying to remember where I had left my revolver, when a man stepped out of the shadows. "Hello, Mr. Baynes," said a voice I remembered from another time and another place.

I looked the man over. His hair was a rich ginger color, as was his thin mustache. His appearance was further distinguished by a monocle which he wore in his right eye. I recognized the fellow at once. "Hello, Smith," I growled. "I am here to take you home. You are to stand trial for fraud."

Fairworthy-Smith gave a mirthless chuckle. "Most of those people had done nothing to deserve their money, you know. Some had inherited it from their parents, whilst others had themselves swindled it from the poor and innocent. I have never shed a tear over taking their money, and I doubt that many of them will have lost much sleep over it either."

"Except those you left impoverished."

"They only have themselves to blame."

"But that does not excuse your crimes."

"And you are merely carrying out your duty. Yes, I know. I was warned that you were on your way, Inspector."

"Warned? By whom?"

"By a friend."

"Then I hope you will surrender yourself to my custody without further ado."

Fairworthy-Smith stood erect and defiant. “I can assure you, Inspector, that you will never take me back to England. I have powerful enemies at home, and if I go back to stand trial, they will take their revenge by seeing me dead within the week.”

“We can offer you protection.”

“Can you protect me from the assassin they’ve already sent here to kill me?”

“Assassin?”

“He arrived on the same ship that brought you.”

It took me only a moment to remember. “Scarrington?”

“I don’t know *who* he is, but I do know *what* he is. And if he suspects that you are here to arrest me, then your own life could well be in danger.”

“He already tried to kill me on two occasions.”

“Then the matter is indeed serious.”

“But you can hardly evade both of us. At least with me, you will stand a chance of surviving a little longer.”

“There are other ways to survive, Inspector.”

“Maybe, but my immediate business if to arrest you.” I glared back at him. “Jason Fairworthy-Smith, I have a warrant for your detention, and I am now placing you under arrest on suspicion of committing crimes of fraud. You will accompany me to the Police Headquarters, where the formal charge will be made. Then I shall take you back to stand trial in England.”

“I really don’t think you will, Inspector,” replied Fairworthy-Smith. “I fear that your journey here has been a total waste of valuable time, which you could have used for more profitable purposes. As I told you, I shall never go back to England.”

“Now you are guilty of the additional offense of resisting arrest.”

Fairworthy-Smith gave me a sour look, made all the more poisonous by the monocle. He then pushed past me, and stomped away down the corridor.

I slumped into the bedroom chair, and contemplated this turn of events. I had found my man, but taking my prisoner back to stand trial would prove to be a more demanding task than I had imagined.

After luncheon in the restaurant downstairs, I sat in the lounge, sipping a fruit juice, and feeling sorry for myself in the unfamiliar heat.

I was nodding off to sleep when Sergeant McAdam arrived.

"Good afternoon, Inspector."

"Oh, hello, McAdam. Please take a seat."

"Thank you, sir." He sat down on another easy chair, and looked at me, expectantly.

"Well, have you discovered anything about our friend, Fairworthy-Smith?"

"Yes, sir."

"Then first allow me to tell you that I found him before you did."

The sergeant's face showed great surprise. "You found him?"

"Yes. He was already in my room, waiting for me. The fellow then left whilst resisting my arrest."

McAdam stood up in alarm. "Then we must lose no time in apprehending the man."

"That might not prove an easy job, now that he knows that I am here. But first sit down, and tell me all you know."

"Mr. Jason Fairworthy-Smith arrived in Barbados in September of last year, sir. He deposited a large quantity of cash at the Central Bank, arranged to hire a small villa on the edge of town, and since then has kept himself very much to himself."

"In that case, we need to begin by visiting the villa. Although I suspect that will be the very last place we will find him."

I returned to my hotel room, slipped my revolver into my pocket, and grasped my straw hat. A few minutes later, we were traveling in convoy along the city streets. Myself and McAdam in the front four-wheeler, and a bevy of constables in a police-wagon behind. We passed along white roads, between avenues of palm and banyan trees, to the attractive city suburbs, resplendent with the rich colors of hibiscus and bougainvillea.

We turned in through an entrance guarded by a pair of stone gateposts and made our way along a gravel driveway. We stopped in the turning circle in front of a whitewashed front entrance and climbed out.

"Here we are, Inspector," said McAdam. "This is the place Fairworthy-Smith has been renting."

I strode up to the front door and tugged on the bell-pull. A large woman answered by opening the door and glaring out at us. Her face carried a look of intense suspicion.

"Yes? How may I help you?"

I showed her my police accreditation, and replied, "I am Inspector Baynes from Surrey, England, now working in cooperation with the Barbadian Police. I am here to see Mr. Fairworthy-Smith. Is he home?"

"Mr. Fairworthy-Smith has not been here for a couple of days now," replied the lady, in a slow drawl. "I am his housekeeper, so I ought to know."

"Do you know when he will return?"

"He didn't tell me."

"May we come inside?"

As the constables gathered around the entrance, the housekeeper scowled and stepped reluctantly aside.

I found the cool shade an immense relief after the heat of the afternoon sunshine. Sergeant McAdam accompanied me as I searched through the rooms, but we stopped the moment we reached the dining room. There we found ourselves confronted by a man reclining a wicker chair, with his feet resting on a footstool.

Not Fairworthy-Smith.

"Scarrington."

"Good afternoon, Inspector," said my erstwhile traveling companion. "You were right when you told me we would meet again. It seems we both have business with the same man."

I indicated the sling he was still wearing. "I hope your wrist will soon be better."

Scarrington glowered back at me.

His presence there confirmed my suspicions, and his attempts on my life now made sense. This man was here to kill Fairworthy-Smith, and my presence would only complicate matters for him, if not bring failure to his entire enterprise.

"I am here to arrest Fairworthy-Smith and return him safely to England to stand trial in a court of law," I told Scarrington. "But your business is surely to kill him."

"But our man has disappeared. That makes us confederates in our search for him."

"I am no confederate of yours," I replied coldly.

"And yet, I am in a better position to find him than you are," said Scarrington. "I have arranged to lodge here, in the house that Fairworthy-Smith has been renting – enjoying his hospitality, so to speak, until he shows his face again."

"If you kill him, I shall make sure you stand trial for murder."

"I am a professional, Inspector." Scarrington picked up a lighted cigar from its ashtray at his elbow, drew deeply upon it, and filled the room with its aromatic scent. "You will never find enough evidence to convict me. Even if you live long enough to see me accused. Which in doubtful."

"I wouldn't be so sure about that. I too am a professional."

Scarrington laughed, and gave a dismissive wave of the hand. "Kindly close the door on your way out."

This was enough for my first day on the island, and without any new leads to go on, I decided to retire early for the night. I dismissed Sergeant McAdam, ate a hearty supper, which contained slightly too much spice for my preference, and retired to my bed, with the mosquito netting firmly in place.

The following morning, McAdam turned up as I was concluding my breakfast, and met me in the entrance hall.

"Now, Sergeant," I greeted him. "Do you have any new leads on our disappearing confidence trickster?"

"Not yet, sir," said McAdam. "But it seems Mr. Scarrington is offering a reward to be given to anyone who can find Fairworthy-Smith for him."

I chuckled. "Why didn't I think of that?"

McAdam appeared shocked. "We must do things the proper way, Inspector."

"I suppose you're right. But we could do with a fresh lead in this case."

Another uniformed man appeared in the doorway, and addressed McAdam. "Excuse me, Sergeant."

"Yes?"

"Dr. Monteith has been called to a death, and he wonders if you and the inspector would care to accompany him to the scene."

I looked out into the street, and saw a man sitting patiently in a four-wheeler parked at the roadside. He was dressed in dark formal clothing, and was clutching a black medical bag.

McAdam looked to me for confirmation.

I nodded. Why not?

I found Dr. Samuel Monteith to be a traditional man of medicine, of the old school, with plenty of experience of life in the tropics.

"I have lived on this island for the last fifteen years, Inspector," he told me, "and I never fail to be amazed at the variety of ways people can find to die in places like this place."

I watched the landscape slip past the window as the four-wheeler left the city and drew up beside a wooden cabin at the head of a small, white-sanded bay. I followed McAdam out of the vehicle and looked around. I noticed a small army of large land crabs, warning us of their presence by the scratching noise they made as they walked along – enough to make the skin crawl.

As I followed the doctor to a small hut, I studied the grove of trees around me. They had a red-gray bark, serrated leaves and bore small, green, apple-like fruits.

"Please do not even touch those fruits, Inspector," McAdam warned me. "They are the fruit of the Manchineel tree."

"Are they dangerous?"

"Extremely poisonous."

I shuddered. "There seems to be an abundance of horrors in this place."

The hut was dark and was haunted by the smell of decaying fish. It had clearly been used in the recent past by the local fishermen as a place for storage.

I watched the doctor approach a makeshift bed, on which lay a man I recognized as Jason Fairworthy-Smith. The man's monocle lay beside him on the straw-filled paillasse.

"He is certainly dead, Doctor," came a woman's croaking voice from the far corner of the room.

I looked across the room, and saw what looked like an elderly woman, sitting quietly in the shadows, watching us with snake-like eyes. She was small, and wore a large, variously colored dress, with beads hanging down beneath a hydra's head of oiled dreadlocks.

Sergeant McAdam leaned closer to me, and whispered, "That is Mama Moon."

"Tell me more."

"She is a local voodoo priestess."

Alarmed, I looked at her with curious respect, and she returned my look with an enigmatic smile.

Dr. Monteith put down his bag, and examined the body. "It seems you are right, Mama Moon."

"He was a stranger to this island," explained Mama Moon, "and he didn't know what was bad for him. He consumed too many Manchineel apples." The priestess pointed to the floor, where the remains of several of the apple-like fruits lay scattered. "The poor man asked me for protection, because he believed that somebody was coming here to kill him. But I was powerless to save his life today."

"If he believed his life was in danger, then he was quite right," I added.

"Ah, yes. Inspector Baynes." She looked directly at me.

"Indeed."

"He considered you to be his enemy as well."

"My intention was only to return him to face justice," I replied defensively. "And now he is dead."

The doctor finished his cursory examination of the body, and began to write out a death certificate. "Cause of death: Manchineel poisoning. Time of death?" he looked at the priestess.

"Not long ago. Say an hour."

"Would you mind letting me have a copy of the death certificate, Doctor?" I asked him. "I came here to arrest this man, so if I am unable to take him back with me, then at least I need proof that he is dead."

"Of course."

As the doctor gathered his equipment together, I looked around the scene. First I examined the body and found no sign that *rigor mortis* had yet set in. Then I observed his face. In the gloom, I noticed unusual markings around the mouth and nose. Interesting. I viewed his body, and noticed a puncture mark where a hypodermic needle had been inserted into the left forearm. Not prominent, but certainly present. I surveyed the floor, and discovered, almost hidden in the darkness, a small piece of gravel. I picked it up and put it away in an inside pocket of my jacket.

All eyes were watching me as I finally stood up, turned to McAdam, and nodded. I was ready to leave. Then I noticed the old woman holding in her lap what looked like chicken wing feathers. Three of them.

"How many times do you think a man should be given a fresh chance in life, Inspector?" the priestess asked me.

"What do you mean by that?"

"Once? We all have one chance, Inspector." She held up one feather. "Twice? Some people are given a second chance." She held up two feathers. "Thrice? Very rarely are we given the chance to live a third time." She held up all three feathers, and looked me in the eye.

"I am not here to play mind games," I replied. "What will happen to the body now?"

"It will be taken back to the hospital, until this evening," said the priestess. "Then it will be cremated. On the beach. Tonight."

I raised my eyebrows in surprise. "Why so soon?"

"There is no need to delay. Particularly in the tropics. We have the death certificate, so obtaining special permission to cremate the body will present no problem. It was Mr. Fairworthy-Smith's expressed wish to be cremated, and his ashes consigned to the deep."

"Am I permitted to attend the cremation?" I asked her.

"I would expect you to be there, Inspector," she replied, "so you can report back to England that all has been done in order, and that your mission here is at an end."

That evening, as the light began to fade, I stood on a slight rise in the ground, looking down at a gathered of people on the white sands of a bay just outside Bridgetown. At the center of the assembly stood a pile of wood with something like a corpse, wrapped in white cloth, resting upon the top. I watched as one of the men lit a flame and applied it to the base of the pyre. The dry wood rapidly caught alight, and flames rapidly licked up around the swathed body.

As I stood watching this ritual, I became aware of somebody beside me. I turned and found Scarrington observing the scene as intently as I was.

"Well, Inspector," said he, "there you have your man. His body consigned to the flames."

I continued standing there until darkness had fallen, the flames had been extinguished by the incoming waves, and the remains finally swept out to sea.

When I returned to my room that evening, I found something lying on my pillow. A single chicken feather. Somebody, apart from the regular hotel staff, had been in my room. I recalled Mama Moon, and the feathers I had seen her holding. He she been here?

I retired to bed a troubled man. I had witnessed the death of the man I had been sent to arrest. I had seen his body burned and his ashes claimed by the sea. And yet, I was not convinced. Fairworthy-Smith was a professional confidence trickster who had deceived dozens of people over the years, all to his own profit, and now I was expected to believe that all I had witnessed here was real. But no – something was wrong. My intuition told me that I had been watching an illusion. A conjuring trick. Was Fairworthy-Smith really dead? Or was he still alive? I had seen it, but I still did not believe.

A few days later, Sergeant McAdam called for me shortly after breakfast. "With your case now closed, sir," said he, "you will be making plans to leave Barbados by the next steamer."

"Perhaps."

"Before you do leave, sir, I have an outing planned for you."

"That is very thoughtful of you, Sergeant. Where do you plan to take me?"

"I have an open invitation for you to visit Codrington College. You might even meet the principal there."

Thirteen miles away, across the center of the island, Codrington College was set in magnificent grounds of colored foliage and avenues of tall palms. With the gentle breeze of the trade wind blowing in from the east, it was very different from the dusty roads we had traveled to reach it, and from the bustle of the west coast city we had left. The principal welcomed me with a friendly smile and a firm handshake, but he was too busy to linger in conversation. Instead, he allocated me a guide, who took me to explore the magnificent college chapel, introduced me to some of the students, and finally took me to visit a small museum.

For several minutes, I examined the exhibits on display there. Each had its own tale to tell. Some were documents relating to the history of the island. Others were fetters employed at one time to shackle the slaves who had labored on the sugar plantations. I also spent a few moments looking up at a pair of spears fixed to the wall above one of the display cases. A label read, "*Arawak spears*".

I turned to McAdam. "Arawak?"

"A race of people who, along with the Caribs, once inhabited parts of South America and the islands of the Caribbean."

"They must have been a warlike race."

"In such a dangerous world, they had to be, sir."

That night, I began to plan my return to England. The steamer would be leaving for home in a few days' time, and I had a copy of Fairworthy-Smith's death certificate with me. But I was reluctant to depart with doubts still haunting my mind.

In the pre-dawn darkness, I was awakened by the sound of shouting in the street outside. I looked out of the window and noticed men and women running. With purpose and direction. I dressed and joined them in the street. There I met McAdam.

"What's happening, Sergeant?"

"It seems that one of Scarrington's men has found Fairworthy-Smith hiding in one of the workers' houses on the edge of town."

"Alive?"

"Apparently so. The whole of Bridgetown is gathering there."

We made our way, as fast as I could manage, in the wake of the crowd, until we stood facing a simple wooden house. The building was surrounded by people, many of whom held blazing torches.

I heard Scarrington's voice. "I know you're in there, Smith. We have the place surrounded, so come out and show yourself."

Neither answer nor any sign of life came from the house.

Scarrington shouted an order, and two men in the crowd threw their blazing torches in through open windows on opposite sides of the house.

"You'd better call in the firefighters," I told McAdam.

"They are already on their way, sir. I had a feeling we might need them."

The fire rapidly took hold, and before long the wooden house had become a blazing inferno. I tried to push my way inside, but the flames forced me back. I imagined Fairworthy-Smith burning to death inside, and watched the firefighters as they cleared a way through the crowd, and tackled the burning building.

After a couple of hours, morning light found the city shrouded beneath a mixture of acrid smoke and gathering mist.

In the gloom, I joined members of the Guard, and the Firefighters, as they sifted through the remains of the wooden house. It was now nothing more than a burned-out shell. A scene of utter devastation. But, of Fairworthy-Smith, we could find not a trace.

I wandered wearily back to my hotel and was greeted by the man at the reception desk, who informed me that he had a message for me. I took the envelope, opened it, and removed a small sheet of paper. It read, "*Meet me at Prospect, at 11.00 a.m.*" It was unsigned.

When McAdam turned up an hour later, I showed him the letter. "It has to be from Fairworthy-Smith," I told him. "Can you get me to Prospect in time to meet him, Sergeant?"

"Of course, sir."

I took the precaution of pushing my revolver into the right hand pocket of my jacket.

The place called Prospect lay to the north of the city and overlooked the ocean, but the views which justified the name were mostly hidden at that moment by mist. However, I was not there to admire the vista.

With McAdam remaining a few yards behind me, I stood on a high point of the land, and looked around.

Then I noticed him. A man in a white shirt and white cotton trousers, sitting on a rock beneath a stand of trees, holding a revolver in his hand.

"Smith," I called out to him. "How does it feel to be a dead man?"

"Better than I imagined."

"Are you ready now to surrender yourself to the law?"

"I would prefer to remain a free man, Mr. Baynes." The man stepped closer. "So, I propose to finish this business here and now."

I watched him stop about twenty feet away, and raise his gun. I was too shocked to respond quickly enough.

"No!" shouted McAdam, hurrying forward.

But he was too late. Above the sound of the waves crashing against unseen coral rocks, I heard the sound of a gunshot cut through the air.

I felt myself thrust back, so that I fell heavily to the ground. A throbbing pain in my left shoulder brought me back to my senses. I realized he had shot me.

Fairworthy-Smith stepped closer and again raised his gun, making as though to finish me off. Instead, I slipped my right hand into the pocket of my jacket, and took out my own revolver. As I struggled against the pain, I lifted the gun in my shaking hand, and fired directly into the middle of the man's chest. Fairworthy-Smith collapsed to the ground. Before I passed out, I watched a drop of blood ooze from the corner of his mouth, and a red stain grow in the center of his chest. This time, he really did look dead.

I awakened to find myself lying in a hospital bed. My left shoulder still throbbed, and I felt weak through loss of blood. I recalled that Fairworthy-Smith had shot me, and that I had replied by shooting him dead.

I also remembered other things. I had a vague impression of having a mask placed over my face before anesthetic gas was given to me. That memory jogged another recollection into my mind: The marks on the face of the man I had taken for dead in the small shoreline hut. Clearly, Fairworthy-Smith had been drugged in order to simulate his death.

Sergeant McAdam came to visit me.

"Well, Sergeant," I began. "If Fairworthy-Smith wasn't dead before, then he certainly is now."

McAdam remained painfully silent.

I leaned on my elbow, to look up at him, but collapsed back onto my bed in agony. "What's the matter, Sergeant?"

"When I went back to collect the body," said McAdam, "I could find no trace of him, sir."

"No trace?"

"Not a sign."

"How can that be?" I gasped. "I shot the man dead."

"As a matter of police procedure, we examined your gun, sir."

"And?"

"By chance, we discovered that it had been loaded with blank cartridges."

Even half-drugged against the pain, I felt stunned. "So I didn't kill Fairworthy-Smith."

"That's the way it seems, sir."

"And he is not dead."

"We can only conclude that the entire incident was deliberately fabricated in order to convince the world that Fairworthy-Smith really was dead. For a second time."

"The fellow is well known as a confidence trickster," I replied. "That is the very reason I came to Barbados. To take him back to stand trial for his nefarious dealings."

I lay back, thinking hard, whilst the sergeant stood patiently at my bedside. The entire situation had slipped out of my control. Things were happening that I failed to understand. I needed a second opinion. I also needed to report back to Guildford.

"McAdam."

"Yes, Inspector?"

"When does the next Royal Mail steamer leave for England?"

"Tomorrow, I think."

"That soon? Then we must move quickly. I need to send a couple of letters. Would you kindly bring me writing-paper, ink, pen, and an envelope? And find me a table and a hard chair."

Fighting against the pain in my shoulder and the weakness in my body, I managed to write down an account of my progress in the case so far. A task I had to endure twice. As the last of my energy ebbed away, I left the price of two stamps on the table, and sealed the letters inside their envelopes. One I addressed to my superior in Guildford. The other, together with a request for professional advice, I addressed to, Mr. Sherlock Holmes, 221b Baker Street, London.

I then collapsed back onto the hospital bed, and knew nothing for the next two days.

At the end of a couple of weeks, with my arm no longer in a sling, I moved away from the hospital, and took up residence at the home of Sergeant McAdam and his family. Their house was small but comfortable, and they treated me with great kindness as I continued to make my steady recovery. The sergeant kept me informed of life on the island and allowed me to make the occasional foray into the city to take the sun and to strengthen my muscles.

I counted off the days until the return date for the Royal Mail steamer, and on the morning of its arrival, I accompanied Sergeant McAdam down to the Post Office, to enquire after any correspondence addressed to myself.

The man behind the counter handed me one letter. It was from my Superintendent in Guildford, reminding me not return home without the man I had been sent to arrest.

"I was expecting another letter as well," I told the man.

"I'm sorry, sir," he replied. "There is nothing else."

"Nor is there any need for it," came a voice from behind me. I turned, and found Sergeant McAdam standing beside a man dressed in a light suit. It took me only a moment to recognize the searching eyes and aquiline features. Mr. Sherlock Holmes.

"Mr. Holmes," I exclaimed. "It is indeed wonderful to see you here."

"It is good to see you too, Baynes."

"When I wrote, I never imagined you would come all this way yourself."

"I am here merely on holiday," replied Holmes, nonchalantly. "A private consulting detective does require time off sometimes."

"Certainly."

"My physician approved of a sea voyage and a few days in the Caribbean sunshine. He said it would do me good. Following the Queen's funeral, I had no pressing engagements, so, with a mystery to be solved, there was no way anybody could prevent me from coming here. Besides, I respect your judgment. When you call for my assistance, I know it is something important."

"We have arranged for Mr. Holmes to stay in the same hotel room that you occupied," said McAdam.

I nodded. "A comfortable room."

"You are feeling stronger," observed Holmes. "But you are staying with Sergeant McAdam for the moment."

"Indeed. He and his family are delightful company."

"Splendid. Then I suggest we repair to their home to discuss our business further."

A few minutes later, Holmes was seated opposite me. "I read your letter with the greatest interest. You have done well. But tell me, have there been any further developments since you wrote it?"

"Very few," I replied. "Jason Fairworthy-Smith seems to have vanished from the face of the earth."

"From what you told me, I imagine he is lying low somewhere. Perhaps not far away from here."

"And Mordred Scarrington is taking out his frustration on everyone else," I told him. "He has organized several criminal activities on the island, and has stirred up a great deal of conflict in Bridgetown, giving the police a particularly difficult time."

"In that case, we must deal with this matter as soon as possible," said Holmes, decisively.

"What should be our next move then, Mr. Holmes?" I asked.

Sherlock Holmes leaned closer and fixed me with his piercing eyes. "We need to have a meeting with the voodoo priestess. Mama Moon."

I felt my blood run cold. "I remember our previous encounter with voodoo practices," I told him, "so I have little wish to look further into that matter."

"Nevertheless, she lies at the very heart of this business," replied Holmes. "After considering the matter carefully for the whole of my voyage out here, I am convinced that we have no choice but to interview her at the earliest opportunity."

I looked round at McAdam, who had been standing beside the door all this time, listening to our conversation. "Can you arrange for us to visit Mama Moon, Sergeant?"

"Of course, sir. When would you like to meet her?"

I glanced at Holmes. "Today?"

"Capital!" declared Holmes.

We found Mama Moon in her small and humble home on the edge of the city. As we entered the room where she was sitting, I could smell something in the air akin to incense. Following McAdam's lead, Holmes and I sat down on the carpet spread out across the earthen floor. I was the one who struggled the most to sit down with any dignity.

The priestess was seated upon a cushion, with her keen eyes studying the three of us carefully. I had a distinct impression that Holmes was studying her every bit as closely.

"Welcome, gentlemen," said the priestess.

I began. "Thank you for agreeing to see us, Mama Moon. We have already met. I am Inspector Baynes of the Surrey County Constabulary. You know Sergeant McAdam. And this is Mr. Sherlock Holmes, a private consulting detective from England."

“The man from my dreams,” she said mysteriously, and then burst into strident laughter, as though to cover her embarrassment. “I am always happy to help the police with their investigations.”

“But I am here purely on holiday,” Holmes pointed out.

“Either way, you are here.”

Holmes watched the priestess like a hawk. “I see from your hands that you are not as ancient as you pretend.”

Mama Moon smiled, intrigued by the man in front of her.

“You appeared here,” he continued, “as if out of the blue, but long enough ago for the people to have come to accept and revere you. Your gown is one object that you brought with you. It is worn, and almost threadbare, but it is still important to you.”

The priestess nodded slowly.

“From the snake-decorated charm around your neck,” continued Holmes, “I would suggest that you came originally from Haiti.”

She chuckled.

Holmes hadn’t finished yet. “I see from your bare feet, Mama Moon, that you value your connection with the earth.”

“Many people here go barefooted.”

“But with you it is deliberate. You are particularly aware of everything that happens in Bridgetown.”

“I like this man,” said Mama Moon, her broad grin showing that his reading of her had been close to the truth. “We could learn a great deal from each other, Mr. Holmes.”

Holmes shrugged. “I merely observe what others fail to notice.”

“But you seem to know a great deal about my business.”

“Baynes and I once worked together on an investigation which involved voodoo.”

I nodded. “No doubt the very reason that Mr. Holmes recommended me for this particular case.”

“Since then,” continued Holmes, “I have made a study of its beliefs and practices.”

Mama Moon turned her piercing black eyes onto me. “This is all very interesting, but how exactly may I help you, Inspector?”

“Tell us where we can find Jason Fairworthy-Smith.”

The priestess sat back and laughed. “And you think I know where he is?”

“I know you do.”

“We have other matters to discuss first.” Mama Moon leaned over a small, low table standing between us and lifted the covering cloth.

Now revealed on the table in front of us, I saw a scattering of flower petals, a garlic clove, and four wax dolls, each approximately the size of a man’s hand. The sight made me shudder.

Looking at me, the priestess pointed to the first one. “Who is this?”

I looked more closely. The figure was slightly plumper than the others, and wore a very small hat, made out of woven grasses. I gasped. “That must be me.”

“And how do you feel about that figure?”

“Sympathetic.”

“And your wishes for this person?”

“I hope he returns home safely.”

The priestess pointed to the next doll in line. This was longer and thinner than the others, and had a small button sewn to the middle of its chest. “And this one?”

“I can only imagine it to be Mr. Holmes,” said I, looking up at her. “Does that button have anything to do with him?”

“Indeed, it does,” interposed Holmes. “A man pushed past me in the crowd on the waterfront, and I realized a moment later that one of my buttons was missing. The man had apparently cut it off with a knife – obviously, a man in our hostess's employ. This has clearly all been planned."

"And how do you feel about this figure?" Mama Moon asked me.

"I have great respect for him, as a wise and extremely competent detective."

"And your wishes for him?"

"That he also returns home safely."

The priestess nodded, and pointed to the next figure. This one had a few strands of ginger hair adhering to its face, like a stylized moustache, and a tiny simulation of a monocle.

"Without a doubt, that has to be Jason Fairworthy-Smith."

"And how do you feel about Mr. Fairworthy-Smith?"

"Nothing personal, apart from the pain he put me through when he shot me."

"And your wishes for him?"

"That he accompanies me back to England to stand trial. He is a crook and a fraudster, and he needs to answer for his crimes."

"One way or another?"

"Perhaps."

The painful silence which followed was broken when Holmes interjected, "The tale is only half-told, Mama Moon. Pray continue."

The priestess pointed to the fourth wax figure. It wore a tiny brown jacket. "And this man?"

"That has to be Mordred Scarrington. A dangerous man."

"And how do you feel about him?"

"I have no love for the man. He tried to kill me twice while we were on the boat. And Fairworthy-Smith believes he has come to Barbados in order to kill him."

"And your wishes for him?"

"I wish he would leave us all in peace."

Mama Moon sat back, and looked around at us with wise and knowing eyes. “Permit me to explain. Mr. Fairworthy-Smith came to this island during the second half of last year. Without giving any details, he told me he was on the run, and he asked me to afford him my personal protection. I agreed. Then, at the turn of the year, I offered a sacrifice on behalf of Fairworthy-Smith. The gods told me that two men were coming to the island in order to find Fairworthy-Smith. One was coming to kill him. The other to take him away. The actions of both men would result in his death.”

I replied, “As I told you, I have no personal hatred for the man. It is simply my job to take him back to stand trial.”

“When you both arrived in Bridgetown, I arranged for Mr. Fairworthy-Smith to fake his own death. Poisoned, as though by ingesting Manchineel fruit. I used a combination of medical gas, and the injection of a combination of drugs found in nature, in order to simulate death. Which was good enough to convince Dr. Monteith to issue a death certificate.”

“I already had my doubts,” I told her. “I could find no sign of *rigor mortis* on the body, but I did notice marks on his face which I later identified as having been made by an anesthetist's mask. I also noticed the puncture mark made by that needle in his arm. At the same time, I found a piece of gravel on the floor, which had most likely come from the pathway outside the hospital. That suggested some equipment had been brought to the site from the surgical department. It must have been an extremely risky business.”

“There was no risk to him whatsoever,” said the priestess. “We took him back to the hospital, and brought about a rapid and safe return to life.”

“Then came the cremation on the beach,” I continued. “We never saw the body, but I now believe it to have been a freshly slaughtered pig.”

"It also failed to convince Scarrington," said Mama Moon. "Hence his attempt to flush Fairworthy-Smith out by burning down the house where he had taken refuge."

"And that meeting at Prospect?"

"Once again, we had to convince both you and Scarrington that he was dead."

"So, he shot me, and I fired directly into his chest. I thought he was dead that time, but then I discovered I had been using black cartridges."

"It was easy enough for me to slip into your room and exchange them for your real bullets."

"And the blood that soaked his chest?"

"A bag of pig's blood, which he could burst easily enough to simulate a gunshot wound."

"And you placed the chicken feather on my pillow."

"That as well."

Holmes had been listening intently. "Now, with Jason Fairworthy-Smith hiding in fear of his life," said he, "and with Mordred Scarrington running riot in Bridgetown, we need to bring this matter to a rapid conclusion."

"The matter is in hand, Mr. Holmes," said the priestess.

"I have no doubts that it is," replied Holmes, "but we need to find Fairworthy-Smith. Am I correct in believing that he is hiding here is this building?"

She nodded. "I promised to keep him safe, and this has to be the safest place on the island. Scarrington has been uttering threats against my life, but none of his cronies dare raise a hand to threaten my safety, nor that of anyone in my household. They are all too fearful of the powers they believe I possess."

Holmes stood up, and call out, "Jason Fairworthy-Smith, come out of there, and face us like a man."

The curtain behind the priestess parted, and Fairworthy-Smith himself stepped into the room. He appeared a mere shadow of the man I had first met in my hotel room. His face had grown thin, his monocle making him look even more pitiable, and his skin appeared almost transparent. "You are two very clever men," he told us. "But I can assure you, once again, that I shall never return to England."

"Perhaps," replied Holmes. "But we shall see."

Mama Moon had the final word. As we turned to go, leaving Fairworthy-Smith in the care of the priestess, we heard her say, "All four of you gentlemen, remember: You only live thrice."

"But you have miscounted," I told her. "Including the fire, Fairworthy-Smith has already died three times, so to speak."

"Not at all," she told me. "They burned down the wrong house."

"Superstitious nonsense," I opined as we made our way outside.

"Agreed," replied Holmes. "But the power of superstition lies in the fact that people believe it."

That evening, Holmes and I enjoyed a meal of local foods, and retired to bed early. During the night, I was roused by the sound of a loud and blood-curdling shriek coming from somewhere outside.

The rays of the early morning sun revealed the dead body of Mordred Scarrington lying in the market place. He had a spear protruding from the center of his chest.

"I recognize that spear," I told Holmes, as we joined the growing crowd gathered around that gruesome spectacle. "It looks like one of the ancient Arawak spears I saw in the museum at Codrington College. I am sure they will confirm it as one of theirs."

Holmes knelt down and examined the body, still soaked with the man's life-blood. "Hello, what have we here?" he asked, carefully removing something clutched in the man's hand.

"It looks like one of those wax figures Mama Moon showed us."

"The one you identified as representing Scarrington himself. The one you had strong feelings against. The man who now lies dead before us."

I looked more carefully at the figure and felt shaken by the implications of my expressed feelings. "Do you think I was responsible for his death?"

"In view of the bitterness he has been stirring up here in Bridgetown, I should have thought Scarrington was entirely responsible for his own demise," said Holmes.

"The police will have to deal with this."

"Quite. But forces are at work here which are beyond the reach or reason of even the island's police force."

When the police arrived, we told them all we knew about the incident, and left them to secure the scene. The time had come for us to reconsider our own situation.

"We still have to arrest Fairworthy-Smith," I reminded Holmes.

"True, but I suggest you forget about him for the time being," he replied. "Our man is as secure now as he would be in any prison. However, I believe his villa is now vacant once more. Perhaps we could use that as a base for exploring the many delights of the island."

The short break improved the health of both of us, but the day of our departure quickly arrived, and, with our berths booked on the next steamer back to England, we made our farewells.

"What about Fairworthy-Smith?" I again asked Holmes. "I still need to secure his arrest."

"That matter is in hand," said Holmes. "Just make sure you board the steamer as planned. With Scarrington dead, Fairworthy-Smith will find it impossible to resist the temptation to venture outside and watch you depart."

"And yourself?"

"I have arranged for the ship's captain to heave-to a few miles along the coast. I shall accompany Sergeant McAdam and his men as they arrest Fairworthy-Smith, and bring him on board the steamer. By force if necessary."

As things turned out, far from resisting arrest, Fairworthy-Smith surrendered without a struggle, finally resigning himself to the inevitable. I bade farewell to my Barbadian sergeant and placed my prisoner in a locked cabin, with a member of the steamer's staff alternating with me on guard outside. Throughout the voyage, I made sure Fairworthy-Smith had all he needed, apart from his freedom.

Our voyage was uneventful, until we reached the Western Approaches and entered the English Channel. I wanted to make sure my prisoner was ready for disembarkation, but when I unlocked the door, I found the cabin empty. Fairworthy-Smith had certainly been there when I checked on him the night before. But since then, nobody had seen him, and even the man on guard outside the door was astounded to learn that his charge had gone missing.

"Everyone on board has been interviewed," I reported to Holmes, "and a search has been made of the entire ship. The crew discovered nothing unusual. No blood. Nobody who ought not to be here. But there is still no trace of our missing man. He has simply disappeared. Along with his monocle."

Whilst I was distraught at losing my prisoner, Sherlock Holmes had no strong feelings about the matter. "Fairworthy-Smith knew he was coming home to face death at the hands of those who had lost money through his fraudulent schemes. They would be eager to finish off the job that Scarrington so evidently failed to accomplish."

"Perhaps his enemies reached out to him even before he landed."

"Or possibly it was his fear of them," said Holmes. "Indeed, the question of what happened here offers a vast scope for speculation. But the only plausible explanation has to be the most simple."

"That somebody released him during the night, and allowed him to leap overboard to his certain death in the ocean."

"Exactly," replied Holmes.

"Thank you, Mr. Holmes. We appear to have reached the solution that I can report to my Superintendent."

"At least you have the man's death certificate."

I gave a wry smile. "Even if it is for the wrong death."

I stood with Holmes one final time in Fairworthy-Smith's untouched and vacant cabin. Although I could see nothing to occupy my attention, Holmes was smoking his pipe, deep in contemplation of the scene before him.

After a few moments, he crouched down, and drew closer to the pillow still neatly occupying the head-end of the bunk. In an instant, Holmes whipped the pillow from its place.

"A-ha!" he declared, as he indicated two objects hidden beneath.

I approached the bunk. "What have you found, Mr. Holmes?"

"A wax figure," declared my companion. "I believe it to be another of those we saw when we visited the priestess. It bears a crude resemblance to our missing prisoner."

"But who left it here? Smith, or somebody else?"

"That hardly matters now," replied Holmes mysteriously. He passed me an envelope. "And this is for you."

I noticed it bore my name, so I opened the envelope, and tipped out the contents into the palm of my hand.

Holmes watched me. "I believe this spells the conclusion to our case, Baynes. Maybe not to our complete satisfaction, but neat enough all the same."

The words of Mama Moon echoed in my mind. "*Remember, you only live thrice*."

It now seemed clear to me that, however he had met his end, Fairworthy-Smith had used up his allotted number of lives. In my hand, I now looked down at the priestess's parting gift to me: Three chicken feathers.

## The Whitehaven Ransom
by Robert V. Stapleton

"Remind me, Watson," said my friend Sherlock Holmes as he looked forlornly up at the lowering sky and around at the cold, gray water. "What exactly are we doing here?"

The exhausting train journey from Euston, via Penrith, had brought us eventually to the small Cumberland market town of Keswick. From there, we had transferred to an open steam launch at the lakeside landing stages, for a journey of only a couple of miles along that most delightful member of the family of English Lakes known as Derwentwater.

"You have had a demanding few months," I replied. "Your work has taken its toll upon your health, and it is my decided opinion that you need time away from the big city. So when the opportunity arose of spending a few days here among the English Lakes, it seemed too good a chance to dismiss."

"And we are to spend a week with your friend, Bushy Barnswick, I believe," added Holmes, without much enthusiasm.

"That is indeed the intention," I replied. "And he's not such a bad chap, in spite of his appearance. As I told you, I know this fellow through my club. He told me he had recently acquired a small property on the shores of Derwentwater. He is unattached, with no family to worry about, or indeed to help him enjoy his good fortune. As a result, he has been kind enough to invite us both to join him here. I know that your list of appointments will allow for a brief absence from Baker Street, and I also have been fortunate enough to free myself from the demands and duties of daily life – at least for a short time."

I was aware that Holmes, as a student of crime, would be lost without a mystery to solve, but I also realized that we both needed a holiday.

I spread my hands to encompass the lake and its surrounding countryside. "A few days in a place of such magnificence can only bring much needed peace to the frayed human soul – both yours and mine."

The man at the wheel, who had remained quiet until now, removed the pipe from his mouth and pointed the stem toward the hills. "You can see Skiddaw towering behind us. He's got his hat on today. Cloud-cover. So we can expect rain before the night's out."

I looked round at the mountain, whilst Holmes seemed to pay little attention.

"Beyond that island ahead of us, you can see Borrowdale," our guide continued. "A green valley, stretching out into the hills. But we're heading to Cat Bells."

Rolling hills rose up in front of us.

"Popular walking country," said the boatman.

"In the right weather," I added.

The man chuckled, and again drew deeply on his pipe. "You'll not have much longer to wait, gentlemen," he added, as he turned the bows of the launch a few degrees to starboard. "Badger's Piece is coming up presently."

As I watched, I noticed the gray slate roof and whitewashed walls of a small but stately building gradually appear above the trees bordering the lakeside now directly ahead of us. I also noticed a small wooden landing-stage, lying below a narrow opening among the foliage. I also recognized a familiar figure standing on this quayside. Although dressed now in tweeds and a floppy hat, rather than the more usual bowler-hat and dark suit, Archibald Barnswick, known to his friends and creditors alike as

"Bushy" in view of his splendid beard, was unmistakable in appearance.

Bushy Barnswick waved and called out his greeting as we approached. The moment the launch touched land, he helped us to disembark, together with our various items of baggage.

"Thank you, Frank," said our host, passing our helmsman a handful of coins.

"No extra for the commentary on the way," added Frank with a chuckle, before he turned the launch around and headed back toward Keswick. And civilization.

Our host seemed delighted to receive us. "Greetings, gentlemen. Welcome to Badger's Piece. I only took possession of the property a couple of weeks ago, so the place is all quite new to me. I bought the house and land from an elderly local man who, unfortunately, had allowed the place to deteriorate somewhat. At the same time, I also acquired an additional parcel of land farther along the lakeside. Nobody else wanted that land, so I picked it up for a mere pittance."

"You are indeed a fortunate man," I replied.

"As I said, the whole place needs renovating, but you are very welcome to join me here for a few days. You are in fact my very first visitors."

Holmes and I followed Bushy through the foliage, which threatened to block our way, and up a slight slope, until we found ourselves standing outside the modestly sized building I had seen earlier, constructed on rising ground.

As we bundled into the entrance hall, we were met by a large woman with an imposing presence. She looked us over for a moment.

"This is Mrs. Henderson, the housekeeper," Bushy explained.

"Good afternoon, gentlemen," said she, with a nod. It seemed that we had been accepted. "I hope you will enjoy your stay here. If there's anything you need, then please let me know."

"We also have a first rate cook, and an efficient kitchen-*cum*-house maid, who helps with many of the chores around the place."

The door opened, and a man stepped in. He was of medium height, thin in build, with a ruddy face and strong, wiry arms.

"This is Wilbert," said Bushy. "Our estate manager."

"Also general workhorse and slave," said Wilbert with a warmhearted chuckle. "As Mrs. Henderson says, let her know whatever you want doing, and she'll get me to do it." So saying, he picked up our luggage and led the way upstairs.

"I've given you the two front rooms," said Bushy. "You'll find a jug of hot water in both of them, so refresh yourselves and join me down here again for supper."

After the evening meal, we sat talking as the soft summer shades of evening fell across the property and the lake.

"Mrs. Henderson tells me we are due for a soaking tonight," said Bushy. "A storm is brewing out in the hills."

The rattling of rain on roof and window-pane kept me awake during the small hours of the night, but I emerged the following morning remarkably refreshed from my first night at Badger's Piece. On my way, I passed the maid in the corridor who was carrying a dustpan and brush.

The girl stopped. "I hope you'll excuse me for saying so, sir."

"Yes, Libby?"

"If you're thinking of going down to the lake in search of that old boathouse, please be very careful."

"Why do you say that?"

"Well, it's a dangerous part of the lakeside. Mrs. Henderson tells everyone that bad things happen to people who go down there. And I wouldn't want any harm to come to you, Dr. Watson."

"Neither would I," I replied. "And thank you for the warning, Libby. But have no fear. I shall be extremely careful."

With her face still displaying acute anxiety, the girl looked back over her shoulder, as though expecting danger, and hurried on her way

A moment later, I stepped outside and made my way down to the lakeside. From the landing stage, I could see the effects of the morning breeze as it whisked away a thin mist that had settled upon the lake following the storm. Then I noticed something emerging through the filaments of haze. A small gaff-rigged sailboat, her brown sails filling with the zephyr. The early morning sun, now glinting on the water, lent an almost magical touch to the entire scene

"He is watching us," came a voice from somewhere behind me.

I turned and found Sherlock Holmes, sitting on a fallen tree trunk, smoking his pre-breakfast pipe. His gaunt face and piercing eyes had regained some of their normal luster.

"The man in that boat has been tacking backwards and forwards across the lake for the last half-hour. He is definitely keeping his eye on this place."

"But who is he?"

"I have no idea, but we shall find out before we leave. Anyway, we must assume that he means us no harm."

Together we made our way back to the house, where we found that the cook had already prepared our breakfast

Bushy appeared as we were finishing off our second jug of breakfast coffee.

"Gentlemen," he declared. "As I told you yesterday, I've come into possession of an additional stretch of land down beside the lake. I'm in need of a boathouse, and this parcel of land possesses one. At least, it's marked so on the map that came with the ownership documents. Would you care to accompany me as I go to investigate?"

We told him that we would be delighted to do so.

Less delighted was Wilbert, the estate manager. When asked to accompany us, he turned extremely awkward.

"I'm not sure I would like to come with you, sir," he declared. "That additional plot of land you acquired lies under a curse."

"A curse? Don't be ridiculous, man. Whatever makes you say that?"

"It's just a local legend, sir."

"Nothing but hearsay."

"Perhaps, sir. But people believe it."

"Yes, mostly ignorant and superstitious people."

"That's as may be, sir, but I'm prepared to bet you acquired that land at a remarkably low price."

"True enough."

"And did you ever ask yourself why that was?"

"Indeed I did, and I told myself that its generous price was down to its isolated location on the shore of the lake. If the low sale price is the result of gossip by those loose-lipped and small-brained old men who frequent that public house in Grange, then I for one will not complain about obtaining a bargain. But I would like you to come along with us this morning, Wilbert."

Still muttering his reluctance, and with a face like thunder, Wilbert joined us as Bushy led the way down to the lakeside, and then continued south along the shoreline. Here we found the foliage growing more densely, and the going becoming more difficult. Overhead foliage blocked out much of the sunlight, and cast the place into a deep gloom. Both Holmes and I were glad that we had brought our stout walking sticks as we forced our way between tangled weeds and overhanging branches.

"Wilbert."

"Yes, Mr. Barnswick?"

"I should like you to organize a gang of men to work on thinning out the foliage along here. Cut back some of the trees, and allow plenty of light to penetrate this dark hole."

"That might not be easy, sir."

"The local lead mines are mostly worked out now, so there must be men in the area who would value a job like this."

"I shall make inquiries, sir."

"I suppose they will all be frightened of the curse, as well."

"There is no denying that, Mr. Barnswick."

Holmes, who had been strangely silent until now, cut in, "When did those stories of the curse begin?"

Wilbert pursed his lips. "Difficult to tell, Mr. Holmes. Perhaps some thirty-odd years ago now, as far as I recall."

"And news of the curse became current at the same time as the disappearance of a local man."

"Why, yes. I seem to remember it was, sir. But however did you know that?"

"It seemed a reasonable deduction to make. Somebody goes missing, for no discernible reason, and people put it down to a curse. Such gossip is always rich breeding ground for idle speculation. There may even be those who wish to benefit from such fears."

By now we had reached the remains of some small building. With a few worked stone blocks lying in a tumble-down fashion around a small inlet of stagnant water, the place looked to have been neglected for very many years.

Bushy stopped, pulled his map from his pocket, and consulted it carefully. "This must be the remains of the old boathouse," he declared, nodding toward the ruins.

The estate manager shrugged. "Must be, sir."

I followed Holmes as he stepped closer to the dilapidated building.

"The roof fell in a long time ago," he declared, examining the surrounding rubble, "and the wooden part of the walls has mostly rotted away. But those stone blocks could provide a stable foundation for it to be rebuilt."

"Then it can indeed by repaired?" asked Bushy.

Wilbert gave an embarrassed cough. "If you want a gang of men to work on this, you're going to have to pay them danger money, Mr. Barnswick."

Before our host could think of a suitable repost, Holmes crouched down and reached his hand into the water that still remained in the basin of the silted-up boathouse. "I can feel something down there," he said grimly, as he laid aside his hat and cape. "A boat of some sort. Old and waterlogged. And I think there is something still inside the boat."

Bushy leaned closer, whilst Wilbert and I watched with deep and growing fascination.

As Holmes and Bushy together pulled on the gunnels which lay just below the surface of the water, we saw the boat begin to rise from the murky depths. "This is far too heavy for us to lift on our own," declared Holmes. "The boat is full of silt, making it feel as heavy as a concrete block."

"And the harder you pull, the more likely it is for the boat to fall apart," cautioned Wilbert. "Then you'll lose whatever is in there."

"The far end of the boathouse has a slope," observed Holmes. "Perhaps the boat might survive being dragged up there."

The estate manager and I added our own strength, and soon we had the boat pulled up the gradient, where it lay above the level of the water.

"Now we need to clear away the silt," said Holmes.

"I know you don't like this place, Wilbert," said Bushy Barnswick. "But we need a bucket. See what you can find back at the house."

With the use of a zinc bucket and water from the lake, we cleared away much of the silt that had built up over the years inside the boat.

I was holding the bucket when I noticed something white in the subdued daylight filtering through the undergrowth.

Bushy gasped, whilst Wilbert gave a groan that came from deep within him.

I stood dumbfounded.

"A skeleton," declared Holmes. "I can hardly say that I'm surprised."

"You thought we might find a body here?" asked Bushy.

"A disused boathouse, the story of a curse, and a missing man. The possibility of a body did seem a reasonable conclusion to make."

As I continued to pour on water, and clear away the surrounding silt, I could see more and more the skull, its white sheen stained by the passage of time and the minerals in the water.

"Leave it, gentlemen," said Bushy, as he stood back and surveyed the gruesome scene. "This has now become a police matter. And they will need to call in the Police Surgeon to see this."

"Certainly," said Holmes. "But first, allow us to make any initial conclusions we can from what is evident."

"But what is evident?"

"Watson, what can you make of our skeleton?"

I stooped to my task and examined the remains. "The skeleton is definitely that of a man. Perhaps in his mid-twenties, judging by the good condition of the teeth. Tall. Nearly six foot in height. Well-built, without being obviously obese. No sign of disease. A good specimen of a man. But I can find no injury that might account for his death."

Holmes now stooped down to examine the remains. "As you say, Watson, there is no sign of anything that might account for his death. But what can we find beneath the bones?" He reached into the silt still covering the bottom of the boat, pulled back his hand, and opened it to reveal four coins. "Two pennies, one farthing, and a florin. They must have fallen out of his pockets when he was placed here. The man was therefore clearly not killed in the course of a robbery. Also, these aren't the coins one might expect to find in the pocket of a working man. Very little remains of his clothing, so it must all have rotted away over the years, but what remains of his boots suggests that they must have cost him a pretty penny."

"He must have been here for at least thirty years," I opined.

"Let us take a closer look at these coins," suggested Holmes. "The three copper coins are dated to the 1840's, but the florin looks new and is dated 1856. We can reasonably conclude that he died shortly after that date."

Holmes thrust his hand once more beneath the silt, directly under the center of the skeleton. This time, he pulled out a small, silver object, which glinted even in this subdued daylight.

"Another coin?"

"No. A small key." Holmes took out his lens, and examined it. "Interesting."

"What is?"

Holmes passed me the key and his lens. I looked carefully. On one side it had a number: "*24*", whilst on the reverse it showed a crest that I didn't recognize.

I handed them back to Holmes.

"Now to work, gentlemen," said he. "Mr. Barnswick, as you said, you need to contact the police in Keswick and arrange for a Police Surgeon to visit."

"That I can easily do," replied Bushy. "Wilbert, please organize a gang to clear away this undergrowth and begin work on repairing the boathouse as soon as the Police Surgeon gives permission for us to move the body. And you, Mr. Holmes – what will you do?"

"Watson and I must try to identify this man. We know that he was tall, reasonably well off, probably not a working man, and disappeared some thirty years ago. Somebody in Keswick must know something about him. They might even furnish us with a name."

"Very well, Mr. Holmes," said Bushy. "Until we can rebuild the boathouse and acquire our own form of water transport, we have no choice but to travel into town by road."

The undulating journey along the western shore of Derwentwater made me realize the value of water transport in that rough and rugged terrain.

From Keswick market square, Holmes led the way to the bar of one of the hotels located in the center of town and asked the barman for permission to make an announcement to those present.

Given permission, and from his place standing at the bar, Holmes looked around at the people who occupied the room. "Gentlemen," he began. "We are trying to identify somebody who went missing some thirty years ago. A man standing six foot in height. Not a working man, but rugged and in good health. Can anyone here help us identify this man?"

"Thirty years ago?" came a voice from the far end.

"Or thereabouts."

"Why? Have you discovered a body?"

"Just a few remains."

"I remember somebody going missing back then," said the same man.

Holmes ordered the man a drink and we joined him at his place beside the empty hearth. "Can you tell us anything more?"

The old man rubbed his chin and screwed up his eyes. "A medical man – a doctor, I think he was. Aye, that's right. He was here working with a medical practice in those days."

"Where was the practice based?"

"A big house at the far end of Market Street." The man chuckled. "But after thirty years, the doctor in charge will be long gone from there now."

Another voice added, "That was in the days when Dr. Letherholm was in charge of the practice. He retired years ago. The last I heard, he had gone to live in a nursing home, but I couldn't tell you which one."

The current secretary at the doctor's surgery pointed us in the right direction, and by early afternoon we found ourselves at a nursing home for elderly patients, situated on the edge of the town.

One of the nurses took us to a residents' lounge where we found a frail and aging man, sitting on a wicker chair, looking out at the garden.

"Dr. Letherholm?" asked Holmes.

"Indeed, sir," replied the elderly man as he looked up.

"My name is Sherlock Holmes. I am a consulting detective."

"Then you're a little out of your territory here, Mr. Holmes."

"I am in the area for a few days' holiday, together with my friend here, Dr. John Watson. We are staying at Badger's Piece, along Derwentwater."

"In that case, welcome, gentlemen. How may I help you?"

"We would like to talk to you about a former colleague of yours."

"Really? Please take a seat, both of you. Now, which one of my colleagues do you have in mind?"

"We understand that this man worked with you some thirty years ago. He was tall, and in his mid-to-late-twenties. He disappeared, apparently for no clear reason, but so far we haven't been able to discover the man's name."

The elderly doctor's face clouded over with concentration, and then lit up again. "You must mean Mortimer Chadwickson. Yes, I remember Mort. And it's true – he disappeared without giving anyone any reason. The gossips believed that he'd run away."

"Why might he do that?"

"In those days, a family known as the Harnecues terrorized the area. They were quite a rough load of villains. Amongst many other things, they had been involved in smuggling operations between the west coast and the towns and villages of north Cumberland."

"And you think Dr. Chadwickson was intimidated by them?"

Dr. Letherholm looked out of the window, but his gaze was far away, in another time.

"Mort joined me as a junior partner in the mid-1850s. He was a good and steady worker, and grew to be well respected by the people we served. Then a medical practice along the coast, at Whitehaven, asked us to help out. Their doctor had been taken ill. Anyway, I agreed to allow Mort Chadwickson to go there as *locum*, until things had settled down again. He returned after a couple of weeks a changed man. He had a hunted look in his eyes, and seemed to be on the lookout for somebody following him. He told me he was terrified of the Harnecues catching up with him. And with him being such a notable figure, there was every chance that they would do just that. I asked him what had occurred in Whitehaven, but he had little inclination to tell me, except that he had been called to the bedside of a dying woman."

"Can you tell us the name of this woman?"

Dr. Letherholm shook his head. "If he told me, then I cannot remember after all these years. But I do remember him saying that it was a most unusual visit."

"We would be most grateful if you could tell us more," said Holmes, quietly but firmly.

"I seem to remember that the lady, who was lying on her deathbed, informed Chadwickson that the town had entrusted her mother with something valuable. The dying woman muttered something about a ransom, and that it was hidden behind a loose brick in her kitchen chimney. She was fearful that, after her death, some local rogues might get their hands on this treasure, and she wanted him to take it from its hiding place and keep it somewhere secure."

"And did he do that?"

"Oh, I think so. But I'm sure that, if he did take the treasure, Chadwickson would never have kept it for himself, let alone run away with it. He wasn't that sort of man. But shortly after that, he vanished altogether."

"We are a long way from solving the mystery, Dr. Letherholm," replied Holmes, "but we have discovered some human remains which are of a man such as I described. And now, thanks to your help, we might have a name."

"We reported Chadwickson's disappearance to the police," said the doctor, "but they could find no trace of him. It was a mystery, Mr. Holmes, and has remained so until this day. But now you're suggesting that my former colleague somehow came to a tragic end. It seems to me that here is a case to be solved, by a detective such as yourself. It also seems upon reflection that the mention of a 'ransom' has to be central to the solving of this mystery."

"I feel sure that you're right, Doctor," said Holmes, standing up to take his leave. "In the meantime, we must bid you farewell. My colleague and I have much to attend to. And be assured, we shall certainly let you know the outcome of our investigations."

Holmes and I returned to the market square, wondering how we would make our way back to Badger's Piece, but we had no need for concern on that score, as we spotted the animated figure of Bushy Barnswick bowling towards us at speed.

"I am extremely glad to have found you, gentlemen," he told us. "The Police Surgeon from Carlisle has arrived, together with an Inspector Armadale of the county police. A sergeant from the local force is arranging for Frank to take us all back in his steam launch. As you have already discovered, the boat is more comfortable than the trackway, so I can let Wilbert take the carriage back by road, whilst we go by water."

It was difficult at first to determine which was the surgeon and which the detective, since the former was a robust, alert-looking man, whilst the policeman was short in stature and round in figure. In the presence of these two heavyweights, the local sergeant kept a low profile, speaking only in mono-syllables when replying to the occasional question put to him by his superiors.

During the short boat journey down the lake, we discussed our observations, together with the day's conclusions.

"Dr. Mortimer Chadwickson?" muttered Inspector Armadale, rubbing his chin in thoughtful contemplation. "It doesn't ring a bell with me. And, after all, you have no conclusive evidence that this is the man you discovered, do you, Mr. Holmes?"

"That is quite correct, Inspector," returned Holmes, "but it seems highly likely to be the man.

"And the cause of death," continued the Police Surgeon. "You say you could determine no sign of violence or other injury that might account for the man's death."

"That is correct, Doctor. But we did manage to discover some coins associated with the body, and found that they dated the death to no earlier than 1856."

"But again, that is inconclusive."

"Quite."

"In that case, we will have to make our separate examination of the body and arrive at our own opinions. We require facts, Mr. Holmes, not speculation."

"I would hope that the two would complement each other."

We arrived at the landing stage directly below the house at Badger's Piece, and Bushy led the way through the foliage toward the remains of the old boathouse. Whilst the sergeant remained with us in the background, the surgeon and the detective began their examination of the skeleton and the scene adjacent to it.

"We have presented the bones as clearly as possible," said Bushy, "without moving them in any way."

The Police Surgeon grunted as he continued his painstaking examination. "An adult male, approximately six feet in height, who appears to have enjoyed a healthy life. As you told us before, Mr. Holmes, there is no evidence of foul play. But the bones have clearly been here for many years."

"I would concur with the dating," added the inspector, juggling the coins we had left piled on the stonework. "Approximately thirty years or so. Again, as Mr. Holmes has already so helpfully ascertained."

"Plenty of time for the bones to have been stripped bare," added the Police Surgeon.

"But there is no way of identifying the unfortunate man," said the inspector.

The two men finished their examination of the bones and stood back to confer, before announcing their conclusions.

The Police Surgeon stood to his full height and gave his decision. "Since I can find no obvious cause of death in this case, I'm obliged to consider it a suspicious death, and I must therefore refer the matter to the Coroner. In due time, he will contact the family and arrange for them to receive the body."

"This is clearly an old case, gentlemen," said the inspector. "But no less important for that fact. It therefore requires dogged and persistent police work." He turned to the sergeant. "I think we can safely leave the matter in the hands of the local police to trace the family and arrange for a proper disposal of the remains. This might be Dr. Chadwickson, or maybe not. We can only judge by the evidence presented to us."

The police sergeant nodded. "Right you are, sir. We'll get on to it straightaway."

Holmes stepped forward, holding up the key. "One more thing, Inspector. We did come across this small key, hidden among the silt at the bottom of the boat."

The police inspector took the key and examined it. "What makes you think it has anything to do with the deceased?"

"Merely the location."

"And what kind of lock might this key fit?"

"I have no idea, Inspector. I was hoping you might be able to enlighten us on that matter."

The inspector shook his head and chuckled. "Scotland Yard tells me that you are a man who enjoys looking into a puzzle, Mr. Holmes. Detective work is for professionals, not amateurs. But if you would like to entertain yourself by looking in the significance, if any, of this key, then you are very welcome to waste your time trying."

The inspector handed back the key and then joined his two colleagues as they returned to the steam launch and set off on their return journey back up to the northern end of the lake.

The following day dawned bright, mild and dry, and a gang of workmen arrived at an early hour to begin the work of clearing the area around the boathouse, and with the further intention of restoring the old building to its rightful use. The body had been removed, and Wilbert took both his qualms and his workmen in hand. Before long, the sound of sawing and digging filled the air.

Holmes announced that he had a great deal to think over. He needed to be on his own, free from distraction, so that he could concentrate his attention more fully upon the matter in hand. Giving no indication when he intended to return, he took his pipe and pouch of tobacco and headed onto the slopes of Cat Bells.

I knew my friend well enough to leave him strictly to his own devices, and instead turned my attention to the various jobs that needed doing around the house of Badger's Piece.

After our midday meal, at which Holmes was conspicuous by his absence, Wilbert announced that he'd arranged a fishing trip for us on the lake.

"A man I know at Grange has promised to take us out in his boat this very afternoon," Wilbert explained. "He has even promised to supply us with the rods, nets, and all the bait we shall need."

As promised, the boat met us at the landing stage and took us out a couple of hundred yards from shore. There we sat down to our battle of wits with the fishes of Derwentwater. For the first hour, our piscatorial adversaries proved to be the victors in the struggle.

Even though the sun wasn't shining, the air was clear, and we all had a perfect view of the lake and its surroundings. With the fishing-line floats bobbing idly among the ripples of the surface water, I looked around.

Then I noticed him. "I can see a man over there, on the shoreline."

"Where?" asked Bushy.

"Toward the southern end of the lake."

"Yes, I see him."

"He's been there for at least the last half-hour, and he's been watching us through a telescope. I can occasionally see light reflecting from the lens."

Bushy screwed up his eyes. "Are you sure?"

"Oh, yes. There is no doubt about it."

Our consideration of the watcher was interrupted by a sharp tug on my fishing line, as the float disappeared below the surface and the rod bent in an arc.

"You've caught yourself something big, Watson!" exclaimed Bushy as everyone in the boat gathered round to offer their assistance.

As I reeled in the fish from its home in the depths of the lake, the boat's owner brought a landing net to bear and soon had the fish on board, where he dispatched it with a fisherman's priest.

"Ugly looking brute," I told Bushy. "I don't like the look of those teeth."

"That, Dr. Watson, is because you have caught yourself a pike," said the boat's owner.

That proved to be my one and only success of the day, but my companions managed to secure a couple of brown trout.

On our return to Badger's Piece, the trout went straight to the kitchen, whilst my pike was dispatched to the taxidermist, and now hangs above the lounge fireplace in Bushy Barnswick's new home. I consider it my thankful offering for his kind hospitality.

I found Holmes, who was in a surprisingly good mood. "How was your day, Watson?

"We have been fishing," I replied. "But a man, standing on the shoreline, was watching us for the whole of our time out on the water."

"Now that is hardly surprising," Holmes replied, with an infuriatingly enigmatic smile.

"And how went your day?"

"I fell into conversation this morning with a fellow walker of the fells," he informed me. "A reverend gentleman, who expressed an interest in limiting the amount of industrial pollution in the area, and in improving the quality of road signs in the county. In return, I impressed upon him the importance of maintaining more generally the quality of the countryside environment, and of safeguarding the beauty of the area for the enjoyment of visitors, the delight of weary souls, and the refreshing of distracted minds. He told me he would give the matter his closest attention."

After supper, Holmes sat back, smiling. "The game is afoot, Watson," said he. "Tomorrow morning, we shall take the train to Whitehaven. The answer to our many questions inevitably lies in that coastal town."

In the middle of the following morning, we alighted from the railway carriage onto the station platform at Whitehaven. We found ourselves in a busy industrial town of elegant Georgian buildings, with the sound and smell of the sea mingling with the scent of coal-dust and the sounds of heavy industry.

"I see that he has come along with us," said Holmes.

"Who?"

"Presumably the same man who was watching you yesterday."

I looked back along the platform and, sure enough, there amongst the crowd was a man who resembled the figure I'd seen on the lakeside.

"Whatever does he want?"

"We shall no doubt find out in due time."

Holmes and I made our way to the center of Whitehaven, and looked around at an unfamiliar townscape.

"What are we looking for?" I asked.

"Oh, do wake up, Watson. A bank, of course."

"In that case, there appears to be one farther along this road."

"Well spotted."

Holmes lingered for a moment in front of the main entrance. "Now do you see it?"

"See what?"

"The crest above the front door."

"Of course. It's the same design we saw on that key. That was a lucky guess on your part."

"Watson!" exclaimed Holmes. "I am disappointed in you. You know better than anyone that I never make guesses."

"Of course. You must have ventured into Keswick yesterday. Doubtless making inquiries."

"All opportunities must be investigated." Holmes smiled indulgently, and led the way inside. "Having found the right place, we now need to speak to the manager."

The bank manager appeared – tall, formally dressed, and sporting a neat mustache.

"Good morning," said my companion. "I am Sherlock Holmes, and this is my friend and colleague, Dr. John Watson."

"And I am Mr. Sheldrake, the manager here. Please come into my office, gentlemen."

"Congratulations on your recent appointment," said Holmes.

"Oh?" The manager raised an eyebrow in surprise. "Thank you, Mr. Holmes."

"The new brass nameplate on your door, and the wood shaving beneath it," explained Holmes.

"Of course."

"Your new responsibility has caused disruption to your family's morning routine," continued Holmes, "forcing you to leave home in a hurry. You were harassed, and were nearly late in arriving today."

Again, an expression of amazement. "All true, but how can you tell?"

"The dog-hair on your coat, and the toast-crumb still on your tie, which neither your wife nor you had time to brush off."

The manager gave an embarrassed cough, brushed his tie, and looked up at us again. "How may I help you, gentlemen?"

“First, Mr. Sheldrake,” began Holmes, “could you please tell me if you recognize the man standing across the street, watching this building?”

The manager looked outside and heaved a sigh. “Oh yes. He’s one of the Harnecue family. They have been involved in all kinds of illegal activities over the years. Has he been bothering you?”

“Not at all, but it is good to have him identified. Now to business. I have two questions to put to you.”

“Pray continue,” said Sheldrake.

Holmes removed Chadwickson’s key from his pocket, and passed it across the mahogany desk to the bank manager. “I believe this is the key to a bank deposit box.”

The bank manager examined the key, and nodded.

“Furthermore, I believe it fits a box currently residing in the vaults of this bank, and that the holder of the key, whomever it is, is allowed to open that box.”

“Again, you are quite correct, Mr. Holmes.” Mr. Sheldrake stood up, searched through the contents of a bookshelf, and returned with an old leather ledger. This he opened, and laid out upon his desk. “Yes. The number on that key corresponds to a deposit made here in 1858, by a man called Chadwickson.”

“Dr. Chadwickson.”

“That was before my time, but our records show that the box hasn’t been opened even once during these last thirty years.”

“Then I should be obliged if we might rectify that situation,” declared Holmes.

“We can certainly do that. But first, you have another question for me.”

“Indeed.” Holmes sat back and riveted the bank manager with his stare. “Can you tell us anything about ‘The Ransom’?”

"This might take some time to explain," the bank manager replied. "Would either of you gentlemen care to partake of refreshments? Tea, perhaps?"

I accepted. Holmes declined.

After his secretary had brought in my tea, the manager sat down and steepled his fingers contemplatively. "In reply to your question, Mr. Holmes, I must first submit you both to a history lesson."

We both settled into our seats.

"You have no doubt heard of the American naval commander, Captain John Paul Jones."

We both nodded.

"Although Scottish by birth, John Paul, who later adopted the name Jones, began his maritime career from this port of Whitehaven. Later, in command of a fleet of enemy ships during the American War of Independence, he wrought havoc amongst the commercial shipping around the shores of Great Britain, culminating in an attack on Whitehaven."

Here was a period of history that I had neglected in my studies.

"On April 17$^{th}$ in the year 1778, John Paul Jones and his squadron appeared out at sea. The Americans were determined to cause devastation in Whitehaven, and to set alight the fleet of more than two-hundred merchant ships in our harbor. If successful, such an act would have caused untold damage to the economy of our town. Even today, the ships in our harbor are mostly constructed of timber, and are vulnerable to fire."

"What cargoes do your ships typically carry?" asked Holmes.

"The town's economy depends mainly upon the export of coal to other areas of industrial activity. The town is built on a coalfield. We even have one colliery designed to resemble a castle, complete with turrets and towers. You can see it standing above the docks. Our industrialists and merchants have a great deal invested in this trade, and in this town."

"As do the people, no doubt."

"True."

Sheldrake looked down at the notes lying upon his desk. "On that particular day, when the people of the town feared the loss of their homes as well as their wealth, the wind came to their rescue, and blew the American fleet right across the Irish Sea, leaving them to cause havoc there instead."

"A fortunate escape," said I.

"Serendipitous, Dr. Watson. But the leaders of the town knew that John Paul Jones and his ships would return as soon as the winds moderated in their favor. Not knowing how long they had to prepare themselves, the merchants decided to organize a ransom to offer the Americans on behalf of the town. They gathered together all the wealth they could muster at such short notice, from poor as well as from rich. This amounted to several thousands of pounds sterling, and they managed to convert this money into cut and polished diamonds. I have no idea how they managed it, or where they found so many gems at such short notice in such a remote area of the country, but, within five days, they had their ransom ready – which was just in time because, in the early hours of April 23rd, John Paul Jones and his men returned to menace Whitehaven."

I sipped my Earl Grey and continued to listen to this tale with rapt attention.

"This time," continued Mr. Sheldrake, "they landed under cover of darkness and began to rampage through the town. But they were badly organized and inexpertly led by Jones's lieutenants. The result was that, before Whitehaven's merchants could arrange to offer the Americans the ransom that they had collected, the people of the town sent the entire landing party packing. True, the invaders did manage to set fire to one of the ships in the harbor, but that was rapidly extinguished."

"The town had another narrow escape," I concluded.

"But I have not yet finished my tale," said the bank manager, now very much into his stride. "The town's people had no guarantee that the American fleet would not return, and ineven greater numbers next time. It was decided to keep the ransom intact, just in case they needed it in the future. They considered keeping it in the vaults of a bank. But, as you can well imagine, the vulnerability of such a scheme lies in securing ownership of the key. Believe me, gentlemen, there were, and still are, plenty of people who have longed to get their hands on those diamonds – thieves, pirates, and smugglers."

"Such as the Harnecues."

"Among others."

Holmes leaned forward. "So the solution was to entrust the ransom to a member of the public who could be relied upon to keep those diamonds secure."

"That's quite correct. The wife of one of our most respected citizens was asked to keep hold of the bag containing the jewels, until further notice." The bank manager once more consulted his notes. "The lady's name was Doris Ferrybridge, and she dwelt in an ordinary house not far from the docks. This lady was well known for her honesty, her compassion, and her philanthropy."

"But the ransom money was never needed," concluded Holmes, "and the bag remained in the care of Mrs. Ferrybridge until the day she died."

"And beyond. With her husband long gone, Doris entrusted the care of the bag to her daughter, until she also died. With no other family to inherit the property, the house was finally demolished. Despite a careful and thorough search of the building, I have to tell you, gentlemen, those diamonds were never found."

"Unless we conclude that somebody moved them beforehand," I interrupted.

"My thoughts exactly, Dr. Watson," said Mr. Sheldrake. "Unless somebody relocated the gems to the safety deposit box here in the vaults of my bank."

"Where they have remained undisturbed for the past thirty years."

"There is only one way to be certain of the matter, Mr. Sheldrake," said Holmes. "We need to go down to the vaults and open that box."

"But remember, Mr. Holmes," Mr. Sheldrake cautioned him. "Those diamonds belong to the people of this town."

"The ownership of whatever we discover in that box would have to be determined by a court of law, Mr. Sheldrake."

The bank manager stood up. "Of course you're right, Mr. Holmes. But I hope that it will be used to benefit the people of this town. Now, gentlemen, please follow me."

Holmes and I followed the bank manager down into the vaults of the bank. The subterranean room smelt musty and felt oppressive, but I soon forgot my discomfort as our attention was directed to the rows of metal boxes which lined the vault. Mr. Sheldrake drew one out and placed it on the table in the middle of the room.

"Number twenty-four."

Holmes nodded. "That is the number on the key. We can only assume that it fits this lock."

"Then I shall leave you in peace, gentlemen," said the bank manager. "Call me if you come across any problem, or when you have finished in here."

As the bank manager closed the door, Holmes approached the box on the table, inserted the key, and turned the lock without difficulty. The lid groaned slightly as he lifted it, and then we were able to examine the contents of the deposit box. All that I could see was a black leather bag, sewn securely shut across the top by a row of leather stitches. Holmes lifted the bag, and felt its weight. Then he slipped it into his pocket.

"Hmm."

"Is that all you can say, Holmes? Aren't you going to open it up and check the contents?"

"There is absolutely no need, my dear fellow. I know exactly what this bag contains."

"But I should like to see."

"Patience, Watson."

"I don't mind acting as your cab service," said Frank as we alighted from his steam launch at Bushy Barnswick's landing stage. "It's always a pleasure doing business with friends of Mr. Barnswick – at least until he gets his own boat.

As we stood on the landing stage at Badger's Piece, watching his launch puff its way slowly back up the lake, we heard the sound of another steam launch, coming from the other direction.

Assuming that this was not meant for us, we both turned, intending to make our way back to the house and prepare for supper. Then we noticed the man, with arms crossed and face displaying dark intent, blocking the pathway.

"Well, Watson, it seems we are to remain here. Perhaps this launch is for us after all."

When the approaching steam launch drew closer to where we were standing, the man on board jumped onto the landing stage, holding the bow line. Here was a man we recognized, the man who had been following us for the last few days.

The other man still blocking our way to Badger's Piece stepped closer.

"Now," he said in a no-nonsense tone. "Would you two gentlemen kindly step aboard?"

We did as requested, although he presented no weapon, and the launch immediately set off on its return journey toward the southeastern end of the lake.

In silence, Holmes and I surveyed the scenery as it passed, and the hills as they emerged from behind closer undulations in the landscape. The air on the lake was calm and mild, but the atmosphere in the boat felt to me as cold as winter.

The steam launch gradually drew toward another landing stage, behind which stood a building constructed of gray Cumberland slate, with white-painted frames giving even greater contrast to the darkness of the windows. Here was a building that had to be at least two-hundred years old.

The engine chugged mysteriously to itself as the launch pulled up at the landing stage and the lines were secured to the mooring posts. Beside the launch lay a small sailboat, with its brown sails furled.

Holmes saw it too and nodded.

Our escorts ushered us off the boat, along the approach path, and into the house by way of the front door.

I could sense the ghosts of history haunting this place, and the very idea made me shudder. I felt that much had taken place in these premises over the centuries. I am not usually a timid man, but it was with a certain amount of trepidation that I accompanied Holmes as we were ushered into the front reception room.

In the middle of the room stood a large chair in which sat an elderly lady, dressed entirely in black. In this respect, if in no other, she reminded me of our dear Queen in her mourning attire.

The woman looked up as we entered, whilst the two men who had brought us here took their places behind the woman's chair, reminding me of guardsmen on formal duty.

Holmes removed his hat. "Mrs. Harnecue, I presume."

The lady raised an eyebrow in surprise. "You know who I am?"

"The matter is no great secret. Your son here has been shadowing us for the past few days, and now you wish to learn what we have discovered in our search for the Whitehaven Ransom."

"That is not the reason I had my sons bring you here, Mr. Holmes."

"No?"

"Certainly not. I am aware that you discovered the key to the bank deposit box when you examined the boathouse. I am also aware that you traveled to Whitehaven to retrieve the goods from the bank."

"Your sons and their informers do you credit, ma'am. Is Mrs. Henderson perhaps the source of your intelligence?"

"Do not think badly of her, Mr. Holmes. She is a local woman, and also a cousin of mine."

"That might explain a few things."

"I have brought you here, Mr. Holmes, because I wish to clear up certain matters in your mind."

It was Holmes's turn to look surprised. "In that case, pray continue."

"You have already ascertained that the skeleton you discovered in Mr. Barnswick's boathouse is that of Dr. Chadwickson."

Holmes nodded.

"The occasion of his death took place some thirty years ago."

"That fact has already been ascertained."

"The truth of the matter is that my husband's family have had a somewhat shady past – smuggling, extortion, and anything underhanded. Over a hundred years ago, when they heard news of the ransom raised to pay off John Paul Jones, and the fact that the money had not been paid over, they were determined to lay their own hands on those diamonds. In fact, Mr. Holmes, it became an unhealthy obsession in this family. They scoured the town of Whitehaven, from one end to the other, but no trace could they find of those gems. The secret of their whereabouts had been kept safe and sound by all involved in the scheme. But as the years went by, the search remained a tradition in the family, handed down from one generation to another. Then, in 1858, the family heard about Dr. Chadwickson's discovery of the Ransom, and learned that he had deposited the jewels in the vault of the town bank in Whitehaven. They realized that, if they were to lay their hands on those jewels, they would have to locate that key. My husband, Jack, together with his two brothers, decided to confront Dr. Chadwickson, and coerce him into handing the key over to them."

"To which end they contrived a meeting down at the boathouse," said Holmes.

"It was relatively secluded, and away from prying eyes, so that is indeed where they met. Whatever was said during that meeting we can only conjecture, but the good doctor refused to hand over the key. Instead, he placed it in the most secure place he could imagine at that moment. He swallowed it. Jack and his brothers decided that the only way for them to obtain that key was to make the doctor regurgitate the contents of his stomach. This they undertook to do, but, in the process, the poor doctor choked on his own vomit and died as a result."

"You are saying his death was a matter of misfortune rather than murder."

“They always insisted upon that. The family may have been rogues, Mr. Holmes, but they were never murderers.”

“But why did they leave the body in that sunken boat? And for so many years?”

“At first, they attempted to find the key. They cut the body open, and examined the contents of his stomach. But they could find no trace of the key in there. But it had to be there. Somewhere. The fools ought to have cut open his throat, and searched his gullet and windpipe. That key might even have been the object that choked Dr Chadwickson to death. Anyway, they knew that if they dropped the body into the lake, it would rise to the surface and be discovered. Even cutting it up into smaller pieces – their act of butchery might well have been discovered. Instead, they decided to allow the body to decompose, so that they could eventually locate the key, and deposit the bones in the deepest part of the lake.”

“That sounds extremely cold-hearted,” I told her.

The woman gave a shrug. “I am merely telling you what happened, Dr. Watson. But they never had the chance to execute their plan. Within a few months of this incident, my husband Jack died, and his brothers had been arrested for various transgressions and sent to prison. The affair of Dr. Chadwickson and the key was forgotten, or at least the memory buried beneath the many other demands of life.”

“And now you want us to hand the Ransom over to you,” said Holmes.

“No, Mr. Holmes,” asserted Mrs. Harnecue, leaning forward and riveting him with her cold gaze. “This is the lake of Saints and Sinners. The saints had the islands, and we were among the sinners. Smugglers and crooks. But we are a decent, law-abiding family nowadays. Our lawless years are over. It is merely our reputation that remains a distasteful memory for many, but that is all humbug. As a family, we are agreed that we must do whatever is the right thing. As far as

I am concerned, Mr. Holmes, you must decide what happens to those diamonds. You may decide to donate them to the town of Whitehaven, or you may give the money to Mr. Barnswick. That is now your concern, not mine."

We took our leave of Mrs. Harnecue, assured that she would be kept well informed of our movements over the coming days.

At supper that evening, Holmes gave the appearance of a man at peace with the world. As the evening progressed, all eyes became fixed upon him, and a tense silence descended upon our gathering.

Finally, I could contain my curiosity no longer. "Come now, Holmes," I cried. "Let us see those diamonds. Open the bag, and show us the contents."

"Oh, the Whitehaven Ransom?"

"Of course the Whitehaven Ransom. That is what this business has been all about, is it not?"

Sherlock Holmes merely smiled, cleared the supper plates to one side, pulled the leather bag from inside his jacket, and laid it upon the table.

There it lay – a bag of black leather, hardened by the passage of time and the smoke from innumerable domestic fires.

Holmes took a knife from his inner pocket, and slowly cut the stitching that sealed the end of the bag. Then, with exaggerated drama, he pulled apart the leather opening and drew out a second bag. This one was made of fine silk, and had survived the years in much better condition.

Holmes now opened the silk bag, and poured out the contents onto the table.

We all gaped, amazed at what we saw fall from its opening.

I looked up at Holmes in astonishment.

"Pebbles," he explained. "From the seashore."

"But, whatever happened to the diamonds?"

"Long gone."

"And you knew that all along."

He shrugged. "It seemed obvious enough. A conclusion confirmed by the stones you now see before you."

"Please explain."

"Use your imagination, Watson. Old Doris Ferrybridge was entrusted with the care of a handful of diamonds worth thousands of pounds."

"Correct."

"Mr. Sheldrake told us that she was a kind-hearted person, known for her compassion and her philanthropy. Can you honestly imagine that she would leave those diamonds concealed in her chimney, apparently forgotten by the world, whilst people around her starved? A man lost at sea leaves his wife and family destitute. What does Mrs. Ferrybridge do? She takes a diamond from that bag and gives it to the family. All is then well. Perhaps a man is injured during an accident at the colliery, and is unable to earn his weekly wage. He and his family will starve. So, what happens? Mrs. Ferrybridge takes a diamond, and gives it to him. The family is saved. An elderly couple fall upon hard times, and face starvation. So Mrs. Ferrybridge gives them a diamond, which will serve them for the rest of their lives. You can be certain that some local jewelry store enjoyed superb business during her lifetime. That good lady was entrusted with those diamonds intended for the benefit of the people of the town. How better could she use that wealth than to provide for the poor and needy? I for one heartily applaud what she did."

"As do I," I responded. "But was that not theft on her part?"

"Hardly. The theft lay in failing to return the money to the people."

"So, when she died, she left her daughter to care for a bag of pebbles. Did the daughter know?"

"Probably not, since she gave Dr. Chadwickson to understand that the bag contained the Ransom itself."

"And did Dr. Chadwickson believe the bag contained diamonds?"

"He believed it contained something of value, though maybe not diamonds. As a man of integrity, entrusted with the care of the leather bag, he took it directly to that bank in Whitehaven, where he left it in a safety deposit box."

"So, the bag had been opened many times since it was entrusted to that lady."

"Certainly. You can see along the opening of the bag that many more holes are present than are needed to thread its present leather cord through and keep it secure. We can only guess at the number of hands that have opened and re-threaded that leather bag."

By the time we were ready to depart Badger's Piece a few days later, Sherlock Holmes was looking a great deal healthier than he had been when we arrived. Bushy Barnswick had enjoyed our visit, and would have much to tell his friends during the winter months, about Sherlock Holmes and the Whitehaven Ransom – to say nothing of my pike.

As our host stood beside us on the railway station in Keswick, he handed Holmes a small wooden box.

On opening it, my companion reached inside and drew out a tie-pin. On top of the pin was mounted a small pebble, ground smooth over many years by the action of the ocean waves.

"I was determined that something of value should result from this affair," said Bushy. "To which end, I had one of the smaller pebbles from the bag cleaned and mounted, so that you might be reminded daily of your time here, and the service you rendered to our community in solving this mystery."

The bright morning sunshine made the translucent pebble appear to glow with some inner light.

"I am honored," replied Sherlock Holmes with a look of obvious delight upon his face, "to share in a legacy from an American hero like John Paul Jones – even if it is mine by default."

# Wolf Island
by Robert V. Stapleton

To this day, I have no idea why my friend, Mr. Sherlock Holmes, decided to accept that particular call upon his precious time. Indeed, as a man of logic and science, his subjective methods of making such decisions often left me baffled. For whatever reason, the selection my colleague made on that bright spring morning in 1887 would lead us both to a case so singular that it would remain seared upon our memories for many years to come.

From the pile of correspondence stacked upon our table that morning, Holmes picked up one item after the other and, after a cursory glance at the contents, dropped each one into the basket of wastepaper. He finally remained holding this one letter, examining it with intense curiosity.

"What do you think, Watson?" said he, handing the sheet of notepaper out toward me.

I took the letter and read it through. Although, because of the brevity of the correspondence, that did not require much in the way of time or energy. "Somebody is calling on you for help," I replied, seeing no specific reason why this missive shouldn't join its fellows in the basket. "And yet that person appears to give little or no information upon which to make a judgment."

"On the contrary. This item of correspondence tells us a great deal."

I turned the letter over a couple of times, examined the envelope, and looked up at Holmes in bewilderment. "Well, I for one cannot make anything of it."

"Employ my methods."

I looked closer. "The post-mark tells us it was mailed in Beaconsfield."

"You are making progress."

"But that reveals little."

"Until you remember that Beaconsfield lies among the Chiltern Hills."

"Buckinghamshire. A pleasant area of rolling countryside. But what else?"

"The letter is brief: '*Help me, Mr. Holmes. The hermit has gone, and now they are coming for me.*' A *cri de Coeur* if ever I heard one."

"But from whom? The note is simply signed '*M*'."

"Let us examine the letter itself," said Holmes, sitting back in his chair and inspecting the dust motes floating in the rays of morning sunshine. "You will note that the paper on which it has been written is of good quality. If you hold it up to the light, as I did just now, you can clearly make out a watermark naming the Black Lion as the likely place of origin – no doubt one of the many coaching inns in that town."

"The handwriting is of poor quality. Suggesting perhaps a member of the waiting staff there."

"Perhaps," he said doubtfully. "The handwriting is undoubtedly that of a woman, whose education is limited. But the fact that she has written to me suggests a young person who is reluctant to reveal her name out of fear for her life."

"Certainly dramatic." I looked up. "But who is this mysterious *M*?"

"Time will reveal it to us, Watson."

"And the hermit?"

"Landed gentry often opened their estates to visitors, with attractions such as flowerbeds, rockeries, lakes, woodlands, and occasionally a so-called ornamental hermit, a man dressed perhaps in a cloak, sitting in a cave, giving his opinion and wisdom for the entertainment of credulous visitors."

I chuckled. "I wonder who might be the more eccentric – the landowner or the hermit?"

"Quite."

"Do you know of any estates in the Chilterns that might fit that description?"

Holmes purse his lips thoughtfully. "I know of one. An estate owned by a gentleman by the name of Andrew Grice Paterson."

I reached for our copy of *Who's Who* and searched through the listings. "Ah, here we are. Sir Andrew Grice Paterson is the elder son of the owner of a shipping line, who inherited the business on the death of his father only a couple of years ago."

"I recall reading of the father's death," mused Holmes. "But the entry suggests there might be another brother somewhere. Pray continue, Watson."

"A note that you added in the margin tells us he has an office in London, to which he commutes twice a week, from his home at Stevendale, some ten miles north of Beaconsfield."

"Today being a Tuesday, he is unlikely to be at his London office. Therefore, it should be easy enough for us to pay the man a visit. I can send him a telegram in advance to warn him of our impending arrival. But first we must call upon our mysterious correspondent. Come, Watson – a day out in the countryside should do us both some good."

Taking the train west from Marylebone Station, we arrived at Beaconsfield by mid-morning, and quickly made our way to the Black Lion Inn. As Holmes had surmised, the building was a typical eighteenth-century coaching inn. The smell of wax polish and cooking, common to such establishments by mid-morning, greeted us as we made our way through the grand front entrance.

The hotel manager, a business-like and well-dressed man sporting bushy side-whiskers, looked thoughtful as we explained the purpose of our visit.

"You are looking for a young woman whose first name begins with 'M'," he mused. Opening the visitors' book, he turned it toward us and pointing out one particular entry. "See, gentlemen. Three days ago – that will be last Saturday – a young lady came to stay here. She gave her name as Mary Smith.

"The young lady confined herself to her room," added the manager. "She seemed to be in fear of something or somebody. But our chamber maid gained her confidence and managed to learn that her real name is Muriel Oakwood."

"And for an address?"

"She seemed reluctant to provide one, but finally gave a location in St. Albans."

"Presumably that of her parents."

"We may assume so."

"And how long was this young woman intending to stay here?" asked Holmes.

"She paid in advance for three nights, with the stated intention of leaving on the fourth day – today. But yesterday afternoon, two men came and escorted her away. By the look on her face, I was certain that she was being taken against her will, but the men told me they were taking her to visit her uncle, so I considered it none of my business to interfere."

Holmes nodded. "May we see the room where she was staying?"

"Certainly." The manager handed him the key. "But she appears to have taken the few possessions that she brought with her."

We made our way up to the second floor bedroom.

With the door closed upon the world, Holmes set about examining the room in his habitual manner, scouring the furnishings for the minutest detail which might prove relevant to his investigation.

"The carpet shows the imprint of several sets of men's shoes. The two visitors and the manager, perhaps. There are also two sets of women's shoes. Muriel and the chambermaid. But no sign of any struggle."

He searched the drawers of the bedside table, and then those of the dressing table. On opening the bottom left hand drawer of the latter, Holmes drew out a printed magazine. "Now, what have we here? A copy of *Beeton's Christmas Annual*. I believe that they publish stories of various kinds."

He handed it to me.

"It has Muriel Oakwood's name on the top," I noted. Then I pushed the magazine into my coat pocket. "I shall keep it safe for her until we locate our missing lady."

"Here is something else that belongs to her," said Holmes as he lifted something else out of the drawer.

"How do you know it belongs to Muriel Oakwood?"

"A crudely inscribed letter '*M*' on the handle makes the suggestion more than likely. But the big question is why a young woman would leave behind such a personal item as her hand-mirror, concealed beneath a magazine."

"She forgot it."

"I hardly think she would forget something so intimate."

"Perhaps it carries a message for us."

"How insightful of you, Watson. Yes. The glass appears to carry some writing on the glass, made with the use of a sliver of soap. The message contains two simple words. '*Wolf Island*'."

"'Wolf Island'. Where on earth is that?"

"Perhaps our visit this afternoon will furnish us with an answer."

After a reviving meal at the Black Lion, Holmes and I hired a four-wheeler and made our way out to the Stevendale Estate, the home of Sir Andrew Grice Paterson. We presented our visiting cards to the butler and followed him into one of the front reception rooms, containing brown furniture and potted plants. I noticed that the walls were lined with pictures, paintings, and photographs of ships, both sailing and steam-driven.

Grice Paterson himself arrived, a man of sartorial sophistication, wearing a dark suit, highly polished shoes, and a wing-collared shirt. He invited us to sit down.

"As you can see, gentlemen," he said, after we had introduced ourselves, "my business lies in shipping. It is a line which involves me in a great deal of work and worry, to say nothing of the demands made upon me by the estate which I recently inherited from my father."

"In that case," began Holmes, "it is extremely good of you to spare us your time."

"You hardly gave me much choice, did you?" he returned acerbically.

"Then we must come directly to the point of our visit."

"An excellent idea."

"This morning, we visited Beaconsfield, in response to a letter we received from one of your employees – a lady by the name of Miss Muriel Oakwood."

Grice Paterson stiffened. "That young lady, if I may employ the term, is no longer in my service, Mr. Holmes. She left Stevendale on a sudden impulse three days ago, and none of us has seen her since."

Even I could tell that the man in front of us was being evasive.

"And I'm surprised that a man of your standing, Mr. Holmes, a man with better things to do with his time, should take seriously any correspondence from a semi-literate house maid such as Miss Oakwood."

"And you have no idea what has become of this lady."

"As I said. And now you tell me she has gone missing."

"So it appears."

"Then I am quite unable to assist you."

"But you have also recently lost another member of your staff – a man who played the part of a hermit."

"You are well informed, Mr. Holmes. I presume you mean Gordon Caldy."

"I don't have his name."

"Yes. I believe Caldy and this young woman were close, in which case, it is hardly surprising that they should both have left at the same time."

"Can you tell me the reason for his leaving?"

"Theft. He simply packed his bags one day and left, taking with him a sheet of paper that he had stolen from my study."

"Can you tell us any more about him?"

Andrew Grice Paterson tugged on a bell-pull. "The estate manager will answer any further questions you might have about Caldy."

"One final question then, if you wouldn't mind my asking: Does the name 'Wolf Island' mean anything to you, Sir Andrew?"

Our host glared back at Holmes and said nothing by way of reply.

The door opened and a man dressed in a tweed three-piece suit entered.

"Ah, Talbot," said Grice Paterson. "Would you please show these gentlemen around the estate, reply to any questions they have about Caldy, and then make sure they leave the premises directly you are finished."

The estate was indeed as we had expected. The house itself was large and rambling and the grounds extensive. An orangery and kitchen garden stood on one side of the house, whilst the front looked out over a landscape of pasture and woodlands.

"What exactly do you wish to see?" asked the estate manager.

"Anything that will help us discover the whereabouts of Gordon Caldy."

"You won't find him anywhere near here, Mr. Holmes," said Talbot. "He was a Scottish man, so he has more than likely gone back north again. The master regards him as a thief."

"What did he steal?"

"A sheet of paper that had been consigned to the waste-paper basket in Sir Andrew's study. You see, Mr. Holmes, all papers generated by the Grice Paterson shipping line, which are superfluous to requirement, are taken outside and burned. By myself. But before I could incinerate that sheet, Caldy snatched it up and disappeared. Rapidly."

"Hardly a crime, one would think."

"Perhaps."

"Do you know what was on the paper?"

"No."

"You say he left in a hurry."

"Very much so."

"Presumably Caldy normally resided somewhere in the house. He would hardly have slept outside in all weathers."

"He did have a small bedroom here. But Sir Andrew told me to empty his room immediately after he left, and burn any papers and correspondence that I found there."

"Where did you burn it?"

"We have a brazier on a patch of waste ground on the far side of the house."

"May we see it?"

"Certainly. For all the good it might do you."

The brazier was full of gray ashes, leaving little hope that anything substantial could be salvaged from among Caldy's belongings. Nevertheless Holmes insisted on searching through the incinerated remains. He finally stood up, slipped something between the pages of his pocketbook, and shook his head.

It was my turn to inquire after the former hermit. "Tell us, Talbot, how did Caldy come to be employed in that position?"

"He was engaged as a general handyman on the estate. He had been with us less than a year when the master came up with the idea of establishing a hermit in the grounds. He thought it might encourage more paying visitors to explore the estate, and therefore had a roughly built grotto cut into the cliff-side down in the woodland. Gordon proved to be quite a character and was indeed popular with our visitors."

Upon our return to London, Holmes insisted that we pay an immediate visit to Scotland Yard. There we found Inspector Gregson ready to hear our story.

"I see no reason for alarm, gentlemen," said the tall, fair-haired inspector. "Two people have gone missing, but you have no evidence whatsoever of any foul play."

"One has gone missing of his own volition, whilst the young woman might have been abducted."

"That sounds a little speculative, even for you, Mr. Holmes."

"Except," said Holmes, as he reached for his pocketbook and removed a small fragment of singed paper, "that I managed to retrieve this one piece of burned paper from the brazier."

He placed the fragment onto a sheet of white paper and examined it in the light of the inspector's gas-lamp.

"It might prove to be nothing at all," said Holmes. "Which is why I said nothing to Watson here, but it carries part of an address in Glasgow. And I should like you to look into the matter for me, Gregson."

The inspector looked closely at the paper. "A complete address would be more helpful, Mr. Holmes, but I can tell you at once that this is most likely to be the offices of the local Customs Department in Glasgow."

"Customs?"

"Coast Guard."

"Interesting."

"I could send a message to them, and mention the name of Gordon Caldy. If there is more to this business than meets the eye, then they might want to speak with you."

The telegram arrived so early the following morning that I was packed and on the train before I was awake enough to completely realize what had happened. The noise and smoke of Euston Station filled the air around me, as Holmes hurried me across the crowded platform and into the waiting carriage.

With the door closed against the cacophony of the station, I sat opposite Holmes and looked to him for something in the way of an explanation.

"We have been invited to travel to Glasgow to meet an official from the Coast Guard," he told me. "They have news for us about our missing hermit. It seems, from what Gregson has to tell me, that we've stumbled into a live and ongoing investigation into a smuggling operation."

"What kind of smuggling? I thought the illegal running of spirits was mostly a thing of the past."

"No doubt all will be revealed when we reach Glasgow. For the moment, though, please feel free to renew your interrupted slumber."

It was early afternoon when we arrived at Glasgow's Central Station. We had already eaten, and were both eager to make the acquaintance of our host north of the border."

A man dressed in a uniform resembling that of an officer of the Royal Navy stood waiting for us on the platform as we descended from the train. He was young, fresh of face and with signs of copper-colored hair beneath his peaked cap.

"Mr. Holmes and Dr. Watson, I presume," said the man. "I am Lieutenant Donald McBruar, a Coast Guard officer working with the Customs and Preventive Authorities to counter the smuggling of untaxed goods."

"Good afternoon, Lieutenant," said Holmes as he shook the man's proffered hand. "We're keen to hear what you have to tell us about our missing Gordon Caldy."

"Ah, yes. Caldy. In that case, please come with me, gentlemen. I have a boat waiting to take us 'doon the watter', as they say in these parts."

"Down the water?"

"Aye. The River Clyde. The lifeblood of Glasgow. We are taking a cutter normally used for coastal and river patrols. Once on board, we can talk more freely about the current business."

"Where are we going?" I asked.

"I am going to show you the Island of Uffa," said McBruar. "That is where you will find the answer to your questions."

I found our journey down the river to be a fascinating experience. Ship-building yards lined the banks, vessels were making their way both up and down stream, and the sounds of heavy industry assaulted us from all directions.

"Now, Lieutenant," said Holmes, as he settled into his seat in the rear of the steam cutter. "Please tell us something about the Island of Uffa."

"It lies to the southwest of the much larger island of Arran, and comes within the estate of the Dukes of Hamilton. It covers an area of just over one square mile, and is divided into three or four crofts, together with a larger building occupied by a man by the name of Grice Paterson."

"A-ha. Is this man any relation of Andrew Grice Paterson of Stevendale, the steamship owner?"

"This is his brother, Alexander. He has been in residence on Uffa for only the last year or so, but we have reason to believe that the two brothers are now involved in a smuggling operation centered on that island."

"Are you suggesting that this man is using his brother's ships to smuggle goods into the country?"

"Not only into the country, but out of it as well."

"Please explain."

"Very well. The smuggling of spirits used to be a lucrative business throughout the United Kingdom. Rum and brandy in particular. And untaxed whisky was also smuggled around the country. It could be a particularly violent business at times, but that mostly ended long ago, with the passing of the Excise Act of 1823, which licensed the distilling of whisky, reduced the tax levied on its production, and opened up free market trade. The smuggling of whisky ceased to be lucrative, but a small amount still goes on."

"But the situation has changed."

"Indeed. In recent years, the French vineyards have been ravaged by disease – the phylloxera beetle, to be precise. Consequently, the production of French brandy has been severely hit, almost to extinction. This has opened up a new area of trade between this country and France: Scotch whisky."

"Including the trade in untaxed whisky," concluded Holmes.

"Precisely the problem we now face, Mr. Holmes. And it is mostly centered on the Island of Uffa. We are convinced that small unlicensed distillers have been transporting their produce to the island for storage until it can be collected and exported in bulk to France. Any profits made would be augmented by the fact that no duty was expended at this end of the trade."

"Can you not simply close them down?"

"We need to catch them in the act."

"And where does our friend Gordon Caldy fit into the picture?"

McBruar set his face hard as flint. "First, you must understand that Caldy is *our* man. He has been acting as an informer for us for several months now. We placed him at Stevendale so he could pass on information about the operation from that end of the business, but recently he believed that Andrew Grice Paterson had become suspicious of him. That's when we decided to remove him from Stevendale, but in the meantime, he had formed an emotional attachment with a young lady there."

"Muriel Oakwood."

"He gave her some money and hid her away in a hotel room with the intention of moving her to somewhere safer as soon as every possible. But we now know that Grice Paterson's men found her before that could happen and have spirited her away somewhere else."

"Have you any idea where?"

"None at all. But Caldy is reluctant to help us, for fear that it might place her life in peril."

"Understandable."

"By such intimidation, they are forcing him to remain quiet and not to rock the Grice Paterson boat."

"Why did you choose Caldy for this surveillance job?"

"Because, Mr. Holmes, Caldy is himself from Uffa. He was born there, and knows the island better than anybody."

"He managed to steal something at Stevendale."

"Oh, he certainly did. We learned that the smuggling operation is to take place imminently. He stole a duplicate letter that was addressed to the captain of one of Grice Paterson's ships, the *Rockhopper*. It instructed this man to collect a cargo from Uffa and transport it to a certain port in France."

"And do you have a date for this?"

"No, but the night of the full moon would seem to be an appropriate opportunity."

"And when is the next one?"

"The thirtieth of this month."

"Today is the twenty-sixth, so time is short."

"Even shorter if they bring the date forward."

"And where is Caldy now?"

"He's on the island. In hiding. Watching."

We passed the various industrial towns lining the river until it widened into the Firth of Clyde. From here it was a long trip down the Firth, along the east side of the Isle of Arran. But the weather was fair and the sights were pleasant, especially when Lieutenant McBruar pointed out the main points of interest. For the rest of our journey, Holmes sat smoking, and keeping his thoughts to himself.

Later in the afternoon, we rounded the southern point of Arran, passed the lighthouse on the island of Pladda, and turned due west.

Facing into the afternoon sunshine, I could see very little, but Lieutenant McBruar explained that our destination lay directly ahead of us. "We are heading for Campbeltown, a port on the east coast of the lengthy Kintyre Peninsula."

"And what is that island to the south-west of us?" I asked, indicating a small island silhouetted against the afternoon skyline.

"That, Dr. Watson, is the Island of Uffa itself," said McBruar.

"And the name?" I asked again. "What exactly does Uffa mean?"

"Apparently, Uffa comes from an Old Norse word for 'wolf'."

"Ah," said Holmes, now taking a keen interest in our conversation. "So, *that* is Wolf Island."

When we reached Campbeltown, McBruar headed for the Customs House, leaving us time to refresh ourselves at the hotel before enjoying an evening meal.

Later, as darkness crept across both sea and land, we joined McBruar outside and together we climbed up onto a high-point overlooking the ocean. As we looked south across the water with the aid of McBruar's telescope, we could see the now dark and somewhat sinister shape of Uffa.

"Tell us more about that place, McBruar," said Holmes.

"The island of Uffa is small, perhaps no more than a mile-and-a-half in length, and one mile in width. The cliffs are steep and rugged, making access limited. The main landing stage is situated directly below the house that you can just see on the clifftop. From here, in good weather, the journey down to the island is easy enough."

I noticed a light flashing against the darkness of the island. "It seems that at least somebody is at home there."

"That will be Grice Paterson."

"He is using Morse Code to communicate with a confederate over here on the mainland," said Holmes. "From their conversation, it seems to be general knowledge that we have now arrived. I should like to meet him."

"You will have the opportunity in the morning," said McBruar. "He'll be here to collect the mails. We may be a long way from London here, Mr. Holmes, but we are still within the reach of civilization. And the payment of taxes."

"I look forward to that meeting," said Holmes, his eyes still fixed upon the flashing light.

There was no denying the fact that Mr. Alexander Grice Paterson was the brother of the man that we had met at Stevendale a couple of days previously – two beans from the same pod, so to speak – except that this one was dressed in tweeds, and had the bearing of a country squire.

McBruar introduced us as if he and the man from Uffa were on the best of terms, but a coldness in their eyes showed that this was nothing more than an illusion.

"Mr. Holmes and Dr. Watson," said Grice Paterson. "Welcome to the west of Scotland. I can only conclude that you are here at the behest of the Coast Guard. I wish that McBruar would learn to leave honest citizens to their own devices without threatening them with unjust interference."

McBruar snorted his derision, then turned and left us to our conversation.

Grice Paterson was engaged in examining the letters that he'd retrieved from the Campbeltown Post Office, having opened and begun to read the one that seemed to him to be most interesting.

"It's from my brother," announced Alexander Grice Paterson, without any apparent change in attitude toward us. As he returned the letter to its envelope, he looked up at us. "Gentlemen, I should be delighted if you would do me the honor of dining with me and my wife this evening."

"On the island?"

"Indeed."

"That would certainly be a great pleasure," said Holmes. "Don't you agree, Watson?"

"Oh, yes, indeed," I replied. "Thank you."

"Excellent. In that case, I shall arrange for my boat to collect you both from this landing-stage at four o'clock."

Holmes and I joined McBruar as he visited one of the licensed distilleries in the vicinity of Campbeltown. We learned about the process of distillation, and the monitoring by the Customs officials. In this way, we passed our time waiting for the hour appointed for our visit to Uffa.

At precisely four o'clock, a steam launch drew up against the Campbeltown jetty. A man, dressed in a smart but practical uniform climbed out of the boat.

"Mr. Grice Paterson has sent us to collect Mr. Holmes and Dr. Watson."

"In that case, you have found them," I said.

"Please, come this way, gentlemen. The master is waiting to welcome you to his domain."

After a journey of several miles, we found Alexander Grice Paterson himself waiting for us as we approached the landing-stage at the foot of an imposing cliff. At the head of this wall of rock loomed a large gray building, which looked more like a castle than a house, with high walls and solid but extensive masonry. It was built of the same sandstone rock that made up the island.

"Welcome, gentlemen, to the Island of Uffa." Our host greeted us with warmth in his voice, and with an outstretch hand of welcome. "Kindly follow me up to the house. We call this place Craigdoon, the 'Castle on the Rock', and you can see why."

Even Holmes was showing signs of wilting by the time we reached the clifftop.

"Is this the only access to the island?" I inquired.

"The island is surrounded by steep cliffs, rising in places to a couple-of-hundred feet," he replied. "Access to the shore is by precipitous descent from any direction. We do however have a winch and pulley system here to raise heavy items, but for the able-bodied, climbing is the only way."

"In that case, you must have very few visitors."

"True. The weather is another limiting factor. Being on such an elevated site, we are somewhat exposed to the elements. But not so much that our residents cannot make a living from the land, poor though the soil might be. We have three crofts, or homesteads, which provide all we need for our immediate needs."

I looked out across the rugged landscape of the island and found it difficult to believe that anybody could survive here, let alone raise a family.

"Come and take a look around, gentlemen," said Grice Paterson. "You will admit there is little here of interest to anybody used to the bustling life of London."

Our host led us across the rough landscape, following the track-ways made by sheep and humans that crisscrossed the island. The homesteads were sturdily built, and each lay surrounded by a plot of thin topsoil which sustained a crop of spring vegetables, and grass which fed several chickens, a few sheep, and occasionally a couple of cows.

As the daylight began to fade, Grice Paterson led us back to the big house, and there we were glad to warm ourselves in the glow of a peat-fire in the grand living room.

Alexander Grice Paterson introduced us to his wife, Thelma, who informed us that dinner would be ready within ten minutes. The couple gave the impression of being people of culture, and our host instantly turned to the drinks cabinet and poured us each a glass of dry sherry.

Small-talk began, and continued as we made our way into the dining room and sat down at the large table.

Alexander placed another set of glasses before us, and proceeded to pour out a plentiful quantity of Scotch whisky into each.

Holmes declined, but I was happy to indulge, not wishing to give offense to our generous hosts.

The evening meal consisted of a warming soup, followed by a serving of venison and various vegetables, and a pudding to finish. As he poured me a second glass of whisky, Grice Paterson began to ask searching questions. "May I ask what brings you all this way, Mr. Holmes?"

"I am a private consulting detective, Mr. Grice Paterson, so that my work frequently takes me into the most unusual places," replied Holmes. "My present client has called upon my services because she was fearful that somebody wished to do her harm."

"Of what kind of harm is she afraid?"

"That wasn't made clear, and the waters were made even murkier when she disappeared."

"Dear me," exclaimed our host.

"There was also another man who went missing," added Holmes. "Our investigations into both disappearances have brought us to you."

"To me?" Grice Paterson appeared horrified. "I fail to see how I can be of any help whatsoever. What is the name of this lady client of yours?"

"Her name is Miss Muriel Oakwood."

He shook his head. "That name means nothing to me."

"And the name Gordon Caldy?"

"Again, it means nothing, Mr. Holmes. I can only suggest that you are here on a wild-goose chase. You would be better returning to London to continue your investigations."

“And what exactly is your line of work, Mr. Grice Paterson?” Holmes asked. “You hardly make a living out of this island.”

“Of course not, Mr. Holmes. My business is in commerce, and involves the import and export of goods. I have an office in Glasgow which, as you have discovered, is no more than a small boat journey from here.”

“In fine weather.”

“We certainly need our sea legs here.”

“And you work in consultation with your brother, presumably.”

“Oh, you have met Andrew, have you?”

“You know that we have, Mr. Grice Paterson. That letter you received this morning no doubt told you about us.”

For a moment, the atmosphere in the room turned icy cold. Then our host burst out laughing. “You are of course quite right, Mr. Holmes. That letter may have mentioned you in passing, but its main content concerned exports.”

“Of untaxed whisky?”

“McBruar and his crew have been leading you astray, Mr. Holmes,” said Grice Paterson. “He thinks he is clever. He imagines that we are storing whisky on this island, in preparation for transferring it to some ship owned by my brother. That is of course quite ridiculous. I have shown you around the island, and I hope you appreciate how difficult it is for anyone to arrive or leave. Quite apart from the landing immediately below this house, the two-hundred-foot cliffs make such a thing utterly impossible

The discussion turned to myself as Alexander Grice Paterson leaned over and refilled my glass with whisky. I had lost count of how many I had imbibed, and I could feel myself losing control of what I was saying. But for some reason, I could hardly stop myself. My garrulous nature took over, and I began to tell tales of my time in the Army.

When the meal was over, Holmes and I joined our host in the withdrawing room, where we smoked and I continued to drink.

It was only when Holmes announced that it was time for us to leave that I discovered to my horror that I was quite unable to stand up unaided.

"Oh dear, Dr. Watson," said Grice Paterson, taking me by the elbow. "I fear that you've had a little too much to drink."

"So it seems," I replied, but the thought crossed my befuddled mind that it was more than mere alcohol that was impeding my movements. I was convinced that some kind of sleeping draft had been mixed with my drink during the evening.

"Well, you cannot go back to Campbeltown in that condition," declared Grice Paterson. "But not to worry. We have a bed already made up in anticipation of visitors, and you are welcome to spend the night there."

"That is very kind of you, sir," I told him. "I have no option but to accept your kind invitation."

"In the meantime, I can arrange for Mr. Holmes to return to Campbeltown."

I noticed a look of deep concern cross the face of my friend, but we both realized that we had no option but to submit to our host's suggestion.

"Dr. Watson can remain here for as long as is necessary," said Grice Paterson.

"And exactly how long will that be?" asked Holmes.

"Until the weather and business allow."

"That sounds like a threat."

"Merely a statement of fact, Mr. Holmes. You will see the matter more logically in the morning."

"In that case, I must reluctantly take my leave of you," said Holmes. "Thank you for a most entertaining evening, and for a delightful meal." He turned to me. "Sleep well, Watson. You will need your strength and wits for the morrow."

The next thing I remember was waking to find myself in a strange bed, with the gray light of a new day filtering in through the window. My head hurt, no doubt as a result of the alcohol and sleeping draft I had taken in on the previous evening. I sat up, sipped from the glass of water that I discovered at my bedside, and then slowly climbed out of bed. I was dressed in a borrowed nightshirt, and my clothes were missing.

I drew open the curtains and looked out of the latticed window. I was facing westward, and I could see the rolling countryside of Kintyre, overhung with heavy clouds racing toward me on a strengthening wind. The ocean looked gray and wild, with waves breaking into a multitude of white horses. Rain rattled against the glass, whilst wind howled down the chimney and whistled through gaps in the woodwork.

As I collected my thoughts together, I tried the handle of the door. It was locked. I concluded that I was now a prisoner, or at the very least a hostage – for exactly what reason, I could only speculate. It undoubtedly had something to do with Lieutenant McBruar's presence in Campbeltown, but I had little wish to embark on a small boat journey in this weather, all the way back to the mainland, or anywhere else.

What a fool I had been to drink so much on the previous evening, and to leave myself defenseless against Grice Paterson's scheming. What exactly did Grice Paterson have planned for me? What was Holmes going to do now? And had I made ruin of McBruar's plans to break this trade in untaxed whisky?

I sat back on the bed, and awaited developments.

Within a few minutes, the key turned in the door lock, the handle rattled, and the door opened.

In the doorway stood a man I had met at one of the crofts the previous evening.

"Good morning, Dr. Watson," the man said. "My name is Donald, and the master has sent me to invite you to take your breakfast downstairs in the kitchen."

He stood aside to allow a young girl of no more than thirteen years of age to enter, carrying a jug of hot water which she placed upon the wash-stand on the far side of the room. Then she turned and left.

I noticed that Donald was carrying my clothes, neatly ironed and folded. These he left on the wooden chair standing beside the window.

Before I had time to interrogate him further, Donald had taken his leave, but this time closing the door without locking it.

Downstairs I enjoyed an ample breakfast, and was just finishing off my second cup of coffee when Alexander Grice Paterson himself appeared in the doorway of the kitchen.

"Ah, Dr. Watson. I see you are being well provided for."

"Indeed, thank you" I replied. "But I do wonder what you have in mind for me now."

"My plans are merely for your safety and convenience," he told me. "As the weather is inclement, you will remain on this island. Please feel free to make yourself at home here at Craigdoon. You're free to occupy the living room, the kitchen, the library, and your bedroom. Only you must not venture outside. At least, not on a day as stormy as this."

With little else to do, I made my way into the library, and settled down with a copy of Mr. Stevenson's recently published novel, *Kidnapped*. It seemed most appropriate to my present predicament.

Alexander's wife, Thelma, joined me in the library and sat at the far end of the room, knitting. It was clear that she was keeping an eye on me. I felt isolated. I had no way of contacting Holmes, so I resigned myself to spending the morning, and perhaps most of the day, in reading, and trying to dampen down a developing sense of paranoia.

I joined Alexander and Thelma around their table for the evening meal. The master asked me about my day, which I was able to answer in very few words. He was equally unforthcoming about other events on the island. Thus, with darkness fallen, I finally bade a goodnight to my hosts, and made my way to bed.

By now, the wind had eased, and I felt content to entrust myself into the arms of Morpheus for the night. Perhaps the god of dreams might help me make sense of whatever was going on here.

In the darkest part of the night, I was awoken by the sound of scraping. I sat up, and looked around at the darkness. "Is somebody there?"

I became aware of a movement in the gloom, and of a figure walking across the room toward the door. Light from a dark lantern illuminated that half of the room.

"I see they've locked it again," came a man's voice, carrying the lilt of a lowland Scotsman. "Good. That is hardly surprising, but it will do nothing to confine us to this room."

"Now, come along," I exclaimed. "Who the blazes are you?"

"Me? I thought you might have guessed by now, Dr. Watson. I am Gordon Caldy."

"Ah, Caldy. McBruar told us you were on this island."

"Keeping an eye on the Grice Patersons. I have been living in the ruins of an abandoned croft on the far side of the island. It might be a bit exposed, but nothing to a man whose job has been sitting outside in a hermit's cave."

"How did you get in here?"

"There are passageways in this house that even Grice Paterson himself knows nothing about. As somebody who was born and raised on this island, I know this place better than anybody else alive. One of the panels in this room opens onto a stairway that leads down to ground level."

"And what are you doing here in the middle of the night?"

"I have something to show you, Doctor. Now, get dressed as quickly as you can and follow me."

In the thin light of Caldy's lantern, I followed him into the hidden passageway and down a flight of stone steps, until he pushed open a small doorway and led me outside into the cold night air.

"Now where?"

Caldy held his finger to his lips and put out the lantern. "Hush. Our lives will be in danger if anybody finds us out here."

As quietly as possible, and crouching down to reduce the chance of being observed, we followed the top of the cliff along the western edge of the island. After several yards, Caldy stopped abruptly and, in the light of the nearly full moon, I noticed that the edge of the cliff had been eroded at this point.

Caldy led the way down a slope, until we reached a flight of steps cut into the rock.

"Grice Paterson assured us there was no other way onto the island," I said.

"You didn't believe him, did you?"

I followed, trying to keep alert to any danger.

Caldy proved more alert than I was. He stopped, listened, and then pulled me aside so that we both stood with our backs against the bracken-crowned rock, but with our presence concealed by the night.

Through the blackness, I could make out three men, climbing up the steps toward us. They were talking. Trying to keep my breathing steady, I watched as the men drew closer. I recognized one of them. It was, without doubt, my host, Alexander Grice Paterson. I could hear very little of what they were saying, but one phrase stood out. "High-tide." That sounded significant.

After the three men had passed us and had disappeared beyond the top of the pathway, we waited for another couple of minutes before continuing our descent.

At the bottom, we reached a small cove, with encompassing cliffs making its entrance all but invisible from the open sea. Behind a narrow shingle beach, I noticed a cave, also well concealed, stretched back beneath the cliff-side. The overhang hid this cave from both the weather and from observation by anybody approaching it from the sea. On closer inspection, I noticed that the cave contained casks and barrels stacked together.

"Contraband," breathed Caldy.

To one side of the beach, we reached a concrete landing stage, which gave access to a wooden jetty stretching out some fifty yards toward the sea and hidden by the rocks.

Just visible through the darkness, I could see a small fishing boat slowly making its way out into the Kilbrannan Sound, and heading west.

"They have offloaded their whisky for the night," said Caldy. He relit and uncovered one segment of his lantern, and was rewarded by an answering light from several yards away to the north-west.

Another small fishing boat approached the calm waters of the cove and crunched onto the shingle beach. The boat appeared to be full of fishermen. A rougher looking bunch I never wished to meet on such a dark night.

The toughest of them jumped down from the boat, and approached me. “Ah, there you are, Watson,” he said.

“Holmes. I never would have recognized you dressed like that.”

“I trust you had a restful day as a guest of the Grice Patersons.”

“I used it as best I could, but there was one thing of note that occurred during the afternoon. Grice Paterson received a couple of visitors. He took them to his office, so I had difficulty following what they were saying, but I am sure they were speaking French.”

“French, eh?”

“But more importantly,” Caldy chipped in. “We heard Grice Paterson mention high-tide.”

“We can only assume he means the one tomorrow night. Then, high-tide will be at about midnight. That has to be the time of the scheduled transfer.”

“So,” I said, “you plan to return tomorrow night.”

“Not just my plans, but those of McBruar as well. Success now depends upon keeping secret that we know their intentions.”

“But they will know when they find me gone.”

“Then you will have to return to your room, Watson.”

“And remain a prisoner? Surely you cannot be serious.”

“Never more so.”

“Don’t worry, Dr. Watson,” said Caldy. “I’ll take you back the way we came, and collect you again tomorrow night.”

A low whistle sounded from the other end of the beach. We saw one of the fishermen stand up and wave. “Mr. Holmes. Dr. Watson. You must come here, now.”

As we approached the wooden jetty, we could both see something floating in the water, bobbing among the waves. I had seen enough human bodies to immediately recognize it as such.

It was Gordon Caldy who waded into the water to retrieve the corpse, and drag it to land.

I turned the man onto his back, and quickly confirmed that he was dead. "His throat has been cut. And not very long ago, judging by the way the blood is still oozing out."

Caldy knelt down and looked the fellow over. "I know this man," he said, with bitterness in his voice. "His name is Alan Randlestone – one of the few people left who were born on the island. He was always a man of honor, and perhaps objected to whatever was going on here."

"So they killed him," said Holmes.

"And left his body to drift out to sea," I added.

"Most of the people on the island now are incomers," explained Caldy. "Strangers. People intent on making gain rather than retaining any love for the place."

"The finger of guilt inevitably points to Alexander Grice Paterson," growled Holmes. "Either he committed the murder himself, or else he knows about it. He is a dangerous man."

"We have to take the body with us," said Caldy, reaching down and lifting the corpse into his arms. "Not only was he my friend, but his body is our evidence against Grice Paterson."

"And you still want me to spend another day in that house?" I asked Holmes.

"We have no choice, Watson," he replied. "But take this with you."

He handed me my service revolver. In the dim light of the lantern, I checked that it was loaded, and slipped it into my pocket.

I felt a sense of disappointment as I watched the small boat push off from the beach, taking Holmes with it, and heading back toward Campbeltown. I was alone once more – albeit with Caldy still on the island. But this time, I knew myself to be grave danger.

The following day passed much the same as the previous one, with the exception that I now regarded Grice Paterson through more guarded eyes, as one would a coiled snake or lurking tiger. From time to time, I could hear people entering and leaving the building. Indeed, I gained the impression that the number of people on the island had somewhat increased. I could see men outside, coming and going with singular intent. I had a distinct impression that they are working up to something significant.

At supper that evening, I thanked the Grice Patersons for their hospitality. "But when exactly will I be able to return to the mainland?"

Alexander leaned over and refilled my whisky glass. I gained the impression that they were trying once more to render me intoxicated. But this time I was more diligent in counting the glasses.

"Tomorrow morning," replied Alexander Grice Paterson. "I promise you, Doctor. By then the weather will have improved sufficiently to make the crossing smooth enough so as not to inconvenience you with the danger of seasickness."

With the encouragement of my hosts, I retired as soon as the clock in the entrance hall chimed ten. With the bedroom door once again locked, I lay on the bed, fully-dressed, and waited. Then, in the light of my candle, I noticed him. Sitting in the chair by the window, with bright eyes patiently watching me.

"Holmes," I gasped. "What are you doing here?"

"Keeping an eye on you, my old friend," he told me. "I had no intention of leaving you alone for a second night in the same house as that murderer."

"Have you been here all day?"

"Much of it. Caldy knows every corner of this building, including a place where one can rest in peace and remain undisturbed by the rest of the household." He allowed a knowing smile to cross his face. "He showed me another room, almost empty, but with signs of recently having been filled with bags of tobacco and boxes of cigars."

"Contraband?"

"It looks like it."

"So the smuggling is going out as well as coming in."

"We're in dark waters here, Watson. This is becoming a much bigger enterprise than anyone first imagined."

At that moment the hidden door opened, and Gordon Caldy appeared as if by magic, looking pleased with himself. "Are you both ready?"

"Indeed I am," I told him.

Holmes stood up, and nodded. "Remember to take your revolver with you, Watson."

"You will also need to wrap your coat tightly around you," added Caldy. "The weather has turned cold again, and we might have a long wait, though I suspect not."

Once more down in the cove, I noticed that the collection of fishing boats had increased in number. At the far end of the line of vessels, I found the one Holmes had been using the previous night.

"Hurry up, Watson," he told me. "This place will be swarming with Grice Paterson's men before long. We must leave before that happens."

The three of us – Caldy, Holmes, and myself – climbed into the small fishing boat, and one member of the crew pushed off from the shore, whilst others raised the darkly stained mainsail.

A few hundred yards out, the crew turned the boat to face shore, took down the sail, and let out a sea-anchor from the stern.

We all sat down to await events.

Soon, the sound of voices reached us from the shore as a couple of dozen men climbed down the pathway and assembled on the shingle beach. With Grice Paterson giving the orders, the men began to move the casks and barrels from their places in the cave and deposit them at the far end of the jetty.

Holmes tapped me on the shoulder and pointed toward the south. I could see a light somewhere across the water, and it was moving.

"A ship," I whispered.

"*The* ship," he replied.

We watched as the vessel drew closer, turned in a circle, and approached the end of the jetty. With her port beam against the pier, the ship was secured fore and aft.

The ship was a small coastal-trading steamship of less than five-hundred tons and perhaps three-hundred feet in length. A central bridge separated the two small holds, with a forecastle in the bows and a long quarter-deck with a tall smoke-stack rising immediately forward of the ship's boat. On the rusted stern, the ship displayed her name: *Rockhoppe*r.

"One of Andrew Grice Paterson's vessels, if I'm not very much mistaken," said Holmes. "The very one mentioned in Caldy's stolen paper."

Caldy confirmed it as the ship was secured fore-and-aft to the bollards on the jetty.

Through the darkness, we could hear Alexander Grice Paterson issuing further orders and could see the small army of men hurrying to load the myriad barrels and casks.

Working with the vessel's crew and using the ship's derricks, they quickly had the cargo loaded into the holds.

Grice Paterson shouted further orders, and the derricks unloaded casks and bundles, onto the jetty.

"Tobacco and rum," whispered Caldy.

From there, the smuggled goods were spirited away, some onto the waiting fishing boats, and some into the cave behind the beach.

All this we observed from our fishing boat, hidden from their view in the darkness of the night.

When all was done, the men in the boats pushed off from the beach, whilst others climbed back up the pathway, leaving Alexander Grice Paterson talking with the ship's captain, and exchanging papers and money.

As the ship prepared to leave, with a plume of pungent smoke billowing from the funnel, Holmes ordered our boat to draw closer to the ship, on the side away from the island.

"It is my considered conclusion," announced Holmes, "that this ship contains our client, Miss Muriel Oakwood."

"If you're going to board that ship," returned Caldy, his eyes flashing, "then I'm coming with you."

Taking my revolver into my hand, I followed Sherlock Holmes onto the deck of the steamer – just in time, for as the ship pulled away, we crossed the deck to where one member of the crew was stowing the ship's mooring rope.

From behind, Caldy wrapped his arm around the man's throat, whilst Holmes pressed his own revolver against the fellow's head.

I could only imagine the look of surprise on the man's face.

"Where is the girl?" demanded Holmes.

The crewman remained silent.

"The logical conclusion has to be that she is on board this ship, somewhere. Take us to the girl, or you will be taking a dip. Do you understand?"

The man nodded, and Caldy loosened the grip on his throat.

"You lead the way, and remember, we are directly behind you."

The crewman led us along the side of the superstructure and in through a doorway. From there, he led us down a companionway until we halted outside a locked door. The man unfastened the door, and pushed it open.

Inside, in the darkness of the cabin, a young woman cried out in alarm at our abrupt appearance.

"Good evening, Miss Oakwood," said Holmes. "I am Sherlock Holmes, and this is my companion, Dr. John Watson."

In the subdued light, Muriel Oakwood noticed Gordon Caldy and, with a cry of delight, threw herself into his arms.

Holmes turned to the man who had led us here. "What were your orders about the girl?"

"We were to take her with us to France," replied the man. "And leave her there, along with the whisky."

"You had better stay out of sight," said Holmes. "I would hate to be in your shoes when your skipper discovers we're on board – which he will do soon."

He turned to me. "Are you ready, Watson?"

"For what?"

"We are taking over the ship."

"Oh, is that all? Of course I'm with you."

As we made our way farther along the quarter-deck, I heard the sound of the engine change, and felt the ship turn sharply to port.

"What now?" I asked.

“We have company,” cried Holmes. “Look. A thousand yards away, off the starboard bow. Another ship.”

I strained my eyes. “Now I see her. She’s rounding that headland. And I am prepared to bet she’s a warship, Holmes. A cruiser.”

“She ought to be. Our friend McBruar is supposed be organizing a reception for this ship.”

“Well, bravo for McBruar, and the Royal Navy, for turning up right on cue.”

I followed Holmes along the deck, and then up a ladder toward the bridge, an open structure, protected from the elements by nothing more than a canvas skirting.

I hung back as Holmes stepped up onto the bridge.

There he found the captain standing beside the ship’s coxswain at the helm. Holmes pointed the revolver toward the captain. “You have no hope of escape, Captain. You can never outrun a warship.”

The captain turned round, greatly surprised to find Sherlock Holmes behind him, and regaled him with a torrent of choice phrases. “We’re not finished yet!” he replied. “And you’ll not live long enough to enjoy any victory!”

From where I was, standing unseen in the shadows, I noticed another figure emerge from the far corner of the bridge. A man. I saw him approach Holmes from behind, and reach beneath his jacket. I realized he was about to bring out a gun. I slipped silently onto the bridge, and immediately pressed the muzzle of my revolver against his neck. The man stopped, and allowed me to reach in and extract the gun – a heavy automatic.

“I see that the mate has joined us, Holmes,” I cried.

Holmes turned and nodded. “Good work, Watson.”

A megaphoned voice reached us from across the water. “I call on you to heave-to, and prepare to receive a boarding-party.”

"That sounds like McBruar's voice," I said, pushing the mate to join his companions in the center of on the bridge.

"Do are he says," Holmes growled to the captain.

The captain rang the telegraph, and the ship slowly drew to a halt, bobbing in the swell coming in from the Atlantic Ocean.

A few minutes later, a steam-launch arrived and a party of sailors swarmed onto the ship.

"Welcome aboard, Lieutenant McBruar," called out Holmes. "I'm glad you could make the appointment. I have already taken over the bridge and command of the ship."

"Mr. Holmes," the other man shouted back. "You have done a good night's work, but we are here now to take over from you."

Holmes looked down onto the deck below. "It seems, Watson that this most singular case of ours is now at an end."

I also looked down, and noticed two figures, embracing, oblivious to whatever was going on around them. "Gordon Caldy and Muriel Oakwood," I noted. "The hermit and the house-maid. I hope they have a happy future together."

"After all those two have been through, they certainly deserve it, Watson," replied Holmes. "Which is more than can be said for the Grice Patersons of Uffa. Smuggling is one thing, compounded by abduction, but murder is quite another matter altogether. They are about to face justice. Their singular adventures are finally at an end, and we can safely say that Craigdoon will shortly be looking for a new tenant."

> *The year '87 furnished us with a long series of cases of greater or less interest, of which I retain the records. Among my headings under this one twelve months, I find an account . . . of the*

*singular adventures of the Grice Patersons in the island of Uffa . . . .*

– Dr. John H. Watson
"The Five Orange Pips"

# The Black Hole of Berlin
by Robert V. Stapleton

Over recent years, I have accompanied my friend Mr. Sherlock Holmes on numerous ventures and investigations, but at this precise moment I craved the homely setting of our rooms in Baker Street, together with its warm fireside, Mrs. Hudson's satisfying meals, and an absorbing English newspaper.

We had journeyed together from Liverpool Street Station to Harwich, thence by overnight ferry to the Hook of Holland, and now we were on a train, in the mid-winter of early 1885, and somewhere in the middle of Germany. We were on our way to Berlin, and the winterscape outside the window made me feel depressed, even when the gray fields gave way to the dismal buildings of yet another area of urban development.

"You are bored, Watson," observed Holmes.

"I was pondering that invitation you received for us to visit the German capital city," said I. "And wondering about its purpose."

"The matter is simple enough. A representative from the Foreign Office has invited us both to join him for a meal at a certain city-center hotel there. A comfortable place I have previously heard of in the *Friedrichstrasse*."

"But the purpose remains a mystery."

"Not at all," he replied. "As you know, the West African Conference is currently being held in that city. It is being hosted by the man in charge of the New Germany – the German Chancellor himself, Otto von Bismarck. And our man is numbered among the British delegation attending that Conference. Whatever our friend has in mind in making this invitation, it unquestionably has something to do with the events taking place there at the moment."

"Then I hope it will be worth our traveling all this way."

"I'm sure the matter is serious enough to warrant our undertaking this journey. He obviously anticipates trouble, and would value my presence there."

When the train ground to a halt, I looked for some indication of where we had arrived, however temporarily.

"Hannover," said Holmes, reading my thoughts.

I groaned at the thought that we would be making no further progress in our tedious journey for several more minutes.

"It is clear," continued Holmes, "that you need something to distract your attention. And, unless I am greatly mistaken, I believe that the distraction you're looking for has just stepped onto the train."

I looked out onto the platform, but could see no sign of anything or anybody unusual, apart from the normal idiosyncrasies of a German city in mid-winter: Heavily clad people standing stoically on the platform in the cold wind, notices printed in Gothic script, and an official strutting along the station platform making strident announcements in an unintelligible language.

"I give the man three minutes to locate us," said Holmes, lying back and stretching his long legs out in front of him.

As I watched the station clock reach the three minute mark, I heard someone open our compartment door and step inside. I turned and was immediately astonished. The man was tall, slim, dressed in a gray suit beneath a heavy overcoat, but otherwise bearing a noteworthy appearance.

"Good afternoon, gentlemen," said our visitor, in an accent as English as any Cambridge professor. "May I join you? This train appears to be more crowded than I had imagined it might be."

Holmes waved his hand toward the empty seats beside us. "You are indeed welcome to join us," he said. As he sat down, placing beside him his valise and the document case he was holding with protective care, the newcomer unbuttoned his coat and gave a smile so broad that the white of his teeth lightened up his dark face. "My name," said the man, "is Bagamoyo."

"Swahili," noted Holmes.

"Indeed. But my baptismal name is Jonathan."

"My name is Sherlock Holmes," explained my companion, "and this is my friend and companion, Dr. John Watson."

As the train began to move away from the station, Holmes sat back and studied our new traveling companion more closely. "And now you are on your way to Berlin."

"That is easily deduced, since this train is bound for the German capital."

"Certainly, but you have just this moment joined us after changing from the train which brought you here from Paris."

"True, Mr. Holmes. I have to admit that is not so readily deduced."

Holmes laughed. "I merely noticed the ticket you have hurriedly slipped into the top pocket of your jacket. The emblem of the French railways is partially visible. But you are not French or Belgian, nor are you from those parts of Africa over which the French or King Leopold currently hold sway. Your appearance suggests rather that you are from East Africa."

"I have to admit the truth of it," said Bagamoyo. "Allow me to explain. Several years ago, I left my home village and joined the crew of a ship sailing from Mombasa with a cargo of spices. I pulled my weight, so that discrimination against me by the mixed-race crew was kept to a minimum. I ended up in London, where I settled down, earned a modest living, made the right kind of friends, and was granted British citizenship. In the meantime, I read of the adventures of white explorers as they journeyed through the continent of Africa, bringing European ideas and culture without ever considering their detrimental effects on the native peoples."

"I fail to see that this is such a crime," I said. "The intention to bring civilization, medicine, religion, and a decent standard of living to the poor people of Africa has to be a laudable ambition."

"Indeed," said Bagamoyo. "I am not opposed to European civilization, wherever appropriate. I myself have reaped the benefits of it as much as anyone. But human greed threatens to lead to exploitation of Africa and its inhabitants on an industrial scale. At present, only the coastal areas are under European sovereignty, but that will change if this current Conference has its way. The British, for example, seek political power, and access to natural resources which will benefit the people of Britain rather than the Africans. Land for settlers. Markets for the products of our industrial machinery. Yes, jobs and employment for the masses, but they must take account of the people who are living in Africa now. People who have rights to be respected, and social networks that are far too unstructured for European bureaucracy to cope with, or ever to understand."

"And now you are on your way to Berlin, with the aim of influencing those currently involved in planning the future of the African people."

He nodded. "These people represent the traders and industrialists whose eyes sparkle at the very prospect of making money from what they call the 'Dark Continent'. The so-called 'civilized' nations have been exploiting the African people for many years – selling millions of our men and women into cruel slavery, just as the Arab traders have been doing for centuries, in order to promote the lucrative trade in sugar, coffee, and cotton."

"But cultural development would surely put a stop to such corruption," I suggested.

"Theoretically, perhaps – if the people are ever allowed to exercise such power, which is doubtful. Just look at the British in India, for example."

I coughed in order to cover up my misgivings about that point of view, but the comment contained enough painful truth that I said nothing by way of reply.

"I am now acting as a representative of the African peoples who wish to present their demand that the present social and cultural life of the African peoples be respected," continued Bagamoyo, "and that no development be entered into without the full agreement of the native peoples affected. We are perhaps fighting a losing battle, but my colleague, a man called Gaston Coss, a French national himself, has spent several weeks this winter trying to explain to those present at the Berlin Conference the serious threat that their proposed activities pose to the native peoples of Africa. The trouble is that most of the delegates are more interested in gaining wealth than in spreading the message of justice, freedom, and democratic accountability among the indigenous population."

"But what can you or anybody else accomplish against such powerful adversaries?" I asked.

Bagamoyo took the case from the seat beside him, opened it up, and held up a bundle of documents. "We are preparing to do battle, Dr. Watson. I am now on my way back from Paris with documented demands for their views to be heard and respected, together with fresh and shocking documentary evidence of ill-treatment of the Africans by Europeans already operating in that continent. One would hope that such evidence will be sufficient to prick the consciences of all civilized people, including those sitting at the Berlin Conference. But be in no doubt: Unless we can rein in their ambitions, these people are planning a free-for-all across the entire continent."

We parted company with our African friend on the platform of Berlin's *Friedrichstrasse* Station and stepped out into the cold Prussian winter, made even colder by the biting wind blowing in from the Baltic. I was glad of my heavy overcoat, and the Astrakhan hat I had purchased for the journey. We made our way on foot the short distance to the hotel mentioned in our invitation – a large and austere building. There we discovered that Holmes's Foreign Office contact had pre-booked rooms for us both.

After unpacking our luggage, we returned downstairs and prepared for our evening meal. Speaking for myself, I found that the journey had confused my constitution. With Berlin on Central European time, one hour ahead of Greenwich Meantime, I found that the missing hour was later than my appetite had imagined. I felt ready for a restorative meal, and was glad when Holmes and I were called to the dining room.

We found ourselves escorted to a table laid for five. I failed to recognize the Foreign Office representative, although it was clear that Holmes knew him. The man was standing waiting for us as we approached the table. He was accompanied by two guests.

"It is good to see you again, Mr. Holmes," the official said by way of greeting.

"And you too, Sir Michael," returned my companion.

"And this must be Dr. Watson."

I smiled and shook his hand.

"Now," added Holmes, "I am intrigued to learn the exact reason for your bringing us here. You need my help, but you have so far been evasive about exactly in what way I can assist you."

"That is a matter we will deal with after dinner," replied Sir Michael. "First, allow me to introduce you to my two other guests. Monsieur Gaston Coss is a Frenchman, with a great interest in the events taking place at the Berlin Conference."

We shook hands with the Frenchman mentioned to us by Bagamoyo. He appeared affable enough, even if slightly too passionate for my taste. He was small in stature, well-dressed, and with black hair above a receding hairline. I estimated him to be in his early forties.

"We have already met your other guest," said Holmes. "Bagamoyo joined us at Hannover, and we have learned a great deal from him about the purpose of this gathering in Berlin."

Holmes was never much good at small-talk, but he appeared considerably happier when we later retired to the smoking room. When we were all seated comfortably, he took out his pipe and sat smoking attentively whilst he prepared to listen to the Frenchman and his African companion expressing their discontent about the Conference.

"You are smoking a distinctive tobacco, Monsieur Coss," Holmes observed. "I have made a study of tobaccos, and I find yours to be a singular concoction."

"These cigarettes are one of my few indulgences, Mr. Holmes," replied the Frenchman. "I have them specially blended and imported from London."

"Unique, then."

"Certainly."

"I imagine," said Holmes, turning to Sir Michael, "that you have invited us here because you anticipate some kind of trouble at the Conference. Perhaps now we may consider the matter further."

Coss, who had been itching all through dinner to speak in greater detail, leaned forward and took up the conversation. “My purpose for being here in Berlin at this time,” he said, “is to attempt to bring a measure of sanity to the madness of these Conference delegates. To frustrate their evil plans to colonize and exploit the entire continent of Africa.”

“Is there anybody else who shares your misgivings?” I asked.

“Very few who are prepared to express their views. Certainly not the Chancellor, von Bismarck, the man who is hosting the event. It was his idea to hold this Conference here in the first place, responding to a request by the Portuguese. His clear intention is to maintain the international profile of the new Germany.”

“What about the British delegation?”

“There are some here out of a matter of duty,” said Coss, giving a sideways glance at our host, “but the main representative of the British government is the current Ambassador to the German Empire, Sir Edward Malet. He is here to make sure the British receive their fair share of whatever benefits might accrue from this gathering. He is hardly likely to countenance the wrecking of the Conference, or the questioning of its aims.”

I could see that Coss was growing ever more agitated as he turned in his seat and faced each one of us in turn. “Gentlemen, I now have evidence, stronger than ever before, which will prove the inhuman nature of much of the European intervention in Africa, together with a plea to respect the governing structures already in place.”

He pulled from beneath his jacket the very bundle of papers I had previously seen in the document case held by Jonathan Bagamoyo on the train.

“These documents, in fact.”

“And how do you intend to use them?”

"I intend to confront the delegates with them. We seem to be making little progress in our countering of the aims of the Conference, but if I show these to the right people, it will challenge them as no other information can – particularly one man."

"Who is that?"

"To be fair to him, I must confront him first, and see what he has to tell me."

"The matter is pressing, then," said Holmes.

"Indeed. And do you know what these Conference delegates are doing?" asked Coss. "They are currently slicing up the map of Africa like a fruit cake. Europeans love to draw boundaries. But such thinking is alien to Africans."

With that, it was obvious that Coss was unable to restrain himself any further. He jumped to his feet, cast a challenging glance at the man from the Foreign Office, wished us all a good night, and strode from the building, followed closely by an anxious-looking Bagamoyo.

"You were right when you suggested I had anticipated trouble here, Mr. Holmes," our host told us as we continued to sip our brandy. "That man is stirring up a storm, and it bodes ill for the future."

After a couple more brandies, we were all ready for bed.

The following morning, after eating a hearty breakfast, we retired to the hotel lounge in order to await the unfolding of events. We imagined that our first visitor would be our Foreign Office contact, so we were surprised by the appearance instead of quite another visitor: A man of medium height, clean shaven, wearing a long black coat against the cold, and a black, broad-brimmed hat.

He stood in the doorway, removed his hat, and scanned those few of us who were present in the room. Then, identifying us as those most likely to be the ones he sought, he approached us.

"Mr. Sherlock Holmes, and Dr. Watson?"

"Indeed," returned my companion.

"I am Commissar Marius Rossmann, from Cripo – the Berlin Criminal Police. I suppose it must be the equivalent of your Scotland Yard."

"In that case, good morning, Commissar," said Holmes. "Please come and join us."

Rossmann sat down, looking decidedly uncomfortable in those luxurious surroundings.

"You must be the equivalent of our Inspector Lestrade," added Holmes, with a smile tugging at the corners of his mouth.

"You are well informed, Mr. Holmes," said the Commissar. "My superiors chose me to visit you here this morning because my English is better than that of anyone else at Alexanderplatz."

"And better than my German," commented Holmes modestly. "In that case, how may we help you, Commissar?"

"Earlier this morning, the body of a man was pulled from the River Spree."

"I am sorry to hear that. Have you managed to identify the deceased?"

"We have indeed. It is a man called Gaston Coss."

"I am shocked, but not completely surprised," said Holmes, looking at me for unnecessary endorsement. "We were talking to the man only last night, and he was telling us about the tensions which exist between himself and other delegates at the Berlin Africa Conference – one man in particular."

"That is interesting," admitted Rossmann. "Did he happen to mention who that was?"

"No."

I chipped in. "But now you say his body has been pulled from the river."

"Indeed."

"Then presumably the man was drowned," I concluded.

"That is the initial conclusion of the *post mortem* examination."

"Then what makes it a matter for the criminal police?" asked Holmes.

"The death is too convenient to have been a pure accident, Mr. Holmes. We have reason to believe that the deceased went out last night in order to confront another man, presumably the same one you mentioned earlier, over issues concerning the present Conference being held in our city. And now he ends up dead. It may be an accident, but my experience of investigating unexpected deaths makes me highly suspicious of this one."

On hearing this, Holmes looked up with renewed interest. "That is thought provoking, Commissar. You suggest we are looking at a homicide made to look like an accident."

"Those are my initial thoughts," said Rossmann. "As you say, Mr. Holmes, it is very thought provoking."

"Regarding the shooting: Do you have any suspects?"

"We have already made an arrest. An African."

"Bagamoyo," I exclaimed.

"That is the name he gave us."

"But on what charge?"

"None as yet. It is all purely investigative at the moment. But we have certain facts which point to the African being the killer."

"Please explain."

"Our investigations have revealed that he and the dead man were colleagues. Even perhaps friends. But late yesterday evening, neighbors heard the two men arguing loudly."

"You have had a busy night, Commissar," observed Holmes. "But how can we be of assistance?"

"We currently have Bagamoyo at the police presidium on Alexanderplatz," replied Rossmann. "He has asked specifically to speak to you both."

On our arrival at the imposing police headquarters, we were taken to a somewhat Spartan interview room where we found Bagamoyo, now in his shirt sleeves, being guarded by two uniformed policemen.

"Mr. Holmes," exclaimed the African. "It is really good to see you. These people think I killed Coss, but you know I would never do such a thing."

We sat down opposite the prisoner.

"Please tell us exactly what happened," said Holmes.

"When we left you last night, Coss and I went immediately back to our rented rooms. It was clear that he wanted to act without delay. He had been boiling all evening, and now he was ready to blow. He gathered the papers that I had brought and set off by cab to confront someone."

"Whom did he go to see?"

"I don't know. He didn't tell me."

"It must be the same mysterious man he mentioned last night."

"Surely. Anyway, we had an argument. I didn't want him to go, and certainly not on his own. As he was not prepared to tell me who it was, I was forced to conclude that the man he was going to see was potentially dangerous. I was afraid that Coss would be walking straight into the lion's den. I tried to dissuade him, but he was adamant. And, as it turned out, I was quite right to worry."

He paused to collect his thoughts.

Holmes nodded. "Carry on."

"I heard nothing more from Coss, and I slept badly thinking about him, until Commissar Rossmann and a couple of his colleagues knocked at my door this morning. He told me that a body had been found, and they had no doubt, from documents discovered in his pockets, that it was indeed Coss. The Commissar said they had been making inquiries among my immediate neighbours and discovered that some of those people had overheard us arguing. Rossmann considered that enough reason to bring me in for questioning."

Bagamoyo gave a sigh and looked up at my colleague.

"Now I need you to help me, Mr. Holmes. I am an innocent man and I need you to help me prove it."

Holmes stood up. "In that case, I shall do my utmost to make sure you are set free." Then, turning to Rossmann, he said, "We must examine the body. And I should like to speak to the surgeon who performed the *post mortem*."

The police morgue was an oppressive place, as cold as the weather outside, but efficient in a Prussian sort of way. The air was heavy with the smells and chemicals common in such places. Then the deceased was wheeled out for us to examine. I immediately recognized this as the man we had met on the previous evening: Gaston Coss.

The police surgeon joined us there and watched as I made my own examination of the body.

"The cause of death appears to be drowning," I concluded.

"That is quite right," said the surgeon. "I found the lungs to be sufficiently full of water as to have caused death by asphyxiation. It also seems that he had enjoyed a decent meal not long before his death."

"We can vouch for that," I answered.

“So far the evidence suggests that this was an accidental death,” said Holmes, “and the only evidence linking Bagamoyo with the killing appears to be purely circumstantial – the argument between them overheard by neighbors.”

“That is a matter for the police to consider, Mr. Holmes,” said Rossmann, coldly.

Holmes stepped closer to the body. “And yet, look here. The skin around his mouth is slightly blue in color. A suggestion that he might have been overcome by gas prior to his drowning.”

“Gas?” said Rossmann

“Oh yes.”

“That confirms our initial suspicions that this is no mere accidental death.”

“I’m inclined to agree with you, Commissar,” said Holmes. “Judging by the evidence we’ve gathered so far, there may well be more to this case than at first appears.”

“So,” I concluded, “we have a drowning which might have been dismissed as a tragic accident, except that now the possibility of homicide has reared its ugly head. And the police are holding Bagamoyo as a suspect – a man who would not be considered a suspect if it were not for the color of his skin.”

Holmes turned to Rossmann. “Do you not agree, Commissar, that the suspect you have in custody is not yet proven guilty?”

“Perhaps,” replied Rossmann cautiously. “In which case, the mystery appears even deeper than ever. Do we have a homicide or not? And if we do, where might our suspicions be directed next?”

Holmes leaned closer to the corpse. “Look at his hands. The fingertips have been rubbed raw and bleeding. This man was in a desperate situation. Interesting. And look at the palms of his hands. Flakes of rust have driven deep into the skin."

"From an iron railing, perhaps," I suggested.

"Something of the sort is a distinct possibility. Both of these facts suggest he was fighting for his life."

I nodded.

"One more thing," said Holmes. "Could we see the contents of his stomach?"

Holmes gave these a careful examination, and then looked again at the body. "The man's coat has been torn, perhaps in a struggle with his assailant, or in an attempt to escape his fate."

"In which case, what sort of place was he in when he met his death?" asked the Commissar.

"That is precisely the question we need to ask."

Holmes stepped back decisively. "It's clear that two things need to be done now. Firstly, Commissar, could you please find for us the cab used by the deceased last night? I should like to speak to the driver."

"I shall put my men on to finding that information without delay," said Rossmann. "It should be a simple matter of old-fashioned police work."

"In the meantime, I should like you to show me exactly where the body was discovered."

"Very well, Mr. Holmes. Come with me."

"And my thanks to the police surgeon for his help," added Holmes as he departed.

After a short carriage ride through the streets of Berlin, we reached the banks of the River Spree, which flows through that city. The river was moving quickly, and the water high to overflowing as we followed it downstream. The carriage stopped beside the roadway in a less-congested area of the city. We alighted and followed Commissar

Rossmann along a stretch of disused ground until we were standing on the muddy bank of the river.

"This is the place, Mr. Holmes," said Rossmann.

As the Commissar and I tried to keep the cold at bay, Holmes, in his accustomed manner, made a detailed investigation of the scene. "A set of cart tracks shows where police activity occurred."

Rossmann nodded.

"Another set of footprints leading in both directions must belong to the person who discovered the body."

"A local man, taking his dog out for its early morning walk."

"And where exactly was the body found?"

"Floating face-down at the margin of the river, entangled in the drooping branch of that tree."

Although the river itself was flowing swiftly, the relatively still water along the edges was beginning to show signs of forming ice on the surface.

"You were fortunate that the body wasn't swept farther downstream," said Holmes. "As it is, we might conjecture that it hadn't drifted far from where it entered the water."

"How can you say that? We are close to the edge of Berlin just here, where the river flows away from the city. He could have drifted from anywhere along its banks. The possibilities are endless, Mr. Holmes."

Holmes scanned the river more carefully. "A study of the surface of the river gives us information about the flow of water beneath. Sometimes deep, sometimes shallow, depending on the hidden currents. In this case, the middle of the river is flowing fast, but it could have picked up the body from one side of the river, conveyed it several yards downstream, and left it here. The impression might be that it has traveled a long way, but the river can be deceptive. The water flows more slowly on the outer curve of a bend such as this, often leaving behind silt or sand – or entangled bodies."

Rossmann didn't look as though he was convinced by the argument, but for the moment, he remained silent.

Holmes led the way upstream, past a number of buildings, until we returned once more to the bank of the river. Here he stopped and looked around, paying particular attention to the structures on the opposite bank.

They appeared mainly to be industrial buildings. "Tell me, Commissar," said Holmes. "That one directly opposite where we're now standing, on the far side of the river. What is that place?"

The policeman shrugged. "It's a disused warehouse, Mr. Holmes. At least, the river side of the building could be described as such. The other side of the property is an occupied dwelling. It is possible that the two buildings were built back to back, with some kind of access between them."

"Do you know who lives there now?"

Rossmann stood in silent thought for a few moments. Then he said, "I believe it is a businessman called Klaus Grimmen – an entrepreneur who is actively involved in developing trade with various lands around the world. He has a particular interest in the events taking place currently at the West Africa Conference."

"Look carefully at that building," Holmes instructed us. "What do you see?"

I was the one to answer. "A stone wall reaching from below the river level to just shy of the eves. There are several openings along this side, all boarded up."

Rossmann added, "Those openings were used in the past to transfer goods into the building, and out again."

"That could account for the iron rings along this side of the building," I said. "Mooring places for boats transporting produce to and from the warehouse."

"But do you not see it?" interjected Holmes. "At water-level."

"An opening, secured by an iron gate," I said. "A kind of portcullis."

"That could well account for the flakes of rust adhering to the hands of the deceased. If he was on the other side of that gate, he might well have been fighting for his life. Scrambling. I should very much like to take a look inside that building."

We returned to the carriage which had brought us to the riverside and found another uniformed member of the police waiting for us there.

"Commissar," the man said, "we have managed to locate the cab driver who took Monsieur Coss as a passenger last night."

"And did he tell you where he took his passenger?"

"No, sir. He refuses to say."

"Where is the man now?"

"He is waiting for us in the Alexanderplatz."

"Very well." Then, turning to Holmes and myself, he added, "Let us go and have a word with this man."

We found a hansom cab standing close to the Police Presidium. The horse was stamping and snorting, whilst the disgruntled driver was likewise stamping his feet and trying in vain to keep the bitter cold at bay. He appeared miserable, not only because of the cold weather, but also because he was losing time in making money.

A quick-fire discussion in German between Rossmann and the driver revealed the fact that on the previous evening, this cabbie had indeed collected a man from the property occupied by Coss and Bagamoyo. When asked to reveal the passenger's destination, the cabbie refused to do so. He freely admitted that he had dropped Coss off close to the address he'd been given, and the man had told him to wait. But then another man emerged from the building, paid off the cabbie, and told the man to go. He also gave him an extra gratuity of some fifty marks, to ensure that the cabbie remained quiet about the address, if asked. As a man of honor, and not wishing to offend a possible future customer, the cabbie refused to break the confidence so generously bought.

It was Holmes who provided the solution to the conundrum.

"Tell him that he has no need to break the confidence, but merely to drive me and my colleague to within a few yards of the building, and then leave us to reach the address on our own. I too shall reward him well for his assistance."

The cabbie dropped us off a couple-of-hundred yards from a building, to which he directed us. I knew at once that it was the same one that we had observed from the riverside only a few minutes previously. It appeared different from this angle, but it was undoubtedly the same place, this side being the occupied section of the property.

We approached the front door on foot and Holmes rang the bell.

The door opened and a face looked out. A woman's grim expression showed that she was unsympathetic toward visitors. "Yes?"

"My name is Sherlock Holmes," said my colleague, handing over his visiting card. "And this is my colleague, Dr. John Watson."

"English?"

"Yes."

"What do you want here, Englishman?"

"We're looking for a man who went missing last night – a Frenchman by the name of Coss. He is reported to have been heading in this general direction, and I was wondering if you had come across such a man."

"We do not have many visitors here," said the woman.

"May we come inside?"

"A persistent devil, aren't you, Englishman?"

"I have frequently been described as such."

The woman at the door turned away, and a few seconds later a man appeared there. He was small in stature, but bulky and muscular, with a neatly trimmed black beard, dark astute eyes, and a sardonic smirk hovering around his mouth. I could tell at once that Holmes didn't like him.

"Sherlock Holmes," he said, looking down at the visiting card. "Yes, I have heard the name. My name is Klaus Grimmen." He looked up and gave a smile which was not reflected in his eyes. "If you would like to step inside for a moment, I am sure we can quickly clear up this matter to your complete satisfaction. Then you can be on your way. I should hate to be found wasting your precious time unnecessarily."

Grimmen led us up a short flight of steps into a comfortable living room. There he turned and addressed us. "You will have to excuse me, gentlemen, but even though I have a fair knowledge of the English language, I hope I am not misunderstanding what you have to say. Now, for whom exactly is it that you are looking?"

I could see Holmes's eyes darting about the room, so I took up the conversation. "A man we met last night has gone missing, and we're looking for where he might have gone. Yours is one of several places we are hoping to visit today in our search for him. The man is a French national named Gaston Coss. We believe you might have come across him during the course of the Conference."

While Holmes walked around, stopping at one point to look at some objects upon one of the tables, Grimmen gave the impression of thinking the matter over. Then he shrugged. "I have met so many people during the Conference that I really cannot tell with any certainty whether I met this particular person or not. Perhaps there was a Frenchman – several in fact – but none of them meant much to me."

I examined Grimmen's face, but it remained impassive. Either he was telling the truth, or he was an excellent liar.

Holmes now stepped forward again. "Thank you for your time, Herr Grimmen," he said. "I'm sure we shall reach the truth soon enough. In the meantime, good day to you."

We joined Rossmann outside a moment later outside. He'd come to collect us using his own conveyance.

"Well, Mr. Holmes?" said Rossmann as soon as we were out of the biting wind.

"He denies it, of course, but Coss was certainly there. There can be no doubt about it." He held out his hand, and opened it to reveal a small cigarette stub, which he sniffed. "This is the very same tobacco that Coss was smoking when we met him last night. He told us that he had these cigarettes specially made for him, and imported them from England. Nobody else smokes this same mixture of tobacco. It is unique."

"What do you suggest we do now?" asked Rossmann.

"We need to explore that building," replied Holmes "I have to look more extensively around the place. Maybe tonight."

"In that case, you might have to do so illegally, Mr. Holmes. I'm not sure I can obtain an entry warrant before the end of the day."

"Will you come with us either way?"

"And risk my career with Cripo?"

"Or else make a name for yourself in the process."

We clattered off along the road, with the Commissar sitting beside us deep in contemplation.

Whilst at dinner, we were interrupted by the concierge, who brought Holmes a written message.

"Splendid!" cried Holmes. "Commissar Rossmann tells me that Grimmen is away from home for the evening, courtesy of Chancellor Bismarck, who has called a meeting of the Conference. It seems that the servants have been left to enjoy an evening below stairs.

"Then there is no reason for us to delay," I concluded.

"None whatsoever," said Holmes, rubbing his hands in anticipation of action. "In which case, let us be off."

Our cab dropped us within a short walk of Grimmen's house.

As we stood in the gathering darkness outside the unlit building, with Holmes adjusting his dark lantern, we were startled by the appearance of a man who stepped out from the shadows.

Commissar Marius Rossmann.

"Mr. Holmes. Dr. Watson. I'm glad you have arrived so promptly. It is very cold out here." He stamped his feet in an attempt to regain lost circulation. "Good news. I have managed to obtain the warrant we need to enter these premises in a legal fashion. It was not given readily, I can tell you, but whether with bad grace or good, we now have permission to undertake that investigation you were talking about."

"Very well," said Holmes. "Then perhaps we had better try knocking on the front door before we attempt any other method of entry."

Rossmann's knocking on the door brought no response. "To the best of my knowledge, the servants are all in there," he said, "but as they are not expecting anybody tonight. They are all probably halfway to being drunk."

We searched for another entrance, and discovered it round the corner. Using his pick-lock bundle, Holmes had the door open in seconds, and we three were inside the house.

Rossmann opened the partly-covered lantern he'd been carrying and led the way through the gloomy house. We climbed a staircase to the room where Holmes and I had met and spoken with Grimmen earlier in the day.

Using his own lantern, Holmes began a careful survey of the room. Little had changed since our previous visit. The stone floor was still covered with scattered rugs. A number of easy chairs stood around the room, whilst a table stood near a fireplace at the far end.

"This is where I found the cigarette butt left by Coss," said Holmes pointing to the ashtray on the table. "It is the dead man's signature – the evidence that he was alive and in this building at some point within the last few hours. Otherwise, it would have been removed by an assiduous housemaid."

Holmes stooped to examine the hearth and nodded to himself. "Something has been burnt here recently. Papers."

"Coss came here bearing a bundle of papers which he imagined would bring shock to whoever read them."

"If these are the papers he brought, then they are now nothing more than a bundle of black ashes."

"Certainly insufficient evidence on which to convict Grimmen of murder," Rossmann reminded us.

"Is that all we have?" I asked.

"No, Watson, that is definitely not all we have. Far from it, in fact. Can you see that curtain on the wall farthest from the window?"

"The drape stretching across a large section of the wall? Yes, I see it."

As Holmes pulled the curtain aside, I noticed that the heavy fabric hung from a thick curtain-rod, being attached to the rail above by a series of metal hoops. It opened smoothly.

"Now, what do you see?"

"A wall. A solid immovable stone wall, built of solid adamantine stone blocks, stretching across that side of the room without a break."

"The side of the house," said Rossmann.

"But examine the floor, if you will. Can you see anything significant there?"

I pushed aside one of the scattered rugs, and looked carefully at the flags that made up the solid floor. "Scratches gouged into the very stonework of the floor," I replied. "In the form of a wide arc."

"Such as may be made by any ordinary door which is habitually being opened and closed – suggesting that the wall we are looking at may not be as immovable as one might imagine."

Using the scratches as his guide, Holmes examined the wall at closer quarters. "A-ha! What have we here? Just about visible. A break in the wall, with a suggestion of massive hinges buried deep within the stonework. And, at the other end of the wall, we have an iron ring."

"Great Scott! Holmes, you're right. It is a colossal door!"

Holmes pulled the ring, but there was no movement.

Rossmann chipped in. "Look. The door has a keyhole."

"But where is the key?" I asked.

"There," said the Commissar. "Just to the right of the door. Look. A recess in the stonework, and a large iron key hanging on a hook, almost invisible in the shadows."

Holmes grasped hold of the key, inserted it into the keyhole, and turned it. The lock mechanism rotated easily, with almost no sound whatsoever. "It has been kept well oiled," he observed.

Once more, Holmes took hold of the iron ring and pulled. This time, the great stone door opened slowly outward into the room.

"It swings easily," he said. "I would imagine those hinges have been thoroughly and regularly greased, as well as the lock mechanism."

"Just as well," said Rossmann. "Otherwise we would be in danger of bringing the entire household out to see what we are doing here."

"But why would anyone bother to build such a structure?" I asked. "All we have now is another great stone wall facing us. And this one doesn't have a keyhole."

"No," said Rossmann, "but it does have an iron ring, much like the first one. This must be able to swing out the opposite way. Into whatever room or space lies beyond."

"If so, then we must be able to open it just as easily," said Holmes.

Together, we pushed on the wall. This also proved heavy, but once it was moving, the wall continued to swing, carried by its tremendous momentum, until it thudded against something in the darkness.

Holmes stepped beyond the opening and raised the lantern to reveal to our astonished gaze another long but narrow room.

"This must run beside the river," said the Commissar. "Look. Those are the high windows we saw from the far side."

We all three moved around the room, exploring the place as best we could in the dim light of our lanterns.

"Over here," said Holmes. "On the floor. What do you make of it, Watson?"

"An iron trap-door." I pulled on the protruding iron handle and found that the door swung upward and then dropped onto the floor.

We all looked down into the dark hole.

"It drops down to the level of the river," said Rossmann. "You can hear the water sloshing against the stonework."

"And it stretches deep below the level of the water," observed Holmes. "See. There are the iron railings we saw earlier, separating it off from the river."

"Maybe they could be raised or lowered by the use of this," I said, pointing to an iron wheel about eighteen inches in diameter on the wall beside me.

"That would seem logical."

"But what is this shaft?" I gasped.

"Most probably it was used to provide access to and from the river," said Holmes. "If this building was a warehouse at one time, then such access for personnel would be essential."

"But now it is disused," I pointed out.

"For that purpose, at least," said Holmes, rubbing his chin thoughtfully. "But it might have become something more sinister. An oubliette, or a dungeon, perhaps, with iron rungs attached to the sides."

Grasping his lantern, Holmes climbed into the black hole and descended into darkness.

"This is extremely interesting," came his voice from the depths.

"What have you found?" I called down to him.

"You remember I told you that Gaston Coss's coat had been torn."

"I remember."

"I have found a fragment of cloth snagged on the iron grill down here which exactly matches its color and weave."

"I would be obliged if you would bring it up with you, Mr. Holmes," said Rossmann.

"Very well. But now I think we have achieved all we came here for tonight. Perhaps the new day will reveal more."

Early the following morning, I was roused from my bed by a loud knocking upon the door of my room.

"Yes?"

"A man from Cripo is waiting for you downstairs, Dr. Watson." I recognized the voice of the concierge. "Mr. Holmes is already down there."

I looked at my watch on the bedside counter and winced at the early hour. Then, without further delay, I arose, dressed, and made my way downstairs.

There I discovered Holmes, ready for an early morning excursion, together with the Commissar and Bagamoyo.

"The game is afoot, Watson," he told me. "Commissar Rossmann has obtained a warrant for the arrest of Herr Grimmen."

"We still don't have all the proof we need," added the Commissar, "but we have sufficient to bring our suspect in for questioning."

I grabbed a roll from the breakfast room, donned my winter coat and hat, and out into the bitter winter weather. Snow was blowing in the wind as we climbed into a police carriage and set off back toward the riverside residence of Klaus Grimmen.

To Rossmann's knock, the door was opened by the same woman we had seen on the previous day, the only difference being that this time she invited us all to step inside.

"Herr Grimmen is expecting you," she told us, in a manner as cold as the weather.

"This is no real surprise," said the businessman when we joined him in his living room. "I knew that somebody had visited my home last night, whilst I was out at a pressing appointment. The servants reported that they had heard noises, and I am sure that you were the culprits."

Rossmann shrugged. "Since you were not at home, and nobody answered my knock, we considered the matter so important that we had to gain entry."

"By breaking and entering?"

"There was no breaking involved, Herr Grimmen," countered Holmes. "We had a legal warrant to enter."

Klaus Grimmen looked at Bagamoyo, and his face twisted in displeasure. "I see you have brought one of those savages with you."

"I think I am as civilized a man as you are, Grimmen," returned the African bitterly.

"Maybe more," I added.

"On his visit here yesterday," continued the Commissar, "Mr. Holmes asked if you had seen a missing man by the name of Coss. You said that you had not."

"That is the truth of the matter," said Grimmen aggressively.

"And yet we have reason to believe that he did come to this house, and that he was killed here shortly after he arrived."

"Are you suggesting that I am responsible for this man's death?" Grimmen held out his hands in a gesture of innocence. "Do you have any evidence at all to back up this ridiculous notion?"

"Perhaps."

"We should like to investigate the room next-door," said Sherlock Holmes.

Grimmen returned him a guarded look.

"Oh, we know about that room," added Holmes.

"It seems you were indeed extremely busy here last night," commented Grimmen.

After a painful moment of silence, during which time the hissing gas-light on the wall provided the only sound,

Grimmen forced a smile. "Would you gentlemen care to see that room next door – this time in the light of day?"

We all now focused our attention on the owner of the house as, with exaggerated drama, he drew back the curtain covering the stone wall. Now, in the daylight, I could see more clearly the iron ring handle, and the keyhole beside it.

Klaus Grimmen reached up to the large iron key on its hook, and then inserted it into the keyhole. He turned the mechanism, replaced the key, and then pulled open the huge stone door.

As on our previous visit, the enormous stone wall swung easily on its hinges. Seeing it now in daylight, I was even more impressed by the ingenious mechanism.

We all stood facing the second wall, and I estimated that there would be barely a couple of inches separating the two walls of stone when they were both closed. I imagined that constructing the place must have been a massive undertaking.

Grimmen applied his full strength in order to push open this second wall-door. Once it was moving, the stone entrance swung fully open, impelled, as on the previous evening, by its own massive weight.

Our host stepped through into the second room and stood watching whilst we all filed in. Commissar Rossmann arrived first and set about examining the room that was now lit up by daylight filtering in through the high windows on one side. Next came Bagamoyo, followed by myself. I riveted my attention upon the iron trapdoor which I knew led to the flooded shaft. Holmes came in last of all, pulling the first stone door firmly shut after him but leaving the second fully open. The place felt bitterly cold.

Grimmen stood watching us all. "In years gone by, this was a warehouse, holding produce used in the wool trade. Access from the river was via an opening now sealed by those wooden slats that cover much of the riverside wall. The other main access for goods was through the house, and that was the reason for the two stone doors being constructed. To give access when required, and to assure security for those living in the house."

"Ingenious!" I exclaimed.

"Now, gentlemen, may I ask the exactly purpose of your visit here? And what is your interest in this disused warehouse in particular?"

"Monsieur Coss came here with a bundle of papers in his possession," said Rossmann.

"Papers which pointed to unjust and exploitative activities in Africa," added Bagamoyo. "And to yours in particular."

"And he left through that black hole," said Holmes, pointing to the access shaft.

"How can you possibly know all that?" demanded Grimmen. Somehow he did not appear to be surprised.

"We know that the deceased man visited you on the night of his death," continued Holmes. "The night before last. You and Coss spoke at some length. I discovered the stub of one of his cigarettes in your ashtray. So we know that he spent enough time here to smoke it. Somehow, you caused the man to drop down through to this shaft, and into the darkness below. If he was unconscious, then the water down there would have brought him back to consciousness, long enough for him to be aware of what was happening to him. We discovered that his fingernails were torn and his fingers bloodied from scrambling to try to escape. He also had flakes of rust embedded in the palms of his hands. From scrambling against the iron gate barring him from the river, and from the rusted iron rungs lining the shaft."

"The man was drowned, certainly," I continued. "And that access shaft is sufficiently full of bitterly cold river water that no one could survive for long down there. Coss would have been overcome by hypothermia and exhaustion, his hands would have been too numb to enable him to climb out, and he would have drowned within a matter of a few minutes."

"This is all pure speculation," growled Grimmen. "News reports say that the body was found outside, on the margins of the river."

"When the man was dead," said Holmes, "you then raised the iron grill separating the pipe off from the river, and allowed the water to sweep the body away. Unfortunately for your plans, the body didn't travel downstream as far as you had hoped, before it was snagged on the branch of a tree."

"Utter and complete nonsense," thundered Grimmen.

"You might try to convince the world that it was indeed an accident," I pointed out. "But the evidence points to murder, and to you as the man who killed him. When the police suspected foul play, it was convenient for you that suspicion fell upon Mr. Bagamoyo here, and you did nothing to dispel that impression." All this time, Grimmen remained standing near the still-open inner stone doorway.

Bagamoyo's attitude toward the German businessman was now hardening fast into a bitter hatred, and he stepped toward him in a belligerent manner. "You swine, Grimmen!" he growled. "You may have used the river to kill my friend, but you are responsible for his death just as surely as if you had strangled him with your own bare hands. Why? Was it worth it?"

"Africa is there, waiting to be exploited by business interests among the civilized nations of Europe." Grimmen's eyes were blazing with passion. "There is nothing immoral in doing that. The continent is rife with cannibalism and barbarity."

"And you want to replace that with your own kind of barbarity. Is that it?" growled Bagamoyo. I could see that he seemed to be moving more slowly now, as though his limbs were not responding properly.

"Coss came here with similar accusations," continued Grimmen. "He made threats to derail my own plans for German commercial enterprise in Africa. So I had to kill him. You can understand that, can't you?"

"I fail to see how anybody could understand your actions," replied Holmes.

Grimmen stepped back, closer to the open stone door and, from the shadows, he brought out a sword – a sabre – and held it out threateningly toward us. "I would warn you, gentlemen, not to come any closer to me."

I could now feel something in the atmosphere causing my throat to constrict.

"Why?" demanded Rossmann. "What have you done?"

"You will already have noticed that my home is lit by manufactured gas," said Grimmen. "Unlit, that gas is a poisonous mixture of carbon monoxide and other noxious fumes. This gas is now filtering into this room through an unseen pipe above the wall. Soon you will begin to feel it starting to squeeze the life from your bodies. I shall leave you all in here as it builds up, and until it has rendered each of you unconscious. Then I shall come back, allow the gas to escape, and drop each of you in turn down into the dark and cold waters of the delivery shaft. The cold water may revive you, as it did Coss, but by then, as he found out, it will be too late to save you from drowning. Then I shall raise the grill and allow the river, which is flowing swiftly today, to take your bodies far away." He laughed. "That tree that snagged your colleague's body has now been removed. So don't trust to that to save you."

"I fail to understand," said the Commissar, who was having difficulty standing. "Why are you going to such great lengths to kill us all?"

"It was your friend Coss who is responsible," replied Grimmen. "He wanted to disrupt the Conference, and spare the people of Africa from what he considered to be unprincipled imperialism."

"Is that all?"

"Far from it. He also confronted me with evidence of my own activities, which he considered to be crimes against the human race. He threatened to bring the matter before every law-court in Europe. He might well have had me found guilty, but I couldn't run the risk of him delaying my involvement in exploiting the resources of Africa. For that reason he had to die. And for your meddling in my affairs, you too must die – perishing in the freezing waters of the River Spree. At least you will have one advantage over Coss. He had to suffocate and drown alone in total darkness."

As Holmes held Bagamoyo back from confronting the businessman, and both the policeman and the African slumped onto the floor, Grimmen grasped hold of the handle of the inner stone door and pulled it with all his strength. The huge weight of the inner stone door swung on well-oiled hinges toward its closed position, its momentum unstoppable. I noticed that, just before the door slammed shut, Grimmen stepped up confidently to the outer door, and pushed.

The two stone doors met with a gigantic slam, which shook the entire building.

"We could have stopped Grimmen," I cried out, "but now he has got away."

"I think not," said Sherlock Holmes, withdrawing a large iron key from the pocket of his coat. "I took the liberty of locking the outer door on my way in here."

As the horror of what must have happened to Grimmen began to sink in, we all stared at the closed stone doorway, each lost in his own contemplation.

"You had better go and check on our host, Watson," said Holmes softly. "Or whatever is left of him."

I did as asked, pulling open the great stone door. There I discovered the man's body in a hideous condition. The skull had been crushed, as had the ribcage and pelvis. All signs of life had been snuffed out immediately as the door had compressed the man against the cold stone bulk of its fellow. The sword lay beside him, still clutched in his lifeless hand.

"We need to make our way back to the habitable part of Grimmen's house," I told Holmes.

"Indeed." He unlocked the door. "We must close these heavy doors behind us," he said. "We have to allow the gas to escape gradually – otherwise the entire house will go up in flames."

Seized by fits of coughing, we made our way back to the safe side, where we began slowly to recover.

Holmes located and turned off the gas supply to the other room, and then opened the windows to allow in a blast of cold but refreshing air.

From my seat close to the fire, I looked up at him. "And what now?"

"The Berlin Conference will come to its inevitable conclusion on the subject of Africa," he decided.

"And this place?"

"Its fate is now out of our hands. The lawyers will have to decide about ownership, and the future of the servants employed here – unless they have made a rapid escape."

Later, when we had all recovered from our ordeal and the effects of the suffocating gas had worn off, we sat together in the warmth of our hotel lounge. "Jonathan Bagamoyo is the sort of man that the Foreign Office in London could use," said Holmes.

“And help the British take control of half of Africa? I hardly think so, Mr. Holmes,” said our African friend. “I shall make my own way forward in life. My name in the Swahili language means something like ‘lie down and rest’, but I have plenty more to do with my life before I can think of doing such a thing.”

“Commissar Rossmann,” said Holmes as he lit up his pipe and sat back in contentment. “The case is now closed, and you will have the distinction of having solved the murder of Monsieur Coss.”

“But I could never have done it without your help, Mr. Holmes.”

“Perhaps. But the credit must go to you, Commissar. After all, I frequently assist Scotland Yard in the solving of crimes which they are unable to unravel, so why not Cripo as well? After all, I am the world’s one and only private consulting detective.”

## MX Publishing

MX Publishing brings the best in new Sherlock Holmes novels, biographies, graphic novels and short story collections every month. With over 400 books it's the largest catalogue of new Sherlock Holmes books in the world.

We have over one hundred and fifty Holmes authors. The majority of our authors write new Holmes fiction - in all genres from very traditional pastiches through to modern novels, fantasy, crossover, children's books and humour.

In Holmes biography we have award winning historians including Alistair Duncan, Paul R Spiring, and Brian W Pugh

MX Publishing also has one of the largest communities of Holmes fans on Facebook and Twitter under @mxpublishing.

www.mxpublishing.com

## Also from MX Publishing

When the papal apartments are burgled in 1901, Sherlock Holmes is summoned to Rome by Pope Leo XII. After learning from the pontiff that several priceless cameos that could prove compromising to the church, and perhaps determine the future of the newly unified Italy, have been stolen, Holmes is asked to recover them. In a parallel story, Michelangelo, the toast of Rome in 1501 after the unveiling of his Pieta, is commissioned by Pope Alexander VI, the last of the Borgia pontiffs, with creating the cameos that will bedevil Holmes and the papacy four centuries later. For fans of Conan Doyle's immortal detective, the game is always afoot. However, the great detective has never encountered an adversary quite like the one with whom he crosses swords in "The Vatican Cameos."

*"An extravagantly imagined and beautifully written Holmes story"* (**Lee Child**, NY Times Bestselling author, Jack Reacher series)

# Also from MX Publishing

## The Detective and The Woman Series

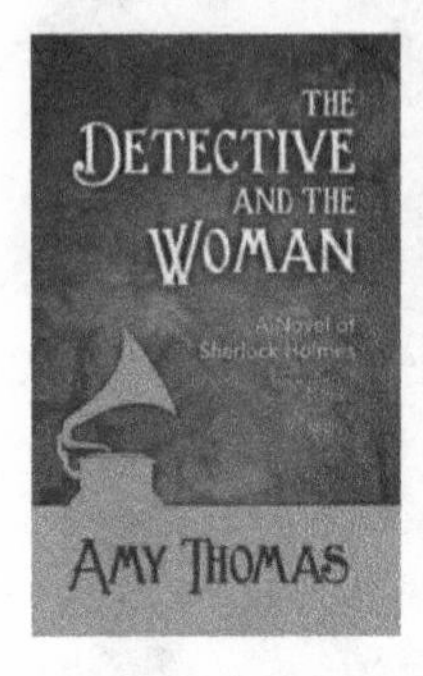

The Detective and The Woman
The Detective, The Woman and The Winking Tree
The Detective, The Woman and The Silent Hive

"The book is entertaining, puzzling and a lot of fun. I believe the author has hit on the only type of long-term relationship possible for Sherlock Holmes and Irene Adler. The details of the narrative only add force to the romantic defects we expect in both of them and their growth and development are truly marvelous to watch. This is not a love story. Instead, it is a coming-of-age tale starring two of our favorite characters."
**Philip K Jones**

www.mxpublishing.com

# Also from MX Publishing

## The Sherlock Holmes and Enoch Hale Series

The Amateur Executioner
The Poisoned Penman
The Egyptian Curse

"The Amateur Executioner: Enoch Hale Meets Sherlock Holmes", the first collaboration between Dan Andriacco and Kieran McMullen, concerns the possibility of a Fenian attack in London. Hale, a native Bostonian, is a reporter for London's Central News Syndicate - where, in 1920, Horace Harker is still a familiar figure, though far from revered. "The Amateur Executioner" takes us into an ambiguous and murky world where right and wrong aren't always distinguishable. I look forward to reading more about Enoch Hale."
**Sherlock Holmes Society of London**

www.mxpublishing.com

Printed in the USA
CPSIA information can be obtained
at www.ICGtesting.com
LVHW041254151023
761121LV00001BB/110